Marley's book
Read by:

Marley 6/09
Jean 2/12
Becky 6/13

Book 2 A Thread of Truth

Book 3 A Thread So Thin

Book 4 Threading the Needle

New Novels (Stand Alone)

Fields of Gold

On Wings of Morning

Ties That Bind

A Thread of Truth

Also by Marie Bostwick

A SINGLE THREAD

ON WINGS OF THE MORNING

RIVER'S EDGE

FIELDS OF GOLD

"A High-Kicking Christmas" in COMFORT AND JOY

A Thread of Truth

MARIE BOSTWICK

KENSINGTON BOOKS

KENSINGTON BOOKS are published by

Kensington Publishing Corp.
119 West 40th Street
New York, NY 10018

ISBN-13: 978-1-61523-129-4

*Dedicated to women of courage everywhere
who have gone from victims to victors
in the battle against domestic violence*

Acknowledgments

This book could not have been written without the guidance of some very special people, including Barbara Spiegel and Nancy Rogers, who, along with the rest of the staff and volunteers at the Susan B. Anthony Project (sbaproject.org), work tirelessly to free families from the scourge of domestic violence. Thank you so much for sharing your insights and for giving me a more complete understanding of the issue of domestic abuse against women.

Also many thanks to Annie Dranginis for helping to clarify the complexities of the legal system in Connecticut.

And, as always, my thanks to "the team"—Audrey LeFehr, Jill Grosjean, Nancy Berland, and associates, Sherry Kuehl, and Adam Kortekas. Without you, I'd just be a lady with a computer and a suitcase of unfulfilled dreams. Thank you for helping make my most audacious wishes come true.

Prologue

The counselor is young, blond, and pretty and obviously nervous. She glances at her reflection in the wall mirror when she enters the waiting room, adjusts her collar, and clears her throat before extending her hand toward me with a wide, rehearsed smile and a request for me to follow her back to her office.

After a quick kiss and a promise that I'll see them in a few minutes, Bethany and Bobby obediently accompany a volunteer to the playroom where they will wait until I finish the intake interview. I follow the counselor down a wide hallway with recessed lights in the ceiling and thick, fawn-colored carpeting on the floors.

This is a strange place. More like an upscale hotel than a women's shelter, at least not like any shelter we've been in before. Everything is so quiet and everyone on the staff is so welcoming, as if they've all been recruited from the ranks of retired desk clerks and children's librarians, kind and purposely calm. Well, almost everyone.

As we approach a turn in the corridor, I hear the sound of two women arguing, politely but heatedly. One voice is strained and restrained, trying to appease another, slightly louder voice that belongs to someone skilled in the art of employing clipped, educated enunciation to intimidate those who disagree with her, the voice of a woman who is used to having her own way.

"Abigail, I'm on your side. You know I am," the first voice says. "But this is a shelter, not a balloon. You can't just blow more women into it like so many extra puffs of air and think it will just keep expanding to make room for the additional volume. I wish we could accommodate everyone who comes through the door, but we can't. We've only got so many beds."

"And *that* is exactly my point. Every month we have more people coming through the door than we did the month before. It's the worst sort of foolishness to think that trend is suddenly going to reverse itself. So why is the board dragging its feet? No! Don't interrupt me. You don't need to say it. I've heard it all before. 'These things take time. We should do a feasibility study. Or take a poll. Or hire a consultant.' Rubbish! We don't need to do any of that. We need to hire an architect and a bulldozer. Today! I am sick and tired of sitting in meetings, listening to Ted Carney drone on about stiffening intake standards while the rest of the board sits and stares at their navels and does nothing! If it's a matter of money, I'll write a check tomorrow. I . . ."

"Abigail," the first voice says wearily, "it's not just about the money. You know that. It's a question of space. We simply don't have it . . ."

My heart sinks. It's the same old story; no room at the inn. I should have expected this. Every shelter has more requests than it can handle, but everyone has been so pleasant since we walked in the door that I dared to hope there might be room for us right away. Maybe if we wait a few days. I dread the thought of sleeping in the car again, but what else can I do? Besides, this is such a nice place, so clean and quiet. If we could stay here, even for a week or two, maybe I'd be able to clear my head long enough to figure out a plan to exit the revolving door that leads from one shelter to the next and get the kids into a real home—at least for a while. I'm so tired of sleeping in a different spot every night. I'm so tired of being so tired, but from the sound of things, there is no place for us here. I should have known better than to get my hopes up.

As we round the corner, I see the counselor consciously straighten her shoulders and smooth her hair. The women halt their conversation as we approach. The counselor's voice lifts to a slightly higher register as she introduces us. The first woman, I am told, the one with a genuine smile and dark brown eyes that match her short cropped hair, is Donna Walsh, the shelter director. The second woman, who doesn't wait for the counselor to do the honors, informs me that she is Abigail Burgess Wynne and she is on the shelter board. They are both attractive, but Abigail Burgess Wynne is beautiful, strikingly so. Tall, well-dressed, and imposing, with platinum white hair drawn into a blunt-edged ponytail at the base of her neck, high cheekbones, arched eyebrows, and a smooth complexion, she might be any age from fifty to seventy.

Donna Walsh puts out her hand and, when I take it, she lays a second hand on top of mine. The gesture surprises me and I have to stop myself from drawing back. It has been so long since I was touched with affection. I don't quite know how to respond. "Hi, Ivy. Welcome. It's so nice to meet you."

"Thank you. It's nice to meet you, too." I haven't had much call for company manners recently, but I still remember how it works.

"Leslie's going to be conducting your intake interview?" she asks, looking a question at the young counselor, who nods. "Well, then you'll be in good hands. I hope we'll be able to help you."

Abigail Burgess Wynne raises her eyebrows to their highest point as she interrupts the director. "Oh, don't worry about that," she says pointedly. "I'm *certain* we will."

Once we get to Leslie's office, I take a seat in a firm but comfortable armchair on the opposite side of the desk. I watch Leslie as she repeatedly presses the top of her ballpoint pen with her thumb while she fills in the forms—name, children's names, dates of birth, and the rest—tapping the pen top several times after she writes down each of my answers.

The clicking sound reminds me of those cheap, plastic castanets Bethany had. She used to put the *Nutcracker Suite* on the stereo, grab her castanets, put her arms over her head, and clack them together, twirling in a circle to the "Spanish Dance." She loved those things. I wish I'd thought to bring them, but there wasn't time. So much had to be left behind.

She notices me noticing the clicking pen, laughs, and admits what I'd already suspected. She is new on the job, just finished her training. In fact, I'm her first client, well, the first one she's handling completely on her own.

"Must be exciting to start a new job."

"It is, but it would be more exciting if jobs like mine weren't necessary." She shrugs. "But, anyway, let's get back to you. You're from Pennsylvania? That's a long way. How did you end up in New Bern?"

I take a breath, deep but not too deep, and keep my eyes focused evenly on hers, pausing now and again as if to collect my thoughts, not wanting to sound rehearsed. I tell her the story I have prepared in advance, the details I've worked out carefully in my mind, the revised history I quizzed Bethany on before we arrived, reminding her that if she got confused or nervous, she should say nothing. After all she's been through, silence is a perfectly understandable response for a child. No one will question it.

Leslie bobs her pretty blond head sympathetically, bent over her clipboard taking notes. She believes me. And I am struck by how easy it is. The lies just slip from my lips like thread from a spool and she believes every word I am saying.

I wish it didn't have to be like this, but I've got to do what I've got to do. With its white clapboard houses and trim green lawns, New Bern, Connecticut, looks like a town lifted straight from a Norman Rockwell painting, safe and secure as can be. But after last night, I don't want the kids to spend one more night sleeping in the car than they absolutely have to while we wait for an opening in the shelter. If it were just for myself, I wouldn't do it, but if lying to this woman is what it takes to protect my children, then that's what I'll do. I have no choice. Still, it bothers me to think how good I have become at getting people to see only what I want them to see.

But why wouldn't I be good at it? I've had so much practice. And it isn't like my life is a complete fabrication. It's close to the truth, just not close enough.

I married at eighteen. I have two children I love. Bethany is six.

Bobby is eighteen months. All this is true and the rest of it is almost true.

We were almost a happy family.

But that word is an abyss that separates happy families from everybody else. Almost.

I wonder if she understands that, this newly minted intake counselor, fresh from training on the care and feeding of women in crisis? She wants to understand, I can see that, genuinely wants to help, but something about her, something about the smooth shape of her forehead and the crisp ironed creases of her trouser leg makes me know she is merely an observer, standing on the edge of the abyss and peering into it. She has not been in the valley herself and probably never will. I hope not, for her sake.

That, too, makes it easier for her to take my story at face value. She won't investigate it and I have all the paperwork, or enough of it, to prove my claim. I am who I say I am—Ivy Peterman. But what I don't tell her is that I never changed the name on my driver's license and Social Security card after I married. Maybe I forgot to. Or maybe, deep down, I knew it would come to this one day. Whatever the reason, I have the documents to prove that I am me.

The rest of the story—the true parts, that my husband abused me for years and that my children and I have been bouncing from emergency shelter to emergency shelter for months now; the almost-true part, that we've got nowhere else to go; and the lie, that my husband was killed in a construction accident—she accepts without question. Even with her training, training that surely included admonitions not to buy into the stereotypes of victims of domestic violence as being poor, powerless, and poorly educated—in other words, not like people this woman lives next door to, not people from nice suburban neighborhoods, or even wealthy ones, with trimmed hedges and late-model SUV's in the driveway—part of her still finds it easier to accept my story precisely because it feeds into the stereotype: poor, teenage girl marries boozing, battering, blue-collar boy she thought would be her salvation, not realizing what she was getting into until it was too late. She finds it easy to believe because it's almost true and because she *wants* to believe it. The whole truth would hit too close to home, send her to the phones and files to verify my background, but this? It doesn't even cross her mind to check my facts. I can tell.

She smiles and gets up from her desk, excuses herself for a moment, and promises to be right back.

In spite of the elegant furnishings and plush carpets, the walls between the offices are surprisingly thin. I can hear Leslie's voice, high and uncertain as she speaks to Donna Walsh in the hallway, mixing with the director's calmer, deeper tones, intersected and frequently interrupted by the clipped, insistent voice of the older woman, Abigail Burgess Whatever-Her-Name-Was. I don't remember anymore. I can't understand what they're saying so I turn my attention to the sounds coming from the playroom next door, where I can hear Bethany and Bobby's muffled voices as they play with the volunteer. I like knowing they are so close and I like being alone in this room. Even with the murmur of voices coming through the walls, this is still the quietest room I have been in for weeks. It feels good to sit here alone and think. Peaceful.

Maybe, if I want to, I can stay here for a while. This seems like a nice town, filled with nice people. People like Leslie. She's just a couple of years younger than me. Twenty-two, twenty-three at the most. Fresh out of college. So weird. All she knows about the world is what she's read in books or heard from her professors. I'm twenty-four but I've seen enough to last three lifetimes. She makes me feel ancient. But still . . . If I lived here, maybe we'd be friends, go to the movies or shopping. Do the things that girlfriends do. It would be nice to have a friend, someone who knows the truth about me and likes me anyway, to stay here for a long time, to live here, maybe forever.

No, I remind myself. That can't be.

We can't stay. Not forever or for long. Even if I'm right and Leslie never checks out my story, or if I'm wrong and she eventually does, it doesn't make any difference. We'll be gone before the truth comes out. We must be.

If we stay too long in one place, he's bound to find us. It isn't safe to stand still. But if I'm careful? Then, maybe? For a while? I'm tired of looking over my shoulder, of carrying my life and my children's lives stuffed into a suitcase constructed of half-truths, and only as large as can be fit into the trunk of my Toyota.

I'm lost in my thoughts and don't hear the counselor when she comes back in the room.

"Mrs. Peterman? Ivy? Are you all right?"

The sound of her voice startles me, jars me back into the moment, and I realize that she's been gone for a good while, at least fifteen minutes. "Sorry. I was a million miles away. Guess I'm tired."

Leslie tips her head to one side, murmurs sympathetically. "I can imagine you are. Don't worry about it. We're almost done here." She puts the clipboard down on her desk and sits down again. "Then we'll get you and the children something to eat and see you settled in for the night."

"You can take us? Tonight?" I can't quite believe what she's saying. Maybe I didn't hear her correctly. "You've got a room right now?"

She nods, pleased that I am so pleased, and beams when she tells me the truly amazing news, like she's handing me a wonderful and unexpected gift. And she is.

"But . . . I thought . . . when I heard them talking in the hall . . . I thought you were full."

"Well, technically we are, but Mrs. Burgess Wynne absolutely insisted that we find you and the children a bed tonight. She said if we didn't, then she was taking you home herself, so Donna did a little shifting and asked some of the single women to double up a few days so we could make room for you and the children now."

"Really? Thank you. I . . . I don't know what to say."

"You don't have to say anything. I'm so glad we were able to find a place for you. And," she grinned, "the news gets even better than that. We have an opening in the Stanton Center. Not tonight but soon."

I look questions at her and she goes on to explain. "The Stanton Center is an apartment building just for women and children who have been victims of domestic violence, the home of our transitional housing program. You can stay there for up to two years while you're getting back on your feet. Initially it's free, but we'll encourage you to find a job as soon as possible and then we'll charge modest rent, a percentage of your earnings. While you're there, we can offer you vocational, financial, and psychological counseling, and child care." She pauses, waiting for me to say something, but it takes me a moment.

"An apartment. A real apartment?" Tears fill my eyes.

She nods. "A real apartment. There's a community room where we hold meetings for the residents and a playground with a swing set and slide for the children. It's in a secret location, no sign in front, and a good security system. Of course, since you're a widow, you don't have to worry about that so much, but the other residents have fled violent relationships and we do everything possible to make sure their abusers can't find them. It's like a safe house."

I blink hard, willing back the tears, trying to stay composed, not wanting her to see the effect those words have on me—a safe house. It has been so long since I even dreamed of such a thing.

"So?" She asks cheerily, already certain of my response. "What do you say? Would you like to take the apartment and stay here in New Bern for a while?"

"Yes," I whisper. "I would. Thank you."

"Good!" She stands up, indicating that I should follow her. "We can finish the paperwork tomorrow, after you've had a chance to settle in a bit."

Leslie opens the door and leads the way through the three right turns of the corridor that will lead us to the playroom that backs up her counseling office, talking as she goes. I'm still in shock, able to offer only short responses to her commentary, the script she has been trained to deliver to new residents.

"You're not required to accept any of the counseling services we offer to residents, but I do urge you to take advantage of them as much as possible—especially the group counseling sessions. Your abuser can't hurt you anymore, but even so, the effects of domestic violence can stay with you long after the abuse ends. Counseling can help you work though that and I think you'll appreciate the chance to develop relationships with women who've dealt with similar problems."

"Yes. I'm sure you're right," I say, knowing that I'll never go to even one of those group sessions. I'm not going to get close to those women. I'm not going to get close to anyone. I can't take that risk.

"Good." She looks back over her shoulder, pleased that I agree. Leslie is a good person. Part of me wants to tell her the truth, but I can't, especially not now, with an apartment on the line. An apartment! A real apartment just for us. I still can't believe it.

"Your timing was lucky. One of our residents, former residents," she corrects herself, "decided to go back to her husband. That's why we have an opening in the Stanton Center." She sighs heavily and shakes her head.

"After all she'd been through, you'd think that's the last thing she'd do, but it happens a lot more often that you'd suppose. It's such a hard pattern to break. Well, at least we don't have to worry about that with you, do we?"

"No."

This is the truth. I'm not going back. There was a moment, one, when I wavered, but not now. In my mind, I see my daughter's face, a dark reflection in the rearview mirror, small and serious and too young to know so much. No. We're not going back.

"Good," Leslie says again, even more firmly. She likes to speak in affirmations. "I hate to think of our other resident leaving, but I'm glad it's worked out so well for you. The timing really was fortunate."

We have arrived at the playroom. She puts her hand on the knob and turns to me before opening the door. "You must be on a lucky streak."

If I am, it's a first.

But, then again . . . A striking, silver-haired woman whose name I can't even remember insisted that room be made for me and my children. A brown-eyed director I'd never met before shifted her charges to make it happen. And now sweet, nervous, well-meaning Leslie has said there is a place for us. A safe house. Tonight. Now. Just a few miles from here, somewhere in this lovely little town where the kindest people on earth live, there is room for us.

Maybe she is right. Maybe, at last, my luck is changing.

❧ 1 ❧

Ivy Peterman

Eighteen months later

Fight or flight? Until recently, it's never been a question. Not for me.

Whenever I feel frightened or threatened, my first instinct has always been flight. I do it pretty regularly.

I was six years old when my father had a heart attack and died. The news sent me running into the woods in the back of our house. I could hear my mother calling for me, her voice raspy with tears and shock and anger, but wouldn't budge from my hiding place in the branches of a half-dead oak. Finally, she sent our neighbor, Pete, out to find me.

Just after my sixteenth birthday, Mom was killed in a head-on collision and Pete, who was by then my stepfather, also became my legal guardian. He and I had never gotten along, but then again neither had he and Mom, not since about ten minutes after their wedding. After Mom died, Pete started to drink even more than before, so I ran away again. Farther this time, buying a one-way train ticket to the city. So far that Pete would never be able to find me, though now I realize he probably never tried.

And, of course, when I was twenty-four, I ran away from my husband. This time I took my two babies with me.

My escape wasn't exactly well-planned.

The day began normally enough, with a trip to the department store and a new tube of lipstick, but by that night I was running. I had to. I was afraid, not just for my life but for the lives of my children. All I took were some clothes, a file with some personal papers, the kids' baby books, some jewelry I sold later, and about $288 in cash, fifty-six of it from the spare change jar we kept on the kitchen counter. That's all. I had credit cards, but I didn't take them. I was worried that Hodge would be able to track us down if I used them.

When we could find an opening, we lived in emergency shelters. When we couldn't, we lived in the car. That was the hardest time. The kids were cranky, and so was I. The things I'd taken for granted while living in a nice house in the suburbs, like being able to keep clean and warm, using a toilet whenever we wanted to, or eating hot food, were concerns that occupied my every waking moment. I had no reserve of time or energy to consider how I was going to get us out of that mess, only enough to survive the day.

One night, I was asleep on the front seat and heard a noise. I woke up to see a figure, a man, pressed up against the passenger side window of the backseat, where my kids were sleeping, trying to slide a hanger wire into the space between the window and the door. I didn't think, just jumped out of the car and started screaming. "Get away from that door! Don't touch them! Get away!"

Somewhere along the line I must have grabbed the metal flashlight from the side storage compartment in the door. Still screaming, I flung it at the intruder and it hit him in the head. He swore and ran off into the alley. The kids woke up and started crying. A tall, scruffy man with a four-day growth of beard—the clerk from the twenty-four-hour mini-mart where I'd decided to park that night, stupidly thinking it was a safe spot—heard the commotion and came outside to investigate.

He took one look at me, tears in my eyes while I tried to quiet Bethany and Bobby's sobbing, and decided to call the police. Over my protests, he went inside the store to make the call. I got in the car and told the kids to buckle up. There was no way I was going to stick around and answer a bunch of questions from the police. If Hodge had filed a report saying I was a kidnapper, they'd lock me up and take the kids away from me forever. That's what Hodge said would happen if I ever even thought about leaving him. He didn't say that out of any kind of love, but just to make me believe that no matter what I did or where I went, he would still be in control. And I did believe it. I'd put hundreds miles of road between us, but even so I could feel his power, the menace of his presence, just like I always had. We had to get out of there.

My tires squealed as I peeled out of the parking lot, my mind racing. Did it made more sense for me to get on the freeway and go to another town? Or better to find a dark alley and park there until the coast was clear? I decided on the freeway.

In the backseat the kids were still crying. I swore under my breath, cursing traffic engineers who were too cheap or too stupid to put up any signs directing out-of-towners to the freeway entrance. Ten minutes later I was still lost. Bethany had stopped crying, but Bobby was still going strong.

I looked in the rearview mirror and saw his face, his chubby baby cheeks flushed and hot, his black lashes clumped and glistening with tears. "Bobby. Calm down, baby. Mommy is going to find a quiet place to park and then you can go back to sleep, all right?"

"Go home!" he wailed. "Go home!"

And for the first time, I wondered if I was doing the right thing. A few weeks before, my children had been living the relatively normal, scheduled lives of children in the suburbs; three meals a day, playing on the swing set in our fenced backyard, watching cartoons, baths at seven, bed at eight. Of course, when it was time for Hodge to come home, they'd get clingy and quiet, feeling my fear, perhaps, as I listened for the grind of gears as the automatic garage door opened and tuned my ears to assess the level of force Hodge used to slam the door of his BMW, a clue as to his mood and what the rest of the evening would bring.

But, I told myself as I drove through the darkness, he wasn't violent every night. Only when I'd done something, or not done something, that made him mad. After all, I was the one he took his anger out on. Not the kids. Maybe they'd be better off if we went back. At least they'd be safe.

But a voice in my head reminded me that it wasn't true anymore.

I remembered that last day, Hodge screaming and swearing and pounding on one side of the locked bathroom door, while we huddled on the other side. I remembered the swelling of my left eye, pain shooting through my bleeding hand, but worse, so much worse, was the memory of the angry red mark on Bethany's pale cheek.

Bethany was used to his rages, used to seeing me holding ice packs on my bruises, or trying to cover up the marks of his fury with extra makeup, but he'd never hit her before. That day, he considered her fair game and I realized that from then on, he always would.

In the backseat, Bethany tried to calm her baby brother. "Bobby, don't cry. We can't go home. Daddy's there."

She was right. I couldn't take them back. Not now. It wasn't safe to go back to Hodge. Not for me and not for my children. But we couldn't go on like this, either. We couldn't keep running. I was tired, and scared, and broke. Somehow or other I had to come up with another plan. But what?

To say that I haven't had a lot of experience with praying in my life would be an understatement, but that night, driving around in the middle of the night without the least clue of where we should go or what we should do when we arrived, I prayed silently, asking God for a sign or at least a hint.

Lost in uncharted territory, I accidentally turned onto the northbound freeway entrance instead of the southbound. By the time I figured it out, I was crossing the state line into Connecticut. And that's how I ended up in New Bern.

After three weeks living in a tiny studio apartment in the emergency shelter, we moved into a much larger two-bedroom unit in the Stanton Center. The counselor talked to me about putting down roots, finding a job, and putting Bethany in school. I nodded, mutely assenting to everything she suggested, but in my heart, I knew we'd stay in New Bern only as long as it felt safe to do so. That was more than a year ago and, believe me, nobody is more surprised than I am that we're still here. If not for Evelyn Dixon and a log cabin quilt, I'd have put New Bern in my rearview mirror a long time ago.

Evelyn owns Cobbled Court Quilts in New Bern. She runs a free quilting class for the women at the shelter. Initially, I didn't want to take the class and had suitcase full of good excuses for not doing so:

1) With two kids, I was too busy for hobbies.

2) I'd never liked crafts, anyway, and any spare time I had really should be spent looking for a job.

3) And wasn't quilting something people's grandmas did? Maybe I'd lived long and hard, but I'm not exactly ready for bifocals and a rocking chair, you know what I mean?

But, none of those were the real reason I didn't want to take Evelyn's class. The truth is; I just didn't want to find one more thing to fail at. There had been so many already.

But Abigail decided to change my mind for me. That's Abigail Burgess Wynne, a volunteer at the shelter as well as a big donor, the woman who insisted that they find room for us at the shelter. Abigail is something of an oddball. Beautiful, in a nineteen fifties movie-star kind of way, all long legs and perfect diction, but an oddball.

She comes off as a snob but, for some reason, she took a liking to Bethany. Out of the blue, Abigail made this gorgeous pinwheel quilt for Bethany and they've been fast friends ever since. She's become not quite an adopted grandmother to my kids, but more of an indulgent great aunt. And I have to say she's grown on me. Anybody who loves my kids is okay in my book and when she gave that quilt to Bethany, I was so grateful that I started to bawl. I couldn't help myself.

Anyway, Abigail is really very sweet deep down—way deep down—but she's also used to getting her own way. She wouldn't listen to any of my excuses about passing on the quilting class, just knocked them all down in that way she has, huffing and puffing out words like "Nonsense!" and "Rubbish!" like the big, bad wolf on a mission, not stopping until your little house of sticks is lying in a heap and there you stand with nothing left to hide behind. Next thing I knew, I was sitting in a room with six other students, listening to Evelyn Dixon explain the techniques for constructing our first project, a log cabin quilt.

It's an easy pattern, just row after row of rectangular strips nesting round and round a center square, stacking one upon the other like those wooden log toys I used to play with when I was a little girl. A simple pattern, maybe the simplest of all. I never expected it to change my life.

Evelyn brought a selection of light and dark fabrics for us to use for the "shady" and "sunny" sides of the house, but for the center of each block, the "hearth," she told us to find our own fabric, to cut the center squares out of something that had a special meaning for us. I chose the outgrown clothes the kids had worn in their pictures with Santa the year before, a red cowboy shirt for Bobby and the red corduroy jumper for Bethany, and cut out little squares, making them as even and perfect as I could, to place in the center of each block.

And then, something strange happened. As I sewed that quilt, stitching strip after strip around those red squares that had lain next to my children's skin and hearts, I started imagining each sunny and shady strip as a piece of a protective wall that was guarding my little ones and somehow, in a way that all my counselor's repeated affirmations never could, the idea that I could keep us safe, that I could make a real home for all of us, started to sprout in my mind. As I sewed, the idea became a belief and the roots of that belief pushed their way through all my doubts and muck to take root in my heart.

I *would* keep my children safe, no matter what. And we *would* have a home, a real home, not sleeping in a car, or bouncing from shelter to shelter and town to town like a bad check, not continually looking over my shoulder, ready to pack up and run every time I had a bad dream or heard a grinding of gears that sounded like a garage door opening. We'd be a family. Everything would be all right. I *would* make it happen.

As this . . . this torrent of conviction flooded my heart, my eyes began to flood, too. I sat at the sewing machine, not sewing, scissors open in my hand, a silent baptism bathing my cheeks.

Across the room, Evelyn was bent over another student's machine, helping adjust a too-tight tension. She saw me but made no move toward me, just looked at me for a long moment, as if trying to see into my real meaning, questioning the reason for my tears but not my right to them.

Seeing her, I sat up a little straighter in my chair, and gave her one quick nod. She smiled, as if knowing and approving that there, among the soft, steady whir of needles passing through fabric and the silent concentration of other women crouched over their sewing machines, bent on making something beautiful and useful out of the discarded scraps of their lives, I had made my decision.

I was done running.

❧ 2 ❧

Evelyn Dixon

Walking out my front door, down the porch steps, through the garden gate and onto the sidewalk on a perfect late spring day in New England, I was reminded again what a great commute I have. Just three blocks from the cozy, two-bedroom cape where I live at a very reasonable rent, to my shop, Cobbled Court Quilts.

My shop! I love saying that. In a week's time, it will have been my shop for two years, but sometimes I still have to pinch myself to believe it's true. Less than three years have passed since, in the wake of a painful divorce and a general upending of everything I'd thought was sure in my life, I got in my car and drove from Texas to Connecticut to see the fall colors.

On its face, there's nothing too remarkable about that, but anyone who knows me knows that spontaneous gestures are not my strong suit. I am a big fan of lists, not just to-do lists but the kind where you write down all the pros and cons of doing something and mull it over for days, weeks, or even months before taking action . . . or not. If you don't believe me, ask Charlie Donnelly, the owner of New Bern's finest restaurant, The Grill on the Green, and my boyfriend.

Boyfriend. At fifty years of age, it feels silly to say I have a boyfriend, but what else can I call Charlie? He's more than my friend and less than my fiancé, which is what he'd like to be, but I'm not ready yet and Charlie knows that.

Initially, when Charlie and I became "a couple" (are there any words for a romantic relationship between two mature people that don't sound so ridiculously precious?) right after my double mastectomy, I wasn't sure I was ready for a relationship. Now, I've worked through a lot of those issues in my mind, but . . . how do I explain it? After a lifetime of being someone's daughter, wife, mother, of defining my existence in terms of who I belonged to, I'm enjoying being just me by myself for a while, steering my own ship. Charlie knows that and he's willing to be patient. In fact, I think he's kind of proud of what I've accomplished. And the truth is, so am I. Not that I got to this place alone, far from it, but none of it would have happened if I hadn't finally decided to tear up my list of lists and take a chance on life and on myself.

Did you ever know, *just know,* that you were supposed to do something, even though, on the face of it, that thing you wanted to do made no sense to anyone else? That's the way it was with me with the quilt shop.

Window-shopping at the end of an absolutely picture-perfect fall day in New Bern during my unplanned escape from Texas to New England, I happened upon an alley paved with old cobblestones that lead into a spacious, square courtyard and found a dilapidated storefront that had been empty for about twenty years. The windows were cracked, the wood casings were eaten away by termites and rot, and the roof was leaky, but, for reasons beyond understanding, I was absolutely sure that my destiny lay in renting this ramshackle ruin and opening it as a quilt shop. So, throwing caution to the winds twice in one week, that's what I did.

Everybody, and I mean everybody, said we wouldn't last six months. They were almost right. In a turn of cosmic irony, on the very night before I was to host Cobbled Court's first Quilt Pink event to benefit breast cancer research, my doctor informed me that I had breast cancer myself. I was sure it was all over, that the predictions of the naysayers would prove true: Cobbled Court Quilts would be forced to close its doors and the door to my dreams would close along with it.

It would have happened exactly that way but for the help of three strangers—Abigail, Margot, and Liza—who became my best friends, supporting me through my cancer treatment and basically running the shop while I was recovering. I owe them everything. Not to mention my son, Garrett, who left a high-paying computer programming job at a big company in Seattle to help me develop and grow our Web business. He works with Margot on marketing strategy. And then there's Charlie, who loves me, encourages me, and who, if I get too tangled up in my lists to move forward, gives me a gentle nudge in the ribs or a swift kick in the pants, usually the latter. Charlie is an Irishman who doesn't suffer fools gladly or at all. He has many fine qualities but subtlety isn't among them.

Abigail, Margot, Liza, Garrett, and Charlie. If not for them, Cobbled Court Quilts really wouldn't have lasted six months.

I almost forgot Mary Dell! Mary Dell Templeton is an old friend from Texas. If she hadn't flown all the way up from Texas to literally pull up the shades in the dark room where I'd been laying and feeling sorry for myself after my mastectomies, I'm not sure I'd ever have gotten up and gotten on with my life.

Mary Dell is as Texas as chicken-fried steak, Dr Pepper, and the Alamo all rolled into one. She's also an amazing quilter. Once she decided to make a quilt with Texas Stadium on it. I watched while she cut out the pieces and then sewed them together without using a light box or even a pencil for outlining, and when she was done it was absolutely perfect; you practically expected to see cheerleaders lining up in the end zone, she's that good. The only piece missing from her quilting talent is . . . well . . . taste.

Mary Dell has pretty much the worst taste of anyone I've ever met. The louder, busier, and more garish the color combination, the more Mary Dell likes it. Fortunately, Howard, her twenty-four-year-old son with Down syndrome, has a highly attuned appreciation for colors, patterns, and textures. Howard chooses all the fabrics for Mary Dell's quilts. Together they make an unusual—and unbeatable—team. Like Mary Dell says, "If not for Howard, I'd be known all over the world for making the best-constructed, ugliest quilts in the state of Texas."

Instead, Mary Dell's quilting abilities and Texas-sized personality caught the attention of the people at the House and Home television network where, every Tuesday and Saturday, you can tune in to watch *Quintessential Quilting with Mary Dell and Howard.* Isn't that something?

When Howard was born, Mary Dell's husband was so upset that the baby was born with Down syndrome that he took off and never came back. In his despair, he left before understanding that, while the Templetons might not have been given the child they planned on, Howard was exactly the child they needed.

Margot would say it just goes to show you that God is in the business of just-in-time inventory, giving us what we need even when we don't know what it is we're running low on. I might not be as vocal about my faith as Margot is, but I can't help but think she's right.

I wouldn't have asked for a divorce after twenty-four years of marriage and I wouldn't have volunteered to lose both my breasts to cancer, either. Nothing about what I've been through was easy, but if I hadn't been through it I would never have fulfilled my dream of owning a quilt shop, or found these friends who have become as dear to me as family, or realized how strong I really am.

It's the same with Mary Dell. She'd never have asked for her one and only son to be born with Down syndrome, but if she didn't have Howard, would she be everything she is today? I don't see how. They fill each other's gaps.

Together, with Howard's gift for color and texture and Mary Dell's gift for design and construction, mother and son create the most beautiful, intricate, stunning quilts imaginable. Quilts that look like symphonies sound. Quilts with the power of poetry, sea air, and homemade chicken soup. Quilts that wrap around you with the warmth of loving arms. Quilts that teach you about love, and living well. Quilts that can heal hurts people don't even know they have and change their lives for the better.

But, then again, I'm convinced every quilt can do that. I've seen it happen before. And, soon, I would see it again.

❦ 3 ❦

Evelyn Dixon

Garrett lives in the one-bedroom apartment above the shop that I occupied before I moved into my rented cape, but I'm the one who opens the shop every morning. I arrive at eight-thirty, a good hour before the other employees.

Garrett is our night owl, working on the computer into the wee hours to process the Internet orders, manage the database, or update our website with our newest classes, fabric shipments, and specials. That's one of the reasons our Web business is coming on so strong; our site has something new to look at almost daily, so people tend to visit frequently. It's a big job and, according to Garrett, it's best done at night when there aren't so many people on the site. This means that Garrett's workday tends to start around noon and end around midnight, but not today.

I walked across the cobblestone courtyard toward the shop, smiling at the sight of the new window display Liza arranged on her last weekend home, an eye-catching collection of gold, yellow, red, black, and green fabrics and a garden of cheerful sunflowers made from wire and papier-mâché to highlight the sunflower quilt class we were offering next month. The lights were already on inside the shop and the red front door was slightly ajar. I pushed it open and the bells jingled merrily to announce my arrival. Someone had already started brewing coffee. I could smell it.

"Hello? Margot? Is that you?" I heard a sound of male laughter coming from the break room. Garrett came out holding a mug of coffee. Charlie trailed behind him, grinning and carrying a plate piled with what looked like fresh cinnamon rolls.

"Morning, Mom." Garrett yawned and ran a hand through his hair.

"Morning, sweetheart. You're up early."

"Yeah, well, Charlie was banging on the door early. I tried to ignore him, but he just stood in the courtyard bellowing that I'd better open up because his rolls were getting stale."

I gave Charlie a quick peck on the cheek, then grabbed one of the cinnamon rolls off the plate and took a bite. "They don't taste stale."

"That's because Garrett finally listened to reason and came downstairs to open the door," Charlie insisted in his teasing Irish brogue. "I've been up since dawn making these just for you. Another five minutes exposed to the cruel morning air and they'd have been ruined for sure. I'd have had to throw the whole batch away."

"Well, that would have been a shame because they are delicious. Thanks. Why were you up since dawn baking? Was there some kind of cinnamon roll emergency?"

Charlie rolled his eyes. "It's your big day, woman! Don't you remember? You've got those movie people coming in today. They're probably used to fancy caterers and champagne at breakfast. You've got to have something decent to offer them, something besides that jar of two-year-old biscotti in their individual, fresh-from-the-factory plastic wrappings you bought at the office supply store." He made a disgusted face. As the owner of New Bern's most elegant and popular restaurant, he was clearly concerned that the town's culinary reputation would suffer at my hands. "One look at those things and the crew will probably pack up their cameras and go back to Hollywood."

I laughed. "First of all, they're from Texas, not Hollywood. Big difference. At least, I think there's a big difference; I've never been to Hollywood. And second, they are television people, from the House and Home Network, not movie people, and I really don't think it's quite as big a deal as you're making it, Charlie. It's not like they're in town to shoot the chase scene of next summer's big blockbuster. It's just a little promotional video. It'll be Mary Dell, a cameraman, and one of her producers—that's all—and the whole thing shouldn't take more than an hour. Mary Dell told me herself. But it was sweet of you to go to all this trouble, Charlie."

"No trouble. Anything for my little starlet."

"Last time I checked, they don't make fifty-year-old starlets."

He put his arm around my waist, squeezed me, and said in a stage whisper. "Well, what do they know? Want to come see my office later? I'll show you my casting couch." I elbowed him in the ribs.

"Ouch! Is that any way to treat the man who got up with the sun to make you breakfast?"

"Don't you have a restaurant to run?"

"As a matter of fact," he looked at his watch, "I do. I've got a meeting with my seafood wholesaler in ten minutes."

Charlie kissed me and hurried toward the door. "You're going to bring Mary Dell and the rest of them up to the Grill for dinner tonight, right?"

I nodded. "Around six. Thanks for the cinnamon rolls. They're delicious. Just like you." I batted my eyelashes.

"Oh sure. *Now* you want to flirt with me. Too late. I've got to see a man about a fish. Bye, Garrett."

"Bye, Charlie."

Garrett, who was looking a little more alert now, took a slurp of coffee and chuckled to himself.

"What's so funny?"

"I was just thinking about Charlie. He told me a great joke this morning."

"Really? What was it?"

"Nothing I'm going to repeat to my mother."

"Ah. Well, in that case, what say we get to work? Can you e-mail a supply list to everybody who signed up for that table runner class? I've got to shelve those new pattern books that came in last night and I'd like to get that done before Mary Dell gets here."

A voice boomed in the doorway. "Then you should have started earlier, Baby Girl!"

"Mary Dell!" I squealed, dropped my half-eaten cinnamon roll, and ran to embrace my friend. "You're here! It's so good to see you! Where's Howard? Didn't he come with you?"

Mary Dell smiled broadly, "Howard's got himself a little girl-friend—Jena. He met her at a Down Syndrome Association dance. Her folks invited Howard to come with them to the rodeo this weekend, so he's staying with them. We're going to film this so quick there wasn't any point in him coming. He'll be out for the broadcast, though. The rest of my crew will be here in a minute. They're hauling in the equipment. Gosh! You look great, Evelyn!"

"You too. But, I thought your flight wasn't supposed to land for a couple of hours yet?"

"Turned out the gal who checked us in at the airport is a quilter. She recognized me and got us onto an earlier flight. First class, too. I do love bein' a television personality," she preened. "And so will you, honey. My camera guy is just going to love that pretty face of yours. It'll be a relief after filming my ugly mug day after day. Every time he turns the camera on it's a wonder the lens doesn't crack." She laughed and hugged me tight before I could argue with her, and I would have, too, if she'd given me the chance.

Mary Dell, with dangly silver and green crystal earrings that hung down to her shoulders, a hot-pink blouse with white cowgirl fringe, leopard-skin pumps that added an extra three inches to her five-foot-ten-inch frame, and fire-engine-red lipstick that clashed with absolutely everything she was wearing, might not be the pic-ture of understated elegance, but she had beautiful brown eyes, thick natural blond hair, a slender waist, and skin so smooth you'd have thought she was closer to thirty than fifty. Mary Dell's mother had been second-runner-up for Miss Texas of 1946. Obviously, good looks ran in the family.

"Whoo-whee!" Mary Dell cried when she finally released me

from her grasp. "You are looking fine! Way better than last time I saw you when you were lying around in that bed, feeling sorry for yourself, and looking like a sick calf. But now look at you!" She stared pointedly at my chest. "If I didn't know better I'd say those ta-tas you got under your blouse were the real deal!"

Garrett choked on his coffee.

"Really, Garrett, doesn't your mama look good? I tell you what, there just ain't nothing they can't do with silicone these days. I might want to get some of those for myself. What do you think?" Mary Dell stood up tall and stuck out her ample chest.

Garrett swallowed hard, trying to catch his breath. He was grinning, but I could see the tips of his ears turn red just the same. "I think you look fine just the way you are, Mrs. Templeton."

"Mrs. Templeton! Listen to you! You're not a teenager back in Texas anymore, Garrett. You're a grown man with a career. You can call me Mary Dell. Your mama says she couldn't run this place without you."

"Don't listen to her," Garrett said. "I handle the Web-related stuff, but Margot deals with all the marketing and accounting . . ."

"And don't forget Liza," I cut in and turned to Mary Dell. "Liza is Garrett's girlfriend. She's going to art school in New York now, but she comes up on weekends to help with our displays and to put together new fabric packs and medleys. She's got a real eye for color. Howard would be crazy about her. Liza's fabric medleys are some of our best-selling items."

"She's the niece of that other friend of yours, isn't she?" Mary Dell asked. "The snooty one? Abigail?"

"Abigail isn't snooty," I corrected. "She's particular. She comes from an old, very wealthy New England family so she's . . . well, it just takes time to get to know her, that's all. People in New England don't open up to strangers quite as quickly as they do in Texas, but Abigail is very kind and incredibly generous. Involved in all kinds of civic causes. She owns most of the commercial real estate in town. She rents me this place, plus Garrett's apartment upstairs, and our new workroom . . ."

"And the new warehouse space up the street," Garrett interrupted.

"And all for ten dollars a month plus the time it takes me to teach a few quilting classes over at the women's shelter. Something I'd have been happy to do for free anyway. So don't you go saying anything against Abigail to me," I shook my finger in mock indignation.

"Ten dollars a month!" Mary Dell whistled. "Well, in case, I take back everything I said about the snooty, old . . ." Mary Dell stopped mid-sentence when she saw the look on my face. "Sorry! I meant to say, I take back everything I said about dear, darling Abigail. Bless her heart," Mary Dell said, employing that old phrase that women of the South use when they want to say something catty about someone else . . . politely.

In spite of myself, I laughed. "Stop that. She may be an acquired taste, but Abigail has helped me and a lot of other people in this town. She can be prickly, I'll admit, but that is changing. She's dating her old attorney, Franklin Spaulding, and he seems to be a good influence on her. Plus, she's very involved with the women's shelter, not just on the board but spending time getting to know the residents. In fact, she's the one who recommended I hire Ivy."

"Ivy?"

"Remember? I told you about her on the phone. She and her kids are in transitional housing at the shelter. Ivy took my beginners' class there. When I needed to hire someone, Abigail recommended Ivy. I'm glad she did. She's a hard worker. Quiet, but cheerful and very dependable. We've got ourselves quite a team now."

Putting down his coffee cup, Garrett boosted himself off the counter and walked over to me, laying his long arm over my shoulder. "Of course, she forgets to mention that none of this would work without the very able leadership of the boss here. When I started working here, I didn't know top stitching from tap shoes, though I'm starting to, which, frankly, scares me a little. But Mom knows every square inch of this place. She knows what the trends are in fabrics and notions, chooses and teaches almost all the classes, and makes it fun for everyone who walks in the door. Half the time, I think customers come in here to talk to Mom as much as to buy quilting supplies.

"Yeah. Yeah." I said, brushing off his compliments. "Don't listen to him, Mary Dell. He's bucking for a raise. Won't do you any good, sweetie. We're doing better, that's for sure. In fact, we're on track to break even this year, but it's way too soon to think any of us will be making more than minimum wage for a good while to come."

"Not if I have anything to say about it, honey," Mary Dell said. She looked out the shop window, where I could see a man and woman coming across the courtyard hauling bags, boxes, and metal poles that looked like light stands. Mary Dell walked to the front door and opened it wide.

"Get in here, y'all! Get that gear set up. Not only do we have to make a promo that will get quilters fired up about Quilt Pink, we've got to make one that'll have folks running to their phones, booting up their computers, and driving halfway across the state to buy their fabrics from Miss Evelyn Dixon of Cobbled Court Quilts. Let's get this show on the road, buckaroos! We're burnin' daylight!"

4

Ivy Peterman

"Oh, come on!" I yelled and slammed my fist against the steering wheel. "This is not happening! Not again!"

I turned the key in the ignition once more, but it sounded even worse than it had the first three times I'd tried it, the halfhearted *vrum-vrumming* of the motor giving way to a low-pitched, lethargic whine. If a car engine could yawn, this was the sound it would make. Clearly, my car wasn't going to start. Not today.

I smacked my hand impotently against the wheel again, silently cursing all auto mechanics.

Ten days before, I had written the garage a check equivalent to two weeks' salary from my job at Cobbled Court Quilts. It was money I'd been saving and desperately needed for a rental deposit. When the kids and I moved into our transitional apartment at the Stanton Center, my counselor made it clear that I had to find a job and start saving for a place of my own as soon as possible. You'd think two years would be plenty of time for me to get my act together and be able to house and feed my own family, but when you start out lying flat on the ground without even a bootstrap to pull yourself up by, learning to stand on your own two feet is harder than it looks. But I was better off than a lot of people; I had the good luck to find a decent job not long after we came to New Bern. Twice in one month, quilting changed my life.

On Abigail's recommendation, Evelyn hired me as the fulfillment coordinator at Cobbled Court Quilts. Basically, I'm the one who cuts and packages up the Internet and phone orders and mails them out to customers. It's not glamorous, but I enjoy my work.

The upstairs workroom, a large rectangular space above the shop with exposed brick walls and tall windows that let in plenty of light, is my personal domain. I spend my days laying out bolts of fabric on the long cutting table, measuring quarter, or half, or full yards of cloth, slicing them off the bolt with a sharp rotary cutter, then packaging up the order and mailing it off to the other side of the state or the other side of the country. Really, it's amazing to see how many places we send quilting supplies to. I've mailed Cobbled Court Quilt Shop orders to every state except Hawaii and Wyoming. Once, we had an order that came all the way from Leicester, England.

As I work, I like thinking about the people who will receive the orders, imagining how excited they will be when their packages arrive and what kinds of quilts they will make from the fabric I've sent to them. It's nice and quiet here in the workroom and I have plenty of time to think. If they get busy downstairs, I'll help in the shop, but most of my day is spent upstairs and I prefer it that way. Not that I'm unfriendly to my coworkers; I smile and try my best to be helpful, to work hard, and to figure out what needs doing before anyone has to ask me to do it, but it's better if I keep to myself.

Evelyn is a great boss. When Bobby came down with the flu, she didn't mind my staying home with him at all. She even made a pot of chicken soup and brought it by the apartment. Garrett is nice, too, very patient when he taught me how to process the computer orders, and Margot is a sweetheart. She's very religious and at first I thought she was trying to make friends with me just so she could convert me, but now I realize that she is just a genuinely kind person. Though she is single and doesn't have any of her own, Margot loves kids and has offered to babysit for me anytime. I can't take her up on that offer, of course, or on her invitations to join her for a movie or dinner. I wish I could. If I ever did have a best friend, I'd want her to be someone like Margot, but I can't risk letting people get too close.

I have gotten to know Abigail a little bit, because of the kids, but that's not as risky, partly because Abigail doesn't work at the shop, she's just a good customer, and partly because . . . well . . . Abigail is Abigail. She likes my kids, but she doesn't seem that interested in me. Truthfully, I don't know much more about Abigail than she knows about me. I know she quilts, is dating her attorney, and is very, very rich. The name Wynne is plastered on half the buildings in town.

Maybe it isn't true of all of them, but I've noticed that very rich people don't seem to be too curious about the not-so-very-rich— adorable children being the exception. Fine by me.

Abigail recommended me for the job at Cobbled Quilts because she was worried about my kids. It had nothing to do with me, but did I care? No. I needed a job and Abigail helped me get one. Not easy in a small town with few openings, especially for someone with no degree and almost no work experience. I'm grateful to Abigail and to Evelyn. They helped me get started and I work hard to show them how much I appreciate this chance.

I'm putting as much money into savings as possible but even though I pay a very cheap rent for our apartment at the Stanton Center, it's hard to save. After paying for rent, food, gasoline, and clothing for two kids who seemed to outgrow a pair of shoes every month, there isn't much left over. In a month when one of the kids has to go to the doctor, there isn't anything left over. But, every time I can make a deposit into savings, I'm thrilled! I've promised myself that by this time next year, we'll be living in a place of our own. Nothing like the house we left in Pennsylvania, I'm sure, but someplace nice. Maybe with a little yard and room to plant flowers.

But when my car broke down, I had no choice but to take money out of savings to have it fixed. It just about killed me to spend that money, but what could I do? I had to get to work. I wrote out the check and hoped that when Larry, the mechanic, promised I wouldn't have any more problems with it, he was telling the truth.

Now, just a few days after taking a deep breath and writing that enormous check, I sat behind the wheel of my stalled car and yelled. "You're a big liar! You know that, Larry? A big, ugly, grease monkey of a liar!"

Larry's garage was miles out of earshot, but I didn't care. It might not have been dignified, but it made me feel better, at least for the time being.

I climbed out from behind the wheel, slammed the door shut, and, after taking a quick look at my watch, started jogging the mile to the bus stop. If I was lucky, I'd be able to catch the 9:11 bus to downtown New Bern and make it to work on time.

I wasn't lucky.

Having run up to the bus stop just in time to see the back of the 9:11 expel a black belch of exhaust from its tailpipe and pull away, I got to cool my heels for another twenty minutes before the next bus arrived.

When I got to New Bern, I took a shortcut down the alley to the delivery entrance rather than go through the front door of the shop. I was twenty-six minutes late. No one saw me come in, and I was glad. I could hear Evelyn, Garrett, and some other people talking in the front of the store. They were probably too involved in their own work to hear the back door open and close and wouldn't realize I was behind schedule.

Not that Evelyn would have given me a hard time for being late if I told her about what happened, but I didn't like the idea of her cutting me slack because of my situation. Evelyn had taken a chance in hiring me and I wanted to show her that she hadn't made a mistake.

On my lunch break, I would call Karen, the woman who lives in the apartment next to mine, and ask her if she would mind picking up Bobby and Bethany from day care when she came to get her little boy and taking them back to her apartment until I got home so I could make up the time I'd missed. That's another thing about living at the Stanton Center—they offer subsidized child care at a very good day care. The program won't end when I leave the Center but will continue for a full year after. Then the subsidy will gradually decline over a period of two more years. Another good reason to stay in New Bern. Without that subsidy, most of my earnings would have gone for child care. But, even with this kind of help, the life of a working mother isn't an easy. When an unexpected problem arose, like today, it was important to be connected to other moms who could help out. Karen would take care of my kids today. Another time, I'd do the same for her.

And if I were careful, no one would be the wiser. I opened the delivery door quietly, crept into the back room, grabbed the pile of order forms that were sitting in my inbox, and looked them over. It was going to be a busy day.

Besides the usual requests for yardage, patterns, and various notions, there were six orders for the pink and green fabric medleys Liza had put together for our weekly special. Those would be easy to do because they were all just fat quarters and we had plenty of fabric upstairs in the workroom. But there were also four orders for block-of-the-month kits. Those would take more time because they included eleven different fabric cuts, all of varying sizes, and I already had nine other kits on backorder because we'd run out of some fabrics. Fortunately, the delivery came in late the day before and the bolts I needed to finish the kits were sitting on the counter.

I loaded my arms up with several bolts of fabric, and then piled the day's order forms on top, keeping the papers from falling by anchoring them to the bolts with my chin.

Keeping my head down and being careful to steer clear of the squeaky tread on the stairs, I carried my load to the workroom, hoping I'd be lucky enough to avoid having my tardy ascent upstairs noticed by Evelyn or any of the other employees.

I wasn't being sneaky exactly. I just figured that since I was going to stay late to make up the time, why draw attention to my tardiness? But, if I could do it all over again, I would have walked in the front door, told Evelyn exactly why I was late, made my apologies, and gone to work. If I had, things would have been so much easier.

5

Evelyn Dixon

Having finished seating and soothing a party of four who were miffed that they couldn't get a booth in the front even though they'd walked in without a reservation, Charlie returned to the table where I was sitting with Mary Dell, her producer, Sandy, and the cameraman, Ben. Charlie pulled up a chair and poured the last drops of a second bottle of pinot noir into my glass.

"Now, wait a minute. Tell me again so I make sure I've got this right. It took you three hours, three *hours* to film a sixty-second promotional spot?"

"Don't laugh," I grumbled as I took a gulp of wine. "I got nervous, that's all. Being on television is not as easy as it looks. I'd like to see you try it."

"Mmmm." Charlie murmured in a tone that was supposed to pass for sympathy but didn't.

"Wipe that smile off your face," I demanded. "I've had a miserable day and there you sit, enjoying my humiliation."

"I'm sorry," Charlie said innocently. "Was I smiling?"

I didn't answer. He knew exactly what he'd been doing.

Charlie said contritely, "Come on now, Evelyn. I was just teasing you. Don't take it so hard. I'm sure it is harder than it looks. I'm sure there are lots of people who've had . . . how many takes was it she needed to film this sixty-second spot, Ben?"

Ben, the big bear of a cameraman, looked up from his plate and, with his mouth full of New York strip steak, answered, "Fifty-six." At which point, everyone but me started laughing uproariously.

"I hate you all," I said. "You're evil and I despise you and that is all there is to it." I put down my wineglass and buried my head in my hands.

"Mary Dell! Why did I let you talk me into this? When you called last month and told me about your great idea to do the show live from Cobbled Court to publicize Quilt Pink, you made it sound so easy. I didn't realize that the second Ben turned on the camera I'd start feeling like I might throw up."

"Actually," Sandy said to Charlie, "she did throw up. Three times. Any chance you're coming down with something, Evelyn?"

"I don't know," I said glumly. "Is stage fright viral? What am I going to do? If this is what happens when we're filming the promotional spot, how am I going to get through an entire broadcast? Live? How will it look if, right in the middle of talking about how to miter a binding corner, I have to excuse myself and run to the bathroom to toss my lunch?"

"A whole lot better than it'll look if you don't excuse yourself," Ben deadpanned, which set the rest of the group to howling again.

"This is serious!" I wailed. "Maybe we should just call this off while we still can."

Sandy made a dismissive face and shook her head. "You'll be fine," she said. "It's just a case of first-time jitters. You'll get over it. You were much better the last hour."

"That's because there was nothing left in my stomach."

"Well, make sure you don't eat before the show."

Mary Dell, who, because she was concentrating on enjoying every last bite of her tilapia, had been uncharacteristically silent all this time, finally spoke up. "Evelyn, calm down. You are making too much of this. Why, the first time Ben turned that camera on me I was jumpy as spit on a hot skillet. Wasn't I, Ben?"

Ben nodded dutifully as he sawed off another piece of meat.

"See? You'll be fine. Trust me. After all, you've got four months until the broadcast. By September, you'll be feeling fine as cream gravy."

I opened my mouth to argue with her, but we were interrupted. Lydia Moss, the wife of New Bern's First Selectman, Porter Moss, approached our table.

"Excuse me," she said, focusing on Mary Dell and completely ignoring everyone else at the table. Not surprising. I've been introduced to Lydia five different times at various community functions and each time she acts like it's the first time. She one of *those* types of New Englanders, the ones that consider you an alien intruder if your family didn't arrive here before 1700.

"Excuse me," she repeated, "but aren't you someone?"

Mary Dell was taking a drink of water. She started laughing when she heard this question and snorted some of the liquid up her nose. Sandy pounded her on the back until she quit choking.

"Well, I suppose so. Aren't you?"

Lydia blushed and cleared her throat. "I'm sorry. What I meant was, aren't you . . . I mean, haven't I seen you on television somewhere?"

"You might have." Mary Dell beamed and extended her hand. "It's nice to meet you. I'm Mary Dell Templeton. My son, Howard, and I host *Quintessential Quilting* on the House and Home Network."

"I thought so!" Lydia said excitedly. "Oh! Miss Templeton, I'm just such a fan!"

Now it was my turn to snort. Mary Dell kicked me under the table. I composed myself but was definitely feeling the effects of my second glass of wine. And, really, wasn't it funny how Lydia hadn't known Mary Dell's name but was suddenly a big fan? If Lydia had ever seen *Quintessential Quilting,* I was sure it hadn't been for more than a few seconds as she was flipping channels. She wasn't a quilter. At least, I'd never seen her in the shop.

Mary Dell, after withdrawing her foot from my shin, went into Moonlight and Magnolias mode. Lydia hadn't fooled her for a minute.

"Well, bless your heart! Aren't you sweet? It's always nice to meet a sister quilter. This is Ben, our cameraman, and Sandy, our producer." Sandy smiled and said hello. Ben just grunted and kept eating. "I'm sure you already know Charlie." Charlie said it was nice to see her again.

"And, of course," Mary Dell continued, lifting her hand toward me, "I'm sure you know Evelyn Dixon, owner of Cobbled Court Quilts? Evelyn is an old friend of mine."

"Oh, yes! Of course! We've met several times at community functions. My husband, Porter, is New Bern's First Selectman. That's something like the mayor in your part of the country, Miss Templeton." Lydia smiled broadly. "How nice to see you again, Evelyn. I just love your shop! It's been such a boon to the town. I said as much to my husband just last week."

I forced myself to return Lydia's smile. New Bern is a small town. There's no sense in antagonizing the First Selectman's wife, even if she is a big liar. "Thank you, Lydia. It's nice of you to say so."

"And before too long," Charlie piped in, "Cobbled Court Quilts will be an even bigger boon to New Bern. Mary Dell is doing a live broadcast of *Quintessential Quilting* from Evelyn's shop. Millions of people will be tuning in to watch Mary Dell and Evelyn, live, at the shop's annual Quilt Pink Day. Millions and millions of them." He turned to me, raising his eyebrows to their full height and grinning impishly.

My stomach lurched. I put my head in my hands again. "Oh, dear Lord."

Lydia ignored my groans. "Really? How exciting! And it's going to be live?"

"That's right," Charlie affirmed. "Filmed live. With millions and millions of . . ."

I snapped, "Be quiet, Charlie!"

"Well! Isn't that something!" Lydia exclaimed. "Will there be an audience at the broadcast?"

"Maybe a small one," Sandy said. "By the time we get all the lighting and camera equipment in, there won't be much extra room. Of course, the women who are participating in the Quilt Pink event will be there."

"Oh! That's wonderful! What a marvelous idea! And, of course, I'll be happy to participate! I couldn't dream of missing Quilt Pink Day, could I? It's one of New Bern's most important events of the year."

Really? Well, of course, I thought so, but if Lydia Moss agreed, it was the first I'd heard of it. I was trying to decide whether to say this or not when Porter Moss walked up to our table, holding Lydia's coat. He nodded to the assemblage.

"Hello."

Charlie got up from this table and shook hands. "Hello, Porter. How was your dinner? Everything to your liking?"

"Delicious as always, Charlie. I'm glad to see the short ribs back on the menu."

"Darling," Lydia purred, taking her husband's arm, "I'd like you to meet Mary Dell Templeton. She hosts a quilting show on television and is going to be filming an episode live from New Bern."

Impressed, Porter reached out and pumped Mary Dell's hand. "Well, that's terrific! A thing like that could really put New Bern on the map! Bring in the tourists. Let 'em know the Hamptons aren't the only place to spend their money."

Lydia nodded enthusiastically. "That's right. And Evelyn has invited me to participate in the broadcast. Isn't that wonderful? Of course, I'm sure she'll want you there, too. After all, you'll certainly want to include New Bern's most prominent political figure in your program, won't you, Evelyn?"

My head suddenly started to hurt and it wasn't from the wine. "Well, yes, normally I would, of course, but it *is* a show about quilting and . . ."

"Wonderful!" Porter boomed. "I'll have someone from my office call you next week. Lydia, we've got to run now. I'm supposed to lead the Pledge of Allegiance at the game. It was nice to meet you, Miss Templeton," he said, grasping her hand again before walking to the door with Lydia on his arm. "Good night, everyone."

"Are you kidding me?" I asked once the door was closed and the Mosses were out of earshot. "Not only has Lydia, who as far as I know can't even thread a needle, horned her way in on this broadcast but now she wants to bring her husband in, too? This is a nightmare. All I wanted to do was raise a little money for breast cancer research and suddenly I'm surrounded by gate-crashers and groupies!

"Seriously, Mary Dell. This is a bad omen. Let's just forget about doing the show here. I know you're trying to do a good deed, but the whole thing is getting out of hand."

"Hush now," Mary Dell said. "Don't go getting your bloomers in a twist. Pull yourself together, Evelyn. So the mayor, or the First Electman . . ."

"Selectman," I corrected.

"If the First Selectman and his wife want to be on the show. Fine. Let them. We'll stick them in a corner somewhere. They're just two people. What matters is that by the time this show airs, Cobbled Court Quilts will be a household name."

"That's not why I agreed to do this."

"I know," Mary Dell soothed. "I know that's not why you're doing it, but think, Evelyn! You've got a chance to really do some good! You could help raise thousands upon thousands for breast cancer research! And did Sandy tell you? We're planning on having your doctor on the broadcast."

"Dr. Finney?"

Sandy jumped in. "That's right. We thought it would be a good idea to have her talk about the importance of regular mammograms and we'll have her use a model to show the viewers how to perform self-exams. Charlie is exaggerating the size of our viewing audience, but it is considerable. Think of the chance to educate people about early detection! This broadcast will be about more than just quilting, it'll be about saving people's lives."

I was silent for a moment, thinking. "But, couldn't you just do a show about breast cancer anyway?"

"We could," Sandy said, "but the story of how you risked everything to open your own shop, and were diagnosed with breast cancer right before hosting your first Quilt Pink Day is so compelling. Women are going to be inspired by your story, Evelyn, and by your recovery. That's going to make them more willing to go in for early screening."

I knew there was something to what Sandy was saying. Sometimes people ignore the signs and symptoms of their disease because they are afraid of finding out the truth. Stories of breast cancer survivors and understanding how treatable the disease can be, especially in the early stages, can make women more willing to engage in early detection, and early detection saves lives.

"Charlie? What do you think I should do?"

His handsome blue eyes were full of encouragement. "I think it's a great opportunity for you to help other people and, knowing you like I do, I suspect you've already made up your mind."

I took a deep breath. "You're right. This is too important to pass up. But, I'm just so nervous."

Charlie put his arm around my shoulder and then reached up to brush the hair off my face. "You needn't be. You're absolutely up to this. And I'll do everything I can to help you."

"You will?" He nodded. "Well, you can start by not saying anything more about millions of people tuning in to watch the show."

"So noted," Charlie said. "So that's it, then? You're going to do it?"

"I guess I am."

"That's the spirit!" Charlie cheered and everyone else joined in, even Ben, who had finished eating and was looking for a waitress, probably wondering what was for dessert.

"This calls for a toast!" Charlie declared, getting up from the table. "Mary Dell, your glass is empty. I'm going to open another bottle of that pinot noir you like so much."

"Oh, no," she protested. "Charlie, darlin', I really couldn't."

"Don't be stupid, woman. You're staying with Evelyn tonight. That's a one-block walk from here. Of course, you can," he insisted as he headed over to the bar.

Mary Dell turned toward me, the sparkle in her eyes matching the sparkle in her crystal chandelier earrings. "I like that man *so* much."

∞ 6 ∞

Ivy Peterman

A champagne-colored sedan pulled up at the bus stop. It was raining so hard that, until she rolled down the window, I didn't realize the driver was Abigail.

"Ivy? What are you doing standing out here in this deluge?"

"My car broke down."

"What? Again?" Abigail pursed her lips and clucked, as if my car breaking down had been a matter of extremely poor planning on my part. Much as I appreciated all Abigail had done for me, her high-handed manner could be irritating. It wasn't like I enjoyed standing at the bus stop in the pouring rain. Of course, it might have helped if, before I'd left the shop, I'd remembered that the buses only ran every forty minutes instead of every twenty after five-thirty. I'd have stayed inside a bit longer before venturing into the downpour.

"Well, don't just stand there," Abigail ordered. "Get in. I'll drive you home. I've got a board meeting to attend at the Stanton Center."

My sodden clothes and hair dripped a rivulet onto the seat. Abigail pursed her lips again, reached behind the seat, pulled out a towel, and handed it to me.

"Here. Franklin insists on bringing his dog, Tina, with us when we go on hikes. She's a big darling of a black Lab but she makes a mess of my upholstery. I started keeping a towel in the car to dry off her muddy feet. It's clean. Use it to dry off a bit."

"Thanks," I said, wrapping the towel around sections of my sopping hair and squeezing out the water. "Sorry about dripping on your upholstery."

"That's all right. It's leather." Abigail pulled into the road quickly and without bothering to use a turn signal, ignoring the protesting honk of a white SUV she'd just cut off, as if she were accustomed to living in a world where others yielded to her. Looking at her, with her perfectly coiffed hair the exact same shade as the string of pearls that circled her long, elegant neck and hung to rest above the pearl buttons of a powder-blue cashmere cardigan that probably cost more than my last paycheck, it was easy to believe that traffic—or crowds, or the seas—parted for her. Abigail, I was sure, had always had things her own way and probably always would.

I flexed my toes inside my shoes and felt water squish out of the stitching. Some people had everything handed to them, I thought. It wasn't fair.

Abigail pulled up to a stoplight, waiting for the signal to turn green, and looked me curiously. "Where is your umbrella?"

"I don't have one!" I said, more sharply than I'd intended.

"Oh." She lifted her chin as she made the turn. "I see."

I sighed. "I'm sorry, Abigail. I've had a bad day. First the car wouldn't start, then I hurt my ankle running to the bus stop, and then I got caught in that downpour. Your coming along to offer me a ride is the first good thing that's happened to me since I woke up. Sorry I snapped at you."

"That's all right. I wasn't trying to make you feel foolish. It just seemed odd to me that someone as bright as you are would have forgotten to bring her umbrella with her on a day when it's raining cats and dogs. It never occurred to me that you didn't own one."

"Well, if you have to choose between buying school supplies for your daughter or an umbrella for yourself, school supplies win every time. Besides, when I left the apartment this morning, I hadn't figured I'd be taking the bus, so even if I had an umbrella, I probably wouldn't have brought it with me. See?" I said cheerfully hoping to ease past the awkward moment. "I'm obviously not as bright as you thought."

Abigail returned my smile, arching her eyebrows as she pressed her foot farther down on the gas now that we were in the less populated part of town where there were fewer police cruisers on the lookout for speeders. "Somehow I doubt that. Bethany is as bright as a new penny and, in my experience, the apple doesn't fall far from the tree. In another situation, I might suppose she could have inherited that from her father. I don't mean to speak ill of the dead, but I'm guessing he wasn't all that intelligent. If he was, you and the children wouldn't be here in New Bern, would you?"

I didn't respond. The last thing I wanted to do was discuss my invented past with Abigail. But I did appreciate her insight. For all her imposing, sometimes intimidating aura of self-certainty, she meant well. And she'd certainly been kind to the kids.

"I'm sorry you're having a bad day. My own hasn't been exactly red letter," she said, launching into an explanation before giving me a chance to ask for one.

"I am *not* looking forward to this meeting. It's just going to be another exercise in futility, everyone sitting around the conference table grumbling and groaning about the need for more emergency and transitional housing to help women like you, and reaching no consensus about how to solve the problem. At the end of three hours, we'll be lucky if we've agreed on so much as when to hold our next meeting! And the whole time we sit there, drinking coffee and doing nothing, the waitlist of families needing our services grows longer. It's so frustrating!"

"Well," I said slowly, not quite understanding why the solution to this problem wasn't obvious to Abigail, "why don't you get a new building? Something bigger."

"Of course, that's what we'd like to do. We've discussed it at excruciating length, but it isn't as easy as just digging a foundation and putting up walls. To begin with, there's the question of money. The kind of facility we'd need would cost millions, perhaps tens of millions. I'd be perfectly willing to pay for it for through the Wynne Family Foundation. But Donna Walsh, the director, feels very strongly that it must be a community-wide fund-raising effort, something that people in town could all get behind. If I just swooped in and paid for it, Donna thinks it could start a backlash against the very families we're trying to help." Abigail drew her eyebrows together thoughtfully.

"I suppose there's something to that," she mused. "We don't want people to start looking at the shelter residents as an alien population that has been imposed upon them without their input or consent. But a big fund-raising effort can take years to mount. We've got people knocking on our door who need help now, not ten years from now!"

"I can see why you're frustrated."

"And that's not the half of it. Even if we had the money in hand today, I'm not sure where we'd find land in a location that would be suitable for a project of this size. We need space to house at least ten families. And in a central location, somewhere close to schools, community services, and public transportation."

This subject hit too close to home. My resolution to say as little as possible melted like an ice cream cone on a summer day.

"You can say that again!" I huffed. "Don't get me wrong, I'm so grateful that we were able to move into the Stanton Center, but it would sure make things easier if it weren't so far off the beaten path.

"Take today; when my car wouldn't start I had to jog a mile to catch a bus and ended up late for work. Evelyn's a good boss—she understands that things happen—but someone else's employer might not. Being late to work even once might cost a woman her job. After housing, transportation is the biggest problem most of us face. We simply can't afford to buy reliable cars, not to mention the gas, insurance, and maintenance to keep them running. If we could live closer in and on the bus line, I'd get rid of my car tomorrow! Everything in New Bern is so close that I could walk to most of the stores. If I didn't have the expense of owning a car, it would make it much easier to save money."

Abigail nodded firmly as she made a hard right into the parking lot of the Stanton Center. "You're right. Absolutely right. But that's the problem. New Bern is an old New England town and all the in-town lots of any size were built on decades ago. The only available building lots around here are either too small for our purposes, or even farther off the beaten path than what we have now. I've racked my brain, but I can't see a solution to this. Not a good one, anyway."

She spied an empty parking spot between two cars, wedged her sedan between them at an alarming speed, and set her parking brake, stomping on the pedal as if it were some sort of poisonous insect. "I'm simply out of ideas."

"It's too bad some of those big mansions in New Bern, you know, those giant places over on Proctor, aren't for sale," I said jokingly. "A couple of weeks ago, we went for a walk down that street. Those houses sure are something. One of those places would be big enough to hold ten families."

I smiled, remembering the day. The calendar had only just turned to spring. Crocuses were blooming in the flower beds that had been covered with snow only a few days before. At one house, the crocuses were sprouting at odd spots all through the lawn, as if they'd just sprung up on their own, like wildflowers in a field, though I doubted that was the case. I couldn't see people in this neighborhood just letting any old flower pop up in their lawn. Probably someone had planted them there to give the impression of wildness, but that was all right. They were pretty, no matter how they'd gotten there.

The sun was warm. Bobby kept pulling off his hat, a knitted stocking cap with two brown and white ovals that made him look like a teddy bear. He looked so cute, but I knew that by this time next year, he'd balk at being seen wearing a teddy-bear hat, just like he was beginning to balk at riding in the stroller. When I was little, my dad used to joke that he was going to put me in a pickle barrel to keep me from getting any bigger. Now I understood what he was talking about. My baby was almost a little boy and my little girl halfway to grown. Make that three quarters.

She'd insisted on being the one to push Bobby's stroller, walking behind it like a miniature mother as we ooohed and ahhhed over the enormous mansions and talked about which houses we'd like to live in if we were ever rich.

My favorite was a sprawling white colonial with black shutters and six dormers tucked into the roofline. The main part of the house was huge to begin with, but it was clear that, over the years, people had added on to the original structure, tacking on a solarium here or a library there as their needs and taste in architecture had changed. It wasn't necessarily the prettiest house on the street, but something about the evolution of this home appealed to me, maybe because I liked to see how each generation built upon the foundation of the one that came before. The roofline was slightly bowed, and yet it looked like it had always been there and always would be.

"You'd never run out of guest rooms in a house like that," I said to Bethany. "On the other hand, maybe you'd have a hard time getting the guests to go home. And of course, there'd be all those bathrooms to clean. Still," I said wistfully, "it would sure be something to live in a house like that, don't you think so, peanut?"

Bethany nodded noncommittally, obviously not as enamored with the house as I was. "I like that one," she said, pointing off to the far right.

"Which one?" I tried to track my eyes in the direction she was pointing.

"There," she said, stabbing the air with her finger. "That little white one next door—that happy house. See? It's smiling!"

I looked again and laughed. She was pointing to a smaller building. Two six-over-six windows sat on either side and slightly above a red front door with three bulls-eye glass panes across the top. The second story had narrow eyebrow windows arranged in perfect symmetry over larger six-by-sixes on the main floor. I saw what Bethany meant; if you used your imagination, the door looked like an open, laughing red mouth and the windows like smiling eyes. "You're right. It's a happy house."

Bethany pointed to the big white mansion next door. "Do you think the people that live here are happy, too?"

"Well, if they're not, they ought to be. I could sure be happy living in a place like this."

"But maybe not," Bethany said sagely. "We lived in a big house before and we weren't happy there, were we, Mommy?"

"No," I whispered, remembering the four-bedroom, two-and-a-half-bath ranch house in an upscale suburban neighborhood where we'd lived for eight years; the house where I'd become an expert in the art of using foundation and concealer to mask my latest bruises because I didn't want to neighbors to know that our house wasn't as happy as it looked from the outside. "No, we weren't."

"I like where we live now." Bethany said, referring to our tiny apartment. "But, if I could, it would be nice to live in a house that smiles."

Abigail smacked the dashboard with her hand, startling me out of my reverie. "That's it!" she exclaimed. "The perfect solution! Why didn't I think of it before?"

"Think of what before?"

"A Proctor Street house! You're right, if it was modeled into separate apartments, it could easily house ten families. The neighborhood is quiet, within walking distance to schools and the downtown area where most jobs are, and it's just two blocks from the bus line! Brilliant idea!"

Beaming, Abigail unbuckled her seat belt and practically leapt out of the car. "Just lock the doors, would you? I've got to run to my meeting. I can't wait to tell Donna about this! It's the absolutely perfect solution to all our problems. Must run. Tell Bethany and Bobby I said hello. Thank you so much, Ivy!"

She slammed the door shut and scurried toward the front door without an umbrella, her high heels echoing definitively against the sidewalk, seemingly unaware that she was getting soaked.

I got out of the car. "You're welcome," I called after her, though I didn't see what I'd said that was so helpful.

7

Evelyn Dixon

"All right, Wendy. The total is $126.75."

Wendy opened her eyes wider and pushed her rhinestone-encrusted glasses up on her nose. "Really?"

"Well, that does include the forty-five dollars class fee as well as your fabric. But, I understand. It does add up."

"Could be worse," Wendy shrugged as she rifled through her enormous handbag looking for her checkbook. "My ex-husband's hobby was drinking and chasing women. Sweetie, compared to that, quilting is a bargain!" Wendy wrinkled up her nose, squashed her lips into an open *O*, and snorted with laughter, her tongue pushing out between the circle of her lips with each snort. I joined in. Wendy's laugh was so unique and so comical that it was impossible not to.

"So, how are things going around here, Evelyn?" she asked as she bent over her checkbook. "How're you feeling these days?"

"Couldn't be better. I just saw my doctor last week. No signs of cancer anywhere. Of course, I'll have to keep going back for regular checkups, but the doctor thinks I'm fine."

"That's great! Wonderful! And the shop? How's business been?"

"Not bad. Not booming, but every month is a little better than the one before. Our Internet business is good and we're getting more walk-in traffic, too. Somebody must be spreading the word. This week I had a group of three customers who were driving from Rhode Island to New York and took a ninety-minute detour just to check us out. Not everyone would go so far out of their way to visit a new shop, but if the word is getting out among the hard-core quilters, it's a good sign."

"That's terrific," Wendy commented and handed me her check. "You've come a long way in two years. Remember when you found this place? I'd been going through the longest dry spell, hadn't gotten a commission check in I don't know how long, and there I was, getting ready to close up for the night and thinking that I'd just wasted another day of my life in the real estate business when the phone rang. It was you, saying you wanted to lease this old wreck of a building and would be over in five minutes to sign the papers. I was so shocked I didn't know what to think! It had been so long since anyone had asked about this place that I had to dig through the archived files to find out what they wanted to rent it for. The paperwork was dated something like 1982! Back in the days when I still had all my own teeth!" *Snort! Snort!*

I put the check in the register and handed Wendy her receipt. "Remember how you tried to talk me out of taking out the lease? Some Realtor you are."

"Well, I was worried about you. You'd just been through a divorce. I thought maybe this was your way of going on the rebound. That instead of taking up with another miserable man who would burn through your money and break your heart, you decided to do the same thing except with a quilt shop!" *Snort!*

"I didn't see how you could make a go of it, not in this location, but I was dead wrong. Forgive me for doubting you."

"That's all right, Wendy. It isn't like you were the only one who felt that way. Do you have your punch card with you? You get a fifteen-dollar gift certificate for every three hundred dollars you spend. You must be pretty close by now."

"Hold on," Wendy said digging through her voluminous handbag. "It's in here somewhere."

The front door jingled. I looked up to see Abigail and Franklin enter with Liza following close behind. "Liza!" I ran out from behind the counter to give her a hug. "I didn't know you were coming home this weekend! Does Garrett know?"

She looked wonderful. She'd gone back to her natural color, a deep chestnut brown with some reddish undertones. It was much more becoming than the dye she'd used when we first met. So much had changed since that day when she dragged Abigail into my first Quilt Pink event. The sullen, angry teenager, the girl with the darting eyes, slumped shoulders and all-black wardrobe had been replaced by a smiling and confident young woman. Of course, she was still our Liza, artistic, a little edgy, blunt, and just as strong-willed as her Aunt Abigail. The two of them could go ten rounds over the silliest things, but these days it was more just for her own entertainment than from any desire to really hurt Abigail. She still liked to wear clothing that got attention, mostly of her own design, like the black jean jacket she was wearing today, embellished with a line of bottle caps she'd grommeted to the shoulders like epaulettes on the uniform of a four-star general. It was an original, just like Liza.

"I didn't have a chance to call him," she said, hugging me back. "My Friday sculpture class was canceled, so on a whim I just hopped the next train headed north."

"*And* she forgot her cell phone in the dorm," Abigail interrupted. "Thank heaven there was a pay phone at the station and that I was home when she called to ask Franklin and me to pick her up. Otherwise, she'd have spent the weekend standing on the platform at the Waterbury train depot. Really, Liza, you must start planning ahead a little. What if I hadn't been home? What if I'd decided to go out of town for the weekend?"

"Then I'd have called a cab to take me to New Bern, found the spare key you have 'hidden' under the flowerpot even though everyone in town knows exactly where you keep it, let myself in, and spent the weekend eating your food and swimming in your pool. Oh. And I'd have called Garrett to come over and spend the weekend with me so we could do a little passionate necking on your sofa. Right before we emptied out your liquor cabinet." Liza rolled her eyes. "Really, Abigail. Do you think I'm ten years old or something? If you'd been gone, I'd have worked something out. Besides, I knew you'd be home. It's Quilt Circle night. You wouldn't miss out on that unless you'd gotten a better offer, like dinner at the White House."

The look on Abigail's face told me she was ready to launch into a full-scale argument with her niece but, thankfully, Wendy interrupted. "Evelyn, I've got to get back the office and I can't find that silly card anywhere. It must be in my other pocketbook."

"That's fine," I said. "Save the receipt and when you find the card, bring it in and I'll punch it for you."

Wendy scurried out the front door just as Garrett came out of the back office. "I was on the phone with a customer, but did I hear somebody say something about passionate necking? Count me in." He winked at Abigail before crossing the room to give Liza a kiss. "I didn't think you'd be here until next weekend. Why the surprise? Did you miss me? So much you decided to come up here to buy me dinner?"

Smiling, Liza reached up, grabbed a piece of Garrett's hair, and yanked it playfully. "You wish. Actually, I came up here to come to my quilt-circle meeting. I may live in Manhattan, but I'm still an affiliate member, you know. However, if you play your cards right, I'll let *you* buy *my* dinner on Saturday night."

"Hmmm. What about the passionate necking part? Do we still get to do that?"

"Maybe," Liza said casually. "If you play your cards right."

"All right, you two." I said. "Enough flirting. Go tell Margot it's quitting time. If she hasn't been able to get the accounts to balance by now, it'll just have to wait until Monday." I walked to the front, turned the closed sign face out, and opened the door. "Franklin, Garrett, nothing personal but—clear out. This meeting is for members only."

Franklin kissed Abigail on the cheek and then turned to Garrett. "They want us to leave."

"Do you think?" Garrett looked at me as I stood holding the knob of the open door.

"Well, fine," he harrumphed. "I can take a hint. I've been thrown out of better places than this. Come on, Franklin. Let's go the Grill and have a beer. I'll buy."

Franklin shook his head. "Sorry, but I can't. I'm headed over to Ivy's to babysit. She doesn't know it yet, but she's about to be inducted as a full member of the Cobbled Court Quilt Circle, with all the rights and privileges herein."

"Rights and privileges? Such as?"

"Such as having Uncle Franklin babysit Bethany and Bobby on Friday nights so she can have an evening out with the girls and do some quilting. At least, that's what they say they do up there. I'm not convinced there's as much quilting as gabbing going on."

"Abigail talked you into babysitting Ivy's kids every Friday night? Wow. You're either the nicest guy or the biggest sucker in the world, you know that?"

Franklin's eyes twinkled as he gave Abigail a glance. "My boy, you don't know the half of it. Why don't you come to Ivy's with me? We can make peanut butter and jelly sandwiches, play Candy Land, and I can tell you about the price of loving a beautiful woman."

Franklin put his arm across Garrett's shoulders and, like Rick and Louis in the final scene in *Casablanca,* the two men walked out into the shadowy evening and into the beginning of a beautiful friendship.

I closed the door. Liza laughed. "What do you want to bet that Ivy comes home tonight to find those two passed out on the sofa asleep, with their fingernails painted red, and the kids still awake, watching TV and eating chocolate ice cream out of the container?"

"I wouldn't want to give you odds on it," I said, "but that's all right, chocolate washes out." I locked the door of the shop.

"Ladies, let's call this meeting to order. It's time to welcome a new quilter into our ranks."

The word "meeting" projects a much more formal, organized gathering than the reality of the weekly gathering of the Cobbled Court Quilt Circle. That's not to say that those kinds of groups don't exist; there are quilt circles and guilds that have roll calls and rosters, agendas and officers, guest books and guest speakers. Over the years and in various locations, I've belonged to such groups and enjoyed them.

But our little circle is as much about companionship as it is about learning the oldest, or latest, or fastest quilting techniques, probably more so.

The Cobbled Court Quilt Circle has just four members: Margot, Abigail, Liza, and me. I started it as a means of thanking the others for supporting me through my breast cancer treatment, but in the end I think I've gotten as much out of it as they have.

These Friday evenings are a welcome break at the end of a long week, something we all look forward to; a safe, private space where we can talk, or laugh, or cry with friends or, if quiet is what we are most craving, just sit and focus our attention on the quilting, working in companionable silence with people who know our stories and understand our stillness. Sometime our meetings are peaceful and calm, marked by low voices, the metallic snip of scissors, and the soft whir of sewing machines. Other nights they are punctuated by raucous, uncontrollable laughter, and the giddy sound of female voices interrupting one another, jockeying to take over the role of narrator for a story they can't wait to tell.

I love Friday nights.

When I was going through my cancer battle, those few hours on Friday were the only times I really felt like myself. For that thin slice of the week, I forgot about the disease that had invaded my body or, if I couldn't forget about it, at least lived with it, embraced by the warmth of good women whose kindness and determination to see me through my darkest hours gave me hope that, one way or another, everything would be all right. And, in the end, it was. Not that I don't still need them, or they me. The scars of my surgery have faded considerably but not completely and the others all carry their own kinds of scars, healing at their own, individual rates. That's the point of Friday nights. The scars don't appear as terrible, or take as long to heal, when you're safe inside the circle of friends. For a while there, Friday nights were the only times I felt lucky.

That's why I wanted Ivy to join our circle. I thought that she needed us.

Ivy has a quick wit but, more often than not, the laughs come at her own expense, poking fun at her own weaknesses with a regularity and fierceness that makes me wonder if she's really joking at all.

I really don't know much about Ivy, but there's something about her, a sadness that lurks behind her ready smile and goes down to the bone. She tries to mask it, but it's there, sadness and something else harder to name. Determination, perhaps.

I saw it clearly one night during the log cabin class at the Stanton Center, as she sat at her sewing machine, holding her quilt block in her two hands as silent tears tracked slowly down her cheeks. Seeing her crying, I started to go over and comfort her, but she saw me looking at her and nodded to let me know she was all right, or would be. Ivy is quiet and careful, but she's also strong. Given what she's been through, I guess she'd have to be.

Since she lives at the Stanton Center, we know she was married to an abusive man, a man who Abigail told me was killed in some sort of construction accident and left Ivy and the children without a dime to live on, but she never speaks of him or of how she ended up in New Bern. I think she's from somewhere in Pennsylvania originally, but I don't know for certain.

Not that she has to share any of that with us, not at all. Our quilt circle isn't a place for gossip, it's a place for honesty. It might take some time, but I think that's what Ivy needs; a safe place where she can be herself and a group of friends who will love and accept her for exactly who she is.

8

Evelyn Dixon

Abigail was indignant.

"No? We're kind enough to invite her to join our quilt circle and she just says no? After all we've done for her! Especially you, Evelyn. Where would she be if you hadn't given her a job?" She answered her own question. "In the unemployment line, that's where! I've never heard of such ingratitude!"

She practically stabbed the needle through the quilt top and batting she was basting together. Looking at her, I decided it was a good thing Ivy had left as quickly as she did. If not, Abigail just might have turned that basting needle into a lethal weapon.

We were in the workroom, Abigail, Liza, Margot, and myself, going on with our usual circle meeting like we normally did, but the evening's previously festive atmosphere had definitely faded.

Margot was working on a quilted tote bag she planned to give her sister for Christmas. Liza was supposed to be sewing a bunch of shells with holes she'd drilled herself onto the back of a jacket, but mostly she seemed to be drinking wine. And I sat at my sewing machine with my head down, using my seam ripper to remove the stitches from a seam I'd accidentally sewn wrong sides together, the sort of beginner's mistake I hadn't made in years.

"Abigail, calm down. It's not like joining the quilt circle is a condition of employment around here. Ivy must have her reasons for not wanting to be part of the group," I said evenly, though for the life of me, I couldn't think what those reasons could be.

I was so sure that Ivy would be happy, even excited, at the prospect of being included in our circle. If not for the quilting, at least for the chance to have an adult evening out now and then. It never crossed my mind that she'd refuse the invitation. I couldn't help but feel a little hurt by Ivy's reaction.

"Well"—Liza shrugged and took another sip from one of the coffee cups we used in lieu of wineglasses—"it isn't like she was rude about it, Abigail. She just said she'd rather not, that's all. You're just mad because someone isn't doing what you want them to do. That always ticks you off."

Abigail glared at her niece. "That's simply not so. I don't know why you always think the worst of me, Liza."

"Then why are you so upset? Why should you care if Ivy joins the quilt circle or not? You don't even like her. Admit it, you're just mad because Ivy isn't doing what you want her to do. You're not happy unless everyone is dancing to your tune."

Oh great, I thought. *Here they go again.*

The last thing I was in the mood for was to listen to Liza and Abigail's bickering. They were each other's only living relatives, thrust unwillingly together when the court had briefly made Abigail responsible for her niece after Liza had experienced a minor run-in with the law. Their relationship was often rocky but they truly did love each other, though Liza knew exactly how to push her aunt's buttons and never tired of doing so.

I never understood why Abigail, so intelligent about so many things, couldn't see that Liza was setting her up, striking the match of her aunt's temper and then laughing at the ensuing shower of sparks.

"Margot, what did you put in that pound cake? It's fabulous. I'm going to have another piece. Abigail, can I get you some more cake?"

It was a weak attempt at a diversion, especially since Abigail hadn't had any cake to begin with, but I was tired; it was the best I could come up with on short notice.

"That's not true," Abigail said airily, ignoring my question. "It makes not the slightest bit of difference to me if Ivy joins us or not. I do think it was rude of her to refuse, but it's no skin off my nose that she did. I'm perfectly happy for things to stay as they are. I wasn't all that sold on adding someone new to the group anyway. I've got other things on my mind besides Ivy Peterman, I can assure you."

A hint of a smiled bowed Liza's lips. "Such as?"

"Such as," Abigail answered haughtily, "my upcoming presentation to the zoning board on the subject of turning my house into transitional apartments for families in crisis."

"What?"

I dropped the piece of cake I'd been serving, missing the plate entirely and scattering crumbs across the floor. Margot sat wide-eyed at the sewing machine, hands in her lap but so shocked she'd forgotten to take her foot off the pedal. The mechanical whirr of the machine underscored our expressions of disbelief.

"You're selling your house?"

"But why?"

"You can't be serious," Liza declared. "This has to be some kind of joke."

This time it was Abigail's turn to smile. Clearly she was enjoying being the one to set Liza off balance instead of the other way around.

"It's no joke," she answered. "I'm quite serious. But, I'm not selling the house; I'm donating it. The Stanton Center is desperate to find a larger facility."

"So you just thought to yourself, 'Hey! I've got an idea. Why not give them the house?' "

"The Stanton Center needs a large building. I do not. At my age, do I really need to live in a house with eight bedrooms, six baths, and a ballroom? No. If the Stanton Center needs the space and I don't, why not give it to them?"

"You're very generous, Abigail," Margot said diplomatically. "But wouldn't it make more sense for Stanton to buy an empty lot and build from scratch? It won't be cheap to convert your antique home into modern apartments. I'm sure you'd have to make all kinds of changes to the plumbing and such. Not to mention the remodeling you'd have to do for it to meet fire codes and handi-capped accessibility requirements. It could run into hundreds of thousands of dollars."

"Oh no," Abigail said assuredly. "It will run into millions. I've already looked into it. But, there are simply no lots that are large enough or close enough to town available. The new center must be close to bus lines, schools, and the downtown area."

Abigail squared her shoulders and lifted her chin. "These women are facing enough problems trying to move beyond the legacy of do-mestic violence without our community making it even more difficult for them to obtain decent housing, and the access to transportation and good schools for their children that they need in order to be-come productive members of the workforce while raising their chil-dren to be responsible citizens. This is an issue that concerns our entire community and it will take the efforts of our entire commu-nity to meet and conquer this challenge!"

"Let me guess," Liza said sarcastically. "You're running for Con-gress. Either that or this is the speech you're planning on making to the zoning board."

"It is. And I'm sure, once they hear my arguments, the board will see things my way."

"Abigail, are you crazy? The neighbors are never going to go for this. The Hudsons? Dale Barrows and the rest of them? Do you re-ally think they're stand aside and let you put an apartment building on Proctor Street? Where did you ever get such a ridiculous idea?"

"From Ivy. I was driving her home a couple of days ago; her car had broken down again. And I was telling her about the problem we were having trying to find a place large enough for the new building, and she said it would be nice if one of the big houses on Proctor Street were for sale. I think she was just making a joke, but as soon as she mentioned that, I could see she was right."

Liza made a noise with her lips, a sputter like a whinnying horse. "You're insane. Really, this is about the dumbest scheme you've ever come up with."

I loved Liza, but there were moments when I could happily have slapped her. This was one of them. But I wasn't her mother and it wasn't my place—it was Abigail's, but she didn't see that. She was too busy sitting in her chair and feeling stung by Liza's out-of-hand dismissal of what was a very well-intended, though less than well-considered, gesture.

Liza grabbed her jacket off the back of her chair. "Hey, I'm gonna run. I want to see if I can find Garrett." She kissed the wounded Abigail on top of her head and breezed thoughtlessly out the door.

There was no point in trying to pretend we were going to get any more quilting done that night.

We shut off the irons and sewing machines and ended the evening as we so often did, sitting around the table eating, drinking, and talking.

"Drink this," I handed Abigail a cup filled with 2003 pinot gris. Abigail took the cup but didn't lift it to her lips. She was still upset.

"I don't understand. Before Liza came into my life, I was capable, erudite, respected. Even occasionally brilliant. Everyone liked me and I liked myself. But as far as Liza's concerned, no matter how good my intentions are, I'm completely inept. How did that happen?"

"You had a baby," I said matter-of-factly. "Not literally, I know, but for all intents and purposes, you're Liza's mother now. Liza still has one foot in adolescence and, trust me, no matter what you do or don't do, an adolescent will find some way of making you feel stupid. It's a stage. She'll outgrow it, but it can take a while."

Abigail finally took a sip of her wine. Actually, it was more like a gulp, as if she'd just realized that she really wanted a drink.

"Well, she makes me feel just awful. Why is that?"

"That," I said as I handed Abigail a plate of cheese and grapes to go with her wine, "is maternal guilt. Unfortunately, it's a stage you'll never outgrow."

Abigail groaned.

"Sorry. But I wouldn't be much of a friend if I didn't tell you the truth.

"Abigail, tell me something. It really is incredibly generous of you to donate your home to the Stanton Center, but Liza does have a point. Do you think all your wealthy neighbors on Proctor Street, all those bank presidents and real estate moguls and movie producers, are really going to be excited about the idea of having a bunch of formerly homeless families living on their street?"

"Well, why not?" she said, sitting up straighter in her chair. "I'll be living there, too."

Margot pulled her chair closer in and pulled a grape off the vine. "But I thought you said you were moving out of the house?"

"I am," Abigail confirmed, "but that doesn't mean I'm moving away from Proctor Street. It's been my home for forty years."

"How are you going to manage that? There aren't any other houses on Proctor for sale. There never are. People always pass those houses down through their families."

Abigail nodded and swallowed her wine before answering. "That's right, just like the Wynnes did. My late husband, Woolley, was born there, as were his father and his father before him all the way back to the 1830s. Since Woolley and I never had children, I always planned on having the house sold and the proceeds donated to charity after my death. Nothing has changed. I'm just donating the house a little sooner than I'd planned on, that's all. I'm going to simplify my life."

"But that still doesn't explain where you're planning on living," Margot said.

"Right where I always have. Well, nearly. That's why I'm going before the zoning board. The first step is to subdivide the property. I'll donate the main house and the larger parcel of land to the Stanton Center, keep the smaller parcel, and move into the carriage house next door. It's smaller, but there are three good-sized bedrooms, a nice kitchen and dining room, a large living room, and lovely gardens. There's no office, but that's all right. I was considering adding on a solarium. And a walk-in closet. I won't have a pool anymore, but I suppose I could always have one put in," she mused. "The ground is fairly flat. It wouldn't be that hard to do."

I bit my lower lip, trying to keep from laughing at the manner in which Abigail Burgess Wynne, the sixth wealthiest woman in the state, went about 'simplifying' her life.

"Abigail, isn't a carriage house a fancy word for a garage?"

Abigail pursed her lips and shifted in her chair. She knew where I was going with this. "In the old days, it was where people parked their carriages so, yes, technically you could call it a garage, but ours was converted to a guesthouse years ago."

I grinned. "So you're moving into the garage?"

Abigail took another sip of wine, peered at me over the rim of her cup and said stonily, "I suppose you could say that."

"And your garage is what? Two thousand square feet?" I guessed.

"Actually," she said imperiously, "it's closer to three."

For some reason, this struck me as hilarious.

"You could fit three of my little cottages in there, Abigail! Can you imagine? My house could fit in your garage three times over. In your garage!"

Abigail frowned, not at all pleased to be the butt of the joke, which only made me laugh harder. Margot joined in, her musical giggle rippling through the air.

"Abigail," she asked sweetly, "would you like to adopt me?"

"Absolutely not!" she growled. "I'm having enough trouble with the adopted child I already have, thank you very much!"

For some reason, fatigue and relief at the end of a long day, or the effects of the wine, or both, this comment sent us into fresh waves of hilarity. Tears were rolling down my cheeks and Margot laughed so hard she laid her head down on the table.

"Oh! You two are ridiculous! Fine. Go ahead and enjoy yourselves. Liza mocks me constantly. Why shouldn't everyone else?"

I gasped, trying to catch my breath and wiping the tears from my eyes. "I'm sorry, Abbie, but it just cracks me up that your garage is bigger than my whole house. And it's got a solarium!"

"Not yet," Margot giggled. "But it will. And a pool. And walk-in closets. Wait! What about a garage?" She feigned a serious expression before collapsing with laughter. "Abigail, don't you need to add a garage to your garage?"

"But that's exactly my point! Why shouldn't I give the main house to those who really need it? The carriage house has everything I need."

"Hey, everybody." Garrett was standing in the doorway. "Where's Liza?"

"Hi, sweetheart. Did you have fun babysitting?"

He shrugged. "While it lasted. We were about ten minutes into a game of Candy Land when Ivy came home. So, Franklin and I went to the movies. I figured you'd all be done by the time it was over and then I could pick up Liza and take her out for a late dinner."

He looked around the room. "Where is she, anyway?"

"She went out to look for you."

"Well, why did you let her do that?" he asked. "How was she supposed to know I'd gone to the movies?" Garrett was the best of sons, but clearly he'd been looking forward to seeing Liza and was irritated to find her missing in action. He looked at the three of us, sitting around an open bottle of wine, drinking and laughing while one of our number was out wandering the dark streets of New Bern, with an expression of disgust. He dug his cell phone from his back pocket, put it to his ear, and headed toward the door.

"Where are you going?"

"To find my girlfriend," he answered in a tone that made it clear he felt that indeed there were such things as stupid questions and then left without saying good-bye.

Yep, I thought. *Maternal guilt. It's yours for life.*

∾∾ 9 ∾∾

Ivy Peterman

Monday dawned bright and clear. The weatherman said the high temperature would be in the mid-seventies with low humidity. The kids ate their breakfast without any complaints. And when we got into the car for the drive to the daycare center, the Toyota started up without any fuss. It should have been a great start to a great day.

But I knew it wouldn't be, not after the way things had ended on Friday night.

I was just putting on my coat and getting ready to leave for the day when I heard the sound of female voices and the hollow clatter of feet on the stairs, several pairs of them. For a moment I was thought it must be quilters coming up to take a class, but then I remembered there weren't any Friday-night classes on the schedule.

The door opened. Evelyn, Abigail, and Margot entered carrying project bags and trays loaded down with platters of cheese, fruit, and other snacks, plus a bottle of wine. Liza brought up the rear carrying a tray with a collection of mismatched coffee mugs I recognized as coming from the break room.

"Oh, I'm sorry," I said, remembering what day it was. "I'd forgotten this was your quilt-circle night. I'll get out of your way." I zipped my jacket and grabbed my purse.

"Not so fast!" Margot declared cheerfully. "Take off your coat and sit down. We have a surprise for you!"

"You do?"

"Evelyn, you tell her. After all, you're our official leader."

"There's a dubious honor, but all right." She cleared her throat as if about to make an important announcement. "Ivy, we are all here to tell you that, after about two seconds' deliberation, you have been voted into the membership of the Cobbled Court Quilt Circle."

"Hear! Hear!" Margot said. Liza and Abigail put down the trays they were carrying and clapped.

I was stunned.

"Oh. Gosh. That's nice of you, really, but I can't. I've got to get home to my kids."

"We've already taken care of that," Abigail reported. "Franklin has volunteered to watch Bethany and Bobby on Friday nights so you can spend your evening with us."

"He did?"

Franklin Spaulding was a very nice man. The kids were crazy about him but . . . "You shouldn't have asked him to do that. It's sweet of Franklin, really it is, but watching my rascals every Friday night? It's too much to expect."

"Nonsense!" Abigail injected, interrupting me again. "Franklin volunteered to do it and, besides, Bethany and Bobby aren't rascals, they're perfectly darling. Franklin loves being with them. After a week at his law office, dealing with the real rascals of the world— bankers, accountants, and, worst of all, other lawyers—your children are an absolute breath of fresh air."

I tried another approach. "But . . . I'm not a very good quilter. I've only made that one log cabin quilt in Evelyn's class."

Liza took one of the mismatched mugs from the tray and filled it. "Okay, now you're just making excuses. Except for Evelyn, none of us knew a presser foot from a pastrami sandwich this time two years ago. Trust me, our standards of membership are extremely low. I mean, look at us," she said, raising her cup. "We're here drinking cheap wine out of cracked coffee mugs. This isn't exactly the Daughters of the American Revolution you'd be joining."

"That wine was *not* cheap," Abigail corrected. "It's a 2003 pinot gris. The last of a very good vintage from my personal wine cellar."

"Well, we're still serving it out of coffee mugs. So, I don't see where Ivy is getting the impression we're such an exclusive club. Heck," she said blandly, "we'll take anyone. We need the dues."

Margot, who was very sharp when it came to marketing and business but was known for being gullible, furrowed her brow. "Liza, we don't charge any dues, do we?"

She turned to Evelyn. "When did we decide to start taking dues?"

"Liza's kidding," Evelyn said.

Liza's eyes sparked mischief as she peered over the rim of the coffee mug. Margot, realizing she'd been duped again, gave her a good-natured nudge in the ribs.

"Ivy, we'd really love it if you'd joined us." Evelyn smiled, waiting for me to say yes.

A moment passed.

"If you're put off by the coffee cups, we can get some real glasses," she joked.

I pressed my lips together, trying to come up with some excuse that they'd buy, but nothing came to mind.

They were all standing there, certain that I would never dream of refusing this gift of time and friendship they were offering me.

With all my heart, I wished I could accept it. But that was impossible.

I swallowed hard. "I'm sorry," I said sincerely. "You're so kind to want to include me, but I really can't."

Their faces fell.

"But, why not?" Margot asked. "You're just worried about leaving the children with someone else, aren't you? I've volunteered to watch them for you a dozen times, but you've never once taken me up on it. Don't worry, Ivy. Bethany and Bobby will be fine with Franklin."

"Of course they will," Evelyn affirmed. "But if you're that worried, we could even bring them over here. I'm sure Garrett wouldn't mind watching them at his apartment as long as Franklin was there to help. That way, if the kids needed you, you'd be right across the hall."

I shook my head. "It's not that."

"Well, then what is it?"

"I can't. I just can't."

The room was silent again. Four pairs of eyes looked at me; the smiles of the previous moment faded. They just stood there, waiting for me to offer some reasonable explanation for my behavior. None existed. At least, none that wasn't a complete lie and I didn't want to lie to them. I was tired of lying.

From the moment I'd come to work at Cobbled Court Quilts, these women had been nothing but kind to me. For no reason other than their own goodness, certainly not because of anything I'd done, they'd accepted me into their community, given me a chance to create a safe home for my family, cared about my kids—even made quilts for them. I remembered how I had cried, actually cried, when Abigail gave Bethany the beautiful pinwheel quilt she'd made herself. No one had ever shown such kindness to my children or, by extension, to me. I was so touched.

But even so, I couldn't permit myself to be drawn further into their circle, opening myself up to the kinds of questions and confidences that would follow if I did. Evelyn might say there were no dues, but she was wrong. The price of membership was honesty and trust, and that was something I couldn't afford. They were good women, kind women, but even so . . . An inadvertent slip, a careless contradiction in my history accidentally passed from me, to one of them, to someone outside could shred my story into confetti.

No matter how much I wanted to, I couldn't accept their friendship. But I couldn't lie to them either. They deserved better than that.

"I'm sorry," I whispered. "I just can't."

Abigail, always insistent on cutting to the chase, pushed the issue.

"Can't or won't?"

I took a breath.

"Won't."

I picked up my purse and went to the door. Their eyes followed me, and the expressions on their faces felt like accusations. Margot and Liza looked confused, and Abigail offended, but it was the wounded look in Evelyn's eyes that stung me most. She was the last person I wanted to hurt.

But at least you didn't lie to her, I thought. *That should count for something. Shouldn't it?*

Maybe it should have, but it didn't seem to make my weekend any easier. When I left the shop, my guilty feelings trailed behind me like a chain. After I got back to the apartment, I thanked Franklin and Garrett for watching the kids but said I wouldn't be needing them anymore. I was so exhausted that I got into my pajamas right away, thinking that I'd just go to bed when the kids did.

I didn't want to think about Monday and what it would be like to go back to the shop and work side by side with Evelyn and Margot, whose feelings I had hurt. And come Monday morning, we truly would be working side by side. Earlier that day, Evelyn said she'd need my help getting ready for the second-anniversary sale that would take place the following weekend. There was inventory to be taken, displays to create, decorating to be done, door prizes and gift baskets to put together, new fabrics and notions to be cataloged and stocked. And this was in addition to all of our regular duties.

Come Monday, I couldn't just sneak in the back door, grab my stack of orders, and tiptoe up to the workroom unseen. I would have to be downstairs with everyone else, trying to do my job while avoiding making eye contact with my coworkers.

I sighed. Monday was going to be just awful. But I didn't have to think about that. Not yet.

I gave the kids a five-minute warning and went into the bathroom to draw water for their baths.

Bethany moaned, "But we're just getting to the good part! The sea witch is going to make Ariel into a real girl."

"I mean it. Five minutes," I repeated. Something in my tone must have told her I was in no mood for argument. She slumped into her beanbag chair and rested her pouty chin onto her hands, but turned off the television without comment when I called out that it was bathtime.

After I finished reading, probably my two-thousandth rendition of *Goodnight Moon* and kissed Bobby, who was already asleep, Bethany asked if she could come sleep in my bed.

I said yes.

She scampered into my room, climbed in next to me and snuggled in, her skin still pink and warm after her bath. I kissed the top of her head, breathing in the sweet, innocent scent of baby shampoo from her hair. I stroked her silky, baby-fine hair slowly. She sighed her contentment and was asleep even before I turned off the bedside lamp. After I did, I closed my eyes, wrung out from a long, emotional day, longing for the oblivion of deep and dreamless sleep.

It did not come.

In my dream, I was standing at the bus stop and the rain was coming down in torrents, like someone was standing on top of the bus shelter and pouring tub after tub of water down upon it. A car pulled up. Abigail's champagne-colored sedan.

The window rolled down, a loud and steady mechanical whine, like the sound of a garage door going up.

"Get in," she said.

"No. That's all right. I'm just waiting for the bus. It'll be here soon."

Abigail shook her head. "No, it won't. The storm is too strong. All the buses are broken down. No one is coming to get you, and you can't stay here. Get in the car."

I didn't want to get in but when I looked up, I saw a crack in the Plexiglas ceiling of the bus shelter. It was already starting to leak and the crack was getting bigger, moving slowly from one side of the roof to the other. If I stood here any longer, it would split in two. All the water would come crashing down upon me, sweeping me away completely. There was no choice. I got into the car.

"You're soaked," Abigail said. "Take this towel and dry off."

I took the towel that was sitting on the seat next to me and dried my sodden hair.

"That's better," Abigail said, glancing at me as she drove down the road. She reached into her pocket, pulled out a shiny black tube of lipstick, and thrust it toward me. "Here. Put this on."

Compliantly, I flipped down the sunshade, peered into the mirror, and dutifully applied the bright red lipstick.

"That's better," she said with a smile. "You'll want to fix yourself up a little. There's someone I want you to meet. I found him. It turns out he isn't dead after all."

I looked into the mirror and saw him sitting in the backseat. Staring at me. He'd been there all along, waiting.

"Hello, Ivy."

I sat bolt upright in bed, gasping for air, my heart pounding. I felt a searing pain in my left hand, as if the heavy crystal vase had smashed down on it only moments before. I put my fingers in my mouth and tasted blood, metallic and sharp, where no blood was, using my hand to keep myself from crying out.

Bethany was in bed next to me, still sound asleep. I bit my lips to push away the nightmare, whispered to myself, repeating the words the trauma counselor had taught me to say when this happened, words I hadn't needed to say in weeks.

Everything is fine. It was just a dream. We are safe. No one can hurt us here.

But I didn't believe it. It was everything I could do not to wake Bethany and Bobby, pack our bags, and sneak off in the night.

But I didn't.

The image of Evelyn Dixon's face, her kind, understanding eyes, held me fast.

I forced myself to lay back down, pulling up the quilt that that slipped to the foot of the bed, the log cabin quilt with the brave red center squares that stood for my heart, my home, my children and everything that mattered to me, tucking my daughter in tight under its sheltering warmth, hiding beneath the log cabin fortress that I had sewn to protect my baby.

It wasn't much, but it was all I had.

❦ 10 ❦

Evelyn Dixon

Even before I unlocked the door of the shop on Monday morning, I knew it was going to be a crazy day.

Cobbled Court Quilts was about the celebrate its second anniversary and, like any good retail establishment, we planned to mark the occasion with a sale. It might not be the most creative way to celebrate our birthday, but I was incredibly proud that, in the face of seemingly unsurmountable odds, we'd actually managed to keep our doors open this long and I was looking forward to this opportunity to thank our customers for their support by offering special prices on the thing quilters love best—fabric!

Over Margot's objections, I'd decided we were going to offer two free fat quarters with every two purchased for two hours on Saturday. Basically, that meant I'd be selling those fabrics at cost, which was why Margot argued against it.

Margot had been a fairly high-level marketing executive at a corporation in New York before she'd been downsized and come to work for me at Cobbled Court Quilts. She had an incredible head for business. Without Margot, Cobbled Court would never have survived to celebrate its first anniversary, let alone a second. Of course, I can't pay her anything like what she was making in the corporate world—I wish I could—but Margot says she's happier working here than she ever was in New York and I do my best to make sure she knows how much I value her. Appreciation isn't something you can take to the bank, but I think people want that as much as a paycheck, maybe more so. On Saturday, after the sale was over, I intended to take Margot out for a very special dinner at The Grill on the Green.

Charlie planned a special menu: Asian pear and ginger salad, black cod with miso marinade, bok choy and sticky rice, topped off with chocolate bread pudding. The dessert didn't quite go with the oriental theme of the menu, as Charlie told me in no uncertain terms, but chocolate bread pudding is Margot's favorite, so that's what we're having, end of discussion. She who pays the check calls the shots.

However, if Margot knew what the dinner bill was going to be, she'd argue with me about that, too, just like she did the profitless fat quarter sale. As the keeper of the books, and therefore the one who posted our monthly profits or, more frequently, our losses, stuff like that just makes her teeth hurt. But if there is one thing I have learned in the last couple of years, thanks to my divorce and bout with breast cancer, it is that tomorrow comes with no guarantees. If you've got something to celebrate, celebrate it now. It might be your last chance. And one of the things most worth celebrating is the people you care about, your family and friends.

Of course, Margot wasn't the only person I was planning on celebrating and that's where things got complicated. I wanted to include everyone associated with the shop—Abigail because of her generosity in letting us occupy the building practically rent-free, Garrett, and, of course, Ivy. At least, that had been my plan until Friday night.

Now I was wondering if I should invite her to join everyone for the anniversary dinner or not. It wasn't something I could discuss with Margot or Abigail.

I needed advice from someone who wasn't involved in the situation, someone patient, empathetic, and sensitive, who had a keen insight into and appreciation of the female mind-set.

Unfortunately, no one like that was available, so I had to settle for Charlie.

* * *

Charlie came over to my house for dinner on Sunday. He can cook circles around me, but he seems to be appreciative, or at least amused, by my efforts and I was determined to show him that I knew my way around a kitchen. After all, I'd made dinner for my family every night for more than twenty-four years before I met Charlie and no one had died of ptomaine yet. I wasn't exactly a graduate of Le Cordon Bleu, but I was perfectly capable of making a nice Sunday dinner for two.

Charlie leaned against the kitchen counter, picking at a bowl of Kalamata olives I'd put out as an appetizer while we waited for the salmon to finish poaching and I told him about what had happened on Friday.

"It was so strange," I said as I leaned down, peering at the flame while I fiddled with the stove, trying to find the exact height of flame needed to induce the 'slow but steady simmer' my recipe called for. "She just said, 'I can't'. No more explanation than that. Well, not quite. When Abigail pushed her, asking if she meant can't or won't, Ivy said 'won't.' It was a very uncomfortable moment."

Charlie made an impatient, clucking sound as he sucked the pit out of an olive and put it on a nearby cocktail napkin. "Well, why did Abigail do that? Isn't her motto 'never complain, never explain'?"

"Hmmm. I think that's her personal motto. She doesn't mean for it to apply to other people."

"Convenient for her."

"Yep." I lifted the lid on the poacher. It seemed to be simmering nicely, so I put the lid back down and started chopping vegetables for the stir-fry I planned to serve alongside the salmon.

"Do you want some help with that?" Charlie asked, looking over my shoulder. "The peppers will cook more evenly if you cut them into strips."

I turned around and gave him a look, still holding the vegetable knife in my hand.

"All right! All right!" he said, backing away with his hands in the air as if suing for surrender. "I was just trying to help."

"You just stay over on your side of the kitchen. I can do this myself. Didn't anyone ever teach you how to be a guest?"

"No," he said and popped another olive into his mouth before continuing.

"So what's the big problem? It was nice of you to want to include Ivy in your quilting club . . ."

"Circle," I corrected, "Quilt circle."

"Okay. Your quilt circle, but she doesn't want to join. Why is that so terrible?"

"It isn't that it's so terrible, not exactly. I mean, at first my feelings were a little hurt. It was like we tried to give her a present and she just handed it back without even bothering to open it, but the more I've been thinking about it, the more it worries me."

"Why?"

"Because it doesn't add up." I picked up a slice of green pepper and ate it. "Ivy likes all of us, I'm sure she does. She's quiet, keeps to herself, but it isn't like she's unfriendly."

Charlie shrugged. "Maybe she's not all that crazy about quilting. Just because she works for you doesn't mean she is. I've got people chopping vegetables in the kitchen of my restaurant, and doing it a lot faster and neater than you are, I might add, who don't like cooking. For me, cooking is a passion, but to them it's just a way to pay the rent. Maybe it's the same for Ivy. By the way, are you *sure* you don't want me to . . ." He took a tentative step in my direction.

I glared at him.

"Never mind. I'll just stay over here and eat my olives."

"Good plan," I said and went back to chopping.

"No, that's not it. I know Ivy enjoys quilting. I knew that when I first met her, in my beginners' class. She was really excited about her quilt. And just a couple of weeks ago, she said she'd like to try an Ohio Star pattern, but she just doesn't have time. So, now she's offered a chance to do something she enjoys, with free babysitting thrown in, and she says no? It doesn't make sense."

"Well, you're right, it doesn't but what can you do about it? Let it go. If she won't join your group, she won't."

"Yeah, but that's just it," I said, scooping up a pile of vegetables and tossing them into the wok I'd had heating on a burner and listening to them sizzle. "Abigail pushed Ivy to say she won't, but I don't think that's it. I think she meant what she said the first time. She can't. Or at least she thinks she can't. Something is holding her back. It's almost like she's afraid of being friends with us. But why?"

"You really need to quit stewing about this."

"I know. I know, but what am I supposed to do now? Ivy doesn't normally work weekends, not unless we have a big sale like we will on Saturday, so I've had all weekend to worry about exactly how awkward it will be when she comes in on Monday. Do I talk to her about it? Do I not talk to her about it? Do I ignore the elephant in the room? And do I invite her to come to the Grill on Saturday night or not? Maybe I should just assume she doesn't want to see any of us outside of work hours," I sighed. "Monday is going to be awful. I don't know how I should handle this."

Charlie shook his head and sighed deeply. "Women. You make everything so complicated."

"Oh, stop it."

"No, I mean it. You'd never find a man wringing his hands and worrying over something like this. Look. This is simple. Just handle this like a man would. Go to work on Monday, do what you normally do and pretend nothing happened on Friday. Do your job and let Ivy do hers. Later, you can invite her to the dinner on Saturday. If she says yes, fine. If not, that's fine too. It's as simple as that."

"But it's not. What if she'd really like to come, but feels awkward about accepting the invitation after saying she didn't want to join the circle? Or what if she really *doesn't* want to come, but feels like she has to because she said no before? It's a complicated situation."

"Arrggh!" Charlie rubbed his face with his hands, as if scrubbing at his frustration. "No, it's not! It's only complicated it you make it complicated!

"Why is it that women, even women who are only bound together by the fact that they happen to work in the same place, aren't happy unless everyone becomes everybody else's best friend?"

I sprinkled the vegetables with salt, pulled a pepper out, and bit into it. Almost ready.

"Because we're social animals, that's why. It's how we evolved. Strength in numbers. Or something like that," I shrugged. "It's just the way we are. Women need the friendship of other women. At least most of them do. Maybe Ivy's different, but I'm not convinced."

Charlie snorted and spit out another olive pit. "Well, maybe she just doesn't want to be friends with the people she works with. Can't blame her for that. You're a pretty scary bunch. Margot's a sweetheart, but Liza looks like she's ready to pose for a biker chick photo op. Empress Abigail refers to herself in the third person. And you? Sure. You may look like a mild-mannered quilt shop owner, but maybe Ivy has caught wind of your dark side. Maybe she's heard the rumors about how you threaten your boyfriend with kitchen knives just because he's trying to help you keep from ruining dinner."

I put the spatula down and turned to face Charlie, my hands on my hips. "I am *not* ruining dinner."

Behind me, the sound of sizzling vegetables reached a crescendo but was suddenly overcome by a loud, long hiss, followed by repetitious staccato clicks; the noice my gas stove makes when something boils over and extinguishes the cooking flame.

Charlie raised his eyebrows. "Actually, you might be wrong about that."

"Oh no!" I turned off both burners, and then grabbed a kitchen towel to lift the lid off the poacher.

"It's ruined." I moaned, peering into the pan. "Why didn't you say something?"

"What? And take my life into my hands?"

Charlie came up behind me, wrapped one arm around my waist and, resting his chin on my shoulder, examined my over-cooked salmon.

"There now, it's not so bad. Not beyond all hope, at least."

"No? So you think I can still serve it?"

"Well," he said doubtfully, "not like that. What do you say to a nice salmon salad? Do you have some vinegar and capers, maybe a bit of fresh dill?"

I nodded.

Charlie clapped his hands together and grinned, back in his element, as delighted by the end of his culinary exile as a major-league pitcher who is called back to the mound after a season spent warming the bench. "Good! Get them out. I'll need a mixing bowl and an apron too."

Glumly, I started looking for the items he requested, but Charlie interrupted my search, kissing me lightly on the lips.

"There now. You're taking this much too hard. Don't worry. I'll be able to salvage our supper." His eyes twinkled as hefted the fish poacher off the stove and poured the liquid down the sink.

"Just like I did last Sunday."

I smiled as I turned the key in the lock and opened the shop door on Monday morning. It was a beautiful, sunny morning, the kind of morning that makes you think that the rest of the day will hold nothing but good.

Maybe Charlie was right. Maybe I was making a mountain out of a molehill.

I had plenty of things to do besides worry about Ivy. The best thing to do was to act as if Friday had never happened and just get on with my day. One thing I knew for certain is that it was going to be crazy busy. But until I snapped on the overhead light and the telephone started ringing as if on cue, I had no way of knowing how crazy.

❧ 11 ❧

Evelyn Dixon

"Ms. Dixon, would you please hold for the First Selectman?"
The secretary pressed the hold button before I had a
chance to say whether I would or wouldn't, and was treated to a
tinny version of "Muskrat Love" while I waited for Porter Moss to
come on the line.

"Good morning, Evelyn!" Porter's voice exuded chummy warmth,
as if we were old friends. "Sorry to keep you waiting. How's everything at the shop? Saw in the paper where you've got a big anniversary sale coming up this weekend."

"Yes, our second."

"Wonderful! You must be proud to have reached such a mile-
stone."

And before I could say if I was or wasn't, he changed the subject.

"Listen, you probably have a million things to do. I won't keep
you. Let me just cut to the chase."

Good, I thought as I eyed the blinking light on my answering
machine and wondered how many calls I'd need to respond to before I could begin cataloging the new stock that had come in over
the weekend.

"It's about this television show . . ."

"Um, yes," I said distractedly, going over my to-do list in my mind. "It's going to be awfully crowded with the cameras and crew and all, but the producer thinks she can squeeze in a couple of . . ."

"Great! Sorry not to have gotten back to you right away like I'd said I would, but I wanted to run a few things by the board before I called. They're very excited about this, as you can imagine. Just full of ideas about how the community can really capitalize on the opportunity."

Something about the gusto of his tone drew my mind back from thoughts of phone calls, catalogs, and to-do. Cradling the receiver between my shoulder and ear, I reached up to rub a kink out of my neck, suddenly certain that my life was about become very complicated.

"What do you mean?"

"I mean," he said so confidently that I could almost see the beam of his self-congratulatory smile streaming through the phone line, "that we've got plans, big plans for this event. It took a little arm-twisting, but I got the board to declare September 26th Mary Dell Templeton Day in New Bern. How do you like that! We're going to have a parade, a picnic on the Green . . . Hey! I just thought of this! Maybe we could have some kind of quilt show. You know, string up some clotheslines between the trees where the ladies could show off their quilts and then Mary Dell could pick the winner! That's a good idea. Gimme a second. Let me write that down . . ."

He finally took a breath and I could hear the scratching of his pencil as he jotted a note to himself.

"Porter," I began slowly, searching for a diplomatic response, "this is all very interesting and I'm sure you've put a lot of thought into it, but I . . ."

"Oh! You don't know the half of it! We're going to put up a giant television screen, a JumboTron, on the Green so that everyone can watch the broadcast live."

Well, at least one of his ideas has some merit. If Porter and Lydia can watch the show from the Green, then they won't be in the shop getting in everyone's way and making me nervous.

"That" he continued, "will be helpful for crowd control, give the average citizens and the visitors that will be coming from out of town someplace to watch but won't make them feel like they're being left out. You don't want to try to film a show with a bunch of people underfoot. I talked to Dale Barrows about it . . ."

"Dale Barrows the movie director? The man who lives three houses down from Abigail on Proctor Street?"

Porter chuckled, clearly delighted that he'd had an excuse to call up New Bern's most famous resident. "Well, he's been retired for a number of years now, but yes. Back in the eighties, Dale directed some of the biggest-budget pictures in Hollywood."

Also, if my memory served me correctly, some of Hollywood's biggest-budget flops. Fabulously forgettable films like *Drive-In Disco* and *Binky and Bunny's Hawaiian Holiday*, movies that explained his early retirement from the glare of the Hollywood spotlight to the sleepy seclusion of New Bern.

"Anyway, Dale says that you need plenty of space for the cameras to maneuver. You can't have a bunch of people hanging around and getting in the way."

I breathed a sigh of relief. "Dale is absolutely right. I'm so glad you understand. I was afraid you were going to be offended when I explained that we really don't have room for a lot of onlookers."

As I was speaking, Garrett came downstairs, his hair still wet from the shower and carrying his cell phone. Catching my eye, he held up the phone, and silently mouthed. "It's for you."

Who would be calling me on Garrett's cell phone? I squashed my eyes shut and held my left hand up flat. I could only talk on one phone at a time.

"Don't you worry about that for another minute," Porter said. "I've worked everything out. We're moving everything into the gym."

For a moment, his meaning didn't register. "I'm sorry?" Surely, I'd misunderstood him. "The gym?"

"Yes, at the high school. There's plenty of room there. You can film on the floor and put the audience up in the bleachers with no fear of them blocking the cameras. You'll have room for 250 dignitaries, maybe more! Don't go getting your hopes up, but I've put a call into the governor's office and I think there's a good chance she'll come."

"What!"

"I know! Isn't that something? But, I've saved the best for last. Dale Barrows himself has agreed to come out of retirement to direct the whole thing."

"He what?" I cried. "You've got to be kidding!"

"I know!" he repeated, completely misreading my reaction and emitting a laugh that was practically a giggle, as giddy as a teenage girl who's just learned that the captain of the football team, the editor of the yearbook, and the student body president all want to take her to the prom.

"This is going to be the most exciting thing that's ever happened in New Bern!"

"Porter," I said, taking a deep breath and trying to get a handle on the situation. "We've got to talk . . ."

"What? Hold on a minute, Evelyn." There was a brief pause before he came back on the line.

"That was my secretary. I'm ten minutes late for a meeting over at the fire department. Completely slipped my mind."

"But, Porter . . ." I protested.

"I know. I know. We've got a lot to talk about. Lots of planning to be done, but there's time. The broadcast is still months off. Don't worry. Everything's going to come off without a hitch. After all, we've got Dale Barrows directing!" he crowed. "Have to run. Talk to you later."

And before I could say anything else, he'd hung up.

My arm suddenly went limp and I stood there open-mouthed, the receiver dangling from my wrist.

"This cannot be happening," I said to no one in particular.

"Mom?" Garrett wore an apologetic look as he held his cell phone out to me. "It's Mary Dell."

"Give me a second."

I hung up the shop phone and laid one hand over my eyes like a shield. It was the same gesture I used when the sun came streaming through my bedroom window too early, a feeble tactic meant to delay the inevitable need to get out of bed and, ready or not, face the day.

I would have preferred a few minutes to process everything before talking with Mary Dell, but maybe now was best. Together,
maybe we could figure out a way to put a lid back on Pandora's box
and save the broadcast before Porter and Dale Barrows decided to
hire Busby Berkeley as Assistant Director and bring Binky and
Bunny in for a surprise on-air reunion. Better yet, maybe we could
just cancel the whole thing.

"Mom?" Garrett looked worried.

"I'm okay." I took two big, cleansing breaths, nodded my pre-
paredness, and took the cell phone from Garrett's outstretched hand.

"Hey, Mary Dell," I said, slipping into the traditional Texas salu-
tation.

"Hey, yourself, Baby Girl. Where've you been? I must have left
about ten messages on your machine before I thought to call Garrett's cell. And why'd you keep me waiting so long? I've got two
cameramen and a floor director standing around cooling their heels
and looking at their watches while I waited for you to pick up the
line. Were you off somewhere necking with Charlie? Hope so. Honey,
that is one cute Irishman you've got yourself there."

"I'm sorry, Mary Dell. It's been kind of a crazy morning around
here, but I'm glad you called."

"And you're going to be even more glad I called once I tell you
the news. Flip on your TV set, darlin', and get ready to be a star!
The first on-air promo is going to run on this morning's show.
Should be on in about forty-five minutes."

My knees felt weak. "It's running today?"

"Yes, it is. And don't sound so nervous. I saw the tape and you
look great. Gather up the troops and watch. Gotta run. Sandy is
wearing her 'time is money' face."

Click.

I looked at Garrett. "What time is it?"

He glanced at his wristwatch and said, "Ten minutes to nine."

"Really? Are you sure?"

"Yeah," Garrett said cautiously, as if worried that his normally
reliable mother was about to slip over the edge of sanity. Which, at
the moment, was a distinct possibility. "Why do you ask?"

"Nothing. I'm just can't quite believe so much could go so wrong so early in the day."

No one was interested in my tales of woe regarding Porter Moss, Dale Barrows, the Governor of Connecticut, and the many sound reasons I had for wanting to cancel the broadcast now, before things got even more out of hand than they already were.

As soon as Garrett and Margot learned that the first promotional spot was to appear that morning, they didn't hear another word I said.

The next thing I knew, Garrett was ferreting around the back office, moving piles of shipping boxes, papers, bags filled with empty soda cans that we always said we were going to take to the recycling center but never did, trying to unearth the small television that no one ever watched from a back corner shelf.

Margot followed him into the office. I followed Margot, holding Garrett's cell phone and hitting the redial button.

"Isn't this exciting!" Margot chirped

"No! It's not. It is the opposite of exciting. It's a catastrophe!"

Garrett pulled the TV from the corner and lifted it up onto my desk where it would be easier for everyone to see the screen. "Actually, the opposite of exciting would be dull or maybe boring. It's neither of those. Margot, can you hand me a kitchen towel or something? I want to wipe the dust off the screen."

"Sure." She opened a drawer, pulled out a dish towel, and tossed it to Garrett. "How much longer?"

Garrett looked at his watch. "About six minutes."

Margot squealed. Actually, it was more like she trilled; clapping her hands together and emitting this half-whistle, half-hoot that was her signature sound for expressing excitement.

The TV in place and free of dust, Garrett declared that he was going to run over to his apartment and get his video recorder. "That way we can watch it again later."

"Good idea!" Margot said.

"Didn't either of you hear anything I said?" I pulled the phone away from my ear, stabbed the end button with my forefinger, and hit redial yet again.

"Porter Moss is trying to turn this whole thing into some weird mixture of three-ring circus, quilt show, and campaign rally! We've got to call it off before it's too late. Or at least postpone airing the promo video until we can figure out how to put a lid on this thing."

With the phone back at my ear, I paused a moment, waiting for an answer, and then growled my frustration when none came. "But how am I going to do that if Mary Dell won't answer her stupid phone so I can tell her not to run the video?"

There were only six minutes left to airtime—now more like five. I simply had to get hold of Mary Dell and tell her to put the video on hold. If not, there would be no going back. We'd have to . . . I'd have to go through with the live broadcast in September. It had been a distressing prospect before. Now, after my one-sided conversation with Porter, it was a terrifying one.

I punched the redial button again, held the phone to my ear and chanted, "Pick up, Mary Dell. Pick up. Pick up. Pick up!"

Garrett, returning with the VCR, laughed and turned on the television set. "Mom, calm down. She's not going to answer; she's probably taping a show and turned the phone off. Even if she did answer, I doubt she could stop the video from airing. They probably get these things set way in advance. There's nothing you can do to stop this. Deal with it. Better yet, enjoy it. Personally, I think it's pretty neat."

I looked at my watch. Two minutes left. Garrett was right, it was too late. As he fiddled with the volume control, I could hear the *Quintessential Quilting* theme music. The horse was out of the barn now and there was nothing I could do but hang on for the ride.

Margot walked toward me and took the phone from my hand. "Come on. Sit down and watch the show."

Grabbing my shoulders from behind, she steered me to a straight-backed chair near the set and pressed me into it. My knees folded under me and I sat, reluctantly ceding control of the situation.

The back door opened and Ivy came in. Everyone turned, briefly noted her presence, and then turned their attention back to the television screen, where Mary Dell was sitting at her sewing machine, talking about a technique she'd learned for simultaneous piecing and quilting that she couldn't wait to share with us.

"What's going on?" she asked.

Margot turned and grinned. "Mary Dell phoned. They're running the new promotional video today."

"Really? Cool!" Ivy pulled up an empty chair and sat down next to me, squeezing my arm encouragingly even though her eyes were glued to the screen.

I thought to myself that, even if this video was the harbinger of disaster that I was absolutely certain it was, at least it had gotten us past the awkward events of Friday night.

Mary Dell looked straight into the camera and smiled genuinely, speaking to her invisible audience of viewers (millions and millions of them, as Charlie would say) as if they were old friends. She looked so comfortable, as if she did this every day, which, I reminded myself, she did. But still. She hadn't always been a television personality.

Back in Texas, when I first met her, she was just plain, old Mary Dell . . . no. Not plain. Mary Dell was a lot of things but you could never have called her plain. Nothing, from the pointy tips of her pink faux leopard print pumps to the wide streaks of blond on her newly highlighted hairdo, was plain. It never had been. Even in the ordinariness of her pre-celebrity life, taking care of Howard, shopping for groceries at the Piggly Wiggly, hanging out in my sewing room while we quilted, and laughed, and talked each other through the peaks and valleys of life, including my divorce, Mary Dell sparkled.

I smiled as I watched her holding up a quilt block she said she'd worked on that weekend, telling the cameraman to zoom in close so everybody could see what a wreck she'd made of it.

"Just look at those points," she clucked and shook her head. "They aren't within a mile of meeting at the center." And she was right; they weren't.

"Well," she laughed, "it just goes to show you. If you're just dying to try out a new recipe for mojitos, don't do at the same time you're trying to sew the points on an eight-pointed star, you hear what I'm telling you?" Her expression became mockingly serious. "Learn from my mistakes, children. I am not a role model."

She laughed again and everyone—Margot, Garrett, Ivy, and I— laughed with her. It was no wonder that *Quintessential Quilting* had the House and Home Network's fastest growing audience. How many other quilt show hosts would let the audience see their blunders? She gave people permission to take risks, to try and enjoy taking on new, more challenging projects even if the results weren't always perfect. Even people who'd never quilted and never wanted to tuned in to *Quintessential Quilting.* I could see why. Mary Dell was just plain fun to watch.

Look at you, girl. You could give Barbara Walters a run for her money. How did you ever learn to do this?

Mary Dell tossed her pathetically off-center quilt block off to the side with an exaggerated shrug. "Well, that one's a lost cause, but I want to tell you about a cause that's anything but, about a battle that millions of people around the globe are fighting and winning, thanks to the help of quilters like you . . ."

"This is it!" Garrett exclaimed and turned the volume up.

Everyone leaned toward the screen. I shifted nervously in my chair, rested the point of my chin on my balled up fist.

"On September 26th, quilters across the country will head to their local quilt shops to participate in the annual Quilt Pink Day. Working together, they will create thousands of quilts that will be auctioned online with one hundred percent of the net proceeds being donated to Susan G. Komen for the Cure and their fight to end breast cancer."

Now it was Mary Dell leaning closer to us, her eyes warm, her teasing Texas twang modulated into softer, more subtle tones.

"Chances are that you, or someone you know, has been affected by this disease and, naturally, many of us are looking for a way to help. One of my dearest friends, a woman named Evelyn Dixon, owner of Cobbled Court Quilts in New Bern, Connecticut, is doing her part by hosting a Quilt Pink event." Mary Dell smiled. "Evelyn is a very special lady with an amazing story that I think she should tell you herself."

The tape rolled, showing Mary Dell and I sitting around a cutting table in the shop, hundreds of bolts of fabric serving as backdrop. Mary Dell looked gorgeous and relaxed. I looked like exactly what I was, a woman who had no experience with cameras and found them terrifying, a quilt shop owner who was so busy tending to business that she hadn't been to the gym in eight months.

That's it. I'm going for a long walk first thing tomorrow. And I'm buying a scale. Look at me. I'm white as a sheet. Looks like I could lose my lunch at any moment, I thought to myself and then smiled a little, remembering that, not too long after that take, I'd done exactly that.

Mary Dell began, sweeping one hand, bejeweled with several enormous gemstone rings, wide to encompass the whole shop, "As you can see, I'm here with my friend Evelyn Dixon in her absolutely beautiful shop, Cobbled Court Quilts in New Bern, Connecticut." She turned to me. "Evelyn, a couple of years ago you hosted your first Quilt Pink Day here at Cobbled Court Quilts. What made you decide to do that?"

On the tape, I nodded and swallowed hard before beginning. "Um. Well . . . I'd picked up a magazine and seen an announcement for Quilt Pink Day and thought it would be a wonderful way for quilters in my community to come together in support of a very important cause. After getting more information, I registered Cobbled Court Quilts as an official site for Quilt Pink, one of hundreds of such sites across the country. I was very excited and very proud to be part of such a wonderful event, but at the time, I had no idea of how deeply Quilt Pink would come to affect me personally."

"And then?" Mary Dell prodded.

"Then, on the day before the event, my doctor diagnosed me with breast cancer . . ."

It was hard, harder than I'd thought it would be, to watch video me recount the story of the early days of my diagnosis, the disbelief and fear, the denial, the sense of complete loneliness that enveloped me, newly divorced, newly relocated, broke, struggling to keep my business afloat, and facing a pronouncement of cancer in a town where I had not one close friend or family member, and how completely unprepared I was for what had come next.

I pressed my lips together and balled up my fist to cover my mouth.

Keep it together, I coached Video Me. *Do not cry with all these people watching.*

She did hold it together, but only just. People watching her probably thought she was swallowing back tears of fear as she relived those days, but it wasn't that. The hesitant catch in her voice, the threat of tears that shone in her eyes didn't come from fear, but from gratitude, from reliving a memory of a time that still amazed her, a time when three strangers, who'd come into the shop that day, each for their own reasons, with the intent of doing nothing more than making a quilt block and going home, rescued her.

Margot, Abigail, and Liza. They were the last three people in the shop that evening. They didn't know me, but when I could no longer keep down the fear I'd been forcing back since the day before when the doctor had told me about the cancer and I crumbled into a million pieces, they scooped up the broken shards, glued them back together, and stayed with me through every step of the journey. They'd rescued me.

Thank God.

Margot, efficient, sensitive, and cheerful. Abigail, stubborn, connected, and proud. Liza, raw, tender, and determined. Thank God for all of them. Remembering those three, how could I have kept my eyes from filling? People on the far side of the television screen might not have understood, but I did.

And now, I realized, Mary Dell did too.

I shifted in my chair again, sat up straighter, as I pulled myself back from memory, not reliving the story now, but observing, seeing the tale play out exactly as Mary Dell had known it would.

At that moment I knew that many of those "millions and millions" of people I'd been so frightened of were leaning in closer, wanting to hear the rest of the story, hoping against hope that it ended well, silently cheering when it did. Some of them were sitting home alone, reaching up with tentative fingers to touch the lump they'd been trying so desperately to ignore, and then, finally resolved, reaching for the phone. Others were searching for a pad and paper, scribbling down phone numbers and Internet addresses, happy that they'd found some way, however small, to support the battle, or honor the memory, of someone they cared about. In big cities and small towns, right at that moment, people I'd never met and never would were making decisions, taking action.

Mary Dell was right.

I hadn't wanted it, hadn't chosen it, but this was my story. It wasn't about Porter Moss or Dale Barrows. It wasn't about Mary Dell Templeton Day or speeches by the Governor. It wasn't about increasing sales at Cobbled Court Quilts. And it wasn't about me.

It was about them.

As much as I hated, truly hated sitting in front of a television camera to the point where it made me physically ill, I knew that was going to be the easy part. From now until Quilt Pink Day, I was going to have to keep fifty plates spinning in the air, balancing a mix of logistical, political, personal, and operational nightmares with the determination of a commanding general and the patience of Mother Teresa. Nothing about this was going to be easy for me. Or fun. But it wasn't about me.

It was about them. About debts that can never be repaid. About doing unto others as you would have done unto you. As has been done unto you. Because whether we know it or not, we all depend on the kindness of strangers.

Ready or not, I was in.

As the camera panned from me back to Mary Dell and then backed away to a wider shot that took in the back wall of the shop, I was lost in my thoughts and resolutions. So lost that I no longer really heard the words that Mary Dell was speaking into her lapel microphone and paid no attention to the figure in the background.

She was only there for a moment and I was so lost in my thoughts that I barely noticed her, a woman with strong arms carrying a heavy load of fabric bolts up the stairs to the workroom. She had a light tread and blond hair that brushed her shoulders and blocked her face.

It wasn't until she twisted her neck hard to the right, flipping back her hair to expose her face and I heard the sharp, shocked intake of breath and Ivy crying out, "Oh God! Oh no!" that I realized something was wrong.

~ 12 ~

Ivy Peterman

The television was still on, but no one was watching it.

I was surrounded by faces, and voices, and questions, the concerned voices of people trying to understand why my hands were shaking so.

"Stupid," I whispered angrily "So stupid. I didn't think about the cameras. I didn't know it was on. Oh God."

My throat felt tight, as if someone was trying to cut off my breath. The old suffocating feeling was back, the sense of dread that used to come over me when I heard the whine of the garage door opening and waited, stretched tight as a bowstring, for the door to open and reveal which Hodge had come home that night. Would he be distracted and dismissive, ignoring me completely? Impatient and critical, ready to find fault with my smallest error, omission, or careless word? Angry and aggressive, violent, looking for a place to unleash his pent-up frustration and disappointments? Or charming and light-hearted, as he'd been when I first met all those years ago, the man who, at the time, had seemed my salvation? Until the door opened, there was no way to predict who was going to come through it, and I think he liked it that way. He liked keeping me off-balance. In the last couple of years, he'd taken to showing up early or later than I'd expected him. Sometimes he'd say he was going to be in meetings all day and then show up again three hours later, or one, and rage at me because I hadn't finished everything on the to-do list he'd left for me. Once he'd said he had a dinner meeting at the club and not to fix anything for him, then showed up unannounced at six o'clock and thrown the pot of macaroni and cheese I'd made for the kids against the wall, leaving a sick, orange-yellow smear snaking down the wall with little white tubes of macaroni clinging to the it, like a canvas of bad abstract art.

There was never a moment when I could relax and be myself because I was always aware that he could walk through that door at any moment and if he didn't like what he saw, there would be consequences. Inevitable, unpredictable, irrational consequences. No matter where he was or wasn't, a sense of his menacing power stayed with me. He knew that. That's how he wanted it.

I'd never been entirely free of that feeling, not even after all these months of refuge in New Bern, but with each turn of the calendar page, and the passing of each succeeding season with no sign of Hodge, the feeling had faded. Sometimes I imagined myself as a character in one of those action movies, squealing around a corner and disappearing into a blackened alley just in time to see the car that had been chasing me speed by. After waiting a minute and another, I'd smile and say, "I think I lost him."

What I'd forgotten was that in those movies, that moment of relief was inevitably followed by panic and terror when the prey pulls out of the shadows only to realize the predator was close behind and closing fast.

There was no place hidden enough.

It was back again in full force, the hopeless dread, the invisible but potent presence, leaning over the back of my chair and close to my ear, his voice intense but quiet, hissed contempt. "Did you think you'd done it, Ivy? Did you really think you'd disappeared? I've known all along. It was only a matter of time."

It was my nightmare coming true, like sitting in a small, enclosed space, a place I'd thought was shelter against the storm, and then glancing backward in the mirror to realize he was there all along.

There was nowhere far enough away. Nowhere he couldn't touch us. I had been fooling myself.

Fingers splayed apart, my voice was reedy and small, slipping through the gaps, as if speaking through a locked grate.

"He saw it. He knows."

Evelyn crouched down close to my chair and took my hand in hers. Her voice was soft, gentle, like she was speaking to a frightened animal. "What is it, Ivy? Tell me. Who saw you?"

"Hodge. He saw it. I know he did. He's coming."

∽ 13 ∽

Evelyn Dixon

I should have known. Almost from the first I'd sensed that Ivy was holding something back. Thinking about it later, it all made sense—her reticence, how she deftly changed the subject whenever anyone asked her about her past.

Now that she'd confessed the truth about her situation, the circumstances and reasons behind her arrival in New Bern, I began to understand what she'd been going through all these months. The poor girl. She lived every moment of her life looking over her shoulder, afraid of what she'd see if she looked in her rear view mirror, her pulse racing every time she heard a knock on the door, terrified of who might be standing on the other side.

She was so completely convinced that her husband was on to her, that at any moment he might arrive in New Bern and . . . I didn't know what she really thought he could do to her. After all, this was a free country; if she didn't want to stay in her marriage there was nothing her husband could do to stop that, but no matter how many times I tried to convince her of this, my words rolled off her like rain pattering on a pane of glass. She saw her husband as a looming, omnipresent being. Her fear of him went beyond all reason and logic, qualities that, in other circumstances, Ivy had always possessed in abundance. But this Ivy, this cowering, frightened girl whose hands shook as she told us her story of her life before New Bern, or at least the outline of it, was nothing like the reticent but capable, intelligent young woman I knew. This Ivy was a stranger to me.

As soon as the broadcast ended, I called Mary Dell and explained the situation. She assured me that they'd pull the tape immediately and edit out the part with Ivy in it. When I hung up, I told Ivy what Mary Dell said, but it didn't seem to comfort her. Margot tried to reason with her.

"Sweetie," she said putting an arm around Ivy's shaking shoulders, "try to calm down. Think. You told us he's a businessman . . ."

"He owns a nursing home," Ivy said in a flat voice.

"Right. So, he's not going to be sitting home on a Monday morning watching television. He's in his office, working. And even if he were at home, would he be sitting around watching a quilting show? I don't think so."

Ivy didn't say anything, just stared straight ahead, as if she hadn't heard a word. Margot gave me a look, raising her eyebrows to indicate she'd appreciate a little backup.

"Of course not," I added. "Ivy, listen to us. There is no way in the world that your husband saw the show. No way at all. And since that tape is never going to air again, he never will. Nothing has changed. Your husband has no more inkling about your whereabouts now than he ever did." I squatted down in front of the chair she was sitting in and met her eyes. "Do you believe me?"

Silently, obediently, she nodded, but I could see the doubt in her eyes and the tremor in her hands. No matter how unreasonable her fear seemed to me, I could tell it was real.

Garrett had been present during this entire scene but seemed at a loss as to what he could do or say. Who could blame him? This was so far out of the realm of my experience that I was feeling at a loss myself, but at least I had age and gender working for me. For a twenty-six-year-old male without a violent bone in his body, the drama being played out in front of him must have seemed a bit unreal. He'd gotten Ivy the glass of water that she held in her trembling hands but hadn't drunk, but after that had stood by as a silently supportive but helpless observer.

Now he glanced at his watch and cleared his throat apologetically. "Mom? It's ten after ten. I think there's someone waiting outside the shop."

I stood up and peered out the office door into the shop. He was right. Wendy Perkins was pacing in front of the door, undoubtedly wondering why it was still locked ten minutes after our posted opening time.

I switched into boss mode.

"Okay, let's pull ourselves together here. The best thing to do is go on with our day and go back to work. Garrett, please unlock the door. Margot, can you boot up the computer and print out the online orders that came in since Saturday? Ivy, you come upstairs with me," I said. "We had a new shipment of reproduction fabrics that came in on Saturday and I'd like you to help me decide which to include in the new fat quarter collection we're going to offer as our online special of the week."

All of that was true, but the real reason I wanted Ivy to follow me upstairs was so we could talk in private. I grabbed the stack of orders that needed to be fulfilled from the in-box and headed out the door, hoping Ivy would follow.

She trooped dutifully up the stairs to the workroom and sat down at the cutting table. Her hands had stopped shaking, but her gaze was still flat and frightened. She looked up at me.

"What should I do?"

"Right this second? Nothing. Just work on these orders and try not to think too much. Later, tonight or tomorrow, you're going to have to see Donna Walsh, the director of the Stanton Center, and tell her the truth."

If it were possible, Ivy's already pale face seemed even more drained of color.

"Don't worry," I said. "She's not going to throw you out on the street. I can't imagine you're the first person that's come through their doors who's been less than completely honest, but she needs to know the whole story. If nothing else, so she can make sure you have the security you need and help you file whatever notices or complaints you should make with the police, maybe find a lawyer."

"The police?" she asked weakly.

"Yes," I said, trying to keep my tone firm without scolding. "You have to. If your husband were to show up today . . ." her eyes grew wide with fear and I backpedaled a bit. "That's not going to happen, but if it did, he could claim that you kidnapped his children. Maybe in retaliation over an extra-marital affair, or maybe just out of spite. Right now, he can accuse you of anything. Unless you document what happened, explain that you ran and took the children with you because you were afraid for your safety and theirs, there's no reason for anyone to believe your story over his."

"I can't talk to the police, Evelyn. I just can't. Hodge always said that if I ever tried to run, he'd follow me, find me, and take away the kids. He promised that he'd make sure I never saw them again."

As far as I was concerned, it was obvious that he'd never be able to do anything of the kind, but it was just as obvious that Ivy believed he could. What had he done, how had he beaten her down to make her believe he had this kind of power over her? I couldn't understand it.

"Ivy, he can't do that," I promised. "You're a wonderful person and an ideal mother. I've seen how you handle the kids, how devoted and patient you are with them. I'd testify to it in court, if it came to that. What could he possibly accuse you of that would make a judge decide to give custody of your children to him over you? Especially once you've told the police about his history of abuse?"

She didn't answer and I backed off a bit. "Let's not worry about the police just yet. All you need to do is get through this day and talk to Donna Walsh. Donna has dealt with situations much more complicated than this; it's her job. She'll know exactly what you need to do." I reached across the expanse of the table between us and covered her hand with mine.

"And I'm going to be with you every step of the way. We all will. Margot and Garrett. Abigail, too."

"Abigail? I have to tell her, too? Don't you think she'll be mad when she finds out I've been lying to everyone?"

I nodded. "Probably. At first. But, Abigail is a good egg. Once she gets over it, she'll be your most stalwart ally. You see if I'm not right. Besides, Abigail Burgess Wynne is a very influential woman. Her word carries a lot of weight in this town and she knows everyone. One quick phone call from Abigail can open doors that would remain firmly closed to lesser mortals.

"When I got my cancer diagnosis, Abigail went into string-pulling mode and within forty-eight hours she'd gotten me appointments with three of the best, most overly booked breast surgeons in New England, not to mention an entire briefing book on everything you'd ever need or want to know about breast cancer, all catalogued and footnoted with especially relevant passages highlighted in yellow marker. It was amazing. Near as I can tell, she just marched into the library, cleared her throat, and next thing you know, she had four research librarians clicking their heels and making color copies."

Ivy smiled weakly.

"Trust me," I continued. "If you're in a bind, Abigail is someone you want on your side. Certainly a better friend than an enemy," I joked.

"Yeah," Ivy said, "I can see that."

"Good. Trust her. For that matter, trust all of us. We're all on your side, Ivy. From here on out. You're not in this alone. Not anymore."

Ivy looked down at her hands, suddenly shy. "Evelyn, I'm sorry."

"About what?"

"About lying to you. I never wanted to. Never. I just . . ." She faltered, searching for an explanation. "It's just that I've been hiding out for so long. You know?"

I nodded. I thought I did.

"You don't need to apologize. It's all water under the bridge. I'm going to do everything I can to help you, Ivy. We all will. If you'd like, I'll even go with you when you talk with Donna."

"Really?" she asked gratefully.

"Sure. I'll call her and get an appointment for this afternoon. Then we can work out a plan for how to deal with the rest of this," I said confidently. "Everything is going to be fine. You'll see."

Ivy bit her lips and inclined her head to show she believed me, or at least that she wanted to.

"Oh! And before I forget, after we close on Saturday evening, I'm taking everyone out to dinner at the Grill, just as a kind of thank-you for all your hard work. Do you want to come?"

Her eyes flickered. The Grill was one of New Bern's more expensive restaurants and I knew that Ivy had never been there. But her initial expression of enthusiasm faded after a moment.

"What is it? Would you rather not go? You don't have to if you don't want to but I wish you would."

"It's not that. It's just that I don't have anyone to watch the kids and . . ." she looked down at the jeans and polo shirt that constituted her normal work uniform. "Isn't the Grill kind of dressy? I don't have anything nice to wear."

"I'm sure Franklin wouldn't mind watching the children again. If he can't, I'll bet Wendy Perkins would love to do it. She's a grandma six times over, just loves kids. And as far as clothes, I've got an idea. You pick out a few yards of fabric, anything you want, and I'll help you whip up a nice dress. Plenty of time to get it done before Saturday. All you'll need is a pair of sandals and some earrings and you'll be good to go."

Ivy's beautiful eyes filled with tears, but they were happy tears, tears of relief that needed to be shed so I didn't say anything.

"Thank you."

"You're welcome, sweetheart," I said using the same endearment I used for Garrett. She'd never mentioned her mother or her father and I wondered what kind of relationship, if any, she had with them. Grown woman that she was, at that moment Ivy needed a little mothering. I was more than happy to fill the role. "It's my pleasure."

Ivy smiled through her tears.

I smacked my hands against the table and got to my feet. "Well, we'll talk about this more later, but now, we've got work to do, right?"

"We do," Ivy agreed and wiped her eyes. "The anniversary sale and all."

"Don't worry," I said. "As long as we work together we'll get through it."

ᴄᴄ 14 ᴄᴄ

Ivy Peterman

Evelyn was as good as her word.

What with getting ready for the anniversary sale, we'd already known it was going to be a busy week, but even before the day was out, busyness blossomed into pandemonium.

It seemed like everyone in New Bern and a good percentage of the population of New England had seen *Quintessential Quilting* and were either calling and emailing to place orders, or actually dropping by the shop. It was crazy. Customers were five deep at the checkout counter and I had to come down from the workroom to help wait on them, abandoning a stack of unfulfilled orders that was growing taller by the minute. Finally, I called my neighbor, Karen, who had just been let go from her factory job, and asked if she'd like to help us out for a few days. She accepted eagerly and showed up at the shop an hour later, bringing two more of our neighbors, Jeni and Gayle, with her. Evelyn hired all of them on the spot.

The addition of three new workers, especially Gayle, who had retail experience, definitely helped, but we were still swamped. Even so, Evelyn found time to do everything she'd promised to do, right down to helping me cut out and sew an adorable dress from the gorgeous green and violet floral I'd picked out. It had been so long since I'd had anything new to wear and sewing it myself (with much guidance and instruction from Evelyn) gave me a great sense of accomplishment. When I mentioned that it would be fun to make a matching dress for Bethany, Evelyn insisted I take another two yards of fabric. I tried to pay for it myself, but she wouldn't hear of it.

"Consider it your finder's fee for bringing in Karen, Jeni, and Gayle. There is no way we'd be able to get through this week without them."

The shop bells jingled and a gaggle of women entered, grabbed the last wicker shopping baskets from the pile sitting by the door and began loading them up. Evelyn sighed and hauled herself to her feet. "Even with three new pairs of hands, I'm still not sure we're up to it. After two years of financial drought, I'm not complaining, but I'm sure glad for the extra help."

The phone rang yet again. Evelyn grabbed it. "Cobbled Court Quilts. This is Evelyn."

I headed toward the stairs to give the new girls a quick lesson in the use of rotary cutters so they could get to work on the unfilled orders. I glanced behind and saw Evelyn wedge the phone between her ear and shoulder while she hunted for a pen.

She looked so harried. I wondered if she'd remember her promise to accompany me to my meeting with Donna Walsh.

As if reading my mind, she asked the caller to hold just a moment, then took the receiver away from her ear and pressed it to her chest. "Ivy, we've got a four-thirty appointment over at the shelter offices. Be ready by four-ten and we'll drive over together, okay?"

"Okay."

She winked and went back to her call. "We're all out of that Hoffman print, but I'm expecting a shipment in a couple of days. Would you like me to call you when it arrives?"

When we got to the meeting, Donna was reassuring rather than reproachful. She said she wished I'd been straight with her from the beginning, but she understood why I hadn't and promised that she would do everything possible to help me. In spite of Donna's encouragement, I felt anxious and little overwhelmed. Evelyn took notes, listing in order the things Donna said I should do next. It was a good thing because by the time we left, I couldn't remember any of it.

The next morning, Abigail dropped by the shop after yet another meeting with the people at the zoning department, who were no more enthusiastic about the idea of Abigail remodeling her home into more transitional apartments for the Stanton Center than they'd been during the last three meetings. Abigail's intentions were good but, personally, I thought she was fighting a losing battle. There was no way her neighbors, the most prominent and influential folks in town, were going to stand by and let Abigail put an apartment building in their midst, particularly one filled with abused women and their children. Of course, I wasn't going to say that to Abigail, not when she was in such a ticked-off mood—and ticked-off was describing it politely.

Abigail was furious and somewhat incredulous that she'd been unable to get the people at zoning to budge. I suspect it was the first time in her life she hadn't been able to make people in New Bern see things her way simply by smiling and uttering those two most influential of words—Burgess Wynne. Suffice it to say, she was not a happy camper—even less so when Evelyn told her the whole story about me.

As predicted, at first Abigail was supremely indignant at what she termed my unpardonable deceit, but Evelyn calmed her down. After a few minutes and an apology from me, I was pardoned after all. Next thing I knew, she became my staunch ally, transferring all her enmity to Hodge, who she immediately dubbed a "bullying, parasitic louse." A redundant insult but an apt one and every time she said it, I couldn't help but smile. It was nice to have someone on my side for once. And, as Evelyn said, if you were going to pick someone for your side, the first person on your team should be Abigail—particularly if your team was playing in New Bern.

Abigail Burgess Wynne in action was a sight to see. She wielded her address book like a fairy godmother's wand.

Her first call was to Franklin Spaulding. He wasn't in, so she left a brief message explaining what was going on and asked him to call right away. Next, she phoned home and arranged for her housekeeper, Hilda, and Hilda's niece, Gabby, to pick up Bethany and Bobby from daycare at five, as well as the children of Karen, Jeni, and Gayle, and take them over to my apartment and keep an eye on them until we all got home from work. When Hilda asked how they were to transport themselves and seven children from the daycare to the Stanton Center, Abigail called the Dowell Ford dealership. She got the manager on the phone, and said she wanted to rent a new van from him for a month or so and that it had to be delivered to her house by four o'clock.

"My housekeeper will accept delivery," she said. "And make sure the gas tank is filled. Yes, her name is Hilda. Thank you, Gene. You're a darling. Oh! Wait just a moment."

She lowered the phone and looked at me. "Won't we need some of those car seat things for the babies?"

I nodded mutely, more than a bit in awe of way in which Abigail maneuvered her way past roadblocks that would have stopped me in my tracks with little more effort than it took to puff on the petals of a spent dandelion, scattering seeds to the four winds.

She waited for me to say something and when I didn't, frowned and said impatiently, "Well? How many do we need?"

"Oh. Ummm." I did a quick calculation. "Three, I guess."

"You guess?"

"No. I mean, I know. Three."

Abigail put the phone to her ear again. "And Gene, could you be a dear and include three car seats with that order? Well, no, I didn't suppose you had three car seats there at the dealership, but I'm sure you can have one of the salesmen run out and buy some, can't you?"

I shook my head and whispered, "Abigail, you don't have to do that. We all have car seats back at Stanton. I could run over there and . . ."

But, Abigail held up her hand and closed her eyes, making it clear that my interruption was unwelcome.

Evelyn came into the back office, which Abigail had requisitioned as her personal command center in the battle against the bullying parasitic louse (it made me smile even to think it), and whispered in my ear. "How's it going?"

I whispered back, "She's telling them they should go buy three car seats for the babies. They don't need to go to all that trouble. I could run back to Stanton and get them."

Evelyn grinned and leaned in closer so Abigail wouldn't hear her. "Don't worry about it. Just let her do her thing. She's loving every minute of this, especially after getting shot down by the zoning department. She needs to throw her weight around a bit, just to prove she still can."

Abigail's countenance brightened. "Oh, *could* you?" she purred. "Thank you so much, Gene. When Jim Dowell promoted you to manager, I knew he was making the right choice. I'm going to call him as soon as I hang up and tell him so. Bye-bye."

I turned to Evelyn. "I didn't know the Ford dealer even rented cars."

"They rent them to Abigail," Evelyn said.

Abigail's face was all concentration, trying unsuccessfully to summon a phone number to memory. She hung up the phone. "Evelyn, what's the number at the Grill? It's completely slipped my mind."

"I thought you were calling Jim Dowell."

"In a minute. First I'm calling Charlie. I want him to send over a tray of sandwiches. I'm starving, aren't you? I'd intended to take you to lunch, but with that crowd in the shop, I can see you won't be leaving anytime soon and I'm sure no one else will have a chance to take a lunch break, either."

The doorbell jingled again and Evelyn looked over her shoulder to see who was entering. "You're right about that, but at least the phone has stopped ringing off the hook."

Abigail wrinkled her nose thoughtfully. "Evelyn. That clicking sound that you hear sometimes when you're on this phone? Does that mean that someone else is trying to call in?"

Evelyn closed her eyes for a moment. "Yes," she said wearily. "How many times has it clicked since you've been talking?"

"About seven."

"Ivy," she said before returning to the shop floor. "Would you please check the phone messages when Abigail is finished?"

"Sure."

"And the number to the Grill is 5883," she said, using New Bern telephone shorthand. New Bern is so small there is only one telephone prefix, so no one who lives here bothers saying the first three numbers; such knowledge is assumed.

Before Abigail could start dialing, the telephone rang. She picked it up herself. "Cobbled Court Quilts." She paused a moment and smiled at the caller's comment.

"Well, maybe I'm taking up a new career." She laughed again, raised her eyebrows and glanced up at me. "It's Franklin," she mouthed before continuing her conversation.

"Really? That's wonderful, darling. Thank you so much. Yes, she's standing right here. I'll tell her myself. All right. Oh, and don't forget. We've got a five o'clock tee time at the club. We'll only be able to get in nine holes before sunset, but better nine than none."

Her smile faded as she listened to his response. "Well, that's fine, darling. No. Don't give it another thought. I'll just reschedule for later in the week. All right. Goodbye, Franklin," she said and hung up.

"Is everything all right?"

"Oh, yes. Fine. Franklin and I were supposed to play a round of golf this evening, but he's feeling a little too tired to keep our date, that's all."

"Franklin works very hard."

"Too hard," Abigail said. "I keep reminding him that he's no spring chicken anymore. At his age, he should slow down a little, pass off some of the work to a few of his younger, overpaid associates."

"And how does he respond to this good advice?" I asked.

Abigail's lips twitched into a smile. "About the way most men respond to the news of their advancing age—with offended expressions and much sucking in of their sagging stomach muscles. And they say that women are vain about their age," she laughed and her face lit up, partly from the pleasure of female superiority over foolish, boyish men, and partly with the pleasure that comes from being able to call one of those foolish creatures her own. She and Franklin made a good couple.

"Franklin wanted me to tell you that he's already making some appointments for you on Monday. He'd like you to be at his office at ten. He wants to talk with you privately and then you'll have a conference call after. You have officially retained him as legal counsel. You couldn't be in better hands."

"Really?" I bit a little flag of cuticle from off my finger. "Okay. Good."

Abigail scowled. "Don't bite your nails, Ivy. You'll ruin your hands. What's making you so nervous all of a sudden? Franklin is an excellent lawyer. One of the best."

"No, it's not that. I know he is. It's just . . . well . . . is he very expensive? I've got some money saved, but I've been saving it for a deposit and rent on a new apartment . . ."

"Is that what you're so worried about?" Abigail waved her hand dismissively. "Well, don't be. Franklin is doing this pro bono."

"Pro bono?"

"Without a fee," Abigail informed me. "And I'm going to take care of the other expenses. Investigators. Consultants. That sort of thing.

"Abigail, you can't. Are you sure? Oh, Abigail! I don't know how to . . ."

Abigail pursed her lips and frowned, uncomfortable with the sight of tears. "Now, stop that right now. There's no need. Franklin is happy to help you and so am I. If you were in a position to help either of us, I'm sure you'd do the same."

I nodded mutely and Abigail rolled her eyes.

"Oh, for heaven's sake," she said, picking up her pocketbook and looping it over her shoulder. "If there's anything I can't bear, it's weeping. Tell Evelyn I decided to go up to the Grill and get those sandwiches myself. I'll be back soon. In the meantime, Ivy, pull yourself together."

I nodded again and sniffed. I didn't blame her for being irritated with me; I was irritated with myself. I almost never cried, especially not in front of people. Over the years, I'd trained myself not to, having learned that when Hodge flew into one of his rages, the sight of me crying only made him angrier. I'd become very good at distancing myself from any feelings of pain, or even of pleasure, keeping my emotions boxed up and out of sight where they couldn't be used against me. But now that the box had finally been opened, it was hard closing the lid again.

For years, every emotion I'd been entitled to—love, hate, fear, and joy—had been dehydrated, every bit of moisture and meaning sucked out of them until they lay faded and flat, tasteless as sawdust on my tongue. This undeserved kindness from Abigail, Evelyn, Franklin, and everyone else was a sweet and surprising infusion, pumping new life into all my old, petrified feelings, expanding them beyond my ability to contain them until they spilled from my eyes unbidden. I tried to hold them back, but it wasn't easy.

"Sorry," I said to Abigail's back, sniffing again and wiping my eyes on my sleeve.

She paused at the door a moment, then turned around on her heel as sharply as a soldier performing an about face, and approached me, patting my shoulder awkwardly and briefly, the way someone who was bitten by a dog as a child pats a schnauzer on the nose.

"It's all right," she said quietly. "You're welcome."

Abigail left. I pulled a tissue from the box on Evelyn's desk and blew my nose. Everyone was being so nice to me. I didn't deserve such kindness. I knew that. I'd known that since I was a little girl.

But, Evelyn and Abigail didn't and I couldn't let them find out. If they did, they wouldn't want to help me and I needed their help. They were our only defense against Hodge and, in spite of Margot's logical assurances that he hadn't seen the show and wouldn't come looking for me, I knew better. One way or another, he'd find us.

Abgail, Franklin, Evelyn, and the others were the only thing that stood between my kids and Hodge. I didn't like it, but if I had to conceal things from them to keep that shield in place, then I would.

If that was the price of keeping my kids safe, I'd pay it.

∽ 15 ∽

Evelyn Dixon

Even though I had to resist the urge to ask the caller if they wanted "fries with that" every time I answered the phone, Garrett was right; buying a hands-free telephone headset had been a good idea. Sure, it made me look like I was working the drive-through window at a fast food joint, but it was worth it. Not only had the kink I'd gotten from constantly cradling the receiver with my neck gone, I could now simultaneously talk to one customer on the phone while ringing up the order of another standing in front of me. Multi-tasking is a beautiful thing. And if you own your own business, it's absolutely required.

"Hang on," Charlie said. "I've got to put the phone down for a minute. I dropped one."

"One what?" I asked. He didn't answer. He was already gone. When he came back on the line I repeated the question.

"One napkin. I'm sitting here folding napkins for the dinner crowd while I'm talking to you. Two birds with one stone, you know."

I chuckled. "Well, that makes us birds of a feather. While you're folding napkins for the restaurant and talking to me, I'm folding fat quarters for the shop and talking to you."

"Wonderful," Charlie flatly. "What a coincidence. We're practically twins. It's all just so eerie and intimate. In fact, it's probably the most intimate moment we've had in three weeks."

He was trying to make a joke.

No, not quite. What he was doing was griping about the fact that he and I hadn't spent five minutes alone since the promotional video had aired three weeks before and then *pretending* he was teasing when he was really complaining. And if I called him on it, if I said he wasn't being fair and that none of this was my fault, he'd flap up his feathers like a wet rooster and give me a hard time for not being able to take a joke. Why do men do that? If they're irritated with you, then why not just say so? I wouldn't have blamed him for it.

The truth was, I *hadn't* had a spare moment to talk to Charlie for days. Now, during a brief and wholly unexpected afternoon lull in business and with the rest of the staff upstairs trying to help Ivy and the girls finish boxing and labeling the week's outgoing orders, I was happy to have a few minutes to chat without anyone listening in.

Yes, I was going to see him for dinner in just a couple of hours, right before the Planning and Zoning hearing that Abigail insisted I attend so I could lend my support to her proposal, but Abigail and Franklin would be there, too. With Abigail so wound up about the hearing and what she had recently termed the "vast, right-wing conspiracy" to stop her from going forth with her plans, this conspiracy taking the form of a petition circulated by her neighbors, it was unlikely that Charlie and I would have a chance to talk about anything personal. And, knowing Charlie as I did, he'd probably spend half the meal jumping up from the table to sort out some confusion with seating or brouhaha in the kitchen anyway. I understood. He had a business to run. So did I. That meant the time we had to spend together was limited, even more so in recent weeks.

Given that, the last thing I wanted to do with these private few minutes was argue. I changed the subject.

"Charlie, what is it about a television camera that makes normally intelligent people start acting like complete morons?"

"You mean like those eejits who stand behind the reporter who's live on the scene of some terrible house fire," he asked, using his favorite Irish insult, "or freeway crash, or other frightful human tragedy and then jump up and down and waving their arms while they talk to people on their cellphones and say, "Look at me! I'm on the TV?"

I started stacking the fat quarters into collections of six complementary colors and tying them with ribbons. "Well, them too, but I was thinking more about the eejit politicians. They're driving me crazy! I mean, these people are our elected officials! Don't they have better things to do than keep bugging me about getting to sit in the audience of a cable quilting show? Some of them would drop the baby they were kissing to get within five miles of a TV camera."

"Well, every vote counts. It's going to be a tight race and you never know what might turn the tide. The quilters' vote might just be the difference between the state going red or blue. But publicity and goodwill aside, I'm a man that cares about the issues. What I want to know is, where do you suppose Porter Moss stands on the question of machine versus hand appliqué?"

I straightened the ribbon I'd been tying. This time Charlie was joking, sincerely, and it made me smile. That was one of the things I loved about him. He always made me laugh. That was also the reason I was never able to stay angry with him for long.

"Be serious for a minute, Charlie. This whole thing has been a nightmare from day one. Ever since Mary Dell's producer, Sandy, called up Porter Moss and told him that, no, they were not filming the show in the high school gymnasium and that, no, Dale Barrows was not going to direct it, that they already paid someone perfectly good money to do that job, things have gotten even worse. And did I tell you?" My voice dropped into a conspiratorial hush. "Just yesterday some slimy little assistant from the permit office called and hinted that if I couldn't find a seat in the audience for his mother-in-law, I might have trouble getting the permits we need to park the sound trucks. He actually threatened me! Can you believe that?"

On the other end of the line, Charlie howled.

"What's so funny?"

"You are. You've worked yourself up into quite a lather over this thing, haven't you?"

"Oh, fine. Go ahead and laugh, but I think it's disgraceful. A violation of public trust! I mean these people are supposed to be intelligent and wise and humble, dedicated to the greater good, but this crowd we've got now . . ." I reached up and scratched my ear where the headphone was rubbing.

"Oh," Charlie said sagely. I could still feel a smile radiating in his voice. "Intelligent and wise and humble, is it? So tell me, what eighth grade civics book did you lift that from?"

"It wasn't the eighth grade," I pouted. "It was the fifth. And it wasn't a civics book, it was a biography. Of George Washington."

"Ah," Charlie murmured. "Washington. Your hero. For me it was Michael Connelly, but I'm afraid they don't make them like that anymore, my love. You're taking this much too much to heart, Evelyn. It's pretty funny when you stop to think about it."

I shrugged and began piling the assembled fabric medleys into a display basket. "I suppose so, in a way. If I wasn't quite so overwhelmed right now, I'd probably have more of a sense of humor about it."

"Well, what else is bothering you?"

"Nothing really."

"Evelyn Dixon, you're a terrible liar. Come on. Tell old Uncle Charlie what's on your mind. It'll do you good. As my mother always used to say, better out than in."

I made a face. "Yech. Isn't that proverb supposed to be about belching and breaking wind?"

"The principle's the same. Go on. Tell me what's on your mind. Are you still nervous about going on television? Or maybe you're just feeling overworked? Every time Mary Dell says the words 'Cobbled Court Quilts' on the air, you get a tidal wave of customers coming through your door. You must be dead on your feet."

"I am, but you won't ever find me complaining about having too many customers. The memory of what it was like when we didn't have any is still too fresh in my mind," I said. "We're all tired. We're getting so much traffic on the website that it keeps crashing. Garrett was up half the night getting it to work again. And I'm on the phone begging my vendors to ship more fabric and get it here faster, but for the first time in history, we're actually making money, so I'm definitely not upset about that."

"Then is it this business with Ivy?"

I thought for a moment before responding. "No. That actually seems to be going well. At least I think it is. It's hard to know for sure. But, you saw how much fun she had when we all came to dinner at the Grill on Saturday. I don't think I'd ever seen her smile so much. She looks so pretty when she smiles, don't you think?"

"She does," he affirmed. "You should have seen the time I had back in the kitchen. Jason and David got into an argument about who was going to wait on her."

"Well, I can't blame them. She's a doll. And she looked great in her new dress." I sighed as I cut a few more lengths of ribbon to tie the fabric with. "It's so hard for me to understand how such a kind, capable, and lovely girl put up with an abusive marriage for so long. I just don't get it."

"Does she ever talk about it?"

"A little. I still get the feeling she's holding back. After what she's been through, it must be hard to trust other people. But I think she's feeling more comfortable with us every day. Last Friday she surprised everyone by showing up at the quilt-circle meeting and saying that, if the invitation were still open, she'd like to join after all."

"That's good, isn't it? Ivy is doing well. You're making money. So what's the problem?"

I didn't quite know myself. I just had this feeling that something wasn't right.

Years before, when we'd first moved from Wisconsin to Texas, we adopted this cantankerous old tomcat, Arnold Palmer. We called him A.P. for short.

Rob, my ex-husband, had found him sleeping on the fourth green of the local golf course. Rob yelled at him to move, even tossed a club in the air, trying to get this cat off the green so he could finish the hole, but the cat just looked at him and went on napping. Rob finally gave up and decided to skip the hole. When he walked past the green, the cat got up and followed Rob through the whole rest of the course—five more holes. The cat didn't have a collar and no one at the pro shop recognized him, so Rob brought him home, and named him Arnold Palmer, after the famous golfer.

Anyway, A.P. was the laziest cat on earth. He must have weighed twenty pounds. He slept all day and all night, never getting up except to visit the cat box or food dish. But, every now and then, A.P. would get up and start yowling and pacing back and forth across the kitchen with the hair on his back standing up on end. The first time it happened, I tried petting him, feeding him, but nothing could get him to settle down. Finally, a couple of hours later, black clouds started gathering and within a few minutes they let loose a huge, pelting rainstorm complete with booming thunder and lightning flashes so bright it was like we'd turned on every light in the house at the same time.

I'd never seen a storm like that and it caught me totally by surprise. The washing I'd put out to dry on the line was soaked, but A.P. had known it was coming.

After that, whenever I'd see him start to pace, I'd run outside to bring in the washing before the storm hit. Sometimes it took only an hour before it showed up, sometimes more, but one way or another and even if he didn't understand exactly what it was, Arnold Palmer always knew when something bad was brewing. He was never wrong.

That's how I felt now. Like there was a bad wind blowing. I didn't know exactly what direction it would come from one or precisely what it would bring, I only knew it was on the way.

"It's hard to explain, Charlie. I just . . ." I faltered for a moment, considered telling him about A.P. but changed my mind. Charlie loved to tease me and if I told him my cat story that is exactly what he would do, tease me mercilessly. Normally, I didn't mind but this was serious. Charlie might not believe in feline or female intuition, but I did and still do. Some things you just *know*. But, I didn't expect Charlie to understand.

"It's complicated, Charlie. Not the kind of thing I can explain over the telephone."

"Well, wait just a minute, Evelyn. Are you . . ."

The doorbell jingled and the door opened.

"Hey, Charlie, I have to run. I've got customers. See you at dinner. Bye-bye."

I hung up before Charlie had a chance to say goodbye back, but I knew he'd understand. He'd had to do the same to me on other occasions. We were business people and during business hours, customers came first. We both knew that.

❧ 16 ❧

Evelyn Dixon

I pushed the pile of ribbons off the counter and looked up, surprised to see a tall, hard and handsome man of about forty coming through the door—not a customer after all.

That's not to say that men never darkened the door of Cobbled Court Quilts. There are male quilters out there. Two or three are my customers. And of course it isn't unusual for our female customers to enter with men in tow, usually husbands who whistle to themselves or look at their watches while waiting for their wives to finish their shopping, or who make little jokes about how they are going to have to build an addition onto the house just to store all the fabric—good-humored men with open faces and relaxed gaits.

This fellow wasn't one of those.

He wore a hopsack blazer of navy blue, the standard issue jacket of businessmen the world over, but he didn't quite look like a corporate type, either. His jaw was sharp and his arms and shoulders were heavily muscled inside his jacket, making the sleeves bulge. Whoever he was, I was sure he wasn't in search of fabric. Maybe he was looking for the gallery or the real estate office and had gotten lost.

He stood at the door, scanning the room but not spotting me yet.

"Can I help you?" I asked.

He turned toward me and his face instantly split into a wide smile that almost reached his eyes.

"Why, yes. At least, I hope so," he said in a deep, pleasant voice, a voice that was designed to charm. "I'm looking for someone . . ."

He didn't have to say more. I knew who he was and what he wanted. The easy smile and polite manner couldn't disguise it. He was the expected storm. If A.P. had been around, he'd have been pacing and yowling.

"Ivy Edelman. I understand she works here. Could you please tell her I'm here to see her?"

Edelman? As far as I knew, Ivy's last name was Peterman, but it wasn't too surprising to realize that Ivy had given us a false name. No, not false. Likely Peterman was her maiden name. That was the way it was listed on her social security card.

There was no way I was going to let this man know Ivy was in the building. I smiled slightly, trying to make my voice sound innocent and convincing.

"I'm sorry, we don't have anyone by that name working here."

"This is Cobbled Court Quilts, isn't it? The place they keep talking about on that quilting show? The one with that lady and the retarded guy?"

I bristled. Retarded is such an ugly word, a word meant to slice through the value and merit of an entire population of human beings and label them as lesser class of mortals.

"Down syndrome," I said flatly. My pretense to politeness dropped. So did his. "Howard has Down syndrome. He's a very sweet and gifted man, a television star."

"Whatever. I don't care who he is. All I know is that one of my neighbors spotted Ivy on that TV show and that they filmed the segment at Cobbled Court Quilts." Keeping his eyes fixed on me, he reached down to the counter, pulled one of our store business cards out of the holder near the cash register, and held one out to me. I didn't move.

"Says on the card that this is the place. Now, where is she? Call Ivy and tell her I want to see her. Do it now."

His voice was quiet, slow and steady, but with a sharp, razored edge that was more menacing than a scream, a sound like the rumbling, warning growl of a vicious dog, fury held in check but only just. I could see why Ivy was so frightened of him.

He was a frightening man, especially if you were a young and fragile woman, isolated, alone, and desperate to keep from saying or doing anything that might cause his hemmed-in anger from breaking loose.

I am none of those things.

"I won't be ordered around in my own shop, not by you or anyone. I'm going to have to ask you to leave."

He put both hands on the counter and leaned toward me, his arms flexed, straining beneath the sleeved confinement of his jacket.

"Maybe you didn't understand me the first time," he said lowering his voice until it was a whisper. "I'm not leaving without her." He didn't blink. Neither did I.

"Ivy is my wife. Almost two years ago she disappeared with my children. She's a kidnapper and a thief. If you try to hide her, you're going to find yourself in a world of trouble."

"I don't know who you think you are, but I've had just about enough of your threats. Get out of my shop or I'm going to call the police."

He just kept staring at me, refusing to budge. I could tell he was trying to intimidate me with his immoveable demeanor and, though on the inside I was shaking, on the outside I was unflinching.

The skin near the base of his shirt collar was beginning to turn red. He was angry, frustrated at his inability to bully me into doing what he wanted.

Well, isn't that too bad. I thought, working to keep my lips from bowing into a smile. *It's a bit harder going toe-to-toe with an old broad whose been around the block a few times than it is pushing Ivy and your kids around, isn't it?*

I waited one moment more, hoping he'd back down, then straightened my shoulders and reached for the phone.

He beat me to it, clamped his big paw over the receiver and wouldn't let go.

"You need to make a call, Mister?" Charlie asked as he walked in through the open door holding a bunch of white daisies clutched in his fist. "You'll find a pay phone down at the gas station."

Charlie isn't a short man. He works out three days a week and is in good shape, but Ivy's husband had six inches on him in height and Charlie had at least a decade on him in age. Yet, there Charlie was, glaring at this intruder with both his hands balled up into fists and, even though one of those fists was still clutching a nosegay of summer flowers, the pugnacious tilt of Charlie's chin made it clear that he was itching to throw a punch, the perfect illustration of the phrase, "got his Irish up." I do love that man.

Ivy's husband, Hodge, turned around to face Charlie. "Nice flowers."

Charlie took a step forward.

"Hey, I'm not trying to cause any problems," Hodge said calmly. He opened his hands and dropped his shoulders, deliberately taking a less provocative stance as if trying to develop a man-to-man rapport with Charlie. That seemed to be his modus operandi, first try charm and manipulation and, if that didn't work, go for threats and intimidation.

"All I want is to see my wife. I know she's here. Her car's parked outside. I'm not going to leave until I get to talk to her. She's my wife. I love her and I want to see her, that's all."

Charlie spoke before I could stop him. "Yes. We've heard all about how you show your love for Ivy. Fists in place of flowers. Kicks instead of kisses. Quite the devoted husband, aren't you?"

"Is that what she told you? That I hit her?" He shook his head and sighed. "Listen, I love Ivy, I always have, but you don't know her like I do. She's had a hard life. Father died when she was a little girl, mother was killed in a car wreck a few years later. And then there was her stepfather," he huffed. "He was a real prince of a guy, used Ivy for his personal punching bag. She ran away. Started living on the streets. That's when I found her."

His eyes drifted up toward the ceiling, away from Charlie, as if having a conversation with himself, and rubbed his neck with his big right hand. "She was so beautiful. It took me about five minutes to fall in love with her. Less. How could I not? And I . . . well . . . I thought I could rescue her," he said ruefully and then let out a short, self-mocking laugh.

"Love conquers all. That's what I thought at the time, but when a person is scarred like that, so badly and so young . . ."

He started a bit and looked at Charlie again, as if suddenly remembering he wasn't alone. He cleared his throat. "I love Ivy; I always will. She's my wife and I promised to love her and take care of her for better or worse. I know she can be very convincing but Ivy has . . ." he hesitated as if looking for a word that would describe the poor, disturbed bride he was only trying to save from herself without sounding disloyal, ". . . issues."

What a guy. What a performance.

The thing is, I *did* know Ivy. I'd been working side by side with her for over a year and I knew she wasn't the pathetic, mental basket case he was making her out to be. It was everything I could do to keep myself from spitting on Hodge Edelman's shoes and then kicking him in the shins.

The problem was, he was a very good actor, a brilliant one. If I hadn't known Ivy as I did, I might have been convinced by his performance. Even worse, his story sounded almost true. Ivy hasn't told me everything about her past, but enough so that I knew that many of the details he was sharing were accurate. He'd added a few facts, left out some others. Almost true or not, it still added up to a lie, but someone who didn't know Ivy might be inclined to believe his version of the story. In a courtroom, wearing his solid-citizen blue blazer and making his polished delivery, he would make a believable witness. More believable, perhaps, than Ivy, with that hollow and hunted look in her eyes.

Much as I wanted him out of my shop, I needed to hear what he had to say. I needed to study his story and his demeanor because, clearly, this was the tack he was going to take, to paint Ivy as a lying, mentally unbalanced young woman and himself as the long-suffering but devoted husband who'd fallen in love too hard and married too quickly to realize what he was getting himself into, but who wasn't going to back away from his family obligations, no matter how burdensome they'd become.

I didn't believe him, but someone who didn't know Ivy like I did might. A judge might. I listened as long as I could, looking for the chinks in his armor. The best offense is a strong defense.

"The thing is," he continued, turning to me now, trying to win me to his side, or at least cause me to consider the possibility that he was telling the truth, "Ivy sometimes has a hard time separating fact from fiction. It's not her fault. After all she's been through I guess it's understandable, but when she feels overwhelmed or upset about something, her first instinct is to run, you know? She doesn't like confrontation." He sighed again, heavily.

"This whole thing was my fault. We had an argument about something stupid; I can't even remember what now. I got mad. I didn't touch her—I'd never do that—but I raised my voice. I shouldn't have. I know how she gets. But I really didn't think it was that big a deal. I went to work, figured we'd talk it out when I got home but by then, she was gone."

He looked me in the eye, held out his hands palm out, a magician bent on convincing me he had nothing up his sleeve. "Ma'am, I'm sorry I was so gruff with you before. Really. It's just that I've been looking for my wife and my children for months on end. I'd almost given up hope of ever finding them . . ."

He sniffed. The same man who'd leaned across the counter and tried to bully me into giving up his abused wife now actually sniffed and blinked as if now, suddenly overwhelmed by tenderness, it was all he could do to keep back the tears. Watching this farce, *I* was suddenly overwhelmed by a desire to lose my lunch.

"I've been away on business," he continued. "When I got home last night, one of my neighbors came over to the house and told me she'd seen Ivy on that quilting show. It was just for a second, but she wrote down the name of your shop. I got in my car and drove up here right away. Didn't even remember to call the office and tell them where I'd gone until I'd crossed the state line. I was so worried that I'd be too late. Like I said, whenever something upsets her, Ivy's first instinct is to run. And then, when I got here and saw her car parked on the street I was so anxious to see her . . . Well, like I said, I shouldn't have been so gruff with you. I'm really sorry, Miss? Ms.?" He looked a question at me.

I'd found out what I needed to know.

"You don't need to know my name," I said. "You won't be staying that long."

He frowned and I could see his jaw clench as he struggled to maintain his kinder, gentler façade. "I told you. I can't leave. I won't. Not without Ivy and my kids."

Still clasping the now-slightly-wilted daisies, Charlie took three steps to the right, moving solidly into Edelman's field of vision, a pugilist circling his opponent, eager for the bell to sound and the first round to begin. "Well you're going to have to. You're not welcome here. You are leaving. I'd advise you to do so under your own steam. It'll be less embarrassing."

"Less embarrassing?" Edelman said wryly, dropping all pretense of affability. "Less embarrassing for you? Yeah, I can see how you'd be worried about that because, Mister, it's going to take ten guys twice the size of you to get me to leave here without taking what's mine with me."

"Now there's an interesting picture. Not sure we can muster an army quite as big as that on short notice. Instead of ten guys, how about one lawyer?"

Franklin Spaulding, with Abigail close behind, came through the door right on time to pick me up for the zoning meeting. Franklin reached into his pocket and withdrew his weapon.

"My card. Franklin Spaulding." He smiled cordially and extended his hand with his business card in it, as if introducing himself to a potential new client at a cocktail party. "Your wife's attorney, to be more exact. If I'm not mistaken, there are some officers at your home and office right now, trying to serve you with divorce papers."

Edelman took the business card, read it, and scowled. Franklin smiled and inclined his head slightly. "Goodbye, Mr. Edelman. I'm sure we'll be seeing each other again soon."

"Count on it," Edelman growled and shoved the card in his

pocket before heading for the still open door. He slammed it behind him, making the bells ring so hard you'd have thought Christmas had come early.

For a moment, everyone was quiet. Then Abigail spoke, with an
uncharacteristically high and flute-like pitch to her voice.

"My! What a smell of sulphur!" she exclaimed and waved her
hands, Glinda the Good banishing the lingering aroma of her
wicked sister to the west.

That broke the tension.

"Well, that was interesting," I chuckled. "Charlie, when you
came through the door, it was like a scene from one of those old
spaghetti westerns, a shootout between the white hats and black,
but with a bit of a twist. What's with the flowers? Were you planning on beating him over the head with them, then hogtieing him
with a length of florist's wire?"

Charlie looked at the bedraggled bouquet and colored a bit.
"They were for you, of course. You sounded upset and then you
wouldn't tell me why, said it was too complicated to explain over
the phone." He shifted his shoulders defensively.

"I thought maybe you were re-thinking our relationship. So, as
soon as you hung up, I grabbed a bunch of flowers from off one
of the tables in the dining room and ran over here to talk you out
of it."

I came out from behind the counter and took the daisies from
him. "Oh, Charlie, they're beautiful. Thank you. But, you didn't
have to do that. I'm not rethinking anything. I'm afraid you're stuck
with me, sweetie." I rocked up on my toes and gave him a quick kiss
on the lips.

"I can live with that."

"So, Franklin, what do we do now? More to the point, what do
we think *he's* doing now?" I asked, tilting my head toward the door
through which Hodge Edelman had just exited.

Franklin took a handkerchief from his pocket and mopped his
brow, looking drained and a bit less formidable than he had just a
minute before. "Right now? My guess he's driving around, trying to
find a phone booth with an intact set of yellow pages so he can get

himself a lawyer. At least, that's what he'll be doing if he's got any brains at all."

"A question that seems to be in some doubt," added Charlie with a smirk.

Abigail moved closer to Franklin, slipping her arm through his. "Well, it won't do him any good whatever he does. The best lawyer in the county is already working on this case." She looked up at Franklin, her face beaming confidence.

"Mmmm," Franklin murmured noncommittally. "For Ivy's sake, I hope you're right." He pulled on his nose and thought for a moment.

"As far as the next move," he said wearily, "It's mine. There's enough time before the meeting. I'd better go upstairs and talk to Ivy."

❧ 17 ❧

Ivy Peterman

"Because I said so, Bethany, that's why!" I shouted at my daughter.

I felt terrible for yelling, but at the moment I wasn't in the mood to explain my reasoning to her. There wasn't time.

Sniffing, Bethany shuffled back into the bedroom she shared with Bobby and started morosely tossing her stuffed animals into the open cardboard box that I'd left sitting on the floor for that purpose. Bobby laughed and started chucking his building blocks into the box, too, thinking it was some kind of game. Every time one of the blocks made it into the box he'd clap his chubby hands and yell, "Two points! Two points for me!" At least one of my children was happy.

I turned back to my own work, taking the clean clothes from the laundry basket, folding them, and piling them into the empty suitcase that was sitting on the dinette where we'd eaten all our meals for the last year and a half. I pulled a pair of my jeans out of the basket and held them up, trying to decide if I should bring them or not. It was amazing to realize how many possessions we'd accumulated since we'd moved to New Bern. Clearly, we wouldn't be able to take everything with us, but I wanted to make sure I left enough room for the things that really mattered. Something I simply refused to leave behind were the quilts; the two that Abigail had made for the kids and the one I'd made in Evelyn's class. However, the quilts were bulky and that meant less room for other things, like clothes.

I tossed the jeans onto the "leave behind" pile. They were pretty worn and, besides, it was more important to leave space for the kid's clothes than mine. I could get along with a couple of pairs of slacks, some tops, and a sweater or two—that and the sundress that Evelyn had helped me make. I pulled it out of the basket and folded it carefully and hugged it to my chest. It wasn't really practical to bring it along. I could only wear it for a few months a year and didn't have much cause for dressing up. I knew I should put it on the pile with the worn blue jeans and other discards, but I hesitated.

I didn't own a camera. I wanted one but they were expensive. Every now and again I'd buy one of those disposable jobs at the drug store and take pictures of Bethany and Bobby, but I couldn't afford to spend much on developing pictures. And none of the few photographs we did have included me; I was always behind the camera.

Once I loaded our few boxes and bags into the trunk, buckled the kids into their seats, turned on the ignition and pulled out onto the highway, leaving New Bern, Connecticut in my rearview mirror, I would have nothing to remind me of its curbed, orderly streets and peaceful town green, the charming antique homes with painted shutters, and the picketed garden gates that swung wide to welcome visitors and, of course, the people.

But this, this dress with the profusion of violet and purple hydrangeas blooming on the rippling gathers of the skirt and the sage-colored piping that reminded me of late summer in Connecticut's quiet corner . . .

Every time I saw this beautiful dress, or stroked the smooth, fine-loomed cotton with my fingertips, it was like opening a photograph album in my mind. I might never have occasion to wear that dress again, but every time I saw it, I would remember Evelyn, and Abigail, and Margot, and all my friends at Cobbled Court Quilts. I would remember New Bern, the only place I ever lived that felt like home.

If there wasn't enough room in the suitcase for underwear, then that was just too bad. No way was I leaving my dress behind.

I laid the dress on top of the stack, closed and latched the lid of the suitcase, put it on the floor next to a big, black garbage bag loaded with sheets, pillows and a set of towels, and went into my room to get the last two suitcases.

Belly-down and with my head and torso under the bed, I was dragging out the other suitcases when I heard the electronic beep of the intercom, telling me that someone was standing outside the locked front door of the Stanton Center and had rung my apartment, wanting me to press the buzzer that would unlock the door.

When I heard the beep, I tried to scramble out from underneath the bed, yelling for Bethany not to touch anything, but the tail of my shirt got stuck on one of the metal supports of the bedframe. By the time I ran into the family room, Bethany had already pressed the door release buzzer and was chirping happily into the intercom.

"Okay. See you in a minute!"

I was too late.

"Bethany! Didn't you hear me telling you not to touch the intercom? I've told you before! You're not supposed to open the door for anyone! Do you hear me? Not for anyone!"

Bethany tilted her head to one side and frowned. "But it wasn't anyone. It was Margot."

I took a deep breath and let it out again slowly, relieved. Hodge wasn't ascending the steps to the door of our second-floor apartment, but I didn't want to see Margot, either. Things were hard enough as it was.

I looked around the family room and considered hiding the suitcases and bags in the closet but there wasn't time. Margot was already knocking on the door.

"Bethany, go to your room. Decide what books you want to take. You can only bring five. And help Bobby pick out five for himself too, all right?"

"But I want to see Margot," she whined.

I hissed through clenched teeth and pointed my finger in the direction of Bethany's room. "Go!"

She did, stomping her pink and gold tennis shoes and closing her bedroom door hard, not slamming it, but hard enough so I'd know she was mad at me.

Margot was knocking again, calling my name. I opened the door, but only partially, wedging my body in the open space so she wouldn't see the mess behind me, and casually raised my arm to rest against the doorjamb.

"Hi, Margot."

"Hi." She waited a moment expecting me to invite her in.

"The zoning meeting was a mess. Witnesses against Abbie's proposal were lined up out the door. Everybody was interrupting everybody else and the chairman was pounding the table and then Dale Barrows came in carrying a petition signed by himself and everybody else who lives on Proctor Street. Franklin practically had to tie Abigail to her chair."

Margot grinned. "You should have heard what she called Dale's last movie! Next thing you know Dale started shouting that he's going to sue Abigail for libel. Small town melodrama at its best."

"Sorry I missed it."

"Yeah," she nodded.

"Anyway," she continued, filling the silence. "It got to be too much for me so I thought I'd drop by and see how you were doing. Can I come in?"

"Oh, not right now," I said through the crack in the door. "I just put the kids to bed."

Of course, that was the moment that Bobby decided to fling open the door of the bedroom and do a victory lap around the family room chanting, "Two points! Two points! Two points for me!" then run back into his room and slam the door shut.

I looked at Margot—caught—and I dropped my arm down to my side.

Margot peered past me into the disarrayed room, taking in the pile of suitcases and bags, heaps of discarded clothing, and drawers left standing open.

"Oh, Ivy. Ivy, don't," she said softly. Her voice dripped disappointment. I felt like I'd been caught trying to sneak out of a restaurant without paying the check. "Ivy, don't run away."

I stepped back from the door, letting her pass.

"I'm not running away," I said defensively, though of course that was exactly what I was doing. The enormity of the lie hung in the air. "I just . . . I can't stay here, Margot. Not right now. Once this whole thing is settled, the divorce and all, then we'll come back for good. To stay."

It was a lie, yet another one, but I wanted it to be true. Surely that should count for something, shouldn't it?

Margot just looked at me with that open, accepting expressions of hers, a forgiving gaze that made me feel just awful.

"Ivy, please don't do this. Not now, after you've worked so hard and have so much to lose. If you run this time, you'll never stop. It'll always be like this," she said, spreading her arms wide to take in the disordered mess at our feet. "If you're not worried about yourself and what this will do to you, think about the children."

"I am thinking about them!" I was exhausted. I sank into one of the dining chairs and dropped my head into my hands. "I am. But what else can I do? I don't have a choice. You must think I'm a terrible mother," I whispered. "Maybe it's true. Maybe I am."

She pulled up another chair and sat down next to me, dropping her hand onto my stooped shoulders and stroking my back, the way I did Bethany's when she was upset about something.

"No! Don't say that! I know how much you love Bethany and Bobby. You'd do anything for them."

"I do. I would. That's why I've got to leave now! You don't understand. If Hodge takes them away from me . . ."

"Ivy, that is not going to happen," she said adamantly. "Franklin Spaulding is a wonderful lawyer, one of the best in the state. Today doesn't change anything. Your husband's arrival on the scene may have surprised you, but it didn't faze Franklin. He knew you'd have to face him eventually. That's why he's been working so hard with you these last few days, taking down your whole story and helping you build your case; because he knew this day would come. But, he's ready, Ivy." she leaned over my bowed back, close to my ear, urging me to have confidence.

"Franklin knows every judge in the county and not one of them is going to listen to your story, hear what you've been through, and how hard you've worked to make a good home for the kids, and then decide to award custody of the children to a documented abuser instead of a wonderful, hard-working mother like you? You can't run, Ivy! Not now!"

I sat up, dry-eyed, and looked Margot in the face. "Margot, you don't know me. Not like you think you do. No one does. You—all of you; Evelyn, and Abigail, and Franklin too—you've been so kind to me. But I haven't told you everything about me. It's not that I've lied. What I told Franklin was the truth, almost the truth, but there are things I left out."

She sat up straighter and rested her hands in her lap, blank-faced, listening.

"I've done things . . . things I'm ashamed of. No one besides Hodge knows about them. It was a long time ago, and I've changed since then, but if people knew about my past, if a judge knew, he might think the kids would be better off with Hodge.

"I know Franklin is a good lawyer. If anyone could help me, I'm sure he could. But, Franklin doesn't know Hodge at all. He's . . . he's got this power, this way of making people believe whatever he says, you know? I just can't believe that a judge would believe my story over Hodge's. And if he doesn't . . ."

Margot tilted her head back and stared up at the ceiling for a moment. "You're being truthful with me, Ivy, so I won't lie to you. If you stand your ground and try to fight for your kids, it's possible that you'll lose them. I don't believe that will happen, but I suppose it's possible. Almost nothing in life comes with a guarantee. But, there is one thing I know for certain."

She leaned toward me ever so slightly and spoke in a flat, factual voice, with none of the tenderness of tone I always associated with Margot. "If you run now, you'll never, ever be able to stop. And more than likely, Hodge will catch up to you someday. And when he does, when you're all alone in some strange town without friends to help you, you *will* lose the children. You can count on it. And there's something else. If you run now, you don't just risk losing your kids, you risk losing yourself.

"Don't you see? You've run away from Hodge and you think you're free, but all you've really done is exchange one kind of prison for another. The lies may have purchased you a temporary liberty, but in the end, only the truth will set you free!"

Her eyes were open wide as if to underscore her ability to see things as they were, but it wasn't that simple, not for me.

Margot had faith. I'd known that from the first day I'd met her. In the beginning, it had kind of creeped me out. The way she talked so easily and openly about God and her faith, occasionally quoting the Bible to underscore a point, seemed just plain weird to me at first. And she was so sweet. I was sure it had to be some kind of act. No one could be that nice and that happy all the time.

But as time went on, I realized she wasn't selling anything. And she wasn't happy all the time. Like anyone else, Margot had her good days and bad days. What was different about her, I finally figured out, was that she met every day with a kind of peace and assurance that I lacked. It was interesting.

I liked Margot, but she didn't understand what I was up against. How could she? It was obvious to me that we were from two different sides of the tracks and it didn't take much to guess which of us was born on the wrong side.

Margot was so sweet, so innocent. She didn't know how cruel the world could be. Probably she was born into a big, loving family with a nice house in the suburbs and a fenced yard, daughter of a stay-at-home mom and hardworking dad who spent his Saturdays happily pushing a lawnmower or his children on swings at the park. A family who ate dinner together every night and went to church together every Sunday, the kind of Ozzie-and-Harriet fairy tale family I'd wanted for myself and my children, the family that, so many years ago, I'd believed would be mine when I married Hodge.

Easy to believe in fairy tales if, like Margot, your whole life had been lived in one. Easy to talk about embracing the truth when doing so wouldn't dredge up the shame, guilt, and pain you'd spent your whole life trying to bury. Easy for Margot.

I pulled my hand away.

"Margot," I said angrily. "This is none of your business. Just back off and let me handle this on my own, all right? Where do you get off coming over here and telling me what to do? You, with your perfect life and your blind faith," I scoffed. "Listen, I'm happy for you, Margot. You believe and that's great. Really. I don't want to take anything away from that, but you've got to accept that belief comes a little harder to those of us who *aren't* on God's list of favorite children! You don't know me. You never have, so I'll thank you to butt out of my life!"

I expected her to back away. Deep down, that's what I wanted her to do. It would be easier to leave if there were a rift between us, if I could tell myself once and for all that Margot and I had nothing in common.

She surprised me.

"You're right. I don't know you, any more than you know me. We've each been careful to put on our best face for the other. Well, why not? We're both grownups and we know from experience that you can't trust everyone. You've been burned before in that department; so have I. Maybe that's why I haven't been as open with you as I might have. But, you're wrong about me, Ivy.

"My life isn't perfect. Neither is my faith. There are times when I have doubts and, like everybody else, there are times when I carry around my own load of resentments. Sometimes I've been so jealous of you, I could hardly stand it."

"Me? You've been jealous of me?" The look on her face told me she wasn't joking.

She glanced toward Bethany and Bobby's closed bedroom door, blinking back tears.

"Ever since I was so high," she held her hand out flat to a height a few inches below the tabletop, "all I ever wanted to be was a mother. I'd be a great mother," she said earnestly and I nodded, knowing it was true.

"That has been the deepest desire of my heart for as long as I can remember. I always figured that since God must have put that desire there, it was just a matter of time until he fulfilled it by giving me a husband and children.

"College came and went. I left with a diploma in marketing and lots of men friends, guys who thought of me as their cute younger sister, but not even a hint of a proposal. But, I didn't worry. I just packed up my car, moved to Manhattan, and took an entry level job in the marketing department of a giant corporation because I figured in that oceanic pool of potential Mr. Rights, at least one of them had to have my name on him.

"Actually, it didn't even have to be Mr. Right. I'd have settled for Mr. Good Enough. All I really wanted was a family. Is that so much to ask for?" she asked plaintively.

"My twenties passed. I got three promotions, a nicer apartment, and bought a weekend cottage here in New Bern, but still no proposals, not so much as a glint of a diamond. I wasn't too worried; I was still young. Besides, men in Manhattan seem to wait a while before settling down. I don't know why, maybe they're more career-obsessed than other people, or maybe the price of real estate makes them nervous about getting married and starting a family. Who knows? But I figured the guys I was working with would *have* to start getting married once they hit their thirties. And I was right. They did. But guess who they got married to?"

"Women in their twenties?"

"Bingo!" she cried, laughing even while wiping away tears with the back of her hand.

"What's with that? Anyway, you know the rest of the story. Here I am. Looking forty in the face and still no babies. So even after all you've been through, even knowing what you're going to have to go through in these next months, can you imagine how jealous I've been of you and those two beautiful children?"

Yes. I could.

"Did you ever think of adopting?"

She bobbed her head. "Oh sure. But it's hard especially for a single woman. Not to mention expensive. I was actually pretty far through the process, far enough so I was starting to visit stores that carried baby furniture and talking to a contractor about knocking down walls to build a nursery. Then I got downsized, the victim of a flagging economy and a new department head who had a penchant for hiring newer, younger employees with what he called 'a fresh, funky take on the heartbeat of what's happening now.'" She rolled her eyes and made a gagging sound.

"Yes, this is the wordsmith they promoted over me to oversee the writing of all ad copy and marketing materials for all our product lines."

"And let me guess," I said. "These fresh new faces with the funky take on the heartbeat of whatever were all willing to work for way less money than people like you who'd been around a while and actually knew what they were doing."

"Right. So the new kids on the block were in and I was out on the street, pounding the pavement and trying to find a job in the middle of a recession. With no paycheck and no prospects for getting one in the near future, the adoption agency informed me that I was no longer considered a suitable candidate. They took me off the waiting list after I'd spent five years working my way to the top." Her eyes were dry now. She sniffed and made a *c'est la vie* face.

Poor Margot. I'd had no idea. My life was no picnic, but I did have my kids. They made up for a lot.

It struck me that, for all my problems, there were good things in my life. And that, even though from my perspective she appeared to be leading a charmed life, Margot had known her share of challenges and disappointments, too.

I realized that I'd been comparing the inside of my life with the outside of everyone else's; measuring my own fortunes against the cheerful how-are-you-I'm-fine façade that people put on for each other. At least in a small way, everybody lies about who they are because you don't have to be alive very long to understand that, in spite of what they say, most people don't give two nickels for the problems of others. No one in her right mind is going to bare her soul to someone else unless she is reasonably sure that person really cares and can be counted as a true friend.

I dreamed about having true friends, the kind you can trust with your most secret secrets, the way I'd dreamed about winning the lottery; it would be nice if it happened, but I didn't really believe it ever would—especially since I never bought tickets. And as far as having a friend—well, I'd never bought a ticket for that, either. I'd always considered friendship too risky. Friends honored each other with their confidences, the way Margot was honoring me now.

I reached out and took Margot's hand. I felt awkward doing it, but I wanted her to know that I was listening.

"And the thing is," Margot continued, "as upsetting as it was at the time, getting fired was blessing in disguise. I hated my old job, but it paid so well that I probably would never have left if they hadn't made me.

"I'm much, much happier living in New Bern than I ever was on the Upper East Side. And I love everything about working at the quilt shop. I love having contact with our customers, and getting to quilt and be around others who do, and, of course, I'm crazy about my wonderful co-workers." She smiled.

"The only drawback is that it doesn't pay anything close to what my old job did. Not that I'm complaining. Evelyn is paying me as well as she possibly can, even a little more than she pays herself. New Bern is a lot less expensive to live in than the city, so I can pay my bills, but I don't make enough to be able to adopt. Even if I did, it would take me years to climb back up the waiting list. By the time I did, the agency would probably think I was too old to be a mom."

Margot was silent, staring off into space at a spot somewhere over my left shoulder, thinking her own thoughts. After a moment, she exhaled deeply, as if consciously releasing old memories into the air.

"Which brings me back to my original point—I'm not perfect.

"I get jealous of people who have things I think I deserve to have but don't, and there are plenty of times when my faith gets shaky, but in the end I always come back to it because it's the only thing that makes any sense. When I look back over my life, I can see so clearly that God loves me and has always been with me. There are so many good things in my life, so many undeserved gifts, and so many times when something I thought was a curse from God actually turned out to be a blessing. I don't know why God has not seen fit to give me a child, but in the end I believe that there is a reason even for that. It's hard, but I accept it." She smiled weakly and glanced at the bedroom door again. "Some days more than others, but I try."

"But, that just doesn't make sense to me," I argued. "If you want this so badly, and if you believe the desire for a child is something that God planted in you, then why doesn't God let you have one? What could be the harm in that?"

"I don't know," she admitted. "I wish I did, but God is God. He doesn't have to consult me on his decisions." She grinned. "Hey, not that I haven't been known to look out my front window to see if there might be a burning bush out there from time to time but so far—nothing. Maybe someday.

"Maybe this will seem silly to you, but this is the way I've worked it out in my mind. Answer a question for me. What would happen if you let the kids have everything they wanted?"

"Well, let's see," I said slowly, pretending to muse over the answer. "They'd never bathe or go to bed before midnight and probably they wouldn't have any teeth because they'd have rotted out from the diet of straight chocolate and orange soda, not to mention a general lack of dental hygiene."

"Right!" Margot nodded eagerly. "Some of the things your children want are not in their best interests, but they're children and don't understand. They don't have your wisdom or perspective. So sometimes, because you love them, you have to tell them no. Even if it means they get mad at you, even if it means they push you away and are angry with you, right?"

"Of course."

"Well, don't you think it could be the same way for God?"

"I don't know. I never thought about it that way."

It was hard for me to think about God as a loving parent, but some of what Margot was saying made sense. It was worth thinking about, anyway.

Margot gripped the edge of the table, and leaned in close. Her eyes were earnest. "Ivy, I know you don't believe that God has always had your best interests at heart, but if can't believe him, then believe me. I'm your friend and I'm telling you the truth. You can't run away again! If you do, you'll never be able to stop. Is that the life you want for yourself? For your children?"

Her eyes bored right through me. I looked away, catching sight of the quilt that was hanging over the back of a dining chair, the log cabin quilt I'd made in Evelyn's class so many months ago.

I stared at the red centers of the log cabin blocks, those bright spots of red that represented the heartbeat of my life, the center of my being, the best and most beautiful things in my world—my children. With tears in my eyes and solemn conviction in my breast I had sworn to protect them, to keep them safe, and to make a real home for them. Every minute and breath of my life was about keeping that vow. I had tried my best but my best wasn't enough.

Margot was right. If I ran again, Bethany and Bobby would never have the safe, settled home and family life I'd promised to provide, the life they needed and deserved. Why should it be so hard to give my children the simple, safe life that so many other children had? It wasn't fair.

I wasn't asking for myself. The only dreams I had left were for my babies, but now it seemed I'd failed in that, too.

Just like Hodge had said I would.

Two weeks after Bethany's birth and only a month after we'd moved into our beautiful house in a brand new subdivision built on old farmland that was six miles from the edge of the nearest town, Hodge hit me for the second time.

It had been months since the first incident but because Hodge had been apologetic even to the point of tears when it happened, I'd convinced myself that it was just a one-time thing. I was wrong

He came home from work and yelled to me from the kitchen. I was changing the baby and called that I'd be there in a minute. Hodge came stomping into the nursery, grabbed me by the arm, and slapped me, shouting that next time he called me I'd better come and quick. The slap stung but it didn't really hurt me, not the way his blows would later, when he progressed from open hands to fists and worse, but I was furious.

I screamed at him. Told him if he ever, ever hit me again I'd leave him. Hodge curled his lip into a sneer, laughing.

"You're going to leave me? What makes you think you could ever do that? You've got no brains, no education, no talent for anything. You know that, Ivy. I'm the only thing you've got going for you. If you left me, you'd be back in the gutter where I found you in five minutes."

He took a step toward me. I grabbed the baby off the changing table and backed away. "I mean it, Hodge. Don't you touch me ever again! You try that again, we're out of here. Me and the baby!"

His eyes flickered with a hard light, like the blue-hot center of a flame. With Bethany still in my arms, he grabbed my hair, started dragging me out of the nursery and toward the front hallway.

"Is that right? You're out of here? Well, if you're planning on going, then you'd better go now. It'd make things a whole lot easier on me. You're nothing but a millstone around my neck anyway. I only married you out of pity. That and for the sex. Think about it, Ivy. That's all anybody has ever wanted from you. Do you know why?"

He looked at me with that cold fire in his eyes, smiling, drinking in the pain and shame he was inflicting on me before answering his own question.

"It's because that's all you've ever been good for. Since the baby you've gotten so fat and flabby you're not even good for that." He pulled the hank of hair he held in his fist even harder, forcing me to jerk my head up. "You disgust me, Ivy. If it weren't for the baby, I'd have thrown you out by now.

"So you don't need me? You think you're capable of taking care of the baby without me? Well, then go! Get out! We'll see how you do. But, I'm telling you the truth, Ivy. You're nothing! You're trash. You can't even take care of yourself, let alone the baby, but have fun trying."

He opened the front door, shoved me out of the house, and slammed it closed. The deadbolt clicked as he turned the lock.

It was February. There was snow on the ground. I was wearing a T-shirt and jeans, no shoes. Bethany was wearing only a diaper and terry cloth pajamas. She'd been crying from the moment Hodge had come in the nursery but now she wailed, her little face turning red and tears streaming from her eyes. I called to Hodge to knock it off and open the door, that the baby was going to freeze in this weather, but he didn't answer.

It was starting to get dark. The streetlights flickered on as the shadows lengthened, but the houses that surrounded ours were dark and still, most of them half-finished with exposed, skeleton walls and gaping holes where windows were yet to be placed. We were the first family to have moved into the subdivision and it would be weeks before we had neighbors. There was nowhere to go.

I started to bang on the door with my closed fist, pleading for Hodge to open the door. Nothing. I heard footsteps walking away from the sound of my voice and the baby's cries.

A minute later, the light turn on in the upstairs master bedroom. With my back to the door, I sank down until I was sitting cross-legged on the porch, my sobs mingling with my baby daughter's. That's where I was nearly three hours later, when Hodge finally opened the door and asked if I'd learned my lesson.

I had.

And tonight I'd learned it all over again. I wasn't capable of taking care of my children alone. Hodge had been right all along.

I stared hopelessly at the quilt once more, at the rings of interconnecting "logs" that corralled the patches of red, each slightly different than its neighbors, touching at every end and side, stacked row on row, united log on log to build a strong and sure fortress around the small red centers and the words rang anew in my mind.

I'm not capable of taking care of my children alone.

It was true but suddenly the words didn't mean what I thought they had a moment before. I couldn't give my children the safe, secure home I so desperately wanted for them, not by myself. I needed help. But I wasn't helpless.

All those years before, my only option was to let my child die from exposure or beg Hodge to open the door and go through it on the terms he dictated.

That wasn't true now.

All around me, there were sturdy, neat little houses with warm, welcoming fires in the hearths and caring faces at the windows; the faces of Margot, Evelyn, Abigail and Franklin, Wendy Perkins, Charlie, Garrett, Donna Walsh, and many more. A whole community of people peered anxiously out their windows, watching me as I stood in the middle of the street holding my children by the hands, waiting to see in which direction I would turn, hoping it would be toward them, ready open the door if only I could find courage enough to stop running, faith enough to knock.

Now I had choices. Now I had friends.

❦ 18 ❧

Evelyn Dixon

"Well, why shouldn't I sue him?" Abigail blustered. "He threatened to sue me. Am I just supposed to sit there and take it? The only way to deal with this is to fire a shot over his bow! Let him know that he can't push me around. The best defense is a strong offense. I'm surprised you don't see that, Franklin. What kind of lawyer are you anyway?"

Franklin turned to me. "See? Everyone goes around blaming attorneys for these frivolous lawsuits that are clogging up our courts, but there's plenty of blame to go around and much of it should be heaped on the doorsteps of hot-headed clients who insist on suing other people . . ."

He shifted his gaze to Abigail and finished the rest of his sentence very slowly, clearly, and at an increased volume, as if she were hard of hearing. ". . . without grounds for doing so."

Abigail bristled. "What are you talking about? I've got plenty of grounds for a lawsuit. He said I was only interested in donating my house for the tax write-off. He called my intentions disingenuous and implied that I was cheap. He insulted me!"

Franklin laughed. "Well, you insulted him first. But even if you hadn't, so what? So he insulted you; big deal. You insult me all the time. Just this morning you said my tie was ugly. You insulted my taste in haberdashery, which wounded me deeply, but do you see me going off and hiring a lawyer because of it? No. I let it go. I moved on. So should you."

Franklin picked up his knife and sawed a piece of steak. I ducked my head and picked at my salad, keeping my face as blank as possible. There was no way I was going to insert myself in the middle of this argument.

"I wasn't insulting you," Abigail said, looking pointedly at the very wide purple and silver striped tie that Franklin wore knotted around his neck. "I was merely giving you good advice. That tie is ugly and you should throw it away. It makes you look like a mob lawyer. Or, if you simply must wear it, at least don't do so when you're dining with me. Someone might think I bought it for you."

"Do you see how she treats me?" Franklin asked me, sighing, his face a mask of martyrdom. "These continual insults and barbs? And all of them unfounded."

He grabbed the tail of his necktie and held it out from his chest. "Tell me the truth, Evelyn. What do you think of my tie?"

"Well, it does kind of bring the word *consigliere* to mind." I speared a cherry tomato and popped it into my mouth.

Franklin clutched at his chest as if I'd just used my fork to stab him instead of my salad.

"Ouch! You sure know how to hurt a guy, Evelyn. In fact, I'm deeply insulted. And yet," he said, raising his eyebrows and turning to address Abigail, "I shall resist the desire to salve my wounded pride by slapping you with a lawsuit. And why? Because while I am distressed by this unfounded and personal attack, I have suffered no material damages from your insult. What you have said is hurtful, but not actionable. Therefore, a lawsuit would be a waste of everyone's time and money."

Abigail was in no mood to be swayed by logic. She was offended and wanted revenge. Wasted time and money didn't enter into the equation. "But what about him suing me? What about firing a warning shot over his bow?"

Franklin shook his head, took another bite of steak and chewed it at a bovine pace, taking his time before answering Abigail's question. "Nobody is firing a warning shot over anyone else's bow, or stern, or anything else. Trust me. Right now, Dale Barrows is sitting at the country club having lunch with his attorney, George Caldwell, the second-best lawyer in town. George may not be as fine a litigator as yours truly, but he's a level-headed sort.

"As soon as Dale finishes his rant about how *you* insulted *him*," Franklin pointed the tip of his steak knife in Abigail's direction, "George is going to tell him to calm down and let it go because he's got no grounds for a lawsuit."

"And it's true; he doesn't." Abigail huffed. "I said Dale's toupee looked like week-old roadkill. That's not an insult. It's the truth. It's high time someone told him so to his face. People certainly haven't been shy about saying so behind his back. If you ask me, he ought to thank me for helping him see the light."

"Yes," Franklin said sarcastically, "I'm sure that's just the way Dale will look at it. Really, Abbie. Leave it. This won't go anywhere good."

"I don't care," she insisted. "I still think we should sue."

Franklin closed his eyes and pinched the bridge of his nose between his thumb and forefinger. "God give me patience," he muttered before opening his eyes again. "Evelyn, you're her friend, talk some sense into her, will you?"

"I'm touched that you think I've got that kind of influence, Franklin, but you're on your own."

"Listen," I said, "not to change the subject . . ."

"Oh, I wish you would."

Abigail shot Franklin a look.

"But, as much fun as it is sitting and listening to you two discuss nonexistent lawsuits, I was hoping Franklin would be willing to give me free advice."

"Certainly," Franklin said. "Though I warn you, it may be worth exactly what you pay for it. What's on your mind, Evelyn?"

"I'm having trouble getting the permits I need for the sound trucks."

"Let me guess. Cecil Waldgren wants tickets to the show for his mother-in-law?"

"How did you know?"

Franklin lifted his hand in a dismissive gesture. "It's a small town, Evelyn. Everybody knows everything."

"Well, can you do something about it? Call up his boss or something? I mean, this is ridiculous. He can't hold my permits hostage like that. Tell him if he doesn't play ball we're going to sue the town or something."

Franklin clucked his tongue against his teeth. "What's going on today? Everybody wants to sue everybody else."

He picked up his drinking glass and examined it before taking a sip. "Do you think they put something in the water? Look, Evelyn, we don't need to threaten Cecil with a lawsuit. We don't even need to bring his boss into it. All I have to do is pick up the phone and call Cecil's wife, Candy."

"His wife? What would you do that?"

"Because Candy Waldgren is the one who's causing all the problems, that's why. Have you ever met Cecil?"

I shook my head.

"Well, trust me, he's no one to be scared of. He's the most mild-mannered man in New Bern. Wouldn't hurt a fly. But when it comes to his relationship with his wife? Well, let's just be polite and say he's henpecked. Cecil is only bothering you about the tickets for his mother-in-law because that's what Candy is telling him to do."

Franklin reached across the table, took two more pats of butter out of the dish, and worked them into his pile of mashed potatoes.

"I'm still not following this, Franklin."

"Candy's mother is Elizabeth Gage. I think you know her from church."

"Oh, sure," I said. "She sings alto in the choir. But she's not a quilter. Why is her daughter so bent on getting her tickets to the show?"

"Because whether you're a quilter or not, the taping of *Quintessential Quilting* is the hottest ticket in the history of New Bern, that's why."

Franklin swallowed a mouthful of potatoes before going on.

"You see, Candy has a sister, Norah, who is married to a very well-to-do banker and lives in Boston. Norah, being very well-heeled, is forever whisking her mother away on exotic vacations or sending her expensive gifts. Obviously, Candy and Cecil can't compete in the presents department and Candy is sure that's why her mother disapproves of her husband. I suspect it really has more with the fact that Cecil never has more than two words to say for himself than with any failure to provide appropriate expressions of tribute. Elizabeth isn't a bad person. Maybe a little insensitive, but she's all right. And for that matter, so are Candy and Norah. They're just too competitive. I've known the Gages for years. They're a little dysfunctional, but not any more than most other families. I'll give Candy a ring later today. Tell her to call off the dogs."

"But, how are going to convince her to do that?"

Franklin narrowed his eyes and stroked the silk of his ugly tie. "I'll make her an offer she can't refuse," he said in a raspy voice.

He winked at me and turned to Abigail, resuming his normal tone. "Abbie, can you help us out here? What have you got in your back pocket? Something impressive enough to make Candy back down."

Abigail thought for a moment. "Let me see. Elizabeth likes music. Maybe tickets for opening night of the opera season? They can't have my box, but I'm sure I could make a call and arrange for a couple of seats, that way Candy can go with her. Front row on the parterre? And a suite at the Waldorf for the weekend? They'll need a car and driver as well, but I'm sure something can be worked out." Queenlike, Abigail waved her hand, leaving the details for lesser mortals to arrange.

"Abigail," I protested, "I can't let you do that. A weekend like that will run into some money."

"No, no. Not as much as you think. There are people all over town who owe me favors. All I'll have to do is make a few calls and it's done. Really, Evelyn. Don't worry about it. It's my pleasure. Besides, Elizabeth and Candy were a big help organizing the food for the last library fundraiser. They deserve a little reward for their efforts."

"But," she said, raising a warning finger in Franklin's face, "just make sure that Candy tells her mother that I'm doing this in appreciation for the splendid job old Cecil has done in helping me get my permit to subdivide my property. We want Elizabeth to think this all came about from the efforts of her wonderful son-in-law." She dabbed her napkin to her lips daintily.

"He really was a quite a help. He walked me through the process, helped fill in the forms. In fact, Cecil Waldgren is the only person at Town Hall who's been the least bit supportive of my plan for the new shelter apartments."

Franklin shook his head. "He's not supportive. He's just scared of you. Anyway, Evelyn, don't worry. You'll get your permits. Problem solved."

"Thanks, Franklin. No wonder everyone says you're the best lawyer in town."

"The best lawyers are the ones who keep you out of court."

He looked at Abigail over the tops of his glasses. She sipped her water and hummed to herself, ignoring him.

Charlie walked in the front door of the restaurant, carrying several brown paper grocery bags and calling to one of the waitresses, "Gina! Take these back to Maurice, would you? He's waiting for them."

Charlie handed off the bags to Gina, who carted them back to the kitchen. Charlie flopped down into the booth next to me.

"Hullo all. Enjoying your lunch?"

"Where've you been anyway? I was hoping we'd be able to have lunch together."

"The tomatoes are ripe," he said and his whole face lit up.

"Mrs. March called me this morning and said they'd picked most of them and were holding back a bushel for me, so naturally I hopped into my car and drove out to the farm as fast as I could. Wait until you see them! Big! Gorgeous! All organic. And the flavor! Beyond belief! Mrs. March sliced one up for me to taste and I nearly passed out from the sheer joy of it. Amazing! Wait five minutes for Maurice to get them washed and sliced and you'll see what I mean. It's like summer on a plate."

I glanced at my watch. "Five minutes is about all I've got. I told Garrett and Margot I'd be back by one at the latest."

"Well, maybe I'll bring some over to your house later tonight.

We can throw in some mozzarella and good bread and call it dinner. What do you say?"

"It's Friday night. Quilt-circle night."

"That's right. I forgot." He drew his eyebrows together. "Well, maybe I'll bring a platter over to the shop later. You can share it with the ladies instead of me, I suppose."

"Thanks, Charlie. You're a sweetheart."

"Aren't I though," he growled. "But listen, Evelyn, we're absolutely going out on Sunday night. Just you and me. Reservations are light and Gina can handle the door and any walk-ins. I'm taking you to the movies."

"Really? The new Renée Zellweger?"

He made a face and drew back in horror. "No! Lord, no! The old James Bond. They're having a festival at the Red Rooster theater. An entire weekend of Bond: *Goldfinger, Diamonds are Forever, Moonraker, License to Kill.* All Bond. All the time. Not a chick flick in sight."

"Hmmm," I said. "I don't know. Who's buying the popcorn?"

"I am. The big bucket."

"Well, in that case, okay. It's a date."

The kitchen door swung open and Gina came out carrying two plates of tomatoes and basil.

"Ah! Here it is!" Charlie exclaimed. "I know you've got to get back to the shop, but just take one bite of these before you go. Believe me, you owe it to yourself."

But before Gina could put the plates down, the telephone started ringing. Charlie groaned and got to his feet.

"Why is it that someone always calls right when I'm in the middle of something important?"

He picked up the phone. "Grill on the Green. This is Charlie. May I help you?"

"Charlie was right. They're gorgeous." The flesh of the tomatoes was a brilliant ruby red. A sprinkling of verdant basil, sliced into slivers and tossed over the plate like cheery confetti made them appear even more vibrant.

Abigail leaned over the plate and sniffed. "They smell heavenly.

Shall we give them a try?" Abigail picked up a fork and knife and started cutting the tomato slices into bite-sized pieces, but before she was finished Charlie was back at the table. His face was serious.

"That was Margot. You're needed at the shop. You as well," he said, nodding to Franklin and Abigail.

"What is it?" I asked as I took the sweater from Charlie and draped it over my arm. "What's wrong?"

"Ivy was served with divorce papers. He's suing for full custody of the children."

Franklin sighed heavily. "Well, we expected that. I was hoping he'd be more reasonable, but after what Ivy's told me about her ex-husband and how vindictive he can be, that's really no surprise."

"But there's more," Charlie said. "And none of it good. Margot wouldn't tell me much on the phone, just said that she needed you all to come back to the shop as soon as you could."

"All right," I said, and rose up to kiss Charlie goodbye. "I'll call you later and let you know what's going on."

"What are you talking about? I'm coming with you. I care about Ivy and those children as much as anyone else, don't I? You think I'm going to stand around and let that eejit husband of hers take those children from her? Not a chance! Hurry along. I'll be right behind you."

Franklin, Abigail, and I headed for the door.

Charlie bellowed. "Gina!"

She left the table she'd been clearing and trotted up toward the front of the restaurant. "Yeah, Charlie?"

"Get me some plastic to cover up those tomatoes so I can take them with me to the quilt shop. You're in charge while I'm gone."

"Okay, Charlie."

"And Gina? Ask Maurice to make up a tray of mozzarella and some olives. And wrap up a loaf of the good bread too, while you're at it. The Pullman loaf. Make it two. And a crock of butter. If you're going toe-to-toe with trouble, it's better not to do so on an empty stomach."

❧ 19 ❧

Ivy Peterman

This couldn't have happened at a worse time but, then again, that shouldn't have surprised me. Hodge was always so good at knowing how to strike at the most vulnerable place and time, and in a manner that would cause maximum damage.

Friday afternoons were always busy. And on a beautiful summer day like this, we have even more customers than usual. The one saving grace was that there were no episodes of *Quintessential Quilting* included on the Friday television schedule. There would be no airing of the promotional video, no mentions of Cobbled Court Quilts on national television and thus, no influx of telephone calls asking for directions to the shop, or how to spell our Internet address, or how they could get tickets to the show.

All we had to deal with today was the usual customer traffic and the fulfilling of what had become the normal glut of online orders ever since Mary Dell Templeton had set out to make Cobbled Court Quilts a household name. There was more than enough to keep us busy even on a slow day, which this wasn't.

After she'd gotten off the phone with Charlie, Margot went up to the workroom and asked everyone who was working on order fulfillment to go downstairs because she needed the space for a meeting. She asked Gayle to be in charge of the register while Jeni and Karen helped customers and cut yardage.

"I feel terrible about this," I said to Margot as I helped her place chairs around the workroom table for Evelyn and the others who were walking over from the Grill. Garrett was at the bank making a deposit, but would return shortly.

"Why do we have to do this now? During business hours? Why can't we just stick with our original plan and do this at the quilt-circle meeting? And why do we have to include everybody—Franklin and Garrett. Charlie, too?"

"Because they're all your friends and they all care about you. And because many hands make light work. Lighter work, anyway," she shrugged. "Nothing about this is going to be easy, but it'll be easier if we draw on the talent and experience of everyone. When Evelyn was going through her breast cancer diagnosis and treatment, we all worked together to help her through get it. That's what we should do now."

She shoved the last chair in under the table. Its metal legs made a scraping sound against the wooden floor that made me wince, further jangling my already jangled nerves.

"And as far as why now . . . We've got to get on top of this thing right away. Especially for Franklin's sake. It's Friday afternoon. In a few hours his office staff will be leaving, some for the weekend and some to begin their vacations.

"Franklin's got to know the whole truth about what is going on here before the close of business today. That way, if he needs to ask some of his associates to cancel their plans, he can do that before they leave town."

Great, I thought. Now on top of everything else, I could feel bad about being the reason people had to cancel their vacations.

Margot looked at me and squeezed my shoulder. "Cheer up. I know this isn't easy for you, but this is the best way to handle this. Just get it out and get it over with. We've been over and over this, haven't we?"

"I know. I know," I snapped irritably. "The truth will set me free."

"Everything is going to be fine. Trust me. I'm going to run down to the break room and put some water on for tea. Can I bring you a cup?"

"Sure," I said more gently. "Tea would be great. Thanks."

I sat down at the head of the table and stared at the pile of documents and the letter from Hodge's attorney that topped the stack. I picked up the letter and read it again, still not quite able to believe that somebody could have written those words in reference to me.

The truth will set you free. I sure hoped Margot was right because embracing the truth was clearly not a philosophy that Hodge was subscribing to.

I read the second to last paragraph again. How could he tell such lies about me? Sure, I'd done a lot of things I wasn't proud of but nothing as bad as this. How could he say such things about the mother of his children? As much as he wanted to hurt me, hadn't he even stopped to think what effect this might have on our kids?

Disgusted, I tossed the letter back on the pile with the other papers.

At least there was one good thing about all this. Up until this afternoon, I'd been nervous about dissolving into tears when I told my story. No danger of that now. I was too mad to cry.

But still, there was something pathetically, inexpressibly sad about this whole thing. Once, half a lifetime before, Hodge had said he loved me. How in the world had it come to this? Exploitation and escape? Lawyers and lies? Where had it all begun?

Not with Hodge. Before that. A long time before.

I was a daddy's girl.

My father was older than my mother by nearly twenty years. She was from West Virginia, a poor girl. Daddy met her on the one and only business trip he'd ever taken, back when the mill owners were trying to get on the good side of labor and agreed to pay Daddy's way to a conference. He'd have been dressed in his best for something like that. Maybe when Mother met him she thought he was a richer man than he was, her ticket out of poverty, and maybe when she saw our two-bedroom house in the poor part of town and woke up with a husband who wore overalls to work, she decided she'd made a mistake. I don't know. We never talked about it.

And I don't know if any of that was the source of their trouble and the reason I was their only child or if they'd have been just as unhappy together had they been the same age and living comfortably in a white-collar world, but the point is, they weren't happy.

And a part of me liked it that way.

I had Daddy all to myself. He thought I was the most beautiful girl in the world. I thought he hung the moon and stars. What's more, I thought he'd hung them for me alone.

We were two halves of the same coin, my father and I, complementary and complete. My mother didn't enter into the equation much.

She kept the house clean, made indifferent meals, and reminded me to brush my teeth, but I don't remember her smiling at me or talking to me beyond issuing directives concerning the basics and necessaries of daily life. But I didn't care about her. I had Daddy.

He and Mother almost never talked and if they did, I was quick to interrupt, to search out a week-old cut on my finger which I would insist my father kiss and make better, or start doing summersaults across the shag carpet and crying out for Daddy to "Look at me! Look at me!"

And he always did.

I was the one whose name he called when he came in the door from work at the end of the day. I was the one he read the funny papers to on Saturday morning and mine was the opinion he sought out when trying to decide if this tie went with that shirt when he dressed for church on Sunday morning. Mother never went to church, just Daddy and me, so of course I loved going but not because it was church. We could have gone to the dog track every Sunday for all I cared. The part that mattered was that it was just Daddy and me getting in the car together and leaving together. I got to sit up front in the seat that would have been Mother's if she'd come along.

That's how selfish I was about him.

Sundays were my favorite day and Mondays my least, because it was the farthest away from Sunday.

Daddy left for his job at the mill very early, before I was even awake, so at breakfast it was just Mother and me.

She would bring me a plate of eggs or a bowl of cereal and then sit at the table drinking coffee with two sugars. After a while she would ask if I had my homework done and I'd say yes. Then after another while she'd look at her wristwatch and say that the bus was due so I'd get up from the table and go. She'd get up as well, stand and stare out the window toward the street, but she never waved at me. When the bus pulled away, she'd be standing at the window still, looking out. I don't know how long she stayed there after I was gone, but I have a feeling it was a long time.

When I came home from school, she was always sitting on the sofa with her legs curled underneath her, twirling a length of hair into a curl around her index finger, reading. She wouldn't look up from her reading when I entered the room, just tell me to hang up my coat and then answer my question about what was for dinner. That was pretty much the extent of our conversation until my father came home from work and my real life began.

But one day, when I was eight, a water main broke in town. The bathrooms and drinking fountains in my elementary school wouldn't work, so they sent everyone home three hours early.

My mother wasn't expecting me and I was very quiet when I climbed the wooden porch steps to our front door, wanting to catch her by surprise, I think, wondering if I'd find her at her usual outpost on the sofa or if, for once, perhaps doing something else.

It was something else.

The house was quiet when I entered. The couch was unoccupied. No smell of food cooking came from the kitchen. But my parents' bedroom door was open and there were soft, pleading sounds coming from inside.

I tiptoed toward the sound and looked inside, saw the back of a man's head, and naked shoulders, and angled twin peaks that were my mother's legs and bent knees spread far apart under the covers, the long, blanketed body of the man moving between them, and my mother's neck arching back and up, and her eyes shut tight, and her lipsticked lips an open O.

And I hated her.

I did not understand then what my mother was doing but I knew it was wrong.

Quietly, on tiptoe, I backed away from the door, paused to lean against a kitchen chair and slip off my shoes to muffle the sound of my feet even more. Then, still backing away to make sure I wasn't seen, I slipped out the front door and went to sit across the street, hiding under the drapery of a neighbor's newly blossoming forsythia bush, watching until our two-doors-down neighbor, Pete, opened my front door, looked left and right, then walked across the yards to his own door, casually lighting a cigarette as he did.

I stayed under the bush for another hour, until my usual arrival time. Then came through the door, hung up my coat without asking about dinner, and went into my bedroom to wait.

And when my father came home from work, I told him everything.

I don't remember the fight in detail. From inside my bedroom, I couldn't make out the words that were being said, only that they were yelling at each other. Until that day, my parent's unhappiness in their marriage was manifested in long silences and averted eyes, not heated battle. The sound of their raised voices frightened me. I wished I had kept my mother's secret.

I heard a heavy thud, like the sound that the logs made when Daddy would bring them in from the woodpile and drop them near the hearth, then nothing, then screaming. My mother's voice screaming.

I ran out of my room and into the kitchen. Daddy was lying on the floor, his eyes wide open and fixed on the ceiling. There was a little foam of spittle clinging to his lower lip and a dark, wet spot on the front of his slacks. The room smelled of urine. My mother was on her knees, bent over him, pushing on his chest and screaming, "Oh God!" over and over.

After a while, she collapsed on top of him.

I watched from the doorway with dry eyes. Afraid, but not understanding.

After a while, my mother raised herself back onto her knees and looked at me with angry, red-rimmed eyes.

"Look what you've done now," she said. "He's dead. Do you see that? What are we supposed to do now? He's dead and you're the one who killed him."

I ran from the house, down the street, and into the woods than ran between our neighborhood and the rail tracks. I climbed a tree, hid high in the branches and wouldn't come down even when I heard my mother calling for me.

It was Pete who found the tree. He tried to talk me down, but I wouldn't budge, so he climbed up and hauled me down

I didn't want anyone to see me. I didn't want them to know. I was so afraid that, if I came home, my mother would tell everyone what I'd done. But, she didn't. Though I'd given away her secret, she kept mine. She never spoke of it again. Until today, neither have I. I'm so ashamed.

My father and I loved each other too much and I killed him. In the end, I killed everything.

The rest, you already know. Part of it anyway; the parts I've been willing to talk about.

Mother married Pete. She wasn't any happier with him than she'd been with Daddy. Pete was a drinker and, before long, Mother was, too. Unlike the silent, disdain she'd shown my father, her marriage to Pete was one big, drunken fight, very loud and very physical. After one of those battles, Mother got in her car, crashed it, and died.

With nowhere else to go, and still a sophomore in high school, I stayed on with my stepfather. He drank as much as he always had, but I was used to that. As time went on, he started hitting me. I wasn't used to that. One night, I woke to find Pete in my bed, crawling his hand up under my pajama top. I fought him off, bloodying his nose and making him curse me.

The next day, I ran away.

I ended up in the city. At first I did all right. I had some money saved. I found a cheap bed in a youth hostel, but it wasn't long before I was broke. I tried to get jobs, but there wasn't too much available for a high-school dropout. Certainly nothing that paid enough for food and rent. I ended up living on the streets, working when I could, panhandling when I couldn't.

When the weather turned cold it got harder, so hard that I thought about going home, but I didn't have enough money for a train ticket and even if I had, I doubt I'd have gone back. I knew what was waiting for me there.

One day, when I was truly at the end of my rope, had gone two days without eating, I found a newspaper somebody had left at a bus stop and started reading it. There was a classified ad for a coat check girl that promised to pay good money and said no experience was needed. I knew the street, but didn't recognize the address. I walked three miles to get there.

When I arrived, the manager was very nice, said he'd interview me right away. We sat down in a curved, red leather booth and he asked if I was comfortable, and told the bartender to bring me a Coke. It wasn't much of an interview. I should have known what kind of place it was, but I was so happy to be out of the cold and on a lead to a decent paying job that I wasn't thinking very clearly. It had been so long since anyone had been nice to me. I wanted to believe it was all for real.

The manager told me to stand up, to walk across the room and back, and then to do it again but this time to smile. He wanted to know where I was living and I told him that, the night before, I'd slept in a doorway on the corner of Williams and Third. He smiled wide and called to the bartender who'd brought my Coke to tell the kitchen to make up a ham sandwich, chips, and a glass of milk and bring it to me.

He watched me wolf down the food and when I was done, he asked my age. When I said I was seventeen, he held up his hand to his left ear like he was hard of hearing and said, "I'm sorry? What was that, jailbait? How old did you say you were?"

I took the hint. "Ummm. Eighteen?"

He nodded and smiled. "That's what I thought you said, sweetheart. Okay. That's good. We're all done here. You're hired."

"Really? Thanks!"

He reached into his coat pocket, pulled five one hundred dollar bills from his wallet and handed them to me.

"What's this?"

"An advance on your first paycheck. Go buy yourself some clothes and a nice warm coat and use the rest to put a deposit on an apartment. We run a nice place, everything first class. Can't have my new coat check girl living on the street like a bag lady."

He handed me a business card. "Go to this address. Take a cab. It's too cold to walk. When you get there, talk to Vern. Tell him I sent you. He's a friend of mine; he'll rent you a nice studio, furnished and very cheap. Be back here by three o'clock. There's a few things I gotta show you before you start."

Leaving the club, I couldn't believe how my luck had turned; that's how naïve I was. I did exactly what the manager, Jerry, told me to do; took a taxi to the address listed on the card, talked to Vern, rented the apartment for three hundred dollars (Vern said I didn't need to give a first and last month's deposit, that if Jerry said I was good for it, I was), bought a pair of black jeans, high heels, a white sweater with silver beading that I thought looked like what a coat check girl in a first-class place would wear, and a warm coat. After that, I spent twenty-two dollars on groceries, holding back the last hundred dollar bill to get me through until payday, and went back to my apartment to take a long, hot shower in my new bathroom before getting dressed for my first night on the job. I looked myself over carefully in the mirror before I left, examining myself at every angle, smoothing my hair, making sure I looked as good as I could.

I intended to be the very best coat check girl in the history of the Atlantis Club. I didn't want to let Jerry down.

When I got there, Jerry found me in the coat check room, said there was a problem, and asked me to follow him to his office. I was worried that he'd decided I was too young to work there after all, but after he closed the door, he told me that one of their dancers had slipped in the shower and broken her ankle.

"I need you to go on in her place," he said and pulled a costume off a rack, all turquoise blue feathers and sequins and netting, and threw it at me.

I wasn't ready to catch it. The costume fell to my feet and the floor.

"I don't know how to dance."

Jerry smirked and rubbed his nose with his knuckle. "You're cute, you know that? Baby, I don't mean you've gotta *dance* dance. Understand?"

I didn't. He shook his head.

"Wow. You're pretty, baby, but you're not the sharpest pencil in the box, are you?" He waved his hand. "That's all right. For what I need, pretty is better than smart. Listen, all you gotta do is put on that costume, smile, walk around on the stage like you did for me this morning. Well, if you could shake it up a little that'd be good too, but if walkin' is the best you can do for now, that's fine. We can worry about technique later. Then, you take the costume off. Slow. Just one piece at a time. See, baby?"

When I didn't say anything he just smiled. "You got a pretty face and a sweet little shape, nice and big on top but not too much in the hips. I don't care if you can dance or not. Neither will my customers."

I whispered. "You want me to go out on the stage and take off my clothes? In front of people?"

"Hey! What's the matter? Gee, you don't need to go crying about it," he said, then walked over and put his arm around my shoulders. "It's not that big a deal. You're a beautiful girl, gorgeous. That's the way God made you, so what could be wrong with letting people see it? It's perfectly natural. Really, you should be flattered. This is a step up from the coat check job, a big one. Pays 250 bucks a week more. Normally, I'd look for somebody experienced but when this other girl had to drop out, I thought of you right off. You made a good impression on me. It's like I said; you should be flattered."

I sniffed, trying to get hold of myself. I didn't to risk him getting insulted and mad at me. "I am. I guess I am. Really, Jerry. It was nice of you to think of me, but I can't take off my clothes in front of people. I just can't. Please don't ask me to do it."

Jerry lifted up his hands and sighed. "All right. All right. No one is going to make you do anything you don't want to. I just figured you were a sweet kid who was down on her luck and wouldn't mind making some extra money, but if you don't want to do it, then you don't. End of story."

"Thanks, Jerry. Thanks for understanding." I smiled and grabbed the doorknob.

"Wait a minute," he said. "Where are you going?"

"To work," I said. "In the coat check room."

Jerry made a sucking sound with his teeth and moved his head slowly from side to side. "No, you're not. That job's filled."

"But, just this morning you said . . ."

"That was this morning, before this whole business with Yolanda breaking her ankle. Broke as you are, sleeping in doorways, I figured you'd jump at the dancer job. Another girl came in about the coat check job after you left and I gave it to her. The only job I've got now is for a dancer, which you don't want. That's fine. No skin off my nose, but you gotta give me back my five hundred dollars." He opened his palm to me, face up, and wiggled his fingers.

"But, I don't have it anymore. I spent it, just like you said to. I rented the apartment from Vern and bought some groceries and," I said, looking down at my new jeans and sweater, "these clothes. All I have left is one hundred." I reached into the back pocket of my jeans and fished out the remaining bill.

Jerry's lips flattened into a line. "You owe me five hundred dollars. That was an advance on your salary. Either you pay me back, now, or you're gonna have to work it off. If not, I call the police. It's that simple."

There was a hard, heavy knot in my stomach. I thought I was going to throw up. "If the coat check job isn't open, maybe I could work in the kitchen. Or help bus the tables?"

Jerry shook his head, bent over, and picked up the fallen heap of feathers and fabric that lay on the floor.

"I told you before," he said. "I've got one job open here. Only one."

He tossed the dress toward me a second time. This time, even with my head hanging low, I caught it.

Carmel Sunday, the older stripper into whose tutelage Jerry had placed me for two hours of instruction before the club opened at six, stuck her tongue out the side of her mouth as she carefully fed a thin line of glue onto a black, spidery false eyelash before pressing it onto my eyelid.

"Try not to blink," she advised. "You might end up gluing your eye shut."

It made my eyes water, but I didn't blink.

"Like I was saying," she continued, "a good stage name is very important. And if you can pick one that kind of works with your real name, then it's even better. That way if the customers call out to you while you're on stage, you know who they're talking to. You don't want to look around like you're asking, 'Who? Me?'" She laughed with her mouth open wide. She had nice teeth.

"Take me. My real name is Carmelita Espinosa, so I just shortened it and added Sunday to the end. It's a play on words, see? Carmel Sunday, but it reminds you of the dessert. All sweet, luscious, and golden. Just like me. You see?"

"Yeah," I said hoarsely and tried not to inhale as Carmel coated my hair with enough spray to varnish a table.

"And that's why your stage name is going to be so perfect for you—Ivy Rose. That's also why I told Jerry no way were you going out in that turquoise number." She made a face. "It's all wrong for your image and your coloring. For a name like Ivy Rose and a baby face like yours, we need something sweet, and innocent, and pink. Had to be pink. Something makes 'em think about the girl next door. And then! When you pull that ribbon and rip open that lace—just be careful not to pull too hard, okay? The Velcro's a little loose in front. I'll stitch it up for you later. Anyway, when you pull that ribbon off and show what you got? Va-voom! They're gonna *wish* they'd had a girl like you living next door!"

She laughed again. When I didn't join in, her face became serious. She patted my shoulder, rubbing her hand over the costume of pink ribbons and white peek-a-boo lace, like a whore's wedding gown.

"Come on, Ivy. I know this isn't what you wanted for yourself, but it's not so bad. The first time is hard and then it gets easier. You're not doing anything wrong, baby. It's just the way things is. Some little girls are born with a silver spoon in their mouths, others get married to a guy who's holding the silver spoon. But the rest of us? We all gotta pay the rent. And the piper."

She gave my shoulder a final pat.

"Let's go," she said. "You're on."

When Jerry introduced me and the curtain parted, I couldn't see because of the glare of the spotlight. Carmel was standing in the wings. She grimaced, showing all her wide, white teeth and pointed to her mouth, reminding me to smile. I did. I tried to.

The music was "Cracklin' Rosie." Daddy had always like Neil Diamond and sometimes played this on his stereo. But, I tried not to think about that as I walked slowly, making long, graceful arcs across the stage, pulling out the single pin that held up my long hair and shaking my head so it would cascade down the way Carmel had taught me. I closed my eyes, so I couldn't see the hungry eyes of the men in the audience, tracking me as I crossed the stage, listening to the music build, waiting. It wasn't so bad with my eyes closed.

And I crossed to center stage on cue when the drumbeat got louder and the lyrics got to the part about her being a "store-bought woman." That was when I was supposed to pull the ribbon, and then the Velcroed buttons of my bodice to expose my breasts, but I couldn't do it.

I stood in the middle of the stage with my eyes shut tight, pinching the end of the pink satin ribbon between my fingers, and not moving. The music kept playing. And in the wings I could hear, Jerry hissing, "Pull it! Pull it, Ivy! Pull the damned ribbon!"

The customers started yelling at me. Then they started to boo. A big hand gripped my arm. I opened my eyes to see Jerry. His nostrils were angry white and flared as he breathed and his eyes were hard and black. He pulled me off the stage and into the wings. Carmel was standing nearby.

"Oh, let her go, Jerry. Don't be mad at her. It's not her fault. She's just a baby."

"Shut up!" he barked. "I don't need to hear any more out of you tonight. You were the one was supposed to get her ready. You couldn't even do that right, could you? So just get out there and take it off, Carmel. That's all you're good for. I don't need any over-the-hill stripper telling me how to run my business!"

Carmel gave me a pitying look, then pasted on a smile, spread her arms out wide on either side of her ample bosom, and strutted out onto the stage. The audience started whistling and clapping.

Jerry pinched my arm hard as he drug me backstage. It hurt a lot but I was afraid to say so. Instead I said, "I'm sorry, Jerry. I'm sorry. Don't be mad at Carmel. It's not her fault. It was me. I just froze. I couldn't do it. I told you I couldn't." I started to cry. I leaned my back against the wall that separated the stage from the dressing rooms and Jerry's office and sobbed.

"Oh, for the love of . . ." Jerry groaned. "Will you cut that out? If there's anything that gets on my nerves it's a crying broad. You all do it, too. On purpose, I'm convinced. You know I can't stay mad once you turn on the water works."

He reached in his jacket pocket and pulled out a handkerchief. "Here. Blow your nose. You're gonna get snot all over the costume."

I wiped my nose and sniffed. "I'm sorry."

"Yeah, yeah. Like you said, you told me you couldn't do it. Guess I should have believed you. It's all right, baby. Don't cry."

He patted me on the shoulder twice but the third time his hand fell it snaked up and down the full length of my arm. Jerry came closer, shifted his stance and moved his right leg between the long, front slit of the white lace dress, forcing my knees and thighs to open. Then he leaned the weight of his body against me, pinning me to the wall, while the hand that had been stroking my arm reached down low.

I tried to struggle away from him but I couldn't.

"Stop it!" My hand balled into a fist. I tried to punch him but with the wall behind me, I couldn't gather enough force to strike hard. I pounded his shoulder ineffectually. He grabbed my wrist and pinned my arm above my head.

He leaned harder against me and smiled; his voice was low and even, like the voice you'd use to calm a skittish horse. "Easy, baby. Calm down." He squeezed my flesh with his hand.

"What're you so scared of? Huh? Bet you've never been with anybody before, have you? Well, that'll sure be different for me after all these years with this bunch. Normally, I'd make you give it up five times, a hundred dollars a pop, before your bill was paid off. Tell you what, we'll make it three. Your first time's gotta be worth something extra, three hundred. And after the other two?"

He grinned and rocked his hips hard into me. "I'm good, baby. After the other two, you'll want to pay me to do you."

His face was close to mine and his breath smelled of cigarettes. He tried to kiss me and I bit his lip. His reaction was instantaneous; he drew back his hand and slapped me hard.

"You little . . . Don't try that again! You hear me?" He was breathing hard. "I don't know what you've heard from your girlfriends at school, but it's not gonna hurt that bad. You relax and cooperate and I'll be real gentle, I promise. Unless, you want it to be rough? Is that what you're after? Hey, baby, if that's your bag, I'm happy to oblige."

He pushed my pinioned wrist hard against the rough brick wall, making me cry out. "Stop it! No!"

The music for Carmel's striptease was blaring and the applause and catcalls from the audience drowned out the sound of my voice.

Jerry was done talking. He tugged the pink ribbon that held my blouse closed, then pushed the lace back and grabbed the top of the white satin corset that lay underneath and jerked open the tearaway seams.

I was crying again. My fury and panic were replaced by a feeling of terrible powerlessness. "Stop. Please, stop."

"Jerry," a deep, calm voice came from the doorway that led to the dressing rooms. "Jerry, what're you doing? In a place like this, with so many warm, willing women, rape isn't just a low-class thing to do, it's a flat-out waste of energy. You should know better."

Jerry's grip on my wrist loosened and I could feel the formerly taut muscles in his body go slack. Released, I pushed him away and pulled the lace top closed around my chest.

"Mind your own business, will you, Hodge? What are you doing backstage anyway?"

"I just came back to let you know that the guys at table nine are my guests. Put their tab on my bill. Also, I came back to meet this beautiful young lady and congratulate her on reconsidering her career options."

He smiled at me and when he spoke his voice was soft and sincere. "You're much too pretty and sweet to be working in a place like this, miss. As soon as Jerry comes to his senses and lets you go, run home to your parents and stay there."

"Thanks," I whispered gratefully.

"Gee, 'Uncle' Hodge," Jerry said mockingly, "I'm sure we all appreciate your advice, but why don't you just butt out. She owes me five hundred dollars. I gave her an advance for dancing and now she don't want to dance. Okay, so fine. I'm reasonable. I'm willing to negotiate. I'm just taking back what I'm owed in trade, that's all."

"Yeah, Jerry, you're a prince of a guy. Everybody knows that." The handsome man with the kind eyes and soft voice, Hodge, looked at Jerry and then at me.

"You owe him five hundred dollars?"

I was worn out. The situation was too complicated to explain, so I just nodded. "Yes," I said.

Hodge reached in the pocket of his suit, fished out a money clip fat with bills, peeled off five, and handed them to Jerry. "There you go, Jerry. You're whole again. Happy?"

Jerry shrugged and closed the bills in his hand.

"Everyone's happy. Now, Ivy Rose . . . Is that your real name?"

I shook my head. "No. It's just Ivy. Ivy Peterman."

"Well, Miss Peterman, if you'd like to change into your street clothes and gather up your things, I'll be happy to give you a lift somewhere."

I hesitated. His smile was so genuine and he seemed so nice, but I'd thought Jerry was nice at first, too.

"If you'd rather take a taxi I understand. Not a problem. But, my Mercedes is parked right outside and you'll be completely safe with me."

Hodge lifted his hands, his palms open toward me. "I won't lay a hand on you. I promise."

❧ 20 ❧

Evelyn Dixon

I was amazed by Ivy's ability to tell her story so calmly.
But, in a way, it made sense. Probably she'd run out of tears years before. Having been through troubles of my own, my unexpected and, at the time, unwanted divorce followed by near financial ruin, possible loss of my business, and then a breast cancer diagnosis, I understood that misery can become so commonplace that you just can't shed one more tear, that sometimes the only thing to do is distance yourself from the pain. Otherwise, you might lose your mind.

Still, I couldn't help but wonder; if this whole mess ended up in court and she had to testify, wouldn't she make a more convincing witness if she did shed a few tears? I understood her, but would a judge?

Only one time did Ivy show any emotion that afternoon. As she told the story of her "rescue" by Hodge, how he'd helped her collect her few possessions from the apartment she'd so briefly rented, and then offered to let her stay in his guest room until she was "back on her feet," acting the perfect gentleman, treating her kindly, never so much as trying to hold her hand, winning her trust and eventually, her love, Ivy's face grew red and angry, not with Hodge but with herself.

"I was so stupid! Even after all I'd been through, I really believed that he was different! An idiotic little girl who believed in Santa Claus and the Tooth Fairy. Stupid! By that time I should have learned my lesson; all men are the same."

No one but Franklin had spoken since Ivy began talking, and even he said little, occasionally asking a question to clarify some point or other, the rest of the time silently scribbling notes on a yellow legal pad, but I couldn't keep quiet in the face of her outburst.

"Ivy, you were a little girl, or very nearly. And you were alone in the world. How could you have kept from having feelings for an older man who was so bent on winning your affections? You weren't stupid. Just young. And you're wrong. Men *aren't* all the same."

"Ha!" Ivy laughed bitterly. "Sure they aren't."

"Your father wasn't like that."

She didn't say anything to that, just ducked her head and bit her lower lip.

At Franklin's gentle suggestion, Ivy continued the story, telling how she, nearly four months after moving into Hodge's guest room, had been the one to make the first advance, impulsively kissing Hodge one day after he'd come home from work carrying big brown bags of Ivy's favorite Chinese food as a surprise. When Ivy said that nothing more had happened that first night, but related how over the following week that first tentative kiss had led to a few more, then to longer and more passionate caresses, until the lovesick teenager gave herself fully and willingly, my dislike of Hodge Edelman bloomed into red-hot hatred.

He'd known what he wanted and what he was planning from the first moment he met Ivy. He been patient, gained her trust, and waited until just the right moment to make his move. After witnessing the scene between Ivy and Jerry, he'd realized that one false move, one over-eager caress would send Ivy running. He knew how to get what he wanted, that was sure. Poor Ivy never stood a chance.

Just weeks after entering into a physical relationship with Hodge, Ivy was pregnant. She was afraid to tell Hodge about the baby, uncertain about how he would react to the news and worried that he might want her to have an abortion. But when she finally worked up the courage to tell him, he was thrilled. He insisted they get married and, on Ivy's eighteenth birthday, they did.

"I was so happy," Ivy said ruefully. "On my wedding day, eighteen years old and five months pregnant, I was sure that I was on my way to happily ever after. No one on earth could have convinced me otherwise."

Her eyes were unfocused and she brushed a fingertip over the ridge of her chapped lips before shrugging off the memory of that day. "Well. Anyway. You know what happened after that," she said, looking at Franklin. "The rest is just like I told you."

"And that's all? Your marriage, how the abuse escalated, the events that lead to you to run away and take the children? Everything happened as you said it did? There's nothing else?"

"No," Ivy said slowly. "I haven't left anything out. I swear, I haven't. I've told the whole truth."

Franklin nodded slowly and bit the inside of his lip while he read over his notes. "Okay. Good."

He looked up, slid his reading glasses to the end of his nose and looked over the tops of the lenses. "If you're sure you have nothing to add, I think that's enough for today. I need to go to my office, transcribe my notes, spend some time mapping out strategy, and then try to track down some people who can verify your side of the story. Tomorrow, you and I should get together, Ivy. I'll want to ask you a few more questions."

Ivy frowned. "What kind of questions? I've already told you everything."

"There are just some things I think we should talk about in private."

"Why? Everybody here has already heard all my secrets. I've got nothing to hide." Ivy's voice took on a panicked edge. Her eyes darted from Franklin to me.

"What aren't you telling me? He's going to do it, isn't he? Hodge is going to take the kids from me." Ivy gripped the edge of the table and rose halfway to her feet as if ready to run out the door.

I reached my arm out and started to reassure her but Abigail, who hadn't said a word the entire afternoon, beat me to it.

"Ivy, sit down," she ordered. Ivy looked at her uncertainly and then obeyed, sinking slowly down into the chair.

"No one is going to take your children from you because of a mistake you made while you were still a child yourself," Abigail insisted. "Stepping onto that stage might not have been the brightest move you ever made, but everyone makes errors in judgment now and again—especially when they're young. And my goodness! In spite of the trap that awful Jerry person set for you, when push came to shove you couldn't go through with it! So quit saying you worked in a strip club! You didn't!"

Abigail's frustration creased her brow and she glared at Ivy. Abigail's sympathy tended to manifest itself in . . . well . . . unusual ways. Knowing her the way I do, I understood it was her concern for Ivy that caused her to raise her voice, but I don't think Ivy realized that. The poor girl looked like she was under siege.

"If that's the terrible secret that's had you on the run all this time and that's had you quaking in your boots so badly that you wouldn't even let anyone get close . . . !" Abigail shouted and smacked the tabletop with her hand. "Well, that's just the most ridiculous thing I've ever heard. *That's* the big skeleton in your closet? The fact that you went a strip club and *didn't* take off your clothes? Ivy, that's not a skeleton. It's not even a bone! How could you have been so taken in? How could you have been so stupid?"

After an entire afternoon spent keeping her cool, telling the saddest and most intimate details of her past with barely a flicker of emotion, Ivy broke under the strain. Her eyes were glassy with tears and her shoulders quivered from the effort it took her not to sob. "You don't understand. You don't know Hodge. He's very . . . he has this way of making things happen . . . You don't understand."

It was hard to understand how a young woman who was so strong in some situations could be so vulnerable and easily manipulated in others. Just a couple of years before, I'd have been scratching my head over this, but that was before I'd started volunteering to teach quilting at the Stanton Center. Even more than physical violence, it is psychological coercion that keeps women like Ivy under the control of their abusers.

Often, abusers will isolate their victims, taking them far from the influence of family and friends, effectively eliminating their access to support systems and making them utterly dependent on the abuser in every way. That's why the victims of domestic violence so frequently go back to their abusers; once implanted, the psychological dependency between abuser and victim is hard to overcome.

In Ivy, an orphaned runaway with no family to turn to, Hodge had found an easy target. The job of isolating her was more than half accomplished when he found her and, alone as she was and with no way of supporting herself, Ivy had quickly begun to view Hodge not just as her rescuer, but as her only means of survival.

Margot had told me the story of how, the first time Ivy had tried to stand up for herself, Hodge had pushed her and baby Bethany out the door and into the snow and refused to let them back in the house. I was pretty certain that Hodge's choice of neighborhood, far on the outskirts of town, and the timing of his confrontation, before anyone else had moved into the subdivision so that Ivy couldn't seek aid from a kind neighbor, had been entirely intentional. He wanted to make Ivy believe that she owed everything, even her safety and that of her children, to Hodge and that her very existence depended on maintaining his goodwill. It had worked.

That accomplished, Hodge had gone on to convince Ivy that she was so worthless and her past was so shameful that anyone who found out about it would shun her as a degenerate and an unfit mother. Ivy's whole world was her children. And since she was convinced Hodge had the power to take them from her, she had continued to tolerate his abuse in hopes that he would keep her "shameful" secret.

In Ivy's mind, Hodge had an omnipotent, almost godlike power to control her and others.

For someone who hasn't been through it or hasn't been educated about the relationships of abusers and victims, it was difficult to understand. But Abigail, of all people, should have been more sympathetic.

Long decades before, Abigail had been under the spell of a man who used her love for him to control her and get her to do things she wouldn't have otherwise done, things that poisoned her relationship with her family, things she'd been so ashamed of that, like Ivy, she'd pushed others away for fear they'd find out about her past. It wasn't until Liza had come unexpectedly and unwillingly into her life that Abigail had finally been forced to reveal the truth to her estranged niece.

It hadn't been easy but, over time, Liza had forgiven Abigail. The process of Abigail forgiving herself had been more difficult. And I wasn't entirely convinced the operation was complete. In another situation, I might have chalked up Abigail's angry response to Ivy's seemingly unreasonable fear of Hodge to her usual impatience with weakness in all its forms, but I suspected that her harsh reprimand of Ivy was really a reprimand of her younger, more foolish self, the girl who had thrown so much away in trying to hold onto the love of a man who was incapable of loving her or anyone else.

Sobbing, Ivy pushed back from the worktable and jumped to her feet so quickly that the folding chair she'd been sitting on fell onto the floor with a metallic clatter. There was panic in her eyes and she bolted for the door, like a wild animal desperate to escape a predator.

We all jumped to our feet, but Abigail reached Ivy first. She grabbed the frightened girl, wrapping her long, strong arms around her in a grip that was as firm as a vise and as loving as a mother's caress. At first, Ivy fought to break free from Abigail's embrace, but after a few moments she ceased struggling. She raised her shoulders high, taking in a deep breath of air and then letting it out in an anguished, audible sigh, and collapsed against Abigail, resting her head on the older woman's shoulder like a child laying her head on a pillow. She was still crying, but the terrified hysteria had passed.

With tears in her own eyes, Abigail whispered, "Stupid girl. Stupid, silly girl. You're wrong. I do understand. I know. Just calm down. Rest now. He's not going to hurt you anymore or take your children. I won't let him. Calm down now. Breathe."

She sniffed, pulled Ivy even closer, and said firmly, "Hodge Edelman might think he's a tough customer, but he hasn't tangled with *me* before. I am a Burgess. Descended from a long, proud line of the most formidable, cunning, and stubborn Yankee stock in New England. On top of that, I'm richer than Midas. And I promise you, Ivy, I am going to use every ounce of my considerable wealth, power, and personal influence to run Hodge Edelman out of New Bern with his tail between his legs. He is not going to take your children. I'm not going to let that happen! Do you hear me? I'm not going to let it happen!"

Margot stepped forward and lay her hand on Ivy's bowed head. "Neither am I," she said.

I moved close, gripped Margot's hand with mine and added my pledge to the others. "Neither am I."

A moment passed. Ivy wriggled an arm loose from Abigail's death grip and reached out to bring Margot and me into her embrace. By then, we were all crying, but it was all right. These were good tears, the kind of tears that clean out the old junk and, when shed among a company of friends, can water the seeds of powerful and unstoppable resolve.

But the men, of course, didn't realize this. Few men understand the healing benefit and emotional relief of tears. I've never understood why, but nothing seems to make men feel as uncomfortable and helpless as weeping women. I suppose it's because when a woman cries, a man feels like he ought to *do* something, but he hasn't the first idea of what that might be.

Behind me, I could hear a masculine clearing of throats and the shuffling of leather lace-ups. After a few moments, Garrett said, "Uh . . . Mom? It's nearly five. Would you like me to close out the registers and tell everyone downstairs that they can go home?"

I squeezed Ivy one more time and looked up, smiling and wiping my eyes. "Yes. Thanks, Garrett."

Charlie pulled on his nose and looked at his watch. "I've got to be running myself. Must check in with Maurice before the dinner crowd shows up." He gave me a quick kiss on the cheek and scrambled for the door with Garrett close on his heels.

Franklin was next to leave, but he wasn't quite as nervous as the other two. He walked slowly toward Ivy and laid his hand on her shoulder. His eyes were tired but kind. He smiled. "Don't worry,

Ivy. We're all going to do whatever it takes to help you. Abigail is right, so I'll leave you in her capable hands."

He kissed Abigail good-bye before turning to Ivy again. "I'll call you tomorrow," he said and then headed downstairs.

Margot grinned and wiped her eyes with the back of her hand. "Well, looks like we scared them off. So what do we do now?"

I frowned. "What do you mean, 'what do we do now?' It's Friday night. We do what we always do. We make a quilt."

❧ 21 ❧

Ivy Peterman

Frankly, I didn't see how making a quilt was going to help anything. After spending the whole afternoon listening to my pathetic history, I would have figured that I was the last person Evelyn, Margot, and Abigail would want to spend the evening with but they were insistent. Friday night was quilt circle night and the ladies wanted to quilt—end of story.

Over my protests, Evelyn recruited Garrett to babysit. Surely he had better things to do on a Friday night.

"Not really," he said. "Liza has to stay in New York until tomorrow. Trust me, taking your kids out to get some burgers and play a round of goofy golf is the best offer I'm going to get tonight. Otherwise it'll just be me, a bag of Doritos, and the *Gilligan's Island* marathon on the Nostalgia Network."

"Wow," Margot teased. "You really don't have much of a life, do you, Garrett?"

"Tell me about it." He smiled as grabbed his car keys and went out the door.

"There you go," Evelyn said. "We're all set."

"Not quite," Margot said. "We'll need provisions. I'm starving."

"There's all that food Charlie brought," Abigail replied. "Tomatoes, olives and cheese, plus some bread and butter. Everyone was so caught up in the story that we forgot to eat. Everything is still in the kitchen. I'll just get out some napkins and forks and put it out upstairs."

"Let me do it," I said quickly. Everyone had spent their entire day trying help me and I was eager to do something for them, even something as small as setting the table.

I headed downstairs. Margot was right behind me.

"I'm just going to run out for a minute," she said. "Be back in a jiffy."

Fifteen minutes later, I had the food set up on one end of the worktable and was putting slices of tomato and mozzarella onto four paper plates and garnishing each with some of the fresh basil Charlie had left in a separate container in the refrigerator. Evelyn was rolling out fabric from several different bolts and studying color combinations, and sketching something on a pad of graph paper. Abigail was fiddling with the radio, trying to find a classical station. Everyone was busy with something. It was nice. It felt normal.

Margot yoo-hooed cheerfully as she tromped up the stairs carrying a bottle of French bordeaux, a box of chocolate-covered ice cream bonbons, and a corkscrew. "I had these at my house and thought they'd be the perfect additions to our supper."

Abigail took the bottle, examined it, then glanced at the bonbons doubtfully. "Red wine and ice cream? Do you think these go together?"

"Sure they do," Margot replied, pointing to the bonbon label. "It says right here, 'French Vanilla'!"

Evelyn clapped her hands to get our attention. "All right, all right. Are we here to eat or quilt?"

"Can't we do both?" Margot giggled.

"Yes, but let's try to work out a plan for our new quilt before we open the wine, shall we? I've got a feeling the end result will be much better if we do."

"We're making a new quilt?" I asked, thinking about the quilted pillow sham I was making to go with the pinwheel quilt Abigail had made for Bethany. A couple more Friday nights and I hoped to be finished with it.

"We are," Evelyn confirmed. "A group quilt and it's going to be for you, Ivy."

"You don't have to do that." I could feel my cheeks getting warm as the others looked at me. They meant well, I knew that, but I wasn't used to being the center of so much attention and it made me feel uncomfortable, not to mention emotional. The last thing I wanted to do was start crying again. "You've already done too much for me. Really."

"Listen," Abigail said firmly, "there's something you need to understand. Once we asked you to join our group and you finally had the good sense to accept, you became part of the family. When one of us needs something, the others are right there and vice versa. Last year, when Evelyn was dealing with cancer, she needed us most. Right now, it's you. Next year, it'll probably be someone else's turn and you'll be there for them one hundred percent, just like we are for you now. Understand? So quit fussing. If Evelyn says we're making you a quilt, then that's what we're doing."

Abigail lifted her chin proudly and yielded the floor to Evelyn, who smiled.

"I've sketched out a basic design." Evelyn laid the graphed pattern on the table and smoothed it out with her hand. "It's a wall hanging with nine blocks surrounded by a pieced border. Very simple. We can work out color choices later, but the basic idea is to use five house blocks. You'll make the center block, Ivy. That will be your home."

"You want me to make a quilt block of my apartment at the Stanton Center?" I asked doubtfully.

Evelyn shook her head. "No. The Stanton Center is just where you live. I want to make a block that represents your home. Not the home you have, but the home you want to have. The home you see when you close your eyes and dream about the life you want for yourself and your children."

"The house that smiles," I whispered to myself, remembering

the happy little cottage Bethany had pointed to on our walk a few months before, nothing big or fancy, but a solid, safe little house a good sturdy roof to keep out the weather, and a garden with flowers and plenty of grass for my growing children to play on.

"That's right. And the rest of us will each make a block representing our homes. When Liza comes home for the summer she can make one too, so we'll have five altogether. Ivy's home will sit in the middle with one of ours at each of the four corners."

"Oh! I get it!" Margot exclaimed. "It will be like the rest of us are surrounding Ivy, protecting her on every side."

"Right! And the border . . ."

"The border should be trees," Abigail interjected. "Big oaks or rows of tall evergreens, something that represents the beauty of the New Bern countryside. We might even want to try having some flower blocks on the border corners. Perhaps something appliquéd."

"Good idea," Evelyn said. "We can plan that out later, but the most important thing is that, as we're making this quilt, we think about the kind of future and friendship we want for Ivy and the children. As we sew, we'll all pray and ask God to give Ivy the home of her dreams."

I was a little surprised at Evelyn's suggestion and even more surprised to see Abigail nodding her vigorous approval of the idea. I knew Evelyn and Abigail regularly attended services at the little white church that sat at the edge of the Green, but I'd never heard them talk about praying.

"Do you really believe that will help?" I asked.

"Absolutely," Evelyn said. "Prayer always helps. That doesn't mean you'll always get what you're praying for. God's not a short order cook. Sometimes he has better ideas than we do, but I do believe prayers are always heard and answered in some form or another, even if it means just helping us get our plans lined up with God's."

Looking around the room at the many quilts displayed on the walls, I wondered how many had been stitched through with Evelyn's prayers. I liked the idea of having something hanging on the wall of my home, the home I hoped to have someday, that had been sewn with the love, prayers, and best wishes of these wonderful women. I didn't have Evelyn's confidence about all prayers being heard and answered, but then again . . .

I reached across the worktable and ran my fingers over a bolt of emerald green cotton.

"This is what I want for the grass in the yard, with white for the siding, and bright blue where the window openings should be, like smiling eyes. This!" I exclaimed and pulled a length of cerulean fabric from the pile of bolts on the table. "This will be perfect! Exactly the color of Bethany's eyes!"

"I like that," Evelyn said and prepared to cut off a piece of the beautiful blue fabric. "That's a good place to start."

❧ 22 ❧

Evelyn Dixon

"Excuse me. Excuse me. Ooops. Sorry. Pardon me, ma'am." Hugging the largest tub of popcorn I have ever seen in one arm, holding what looked like a magnum of soda in the other, and with his pockets stuffed with several jumbo-sized candy bars, a pile of paper napkins, and two straws, Charlie muttered apologies as he wended his way between the seatbacks and legs of other movie-goers.

He didn't look happy.

"They were out of carrier trays," he grumbled as I took the gargantuan container of popcorn from him.

"So I gathered. Good heavens, Charlie! Look at all this. I don't know how you can eat like you do and stay so trim."

"I've the metabolism of a wolverine."

I shook my head and laughed as he pulled one box of candy after another out of his pockets. How big were those pants pockets anyway?

"Had it occurred to you that you might have bought fewer items, or at least bought smaller sizes? It would have been easier to carry."

"I didn't want to run out halfway through the movie. It always happens that way. Just went you get to the interesting part . . . slurp. You've downed the last drop of soda, so you have to go get another and by the time you get back, you've missed so much you've got no idea what's happening anymore."

"Couldn't you just sit through the rest of the movie without drinking more soda?"

"What? And have your throat go dry from eating popcorn with nothing to wash it down? Next thing you know you're coughing up a storm and everyone in the theater is shushing you. Is that your idea of a fun evening on the town?"

"Well, my idea of a fun evening on the town includes doing something more interesting than just eating popcorn and watching the film," I batted my eyelashes at him and he grinned.

"In that case, maybe we should move to the back row."

"Too late for that," I said breezily glancing around the packed movie theater. "All those seats are taken."

"Tease."

A man in the row behind us said, "Hey, mister. Sit down, will you? The movie's about to start."

"Sorry," Charlie said removing the last candy bar from his pocket, along with the napkins and, finally, his cell phone.

There was a red light blinking on his phone and Charlie stared at the screen.

"Hey," I said, laying my hand on his arm. "We had a deal about tonight. No phones. No interruptions. No business. Remember?"

Charlie frowned, shoved the phone back in his pocket, and grabbed my hand. "Come on, Evelyn. We've got to go."

"Why? What happened?"

"It's a text message from Liza. An emergency. Franklin's in the hospital. He's had a heart attack."

A quick call to Liza confirmed the news. Charlie's expression was grim, almost angry, as he pulled out of the parking lot and headed south. Garrett was driving Liza to the hospital. We promised to meet them there as soon as we could.

"How bad do you think it is?"

"I don't know. Liza didn't have much information. Abigail is still waiting to talk to the doctor. That's all I know."

"He's been looking tired lately."

Charlie shook his head slightly and drew his brows together in a frown. Franklin was Charlie's closest friend and though it sounded like he was scolding, I could see how worried he was. "He works too hard, I told him so a hundred times. Last night, I locked the door to the restaurant at well past midnight and when I was walking to my car the lights in his office were still on. He's always pushed himself too hard. And since this business with Ivy has escalated, he's worse than ever."

It was true.

When Franklin had left the meeting in my workroom the week before, saying he wanted to talk with Ivy the next day, no one except Franklin realized just how serious the nature of Hodge Edelman's suit to gain full custody of Bethany and Bobby had become, nor the level to which Edelman was willing to stoop to accomplish his ends. Of course he'd brought up Ivy's brief and unfortunate history at the Atlantis Club, we'd known that, but he'd embellished the story considerably, claiming that Ivy had not only been a dancer there for several months but that she'd also sold her favors to a select group of club patrons. His lies were difficult to prove or disprove, since the club had closed down several years previously. Franklin had been trying to track down people who had formerly been associated with the club, thinking it would be the best way to cast doubt on Hodge's claims, but so far his efforts had been unsuccessful. Still, what was far more worrying was Edelman's accusation that Ivy was not only mentally unstable, but was abusing drugs!

This was just a flat-out lie. If Ivy had been using drugs, I'd have known it. She didn't even like to take over-the-counter medications unless she absolutely had to. Once during the winter, she'd had a terrible cold and when I'd offered to run up to the drugstore to get her something that would help ease the symptoms, she refused my offer, saying she'd rather just stick with her regimen of hot lemonade with honey because cold medications always made her feel either too drowsy or too jittery. I was absolutely certain there was no substance to Edelman's claims. I'd have staked my store on it. But there was just one problem; Edelman had "proof."

Dr. Clyde Kittenger, Hodge's business partner and the physician at the nursing home they owned together as well as personal physician to the Edelman family, had given a sworn deposition saying Ivy was a drug addict. And, as damaging as that was, it was what Dr. Kittenger was *not* willing to swear—that over the years he'd treated Ivy dozens of times for the various cuts, bruises, and even broken bones she suffered during Hodge's violent outbursts—that really damaged Ivy's case. Without the backup of medical records or her doctor's testimony, it would be difficult to prove Ivy's claims of abuse at Hodge's hands. Franklin was sending Ivy for a thorough physical, including the x-rays that would show evidence of past bone breaks.

But even with x-ray evidence, it would be one doctor's word against another. Franklin was sure Kittenger was lying, but he'd have to convince a judge. Nothing about this case was easy. Franklin had been wearing himself out with work. And now this.

Poor Franklin. And Abigail. I could only imagine what she must be going through. Abigail and Franklin were very much in love though it had taken many, many years, make that decades, for their friendship to flower into a full-blown romance. What would happen to Abigail if Franklin . . .

No. I wouldn't let myself consider the possibility. Franklin was going to make a full recovery. He just had to! But until he did? What would happen to Ivy's divorce case? Franklin was the best attorney in the county, but Hodge Edelman had engaged George Caldwell, who was a close second. If Franklin was ill and couldn't represent Ivy in the courtroom, where would we find a lawyer who stood a chance against George?

Dear God, please let Franklin be all right. Let everything be all right. Please.

Charlie glanced at me quickly. "What did you say?"

"I said please. Please hurry, Charlie."

"I am doing my best, sweetheart," he said, gripping the steering wheel tightly and stepping harder on the gas to make it through a yellow light about to turn red.

"I'm going as fast as I safely can. We'll be there soon." He took his eyes off the road for just a moment and gave me a quick smile. "Don't worry. Franklin's tough. He won't die. Abigail won't let him."

When we got to the hospital, the woman who was sitting at the information desk asked, "You're friends of Mrs. Burgess Wynne? Mr. Carroll, the hospital administrator, told me you'd be arriving soon."

"How is Mr. Spaulding?" Charlie asked anxiously.

She tapped a few keys on the computer to bring up a new screen before answering. "He's in the intensive care unit and his condition is listed as critical. I'm afraid that's all the information I have right now. Mrs. Burgess Wynne and her family are in the Board of Directors' lounge on the sixth floor. Mr. Carroll thought they would be more comfortable there than in the waiting room. Shall I take you there?"

"No, thank you," I said. "I'm sure we can find the way. Sixth floor?"

"Yes. Just take a right off the elevator. You'll see the signs."

The hospital was quiet on a Saturday night and the elevator was empty. "Board of Directors' Lounge," Charlie said as the car ascended. "Sounds like they're taking very good care of Abigail."

"Not too surprising, considering her contributions probably paid for the sixth floor. They'll take good care of Franklin, too. I'm sure they're doing everything they can," I said and squeezed Charlie's hand.

He didn't say anything, just returned my squeeze as the elevator doors opened.

Liza and Garrett were sitting on the sofa, holding hands. Liza's eyes were red; she'd been crying. There were two other men in the room. One, tall and blond, wearing a white coat, was obviously Franklin's doctor. The other man, also tall with rumpled brown hair, wearing a gray suit with a red tie and glasses with wide black frames, I assumed was Mr. Carroll.

Abigail's eyes were clear, but her normally vibrant complexion was white as chalk as she stood listening to the doctor. Charlie and I entered the room quietly, not wanting to interrupt their conference. Abigail was so focused on the doctor that I doubt she'd even noticed us coming in.

"I assure you, Mrs. Burgess Wynne, I'm not trying to be evasive. When I say I'm cautiously optimistic, it's because I am."

"But, what does that mean exactly? I know Mr. Carroll has probably got you people scared witless, telling you that if you kill the . . ." Abigail lifted her chin and swallowed hard. ". . . the close friend of one of this hospital's biggest donors you'll probably be out on the street. Doctor Loring, I don't want you trying to sugarcoat the situation just because you're afraid of Mr. Carroll."

Doctor Loring cleared his throat. "Mrs. Burgess Wynne, I am one of the finest cardiologists in the state, arguably one of the finest in the country. Again, I can assure you that I am not the least bit frightened of Mr. Carroll, or any other hospital bureaucrat."

"Well then give it to me straight and stop all these platitudes about cautious optimism! Whatever that means!" Abigail shouted. "Tell me what I want to know. Is Franklin going to die?"

"No. I don't believe so."

Abigail closed her eyes for a moment and rested her hand on her breast, as if trying to calm her own heartbeat. Liza sniffed and Garrett put his arm around her.

"That being said," the doctor continued, "this was a very severe heart attack. We are doing everything possible to prevent his having another. That's why he's in intensive care. If he gets through the night with no problem, I'll probably upgrade his condition from critical to serious in the morning. If everything goes well after that, I would discharge him in a week or so. After that he would begin a serious and intensive course of cardiac rehabilitation until he is well enough to resume his normal activities. To a great extent, Mr. Spaulding will be responsible for the success or failure of his treatment. He is going to have to make some serious alterations in his diet and lifestyle. From what you've told me, Mrs. Burgess Wynne, Mr. Spaulding is a workaholic of the first order. If he wants to live to see seventy, he's going to have to change his ways."

"He will," Abigail said firmly. "I can promise you that."

"Good. And I will do my part. Mr. Spaulding is getting the absolutely best cardiac care available. I will be on the ward all night. If there are complications, I'll never be more than a few seconds from his bedside."

"Thank you."

The man in the gray suit spoke. "How long will it be before he can return to the office?"

"Depending on the severity of the attack, that can be anywhere from two weeks to three months. In Mr. Spaulding's case, I think we should plan on a recovery period in the two-to-three-month range. And, as I said, even when he does go back to work he simply can't continue working the kinds of hours he has in the past."

"I understand." The man in the gray suit nodded and turned to Abigail. "Don't worry, Abigail. I'll take care of everything until Franklin is back on his feet."

"Thank you, Arnie."

I was confused. Obviously, the man wearing the suit wasn't the hospital administrator. "Who is that?" I whispered to Charlie.

"Arnie Kinsella. He's Franklin's associate. He's been working for Franklin for about three years now."

"Three years? How is it possible that I've never met him before?"

Charlie shrugged. "Well, he lives a couple of towns over, in Chelsea, and Franklin doesn't let him do much. Says he's still too green, still learning, but I think that's just an excuse. For all his appearance of being this relaxed, laid-back fellow, Franklin is a bit of a control freak, at least when it comes to his law practice."

The doctor was preparing to leave. "Just a moment," Abigail said. "When can I see Franklin?"

"Not tonight. No visitors are allowed in the intensive care unit."

"But," Abigail insisted, "I must see him. When they were unloading him from the ambulance, I promised him I'd see him later tonight. Mr. Carroll assured me that he would arrange it."

"Well, since Mr. Carroll is not in charge of the care of cardiac patients in this or any other hospital," the doctor said in a tone every bit as imperious as Abigail's, "I'm afraid you were misinformed. Until Mr. Spaulding is released from intensive care, no one, not even the most generous of donors, will be permitted to visit him."

Abigail's eyes bulged. She was ready to go toe-to-toe with the doctor, but I sensed she'd met her match. I stepped up and put my arm around Abigail's shoulder. Wisely, the doctor took advantage of this momentary distraction and slipped out the door.

"Come on, Abbie. You can see Franklin first thing in the morning. Tonight it would be best to let him get some rest. Wouldn't be a bad idea for you, either. Why don't you go home and get some sleep? Charlie and I can stay here. We'll call you if there's any change."

Abigail shook her head and blinked a few times. "No. I'm not leaving the hospital until I've seen Franklin with my own eyes and know he's out of danger. But the rest of you should go home. Garrett, would you take Liza back home? I don't want her driving when she's so upset."

"I want to stay and wait with you."

Abigail smiled and shook her head, gently. "No, darling. You go home and be back here first thing in the morning. There's no point in both of us waiting up all night and being exhausted; besides, I'm going to need someone to bring me some breakfast. Even a member of the board can't get a decent meal in the hospital." She turned to Garrett again. "Go on. Take her home."

Garrett nodded and helped Liza up off the sofa.

"Arnie," Abigial continued, "you should be getting home, too."

"No. I'm going back to the office for a few hours and get some work done. When you see Franklin, please tell him for me that everything is under control."

"I will. Thank you, Arnie. I'm sure he'll rest easier knowing that."

He shook Abigail's hand and gave her a card. "If you need anything, anything at all, feel free to call. My home number, my cell phone, and my direct office extension are all listed there."

Arnie followed Liza and Garrett out the door. Abigail looked at Charlie and me. "You've both got to go to work in the morning. You should go too."

"Not a chance," Charlie declared. Someone has to stick around here and make sure you don't give that doctor a good poke in the nose." Charlie grinned. "You really don't like that fellow, do you?"

"No, but that doesn't matter. He's arrogant, rude, and he has the bedside manner of a shellfish, but he *is* one of the best cardiologists in the state. I should know, I'm a member of the board that helped hire him, luring him away from several larger and more prestigious hospitals. Franklin couldn't be in better hands, but if you tell that arrogant, rude genius of a doctor I said so, I'll deny every word."

"Your secret is safe with us," I said.

Abigail sank down onto the sofa. "Well, I still think you should go home, but I won't force the issue. To tell the truth, I'm glad you're here." Abigail yawned.

"It's going to be a long night. Charlie, I don't suppose you'd go down to the cafeteria and see if they'd sell you a cup of coffee? Mr. Carroll said he'd bring up a pot, but that was an hour ago. He's probably down in intensive care, personally monitoring Franklin's heart rate. He's absolutely terrified that Franklin will die on his watch and I'll renege on my promise to pay for all new equipment for the physical therapy department." She smiled. "I wouldn't, of course, but Mr. Carroll doesn't need to know that, does he?"

"No reason he should," Charlie said as he left. "I'll be right back."

Abigail leaned her head back against the sofa and closed her eyes. I sat down next to her while, together, we waited.

❧ 23 ❧

Evelyn Dixon

Four days after Franklin's heart attack, Charlie and I headed over to the hospital to bring Abigail some breakfast. Charlie had risen early to bake cheddar dill scones and my contribution was fruit compote made with fresh strawberries and mint I'd picked from the small garden I'd planted in the back of my cottage.

In the days since Franklin had been admitted to the hospital, this had become our routine. Franklin was improving, slowly. His condition was now considered stable and he'd been moved to a private room on the cardiac ward, but since Abigail refused to leave the hospital until he did, all of us—Charlie and I, Margot, Liza, Garrett, and Ivy—took turns dropping by the hospital to keep Franklin and Abigail company and to bring her meals. Poor Franklin had to subsist on the low-fat, low-cholesterol, low-flavor meals brought to him on little trays from the hospital kitchen. Not for long, though. Charlie was working on creating a series of recipes that would meet with the dietary guidelines set forth by Franklin's doctor. It seemed to be going well. In fact, Charlie was so excited about his new creations that he was considering adding a special section of heart healthy "spa cuisine" to Grill's regular menu.

We met at the Blue Bean Bakery on Commerce Street. Charlie ordered a medium black coffee from the teenaged girl handling the register and espresso machine. I got my usual, a large mocha. It was still very early, so we sat down to enjoy our coffee together before going to the hospital; we'd wait to order Abigail's large skim latte until we were ready to leave. The coffee at the hospital cafeteria was drinkable, but it couldn't compare to the brew at the Blue Bean.

It was a beautiful morning, cool and quiet and calm. Except for a few dog walkers, the streets were almost deserted, but in a few hours the summer sun would raise the mercury above ninety and downtown New Bern would be crowded with day trippers and "summer people," as a well as the year round residents.

Mothers would wheel babies in carriages, hoping the steady movement of the wheels would lull their little ones to sleep. Kids who didn't understand that hot summer days were meant for resting under shady trees would play sweaty games of tag on the Green. Residents of the town would meet each other coming and going as they dropped by the post office to check their boxes, a pleasant but necessary daily chore in a town that stubbornly shunned the installation of individual curbside mailboxes. Gaggles of girlfriends would meet for lunch and laughter around big tables in the back of the Grill, while couples newly or long in love would sit holding hands at intimate café tables in the front, enjoying each other's company and the cool breeze that came in through the open French doors facing the sidewalk. Shoppers would poke through stores, including Cobbled Court Quilts, looking for the special, unusual, and even one-of-a-kind purchases they couldn't find in the strings of chain stores that make up the commercial center of most cities, monotonous retail Levittowns that offer consumers anything they could desire except choice, surprise, or a sense of place.

New Bern isn't like that. There isn't a chain store on the entire length of Commerce Street and the citizens of New Bern like it that way. New Bern is unique, simple, authentic, and unapologetically itself. What its residents have they cherish and enjoy and what they don't have, they're content to do without. That's the spirit that made me fall in love with this little village. It's real. That's why I love it still.

Charlie and I took our coffee to a table by the window. Outside,

Mr. Yoelson, who owned the antique shop, walked by with his dog, Bailey, a sweet, white standard poodle who spent her days in the antique store, greeting customers and sticking close to Mr. Yoelson's side. Bailey was one of several "shop dogs" here in New Bern, another quaint feature of our small village.

Charlie wasn't very talkative, but I was determined to enjoy a few minutes of conversation before launching full bore into what was bound to be another busy day.

"Did you read the paper?"

He shook his head.

"The zoning board turned down Abigail's petition. The decision is final. No more appeals. I'm not really surprised. Sub-dividing her property was one thing, but if they let Abigail put an apartment building in the middle of a street of single family residences they'd have to do the same for anyone who applied. Pretty soon there wouldn't be any zoning, but I don't suppose that will make any difference to Abigail. When she gets an idea into her head, she can be pretty single-minded. She's not going to be happy about losing this fight."

"I doubt she'll even notice. She's got more important things on her mind."

"True," I agreed. "But wait until she reads the snotty quote Dale Barrows gave the paper. He didn't name names, but everyone will know he was talking about Abigail. He said it was about time some people in this town realized that having money and influence didn't mean they could bend the rules to fit their personal whims and follies."

I rolled my eyes as I picked up the shaker from the table and put a good dusting of cinnamon on my drink. "Dale's one to talk. He's still mad about my usurping his plans to resurrect his deservedly dead directing career by hijacking the Quilt Pink broadcast. This whole thing is getting weirder by the minute. Yesterday, I was unlocking the door of the shop and some woman jumped out of the shadows and shoved this enormous ream of paper into my hands. Turns out she's written a screenplay; some sort of quilting murder mystery called *A Body Between The Bolts*. She refused to leave until I said I'd read it. Can you believe that? Who does she think I am? Martin Scorsese?"

I paused to give Charlie a chance to jump in with one of his witty quips, but he didn't say anything, just stirred his coffee.

"And then there are the reporters. They keep calling, wanting to schedule interviews with Mary Dell and me. It's gotten so I'm scared to answer the phone, but I've got to get a handle on this. Everybody wants a ticket to the broadcast. Some of my best customers have said if they don't, they're going to take their business elsewhere. I'm being blackmailed by little old ladies! Sweet grandmothers who smell like cookies are threatening to boycott my shop if I don't meet their demands. Mavis Plimpton said if I didn't get her a ticket she was going to start spreading rumors that I get my fabric from sweat shops in the third world that use slave labor and pump dangerous chemicals into the ocean. Can you believe it?" I laughed. "I don't know what to do. There are simply more people who want tickets than there are places to put them. I want to be fair about it, but how?"

I looked at him, hoping for some guidance, but he just shrugged.

It was like pulling teeth to get him to talk. Maybe he was just sick of hearing about the broadcast. Well, me, too. I searched for another topic of conversation.

"Franklin should be able to leave the hospital next week. At least that's what Margot told me."

"Good."

"He's still got a long road to recovery. There's no way he'll be able to represent Ivy at the trial. Arnie will take his place. Margot said he was at the hospital when she brought Abigail's lunch, filling Franklin in on what's going on at the office, especially Ivy's case."

Charlie grunted. "Huh. Must be killing him to leave this to someone else."

"Margot said he was really grilling Arnie. Had a million questions. He got so worked up that one of the monitors started beeping. Abigail told Arnie he'd have to go, but that just made the monitor beep louder." I chuckled. "Poor Franklin. It's so hard for him to let go, but I guess he's just going to have to get used to it. The doctor keeps telling him that even after he recovers, he's going to have to slow down and share more of the workload with his associates. Arnie seems capable, don't you think?"

"Mmmm," Charlie murmured as he slurped his coffee.

"And he's certainly getting lots of help. Margot spends every night after work helping him with the paperwork, transcribing notes. All kinds of things. The firm's paralegal is on vacation, so they're really shorthanded. And now that Liza is home for the summer, she and Garrett are helping too. They're going to drive out to Pennsylvania soon to do a little sleuthing. See if they can find some of the people who used to work at the Atlantis Club, people who can verify Ivy's story. It's a long shot, but you never know. Oh! And did I tell you? Arnie sent Ivy for x-rays and they showed that she had two broken ribs and several broken bones in her hand. They're healed now, of course, but it does help corroborate Ivy's statement about her abuse.

"Still, I don't know how much help that will be without medical records. I can't believe this doctor, Kittenger or whatever his name is, is saying that he has no records that support Ivy's claims of abuse. Ivy says he treated her at least a dozen times after Hodge beat her, but his records only show a pregnancy diagnosis for Bobby and a few bouts of cold and flu. How does he plan to explain away those broken bones? And then he accuses her of abusing drugs? Why would anyone, a doctor especially, lie about something like that? Isn't he under oath to try to help people?"

Increasingly aware that I was doing all the talking, I paused and looked at Charlie, waiting for him to say something, but he just sat there and drank his coffee, still brooding. I tried another tack.

"This is nice," I said blowing on my mocha to cool it down before taking a sip. "Do you remember back when we first met? We used to have our coffee together almost every morning. Why don't we do this more often?"

Charlie looked up at me. He belched out an irritated noise, half-laugh, half-snort. "Probably because neither of us seems to have time to do so much as change our minds these days, let alone find a spare half hour for coffee dates. Do you realize that Saturday was the first time we'd been out together in weeks? Ever since Mary Dell came up with her brilliant plan to shout the name Cobbled Court Quilts over national television you don't have a spare moment for anyone or anything—especially me."

Charlie's stormy expression told me this was a gripe he'd been nursing for some time but I didn't let myself get too upset by his accusation, not at first. Frankly, I couldn't quite believe he'd have the nerve to lay the blame for our current lack of face time on my doorstep.

"Oh, come on, Charlie. That's not fair. It's not like I'm the only one with a busy schedule. You're the one who works nights. During the tourist season, it's every night."

"Well, you're the one who spends every bloody Friday night quilting with her girlfriends!"

"What!" I exclaimed. I couldn't believe he was throwing that in my face. He knew that Friday nights were the one night in the week that I had for myself. I *needed* those few hours of creativity and companionship on Fridays. It was my way of recharging my battery at the end of a long workweek.

"Don't you go throwing stones at me, Charlie Donnelly. It practically took an act of Congress to get you to let Gina take over for you so we could go out on Saturday."

"Well, what do you expect? I've got a business to run!"

"So do I!" I retorted, raising my voice to match his. "And for the first time since I opened my doors, I'm actually making money, so don't go making me feel guilty about my success. You, of all people, know how much that means to me and how hard I've worked to get to this point. You sat here with me at this very table during those first months after Cobbled Court opened, when I was teetering on the edge of bankruptcy, and told me to think outside the box. You told me not to give up, to find a way, *any* way to make it work and now that I have, you're giving me a hard time about it!

"Why do men do that? The second a woman becomes successful and can't spend every moment of every day focused entirely on them they get jealous, or threatened, or some such thing. Well, my business is just as important as yours, Charlie. And I'm proud of what I've accomplished even if you're not!"

Charlie's eyes narrowed and he scowled. "Now who's not being fair? I never said I wasn't proud of you. I am. Of course, I am. How can you even say that?" He hunched his shoulders and glared at me.

"What's going on here, Charlie? When I was failing you were my biggest cheerleader; so now that I'm finally a success, you've suddenly turned into a critic? I don't get it. What's changed between then and now?"

Charlie sat up straighter and banged his coffee cup down hard on the table. A wave of the black brew sloshed over the edge of the cup. "What's changed is that now I love you!" he shouted.

The girl who had been working the counter looked at us nervously and then scurried back into the kitchen, perhaps thinking it might be a good time to make sure the muffins weren't burning. Charlie saw her go and lowered his voice.

"I love you!" he hissed. "When I first met you, I liked you—a lot. I gave you advice because I wanted to see you succeed in your business. Nothing's changed on that score. I still want you to succeed, but now I love you. I want to spend time with you. If I could, I'd spend every waking and sleeping moment of my life with you, you know that. I'd like to marry you, as I've told you a hundred times."

It was true. Well, maybe not a hundred times, but often, especially in the last few months. My anger of the moment faded quickly, replaced by tenderness for this very complicated, very good, and very difficult man.

"I know. And I love you too, Charlie, very much. After my divorce, I couldn't imagine ever wanting to marry again. You've made me rethink that. Still, Charlie, I'm not ready. Not yet. I just think we need to know each other better before we make that commitment. We've talked about this before. I was a teenager when I met Rob. I rushed headlong into marriage without really knowing him, sure that love would conquer all. I'm not going to make that same mistake twice. We need to spend more time together before we consider marriage."

Charlie threw up his hands, "But isn't that just what I'm saying? You say we need more time together before we marry and I agree. But, how are we going to do that if we never see each other? That's my point! I'm not some chauvinistic, knuckle-dragging caveman who expects you to let your business fail just so you can wait on me or because I feel threatened. Nothing could be further from the truth. But somehow or other, we've got to figure out a way to make more time for each other. That's all I'm saying."

"All right. Fair enough. You're right." Charlie gave his chin a quick jerk, vindicated. I took another drink of my coffee. "And I'm sorry I lost my temper with you."

"Me, too," he mumbled. Saying sorry didn't come easy to Charlie. That was as close to an apology as I'd ever get out of him, but I knew he was sincere.

"So. We need to figure out a way to spend more time together."

"Right. And still give our businesses and our friends the time they deserve, but short of giving up sleep, I don't see how, at least not until the tourists leave. This time of year, the restaurant has to stay open every night. And even though Cobbled Court closes at five . . ."

I shook my head. "Six. I've decided to expand my hours through the summer. It's foolish not to. Late sunsets mean that shoppers are staying out late, too. If I close my doors at five, I'm just turning away business. But, you know, the answer really is right under our noses. We used to find time to meet here every morning, why don't we just start doing that again?"

Charlie lifted his cup and wiped off the coffee that had splashed over the side before taking another drink. "Well, it's not exactly a month-long getaway to a tropical isle, but for the moment I guess it will do. I've got another idea. How about if you come and have dinner with me at the Grill a couple nights a week? If you come after the rush, say nine o'clock, I should actually be able to dine without having to get up every fifteen times. What do you say?"

"It's a deal," I said.

He smiled, reaching across the table to take my hand, and lifting it to his lips. The soft, feathery sensation of my fingers brushing across his lips caused a thrilling flutter to rise in my chest and spread through the rest of my body. Charlie was right. It had been too long since we'd made time for each other.

With his head still bent over my hand, I leaned my own low and whispered, "Why don't you order Abbie's coffee now. Let's go."

Charlie looked up at me. "It's only seven-thirty. Visiting hours don't begin for another hour."

"I know. So if you take ten minutes to get the coffee and fifteen to drive to the hospital, that gives us thirty-five minutes alone in the car. Want to steam up the windows?"

Charlie grinned, reached into his pocket, and handed me his car keys. "Go warm up the engine. I'll be right with you."

Visiting hours began at eight but by the time we walked past the information desk and entered the elevator carrying Abigail's now-cold latte, it was a quarter past. We'd lost track of the time.

"Your lips are chapped."

Charlie didn't say anything, just put his arm around me and kept it there during the ride to the fifth floor, home of the cardiac care ward.

When the doors opened, we took a left at the nurses' station and walked down the long hallway. As we rounded the corner we saw a gray-haired man wearing a black shirt, clerical collar, and a solemn expression leave Franklin's room. He didn't look up when he hurried past. Charlie's eyes grew dark as he watched the retreating figure in black. I clutched at his hand.

"Wasn't that the hospital chaplain? Did you see the look on his face? What was he doing in Franklin's room? You don't think . . ."

But before I could ask the question that was so fearsome, just thinking it made my heart pound, we saw Abigail leaving the room.

Abigail's face was pale, drained of color. Her eyes were glassy and unfocused, as if she'd just received a terrible blow.

Charlie and I quickened our pace, the sound of our steps echoing through the empty, sterile corridor. I reached her a split second before Charlie did.

"Abigail, what's the matter? What's wrong?"

Charlie put his arms out to support her and she practically sank into them. For a moment I thought she might faint.

Charlie gave me an alarmed look and jerked his chin in the direction of a wooden chair that was sitting a few feet away. I pulled it closer and helped him guide Abigail toward it.

"There now. Sit down, Abbie. Are you all right now?" Abigail nodded. "All right. Then just take a deep breath. That's right. Now tell me what happened."

Abigail's gaze was wide and unblinking, but she looked right past us as if she were talking to herself. "Franklin had a rough night. He couldn't sleep. Said he was in terrible pain, but he wouldn't let me call the nurse. But he just kept groaning and I was so worried. Finally, about an hour ago, he asked me to call for the chaplain and I did. And when . . ." she paused for a moment and then shook herself before going on, as if trying to collect herself. "When the chaplain arrived, Franklin asked me to marry him. And I did!"

Charlie and I looked at each other, our faces mirrors of disbelief. "You did?"

"You got married? Here? In the hospital?"

I laughed. "Abigail, you must be joking."

Eyes still glazed, she moved her head slowly from side to side. "I'm not. Two of the nurses stood as witnesses. Franklin's voice sounded so weak when we were repeating the vows that I could barely hear him say 'I do' but as soon as the ceremony was over the color came back into his face and he sat right up in the bed. He's in there now right now, calling his daughters to tell them the news."

She looked from me to Charlie and back to me. "I can't believe it," she whispered. "I'm married. I am Mrs. Abigail Burgess Wynne Spaulding."

I leaned down to give her a congratulatory hug but stopped when her lip began to quiver and she suddenly burst into tears.

"Now what am I supposed to do?"

❧ 24 ❧

Ivy Peterman

Donna Walsh facilitates the twice-weekly support group at the women's shelter. Even after four weeks, she makes a point of greeting me personally when I arrive, as if slightly surprised to see that I've shown up yet again. To tell the truth, I find it a little surprising myself. After all, I was the one who swore she'd never, ever go to one of these things and, for a year and a half, I kept my vow. But a lot of things have changed in the last month. It's nothing anyone would notice by looking at me but on the inside? I'm definitely doing some remodeling.

Finally telling Evelyn, Abigail, Margot and the others the truth wasn't easy, but sooner or later, it had to happen.

For so many years, Hodge told me that I was worthless, that no one who really knew me could care about me, and I believed him. Of course, it didn't start with him. Secretly, I'd believed it all along. But I *wanted* to be loved. That's what made me take a chance on the truth. I had to know if there was anything in me, the real me, that anyone else could care about.

When I sat down at the workroom table and told them my story, my real story, I fully expected Margot, Evelyn, and Abigail to reject me. When they didn't, when the voices of the past—Hodge's, my mother's, my own—turned out to be wrong, it made me wonder how many other lies I'd been telling myself.

The answer, it turns out, is a lot. Let's start with one of the big ones: I stayed in my marriage as long as I did because I had to. This lie has many variations involving kids, finances, safety, etcetera; pretty much the same justifications the other women in our support group list when trying to explain why they stayed in their abusive relationships. Sitting in this circle for the last four weeks, I've heard every stupid excuse in the world. Funny how easy it is to spot the lies other people tell themselves about themselves—the more you do, the harder it becomes to believe your own.

So here it is; the truth. Finally.

Besides my father, Hodge was the only one who ever loved me, or at least gave the appearance of loving me. Yes, Hodge beat me, physically and emotionally. He broke my spirit as well as my bones, but he wasn't always like that. Sometimes he could be kind, even gentle. That was especially true during the early years. I kept thinking that somehow, if I could just figure out what I was doing wrong and be what it was he wanted me to be, then things would go back to the way they'd been before. I wasn't trapped in my abusive marriage; I *stayed* in it. I stayed because I wanted Hodge to love me. That was the truth and, in a way, it still is.

I understand now that Hodge didn't, doesn't, won't ever love me, but that doesn't mean I don't want to be loved. I still do, but I don't see how that will ever be possible. Love takes trust and that's something I don't have anymore. I don't mean lack of trust in men so much, though I *don't* trust them. What I'm talking about is a lack of trust in myself. Let's face it, when it comes to men, I have terrible judgment.

If I ever did meet a nice man, someone who I could really care about, how could I ever trust that he really was what he appeared to be? When I met Hodge, I saw what I wanted to see; the looks, the style, the dashing prince on the white charger who rescued me from the gutter and seamy, steamy clutches of the disgusting Jerry—who I also trusted when I first met him. How is that I never thought to ask myself what Hodge was doing at the Atlantis Club? It wasn't like he'd just wandered in off the street by accident. He was a regular, a good customer; good enough that he could come backstage and call Jerry by his first name; good enough to run a big tab for the table full of leering clients. Hodge was in the gutter that night because that's where he liked to spend his time. How could I have failed to see that?

And that wasn't my only blind spot. For so many years, I thought Hodge hit me because of what I'd done or not done, that I deserved what I was getting. But when he turned on Bethany and started hitting her . . . I knew. Hodge didn't hit me because of who I was, but because of who he was. Hodge hit me because he liked to.

Realizing this is a big step for me, but it doesn't mean I've suddenly freed myself from guilt. If anything, I have new things to feel guilty about, like the effect all this will have on my children. For years, they were silent witnesses to the abuse. They watched as Hodge dished it out and I stood there and took it. I exposed them to the rules and roles of abusers and victims. What is that going to mean for them and their future relationships? Will Bethany grow up to be an easy target for men like Hodge? Will Bobby grow up to become an abuser himself? I don't know. I'm doing my best to make sure they don't inherit this destructive family legacy. But there are no guarantees. The odds are less favorable for them than for other children and I've got to live with that. It's my fault.

Also, taking big steps forward doesn't keep me from trying to retrace my footsteps. There are times, especially when I can't sleep, that my mind will hit the rewind button, playing and replaying the tape of my marriage, freeze-framing this decision, that omission, the careless words that escaped my lips, the wiser thoughts that were never voiced, trying to figure out where I made my first mistake, and my second, and all the mistakes that came after, and I try to figure out what I should have done differently.

Hodge hit me because he liked to.

No matter how many times you say it, it doesn't make sense. And so, years after that light dawned in my mind, it still flickers uncertainly as I lie alone in the darkness, looking for reasons, wondering if the blame lies with me.

But when I go the meetings, sitting in a circle on an unsteady folding chair and wondering what to do with my hands, and listen to the stories of other women like me, I'm not so sure.

We're all different: some are poor, others are rich; some have advanced degrees, others are high school dropouts; some like to talk, others prefer to listen; some have unblemished faces; others are marked by purplish bruises fading to sickly green. All of us have scars. All of us are trying to heal. All of us have a long way to go.

In a way that is different than talking with Abigail, or Evelyn, or even Margot, it helps me to tell my story to these women and to listen to theirs. When they tell their stories I can see them trying to make sense of the senseless, trying to figure out how they got to where they are. And often, especially in the case of the newer arrivals, they still think it was their fault and that if they'd said something different, or done something different, or brought the coffee more quickly, or remembered that he'd switched to half-and-half instead of cream, then the man they thought loved them wouldn't have hurt them so.

"He just lost his temper, you see? He's really not like that," they say.

The rules of the group say we have to be quiet when others are speaking and I am, but sometimes it is everything I can do to keep from screaming, "You're wrong! He *is* like that! You didn't do anything wrong. Even if you did, a broken jaw is not a fair exchange for a flubbed coffee order. You're innocent. You didn't deserve that. No one deserves that."

No one deserves that. Not even me.

Sometimes, more often than you'd think, I'll come to the meeting to find one of the chairs in the circle empty; the woman who used to sit in it has gone back to her abuser. It's so sad. She still believes it is her fault and that if she changes, he will too.

But, it's not true. I see that now. And while there are still plenty of things for me to feel guilty about, though the road I must travel stretches beyond the horizon, too far for me to discern where it ends, and though some days I take one step back for every two that lead forward, there is one thing I am certain of: none of my circle sisters will ever come into the room to find my chair empty.

❧ 25 ❧

Evelyn Dixon

I had never seen Abigail without makeup, impeccably coiffed hair, understated but elegant clothes, and carefully chosen accessories. Even lipstick- and jewelry-less, wearing driving moccasins, beige slacks, and a white oxford blouse with a red sweater hanging carelessly around her shoulders, Abigail is still one of the most beautiful women I know, but her casual ensemble, not to mention the shadows of fatigue under her eyes, made it clear that she had more important things than grooming on her mind.

"Go on," Franklin said as he clicked through channels looking for the baseball game. "It'll do you good to get out for a little while."

"Franklin's right," I agreed. "A break will do you good. Just for an hour or two."

"I don't know," she said doubtfully.

Franklin rolled his eyes. "For heaven's sake, Abbie. You'll only be one floor away. Go on and make your quilts. I'll be fine. I promise. Nothing bad is going to happen to me."

Charlie, who was busily arranging a tray of heart-healthy snacks including pretzels with homemade maple-mustard, butterless chili-spiced popcorn, and turkey and veggie subs on whole wheat, looked up. "Oh, I wouldn't be so sure of that. Your Yankees are going to lose this game to my Red Sox, badly. And when they do, my friend, it's going to cost you ten dollars," he grinned and handed Franklin a sandwich. "But, other than that, Abigail, he's right. Everything will be fine, so go on. Work on your quilts and enjoy a nice gab with your girlfriends. Recharge your batteries so you can comfort poor Franklin here after he sees the final score."

Abigail hesitated a moment. "Are you sure you'll be all right?"

"Yes, Abigail. I'm sure. Now will you get out of here and let us watch the game? I promise not to have a heart attack and die before you return."

Abigail scowled. "No one thinks you're funny, you know."

"No one but you," he said and blew her a kiss as she walked out the door.

I pressed the sixth floor elevator button.

"This really is ridiculous," Abigail said. "Moving the quilt-circle meeting to the hospital. Just this once, you could have gone on without me."

"I know," I said and casually pulled a tube of pink lipstick from the side pocket of my handbag, took off the cap, and applied it to my lips. "But we just thought it would be nice for you to get out of Franklin's room for a bit. How are you anyway? How does it feel to be married?"

"I wouldn't know. I'm trying my very best not to think about it."

I laughed. "Oh, come on. Don't be such a grump."

I finished coloring my lips and held the open tube out to Abigail. "Here. Want some?"

"No. Thanks, I'm fine."

"It's a new color; kind of a pinky peach. And it has all these plant extracts that are supposed to make your lips look younger. Try it," I urged, shoving the lipstick tube into her hand, "I want to see how it looks on you."

Abigail gave me an irritated look. "All right. All right. I don't know why you're so insistent." She opened her mouth into an *O*, applied the lipstick in three expert swipes, and pressed her lips together to make sure the color was even.

"There," she said. "Happy?"

"Makes all the difference," I said.

The elevator doors opened and I led the way to the Board of Directors' Lounge. "Mr. Carroll let me set everything up in here. Since everyone is still working on their house block and those are all done by hand, I didn't bring any machines, but we've got everything else," I chattered in what I hoped was a distracting tone, "ironing boards, rotary cutters and mats, notions, fabric—the whole nine yards. You should have seen my car—simply packed. Thank heaven the girls were here to help me unload."

As we approached the entrance to the Board of Directors' Lounge, an impressive and elaborately carved double door with ovals of etched glass in each side, Abigail looked at me suspiciously. "Where are the girls, anyway? And why isn't there any light coming through the glass?"

For a moment she stopped short, adding up two and two in her head and quickly reaching four. "Oh no. Evelyn. Tell me you didn't . . ."

I shoved open the door to the darkened room. Three figures jumped out of the shadows and shouted. "Surprise!"

Abigail shot me a look. "You did."

26

Evelyn Dixon

Abigail sat in a big wing chair, smiling, while the rest of us crowded onto the sofa, the queen surrounded by her loyal ladies in waiting and a pile of opened gifts. Considering we'd had only two days' notice to pull it together, it really was a lovely shower.

We'd settled on a floral theme and the plates, napkins, centerpiece of purple hydrangeas, and even the gifts reflected that. Margot's offering was a beautiful crystal flower vase, very simple with a classic Greek key pattern around the edge. Ivy's gift was a sweet little basket filled with flower seeds and bulbs, a pair of hot pink gardening gloves and matching trowel, plus a homemade gift certificate for three hours of Ivy's weeding or planting services. Liza gave her an exquisite oil painting of daffodils in an old-fashioned gathering basket. It was the final project of her advanced oils class and it was easy to see why she'd gotten an *A* on it. The painted flowers sparkled with diamond drops of dew, looking for all the world like some absent hostess had just picked them from the garden and left them on the table while she went to find the right vase to fill them with. My gift was, of course, a quilt. There hadn't been time to make anything new, so I'd chosen one from my own collection, a vibrant, happy quilt with a center medallion made from pieced posy blocks in four jewel-bright colors, surrounded by a wide expanse of crisp quilted white softened by appliquéd vines and leaves, and bordered with more of the posy blocks each in its own cheery color, like a garden in bloom. It wasn't the most complicated pattern in the world, but I've never been one to think that complicated necessarily equals beautiful and this quilt was beautiful, one of my favorites. I couldn't have been persuaded to part with it for anyone I cared about less than Abigail, but when she opened the box, gasped, and then got up from her chair to give me a lingering hug, I knew she loved it as much as I did.

The company of friends, the lovely gifts, a glass of champagne along with a nice thick slice of chocolate-orange cake with cream cheese frosting, a recipe I knew she loved, had lightened Abigail's mood considerably. But even with her improved spirits, she flatly refused to wear the "hat" Margot had fashioned out of a paper plate and the discarded ribbons from the gifts.

"Oh, come on," Margot begged. "Put it on just for a minute. Just long enough so we can get a picture."

"Pigs will fly before I allow you to take a picture of me wearing that thing on my head. Besides, there has been entirely enough photography going on here tonight. Thank heaven Evelyn got some lipstick on me before I opened the door."

She narrowed her eyes and pointed a scolding finger toward Liza. "If you'd taken a picture of me without my lipstick, I'd have disowned you!"

Liza wrinkled her nose at her aunt, took the champagne bottle from where it rested on the coffee table and got up to refill the glasses. "Ivy?"

"No, thanks," she said looking at her watch. "I've got to get behind the wheel soon. Karen is babysitting for me and I told her I'd be back by nine."

"It's nice of her to watch the kids for you," I said.

Ivy nodded. "Yes, she's really a sweetheart. That's one of the nice things about living at the Stanton Center. Now that I've gotten to know everyone better, there are always plenty of other mothers around to trade babysitting with and if you're in the middle of making dinner and you realize you're out of some crucial ingredient, all you have to do is go into the hallway and knock on a few doors; with eight families in the building, somebody is bound to have what you need."

"That's nice," Liza said. "Sort of like living in a girls' dorm. My roommates and I are always borrowing each other's clothes."

Ivy shrugged. "I suppose it's something like that, but I wouldn't know. The furthest I got in school was tenth grade."

"Have you ever thought about going back?" Abigail asked.

Ivy shook her head dismissively. "I was never much of a student and now, after all this time . . ."

"Well, what does that have to do with it? Goodness, Ivy! You're not even thirty yet! There are plenty of women twice your age who go back to school. I know some people who could help you. Would you like me to make a few calls?" Abigail's eyes brightened and she leaned in, eager as always to use her influence for some good purpose.

"I know the president of the university quite well. He was a friend of my late husband, Woolley Wynne. We used to play bridge together," Abigail continued excitedly but then paused a moment, reconsidering.

"But, perhaps we should wait a bit on that. You'll need to pass your high school equivalency examination before enrolling in college. Maybe I could call Carol Devine, at the community college. I'm sure she could put us on the right track."

Abigail narrowed her eyes and drummed her fingers against the armrest of her chair thoughtfully. "You know, we really might be onto something here. I'm sure you're not the only woman at the Stanton Center who had her education cut short. Perhaps the university would be open to creating some kind of adult education program for victims of domestic violence. If the Wynne Foundation were to get the ball rolling, perhaps create a scholarship fund . . ." She looked at Ivy and beamed.

"You know, this could really be exciting! Of course, first we have to start with you. On Monday morning, I think we should . . ."

Ivy held up her hands like she was bracing against the impact of an oncoming steamroller, which wasn't too far from the truth. "Abigail! Whoa! Just hold on a minute, will you please?"

Abigail frowned, displeased by the interruption.

"As far as creating a program, I think you should go for it. A lot of the women I know would jump at the chance to go back to school. Maybe I will, too, someday, but not now. I can't. The only thing I can focus on right now is getting through this divorce and keeping my kids. Period. When and if I clear that hurdle, then I've got to find a place for us to live. My time at the Stanton Center is almost up. But, for now, even finding a new apartment is on the back burner."

Despite this gracious refusal and the logic behind it, Abigail still looked miffed. I decided it was time to change the subject.

"How are things going with the divorce? Has Arnie turned up anything new?"

These questions weren't entirely diversionary in nature. With each of us taking our different "shifts" at the hospital and the business at the shop at record levels, we hadn't had a chance to catch up in several days.

Ivy reached up and began playing with her hair, an unconscious habit I'd noticed she fell into whenever something was really bothering her. "Not really. But he keeps telling me not to worry. He says that Hodge can bring in all the papers and witnesses he wants, but he's still a liar and, eventually, liars always make a mistake." Ivy sighed. "I sure hope he's right."

Margot was sitting next to Ivy on the sofa and reached over to give her hand an encouraging squeeze.

"He is," she said earnestly. "I know things look pretty bleak right now, but we're not giving up. Arnie says that Hodge's whole case is like a piece of fabric woven from lies and that all we have to do is find one stray thread that Hodge has been too careless to clip, give it a good tug, and the whole thing will unravel."

"Sounds like you and Arnie have been spending a lot of time together," Abigail said.

"Oh, yes. Every night after work I go pick up some dinner for us at the Chinese place, then go over the law office and help work on Ivy's case. Arnie is very smart, a wonderful lawyer," she said.

"How nice for you," Abigail said gave me a knowing look.

"It's nothing like that. He's glad to have an extra pair of hands but once this case is wrapped up I'm sure we won't see each other again. We're just friends; that's all."

"Why do you say that?" Liza asked. "What makes you think you couldn't be more than friends?"

"Because," she said firmly, "that's what always happens to me. Men like me as a friend. They enjoy spending time with me and confiding in me but, in the end, they think of me as a favorite kid sister, cute and sweet but not someone they could be interested in romantically. Trust me. It used to be, every time I made friends with a man I'd get my hopes up only to have them dashed. Well, no more. I've learned my lesson fifty times over. So let's leave it at that."

"Fine," Liza said. "Have it your way."

"Thank you, I will." Margot said primly and then took a ladylike sip from her champagne glass before going on. "Anyway, as I was saying, it's only a matter of time until we find the loose thread that will unravel this whole thing. You'll see, Ivy."

"Yeah," Liza added. "Garrett and I will be heading out to Pennsylvania next week. Maybe we'll find out something that will help. You never know."

"I hope so. I really appreciate you trying," Ivy said and twisted her hair into a tight corkscrew around her index finger.

"There's just something about this whole thing that doesn't feel right," she mused.

"I'll say," said Liza.

"No, I don't mean that way. Nothing about what Hodge is doing is right, but that's no surprise. What does surprise me is that, other than that one time when came into the shop, he hasn't shown his face in New Bern."

"Well, there isn't much he can do here, is there?" Margot reasoned. "He's got his lawyer handling everything and he's got a business to run that's miles away. Not to mention the restraining order. He's not supposed to come within 200 feet of you."

Ivy laughed bitterly. "Restraining order? If Hodge Edelman decides he wants to do something, there's no piece of paper that will stop him. He considers himself above the law. And as far as his business . . ." Ivy shrugged. "I suppose you could be right. Maybe that's why he's let me be so far."

Her forehead was creased in thought and I could tell she wasn't as convinced by Margot's logic as her words indicated. Ivy pulled her finger out of her hair, leaving a perfect curl behind, the hair twisting of its own accord, corkscrewed by the memory of Ivy's nervous fingers.

"Anyway," she said, "enough of that. This is a bridal shower. I want to hear more about this wedding."

"Good point," I said, following Ivy's lead. "Abigail, you've barely told us anything about your plans. Have you and Franklin decided where you'll live after he gets out of the hospital? What about a honeymoon? You and Franklin should go off to a tropical island somewhere."

Abigail made a face. "A honeymoon? That's the last thing on my mind. I'm still not convinced this wedding was even legal. Franklin tricked me! And that chaplain. I bet he was in on the whole thing! They plotted it together, the minister and Franklin. The doctor says I should avoid saying anything to upset Franklin, but if it wasn't for that, I'd certainly give him a piece of my mind!

"Wedding indeed," she harrumphed. "That was no wedding. There were no flowers, no music, no church—not even a ring!

"When Woolley and I got married, he wanted a big wedding, but I insisted on eloping. I couldn't bear to endure the farce of a big church wedding, all those people congratulating us and saying how much in love we were when I knew it wasn't true. I wasn't in love with Woolley. He knew it, but he said he didn't care. My mother was thrilled, of course, because he was so rich, but still I'd never have gone through with it if I hadn't been so recently disappointed in love. I married Woolley on the rebound and that sad little ceremony in Reno was simply awful. It felt more like forming a business partnership than getting married."

She shrugged. "Well, in a way I suppose that's just what it was.

Don't get me wrong, Woolley and I were happy enough. We liked each other and I was as good a wife to him as I knew how to be, but it wasn't a marriage in the true sense of the word. I always promised myself that if I ever did get married again, I'd only do so out of love and in a proper church ceremony with flowers and friends and a cello concerto for the processional, a real wedding with bridesmaids and groomsmen and me wearing white. Or," she said after a moment's reflection, "perhaps ivory. And a lovely reception at the club afterwards with canapés and cold lobster and champagne toasts, a party that goes on past midnight with a full orchestra and dancing under the stars."

"*If* I'd planned on getting married anytime soon, which I didn't," she declared imperiously, "*that's* the sort of wedding I would have wanted. Instead, I got a slapdash affair that I agreed to on the basis of pity and a feigned deathbed proposal, conducted by a mumbling hospital chaplain who sandwiched the ceremony between administrations of the last rites, witnessed by two sleepy nurses finishing up the night shift, with music provided by the dulcet beeps of Franklin's heart monitor!"

Abigail put down her champagne glass and got to her feet. "Don't let's talk about this anymore. It was sweet of you to go to all this trouble for me, but Franklin Spaulding tricked me into marrying him and that's all there is to it."

She looked at her watch and frowned. "Speaking of Franklin, I really must be going. I don't like leaving him alone for so long."

Liza, who had been listening with her arms crossed over her chest and an amused expression on her face, got up off the sofa to block her aunt's departure.

"Hold on just a minute," she said, putting both her hands on Abigail's shoulders and pushing her back down into the armchair. "You're not leaving yet. Franklin will be fine for a few minutes; Charlie can take care of him, not to mention that extra private duty nurse you hired to stand by in case the other six cardiac nurses weren't enough. So, before you go running out the door, let's just get a few things straight."

I took the flowered paper napkin I had in my hand and raised it to my mouth, choking back my laughter and trying to disguise it as a cough. Nobody but Liza could talk to Abigail this way, but with a blunt style that proved her apple hadn't dropped far from the family tree, she said exactly what the rest of us were thinking.

"First off, nobody is buying this whole 'I only married Franklin out of pity' routine. Deathbed request or no, nothing could have made you marry him if you didn't want to. You married Franklin because you love him and only because you love him. Admit it."

Abigail sat under this barrage with a face as petulant as a rebellious teenager's. For a moment, she refused to say anything, but Liza just stood in front of her and grinned, making it clear that she was willing to wait as long as necessary for a response.

"All right. Fine. It's true; I do love Franklin. Of course, I do.

"But," she said, sticking out an index finger to underscore her point, "that doesn't mean I'm not mad at him. And no matter what you say, he *did* trick me. If he'd have asked me to marry him another time, when he wasn't ill, I'd have insisted on a proper wedding. Franklin knew that, but he played on my pity and fear so he could get out of having a real wedding. And the minute he got what he wanted—boom! There he was, sitting bolt upright in bed and miraculously cured. Lazarus couldn't have pulled off a more convincing resurrection. He tricked me, I tell you!"

"Abigail," Margot chided gently, "Franklin would never do something like that. I think he really was feeling terribly weak and ill and worried that he wasn't going to pull through, so he asked you to marry you because he didn't want to leave this world without making you his wife. But, when you accepted his proposal, he probably felt so happy that it sped his recovery." She giggled. "Really, it all sounds terribly romantic to me. Wouldn't it be better to think of it that way?"

"Margot, it's a good thing you're single, because the sum total of what you don't know about men could fill an ocean. Franklin is a good man but, even so, he cheated me out of the wedding I wanted.

Eventually, I may be persuaded to forgive him but at the moment I'm mad about it and I expect to stay that way for a good while."

"Oh, Abigail. Come on," I said. "After all you've been through with Franklin this week, haven't you learned that life is too short to go around holding grudges? Especially against a man you're in love with."

That took the wind out of her sails.

"Well . . ." The angry look faded from Abigail's face but was replaced by an expression I couldn't quite read. Something was still bothering her, but I couldn't tell what it was.

"Evelyn has a point. At your age, especially," Liza teased, "you've got to make the most of every moment you have left. And to those ends," Liza walked over to a potted palm that stood in the corner and pulled out a white dress box tied with pink and green satin bows. "I have one more present for you."

She walked to the armchair and placed the box in Abigail's lap. "Go on," she urged. "Open it."

Abigail pulled on the satin ribbons, lifted the lid off the box, removed the tissue paper, and held up the gift, a white negligee with a long, shimmering satin skirt that gave way to a see-through lace bodice with a plunging neckline.

She glared at Liza. "You don't imagine for one moment that I'm going to wear this, do you?"

"Well why not? You said you'd wanted to get married in white."

Margot giggled. Abigail shot her a look that could have shriveled a cactus.

"You know," Liza said, "there's a matching garter belt and white fishnet stockings that go with that negligee. I can order them for you if you'd like."

Everyone laughed, but Abigail was not amused.

"Ha! Glad you're all having such fun at my expense. Now, if you'll excuse me, I really must be going. Thank you all for the party. Up until now, I enjoyed myself."

"Oh, come on, Abigail. Don't be mad," I said. "Nobody is making fun of you. It's just a little good-natured ribbing, that's all. It's practically required at bridal showers. You should have seen the get-up my bridesmaids gave me when I got married. It was lime-green polyester lace with cheap black velvet ribbons and many strategically placed cut-outs; the most garish, vulgar, completely hilarious lingerie imaginable. This, one the other hand, is beautiful and in perfectly good taste. I think you should wear it on your honeymoon. You'd look simply lovely in it and, honestly, I think Franklin would agree."

Abigail pressed her lips into a thin line and said nothing, just looked at me with that same tense expression whose origin I'd been unable to pinpoint before but now I thought I understood.

"Abigail, is that what's bothering you? Is that why you keep saying you don't want to think about being married? You're not worried about having sex with Franklin, are you?"

Abigail's eyes darted from my face to Liza's and back nervously.

"Well, wouldn't you be if you were me?" she practically shouted, all her objections and concerns spilling forth like floodwaters breaching a dam. "Do you have any idea how long it has been since I was intimate with a man? Thirty years, that's how long! Ever since Woolley died."

The laughter of a moment before faded into silence as we all realized that, for Abigail, this was no laughing matter. She was truly distressed about this.

"And what about his heart? He keeps joking that once he gets back home and we start sharing a bed that we'll have to keep a defibrillator in the closet in case the throes of passion throw him into cardiac arrest."

Despite my best efforts to keep a neutral expression, I couldn't help but smile a bit at this; the play on words was just so entirely Franklin. For a lawyer, he was actually pretty funny. But, Abigail didn't think so.

"How can he joke about a thing like that? It could actually happen, you know."

"But," Margot interjected, "I'm sure the doctors won't let him . . ." She blushed. "Well . . . you know. I'm sure they won't let him engage in anything that's too strenuous until they're sure he's completely recovered."

"Doctors!" she scoffed. "What do they know?"

"Margot's right," I said. "Franklin has an excellent doctor. You know that, Abbie. You helped hired him. I'm sure he's not going to let Franklin take any unnecessary risks. Really, you just need to trust the doctor's judgment and relax. Put the whole thing out of your mind, at least for now. It'll probably be some weeks until Franklin is well enough for any kind of sexual activity. In the meantime, enjoy each other's company. And celebrate your good fortune! After all, you're one of the luckiest women in the world. And you're married to the one of most wonderful men in the world!"

Abigail let out a breath and nodded slowly. "He is, isn't he. The most wonderful man in the world. It's just that . . . well . . . I'm worried that he'll be disappointed."

"He won't be," Ivy said. "He'll understand that the two of you will have to wait until he's fully recovered."

"No, it's not that . . . Franklin is patient. That's not my concern," she said softly. Her eyes were downcast and for the first time since I'd known her, she sounded vulnerable. "I'm just afraid he'll be disappointed in . . . well, you know . . . in *me.*"

Liza made an impatient clicking sound with her tongue. "Disappointed in you? Are you kidding me? Franklin Spaulding has been in love with you for decades! I knew it within about fifteen seconds of meeting him just from the way he talked about you. And have you seen what happens when you walk in a room? His whole face lights up. Franklin is yours, heart and soul. There is no way on earth he could be disappointed in you. No way."

Abigail still wasn't convinced. "That's easy to say, but men pin huge expectations on sex. Woolley certainly did. I disappointed him on plenty of occasions and he had no qualms about telling me so. At first things seemed to go well enough, but after a few months . . . I don't know exactly what he expected of me but, knowing Woolley, I'm sure he felt he'd paid a high enough price for me that I should have fulfilled his every fantasy. Well, I didn't. I couldn't. I'm not sure anyone could have. I tried my best to please him, but . . ."

Abigail picked up her champagne glass and shrugged her shoulders nonchalantly before taking a sip, as if it was all water under the bridge. I wasn't convinced. Even after all these years, the memory of her husband's dissatisfaction still stung. No wonder the prospect of intimacy with Franklin had her so tied up in knots.

"People make sex into such a big deal," she continued blandly. "Personally, I've never quite understood why. At the end of the day, its just biology, a basic physical urge designed to ensure the continuation of the species. Nothing more."

Ivy nodded her wholehearted agreement to this, but I couldn't let Abigail's assertion go unchallenged.

"Oh, come on, Abigail!" I laughed and took another sip of champagne. "You make sex sound about as appealing as eating a ham sandwich and far less romantic. Biology my eye! You know there's more to it than that, much more. It's an important part of how couples connect and find emotional intimacy. At least . . . it is when you're in love."

I stopped, realizing I should have been a little less mocking in my tone. I looked into the bottom of my glass and chose my words more carefully. "Is it possible that perhaps your first husband's dissatisfaction with your sex life had more to do with what you weren't *feeling* than what you weren't *doing*? You say that he knew you didn't love him and accepted that, but I can't quite buy that."

Abigail started to interrupt, but I wouldn't let her.

"I'm not saying it didn't happen the way you say it did, I'm just suggesting that he wasn't entirely honest—either with you, or himself. If all he wanted was sex with a beautiful woman, I'm sure a man as rich as Woolley Wynne could have easily attracted scores of women who would have been happy to accommodate him. It doesn't matter what he said; in his heart, Woolley wanted your love. Possibly he thought that once you were married, you'd learn to love him, but it didn't happen. I know you tried your best to make him happy, Abigail. I don't doubt that you were attentive, charming, beautiful, entertaining and a delightful companion. But when you were in the bedroom, he must have known he'd bought your body, but not your heart. There are some things you just can't fake. Love is one of them.

"So, yes, I can easily imagine that Woolley was disappointed because all his wealth couldn't buy what he was really after—your love. He took his disappointment out on you, but that's not going to happen this time, Abigail." From my spot on the end of the sofa I leaned forward and took my friend's hand. "You love Franklin."

"I do," she admitted grudgingly. "Don't get me wrong; I'm still mad about this wedding, but I'll get over it. Because I do love Franklin, very much indeed."

I smiled. "Then you don't have a thing to worry about. You don't need to do anything or be anything other than what you are—a woman in love. That's the only thing Franklin wants from you. You know I'm right because, that's all you want from Franklin, isn't it?"

A tight little smile bowed Abigail's lips as she nodded in agreement.

"In that case, you can relax. Everything will be fine—far better than fine. You'll see. When you and Franklin make love for the first time, whether it's next week or next year, it's going to be a beautiful, intimate, memorable experience—for both of you. Trust me," I said with a smile, "by the next morning you're going to wonder why you didn't marry Franklin years ago."

"I hope you're right, Evelyn but . . . I don't know. It's been so long. I'm not even sure I remember how it all works."

"It'll come back to you. Trust me."

"And then there's this," she said, picking up the white lace negligee from where it had been resting on her lap, pinching it between her thumb and forefinger as if it might bite. "Put me in a nice St. John's suit and a good pair of shoes and I look, if not beautiful, at least well-groomed."

"At my age," she said examining the satin confection with doubtful eyes, "I won't even wear a sleeveless top. If I don't think it's fair to inflict the sight of my aging upper arms on others, why would I want to subject poor Franklin to the sight of my sagging flesh? It might be enough to bring on a second heart attack."

She looked at Liza in mocking reproach. "And if it does, I'll know exactly who to blame."

Everyone chuckled, not so much in response to Abigail's humor but because the moment had passed. Abigail was still feeling anxious about her first tryst with her groom, but it was the kind of anxiety common to any bride: part nerves, part anticipation. She was going to be all right.

"Just look at this thing!" She clucked and held the negligee up high so everyone could see. "That satin is going to cling to every bump and bulge. Liza, what in heaven's name made you pick this? Did you get a gift receipt? Is it too late to exchange it? Maybe we could find something more appropriate, something in a nice, heavy flannel."

"Not a chance," Liza said with a grin. "This particular lingerie store has a strict 'no return, no exchange' policy."

"Well then," Abigail said as she folded the negligee carefully and put it back in the box, "looks like we're stuck. I guess I'll just have to go through with it."

"Guess so," Liza said and then leaned down to give her aunt a kiss.

27

Evelyn Dixon

"Now this is more like it," Charlie said as he snuggled closer to me in the booth. He picked up a golden brown shrimp tempura by the skewer, dragged it through the ginger sauce that Maurice had drizzled artistically around the edge of the plate, fed half of it to me, and finished off the rest himself. It was delicious.

"Look at us," he said, amazed. "We're having a real date, the way people do!"

"Not quite. We're having a real date the way restaurant owners do, hiding out in the darkest corner of the dining room, hoping that nothing goes wrong in the kitchen, or at the hostess station, and that none of the customers spot you and come over to complain that the meat was overcooked, or the portions too small, or the bill too big."

"You're a cynical woman, do you know that? My mother and sisters are just the same. Are you sure you're not Irish?" He picked up the wine bottle and topped up my glass before refilling his own.

"You know it's true," I said, laughing. "I'll bet you five dollars that within the next twenty minutes—no, make it fifteen—somebody, either an employee or a customer, is going to come looking for you."

"Five dollars? It's a deal. But I'm telling you right now, you're going to lose. I have given strict instructions to the kitchen that if they bother me about anything less monumental than a flood, famine, or fire—and I made it clear that in the case of fire, it'd better be a big one, two alarm at least, none of your little grease flare-ups—I'll sack the lot of them. And I told Matt, that new waiter who I promoted to maître d' for the evening so Gina could have a night off, that if there are any problems with reservations he is to solve them and that should he spy any irate customers approaching out table he is to intercept them. Failure to do so will mean that his first night as maître d' is also his last. I explained it very clearly. Trust me, Evelyn, no one is going to bother us tonight."

"You feel pretty sure of that, do you?"

"I do."

I sighed heavily. I'd tried to warn him, but if he insisted on taking sucker bets there was nothing I could do about it. "All right then. Let's see the color of your money."

I reached into my handbag, pulled out a five dollar bill, and laid it on the tablecloth. Charlie dug out his fiver and laid it next to mine.

"Let me see your watch."

He held out his arm and pulled up his shirt cuff. I squinted to see the dial in the dim candlelight.

"The current time is nine fourteen. If no one comes to bother you before nine twenty-nine, then you win, but if they do, the kitty goes to me. Agreed?"

"Agreed."

"In the meantime," I said taking another shrimp off the plate, this time feeding it to Charlie, "let's relax and enjoy ourselves because you know something, Charlie? I'm really having a lovely time."

"Me too."

At nine seventeen, the waitress brought our salads to the table along with as a two-and-a-half-foot-tall piece of carved black wood that looked like a piece of fancy stair railing that turned out to be Charlie's new pepper grinder. He took great delight in showing me how it worked. Charlie loves new kitchen gadgets the way I love new sewing notions.

A nine twenty-one, there was a tremendous flash of lightning outside, followed by a boom and a flickering of the lights inside the restaurant. A few diners gasped, then laughed at their startled response to the thunderstorm, after which everyone continued eating, drinking, and talking.

At nine twenty-four, Gina ran in the front door. Her eyes were wild and her hair was dripping wet. She stood near the maître d' station, squinting as she scanned the restaurant looking for a particular face.

I clapped my hand over the two five dollar bills and pulled them toward me. "Too bad. Another five minutes and they'd have been all yours."

Charlie groaned and raised his hand. "Over here, Gina."

Gina turned toward the sound of his voice and scurried to our table. "There you are! I've been looking all over town for you!"

"Why?" Charlie said. "Where else would I be?"

Gina shook her head, making drops of water fly through the air. "Not you, Charlie. I was looking for Evelyn."

"Evelyn?" Charlie clapped his hand over mine and smirked. "Not so fast there, Jimmy the Greek. The bet was that someone would come looking for me, not you. I'll thank you to leave the kitty on the table."

I let go of the money. "What is it, Gina?"

She pulled a soggy newspaper out from under her jacket and thrust it to me. "I was picking up some milk at the mini-mart and there was a guy delivering the newest edition of the *Herald*. Have you seen it?"

I took the paper and scanned the page, wondering what in the world could be written on the editorial page that would make Gina come out in the middle of a thunderstorm to find me. And then I saw it.

> *To the Editor:*
> *Twenty-six years ago, I came to visit New Bern on a day trip, fell in love with it, and decided to make it my home.*

Beverly Hills, California, is far from New Bern, Connecticut, in so many ways but, like so many others who have relocated to New Bern from big cities, I realized that the culture, history, tradition, and values of this little village were what made it special. Knowing this to be true, I set about adjusting myself to New Bern rather than demanding that New Bern adapt itself to me, embracing its history, respecting its traditions, and (especially as a newcomer) learning from the experience of our town's lifelong residents.

Would that every newcomer to our village adopted this philosophy.

Evelyn Dixon, owner of Cobbled Court Quilts, moved to New Bern from Texas just three years ago. In typical New Bern fashion, always eager to embrace new members of our community, always willing to provide assistance and advice to local business owners, our village has opened its arms to Ms. Dixon, showing support for her and for Cobbled Court Quilts, helping it grow from a risky venture that many felt was doomed to failure into a thriving local business. One would suppose that Ms. Dixon would be grateful for our support but, sadly, this is not the case.

In just a few weeks, Cobbled Court Quilts will host a live broadcast of the popular cable television show, Quintessential Quilting. This program, which will be seen by viewers all across the country, could be an outstanding opportunity for the village of New Bern, a chance to tell the world that our community is a wonderful place to shop, take a vacation, or locate a new business. But, because Ms. Dixon seems determined to let the spotlight shine on herself alone rather than serve as a booster for the community that embraced her in her hour of need, that will not happen.

Many in our town have offered to help Ms. Dixon turn this broadcast into an event that could benefit us all, but she has refused all offers. She seems determined to go it alone, cutting New Bern out of the picture entirely, even to the point of failing to return the phone calls of reporters asking for interviews about the broadcast and refusing to let locals, including of many her own best customers, have tickets for the broadcast, preferring to limit the audience to a small number of her personal friends and cohorts.

My question to the citizens of New Bern is this: is this the sort of person or business we should be lending our support to?

Respectfully,
Dale Barrows

I was so astonished by what I'd read that I was literally struck dumb. For a moment I couldn't do anything but sit with my hand over my mouth. Charlie, on the other hand, had less trouble finding his voice.

"That pompous, sneaky, lying . . . ! I'm going to kill him! Do you hear me? I am going to hunt him down and kick his pompous, sneaky, lying carcass from here back to Beverly Hills!"

"I can't believe it," I whispered hoarsely. "I can't believe he'd write something so vindictive and then actually get it published in the paper."

Gina looked pained. "I'm sorry, Evelyn. Maybe I shouldn't have told you, but I figured you'd find out sooner or later."

"No. It's okay, Gina. You did the right thing. By ten o'clock tomorrow morning, half the town will have read this and the other half will want to. That means I've got to figure out what I'm going to do tonight." I looked at Charlie. "What *am* I going to do?"

His face was red as a poker that's been left in the fire. "*You're* not going to do anything! I told you. *I'm* going to hunt him down and kick him into next week!"

"Charlie, be serious. You can't do that."

"Oh, can't I? Watch me." In one infuriated motion, he pushed away his salad, slid from the booth, and leapt to his feet.

"Gina, you stay here with Evelyn and keep an eye on the restaurant. I'm going to go out and find that sniveling, putrid excuse for a man who was belched up from the bowels of Beverly Hills and beat him senseless. And then . . ."

"Charlie, sit down. Be reasonable. I'm touched that you want to defend my honor and all, but you can't just go out looking for Dale Barrows and challenge him to a duel."

"Well," said Gina, looking toward the front of the restaurant, "if he does, he won't have to look very long."

Sure enough, Dale Barrows, Porter Moss, and Lydia Moss came through the door, laughing and shaking the rain off their coats.

"Charlie, don't." I leaned out to grab his arm but I was too late. With an expression as roiling as the storm outside, he grabbed the long black pepper mill from off our table and, brandishing it like a club, strode toward the maître d' station where Dale Barrows and company were talking to Matt.

"Ah! The innkeeper himself!" Barrows boomed. "Just the man I wanted to see. This young fellow tells me that the kitchen closed at 9:30, but I've assured him that, for frequent customers like ourselves, Maurice won't mind staying a few minutes longer. We can order right away, can't we, gang?" He looked at the Mosses, who nodded.

Charlie wasted no words.

"Get out! Get out, the lot of you, and don't come back!"

Porter Moss smiled and took a step forward, holding his palms out in a conciliatory gesture. "Hey, Charlie. Come on now. Surely you can keep the kitchen open an extra five minutes, can't you? What's the big deal? After all, we're old friends. You voted for me in the last election."

"A decision I have lived to regret." Charlie gripped the pepper mill so tightly his knuckles went white.

I decided I'd better get up there before he did something we'd both regret later. There are certain things it is never wise to do; frying bacon in the nude is one, clubbing an elected official with a pepper mill in front of a restaurant filled with witnesses is another. I came up and stood next to Charlie, gently pressing my hand on his arm so he'd drop it to his side.

"Hello, Porter," I said and before acknowledging the others. "Lydia. Dale. How are you? Charlie and I were just sitting here reading tomorrow's paper." Unblinking, I turned my gaze on Dale and was gratified to see him blush. At least he had some sense of shame, though I could tell from the way he jutted his chin out that he wasn't planning on apologizing.

"Hello, Evelyn. I take it you read my letter to the editor?"

"I did."

"Well, I'm sorry if it offends you but . . ."

"No, you're not," I said. "But you should be."

Lydia gave Porter a nudge in the ribs. He stepped forward. "I saw that letter, Evelyn and, for what it's worth, I thought it was out of line. Dale has some gripes with you, but he shouldn't have sent that in and I told him so."

I believed him. Porter wasn't necessarily somebody I wanted to make my new best friend, but he was okay and he worked hard at a fairly thankless job. "Thank you, Porter."

He cleared his throat. "Maybe we should all sit down and talk this thing out."

Charlie jumped in before I could respond. "Not tonight, you're not! And not in my restaurant! Out!"

Porter gave Lydia a sidelong glance and tilted his head toward the door. She took the hint and left. Porter was right behind her. "Good night, Charlie. We'll come back another time."

Dale spun around to watch the Mosses' retreat. "Wait a minute! Come back here! We're not putting up with this! We should demand to be seated and served!" But when Porter ignored him, he turned back to Charlie and stuck his chin out so far that you could have used it to open cans.

"This is a free country with a free press," he declared. "And I've got a right to express my opinion."

"That may be," Charlie said, "but this is a privately held restaurant and as you were told before, the kitchen is closed. And even if it weren't, it sure as hell would be to the likes of you. Now get out!"

Charlie raised the pepper mill, stabbed it into Dale's chest like a swordsman preparing to run his enemy through, and forced the sputtering Barrows to back out the door into the rainy street and then clicked the deadbolt into the lock position with a flourish.

The restaurant had been silent as the diners watched the drama unfold, but now one of the regulars quipped, "Gee, Charlie, I was going to ask to see the dessert menu but now I'm having second thoughts. Too risky."

A round of tentative laughter rippled through the dining room

Charlie pasted a grin on his face and turned toward his customers, "Well, Jim, if you'd been adding extra notches to your belts the way I have lately, I wouldn't recommend it. However, you seem fit enough. I think you can chance it."

"All right, Charlie. But let me ask you something first; can I get mine without pepper?"

Tensions eased and the wave of laughter that followed was full-throated and long.

"Matt!" Charlie shouted jovially. "Bring Mr. Snelling an order of chocolate bread pudding, on the house—no pepper. While you're at it, offer everyone a dessert with my compliments. Enjoy your evening, everyone!"

There was a murmur of appreciation as waiters began bringing dessert menus to the tables. Charlie kept smiling as he took my arm to guide me back to our table in the back corner of the room. When we sat down, his stormy expression returned.

I was just as upset as he was, more so. After all, I was the one whose name and reputation was being disparaged in the local paper, not Charlie's. But nursing grievances wouldn't do me any good and getting sucked into a public squabble with Dale Barrows could only make things worse. It was time for cooler heads to prevail.

I squeezed Charlie's arm affectionately, pried the pepper mill from his grip, and placed it back on the table.

"That was very gallant of you, Charlie," I said breezily. "A little insane, but gallant. I may be the only woman in history who has had her honor defended with a kitchen gadget."

As I'd intended, Charlie was momentarily distracted from thoughts of Dale Barrows. His eyes bulged, incredulous and insulted.

"Gadget? Did you just call my brand new three-hundred-dollar Peugeot pepper mill, crafted from genuine olive wood with a steel mechanism that adjusts from coarse to fine grind, a gadget?"

"Yes, I did. Like I said, it was very gallant of you. Thank heavens Dale backed down or things could have gotten dangerous— blenders at fifty paces." I picked up my fork and resumed eating my abandoned salad.

"This is good, but it needs something." I feigned a moment of deep concentration, then reached for the pepper mill and ground some onto my salad.

"You're trying to make me laugh. It won't work. Just wait until I get my hands on that . . ."

Obviously, he was not going to be humored out of this mood. I cut him off. "Charlie, I appreciate your willingness to commit battery on my part, really, but right now we both need to calm down and think."

"What's there to think about? That slime-ball Barrows is dragging your good name in the dirt!"

"Yes, I'd noticed that," I snapped. "Charlie, calm down and listen to me. Aside from those years in Dallas, I've lived my whole life in small towns and so have you. We know that in small towns, a little squabble like this can blow up into a full-fledged feud if it's not nipped in the bud." I pushed the salad plate away, my appetite spoiled, and rested my chin on my hand.

"And the thing is," I mused, "Dale may not be entirely wrong."

"Are you kidding? How can you say that?"

I sighed heavily, a bit weary of Charlie's indignation on my be-half. "Look, his methods were wrong, no question about that. Not to mention underhanded, but I shouldn't have been so quick to shun his ideas and offers to help. And if I wasn't feeling so over-whelmed by everything, the broadcast, this huge surge in business, Ivy's divorce, and Franklin's heart attack, I might have realized that sooner.

"That doesn't mean I have to let Dale and Porter turn this into some kind of three-ring circus, but he has a point. This is a big deal—especially in a town this size. Naturally, people want to be part of it. If I don't figure out some way to include them, they're going to resent me for it. I'll be persona non grata in every home and busi-ness in town."

"Not at the Grill, you won't," Charlie declared righteously.

"Thank you, my love, but don't you see? If this thing goes any further, it'll hurt you and the Grill, too. That's the blessing and curse of living in a small town; nobody is anonymous. Everyone knows everyone's business and, when there's a controversy, everyone takes sides. Everybody knows you and I are a couple. A boycott of Cob-bled Court Quilts could easily spread to the Grill and damage both businesses."

Charlie grunted, a grudging admission that I might be right.

"More importantly, it could end up hurting the town. I don't want to be responsible for that. No matter what Dale Barrows says, I love New Bern as much as anybody. This is my home. If eating a little crow is the price I have to pay for living in peace with my neighbors, so be it."

I got up from the table and kissed Charlie on the top of the head. "Thanks for dinner."

"What are you going to do?"

"What I should have done from the beginning. I'm going to call Mary Dell."

❧ 28 ❧

Evelyn Dixon

"The front page? Really?" Mary Dell drawled.

I tucked the telephone receiver in tighter under my ear so I could hold that morning's edition of the *New Bern Herald* in both hands. "Yup, above the fold, no less. The headline says QUILT PINK DAY: NEW BERN TRADITION HITS TV AIRWAVES. There's a picture of Howard and your lovely self standing by a sewing machine . . ."

"That's the publicity photo. Sandy sent one to the reporter."

"And then there's a picture of Dale Barrows, Porter Moss, and me with a caption saying, 'Co-chairs for the upcoming Quilt Pink Day to benefit breast cancer research discuss plans for this year's celebration and live cable television broadcast.' There's a big pink quilt in the background and we're all looking at the clipboard I'm holding and grinning like the best of friends. Dale even has his arm draped over my shoulder."

"Honey, you may have overdone it. What does the article say?"

"It starts out telling all about how I'd decided to host our first Quilt Pink event soon after opening the shop only to be diagnosed with breast cancer myself the day before the event. Then it talks about you, how we were friends in Texas before you became a great big, huge, glamorous television star," I teased.

"Oh, hush up with all that. Did Barrows apologize like he said he would?"

"More or less. Hold on a second." I scanned the page searching for Dale's quote.

"Here it is. 'After some initial misunderstanding regarding her plans for Quilt Pink Day, I'm honored and delighted that Evelyn Dixon, Porter Moss, and I are working together. This will be a proud day in New Bern's history; one that will to be instrumental in finding the cure for breast cancer and in raising breast cancer awareness across the country. Of course, I'm happy to lend my talents in support of this worthy cause, but most of the credit has to go to Evelyn. She's a real asset to our community.'"

Mary Dell let out a peal of laughter as deep and booming as brass bells. "Well, what'd I tell you, honey? You want to get people to cooperate, just give 'em a title and put their picture in the paper."

"Well, I think that conference call you organized might have helped a little bit, don't you? You charmed the pants off old Porter and Dale."

"There's a mental image I could sure live without, 'specially right after breakfast."

"Really, they were absolutely starstruck. After you hung up, they couldn't stop talking about you."

"Don't be silly," she puffed. "Dale worked in Hollywood all through the seventies and eighties. He's not impressed by any little old D-list celebrity cable quilt show host. That man knows some *real* stars and has directed plenty of them, even if most of his movies were lousy."

"Maybe, but he still likes you an awful lot."

"And I like him. Once you two kissed and made up and he got that chip off his shoulder, he turned out to be all right. You know, I don't think he really is a bad director; he just got handed bad scripts to work with. The best director on earth couldn't have turned *Disco Drive-In* into Oscar material. He'll do a great job shooting the montage."

From the first, Mary Dell and Sandy, her producer, had planned on including a pre-filmed montage about New Bern as part of the broadcast. It would include a quick video tour of the town, a short interview with me to explain about my battle with breast cancer and Cobbled Court's first Quilt Pink Day, plus a few waves and very short greetings from people around town, including all the state and local dignitaries who had been nagging me for tickets to the show. In one fell swoop, Mary Dell had solved myriad problems, appeasing not only Dale Barrows but also scores of other people I'd inadvertently offended.

"Mary Dell, asking Dale to direct the montage was a stroke of genius."

"That was really Sandy's idea. Saves her and our crew from making another trip up there to film. She was happy to have Dale do it. Don't let those blue jeans and baseball cap fool you. Sandy's society, Baby Girl, made her debut at the Idlewild Ball in 1997, and was crowned Miss Dallas of 1999, a real Texas belle. If she goes more than forty-eight hours without sitting down to a plate of chicken fried steak, she gets the shakes. Not that you could tell to look at her. That girl is thin as a nun's smile. "

Mary Dell laughed and so did I. New Bern is my home for now and forever, but the one thing I do miss about Texas is Mary Dell. She's the original Yellow Rose with all the warmth, humor, enthusiasm, generosity, grit, and growl that marked a true-blue Texan, the finest kind. On top of that, she has a brilliant head for business, and diplomacy. The events of the last few days had made me think she ought to run for president. Seriously.

When our conference call began, Dale, Porter, and I were speaking, but barely. Mary Dell's idea of getting everyone together seemed a good one, but that didn't mean I was happy about it. I imagine Dale felt the same way. But when Mary Dell and Sandy came on the line everything changed. Mary Dell told a few jokes, unruffled a few feathers, and within ten minutes had us all brainstorming and working together as a team.

Besides handing off the montage filming to Dale, a idea that solved a number of problems, she had also gotten rid of my publicity headaches by getting Porter to handle calls from reporters and giving interviews, something I had no time for or interest in but which Porter loved. Sandy liked his idea of setting up a giant screen on the Green so people could see the show and having a barbeque after and built on it, suggesting they bring an additional camera crew and station them on the Green so they could do cutaway shots from time to time.

"It'll give the show some color, you know, a nice home-town feel as the cameras scan over the crowds. Everyone will feel like they're part of the show."

"Good idea!" Mary Dell piped in and then added, in that praline sweet voice of hers, "And Porter, darlin', would you mind if we put a microphone on you and had you serve as a kind of emcee for that part? Like those cheery weathermen they have on the network morning shows, you know what I'm talking about. I'll ask you how it's going out there and you'll talk about what an exciting day it is and how the wonderful citizens of New Bern have come out in full force to support Quilt Pink Day, then you'll tell everybody to wave and the cameras will scan the crowd. I know it's a terrible imposition, but I think you'd be perfect for the job. Would you mind?"

He didn't mind at all. And, once again, Mary Dell had killed a number of birds with one stone. She'd figured out a way to appease everyone who wanted to be part of the broadcast, boosted Porter's ego, and, most importantly, gotten him out of my quilt shop and my hair during the broadcast. Genius.

After I'd thrown out the idea of distributing the few tickets we had for quilters inside the shop via raffle, Mary Dell suggested we set up a satellite studio in the high school gym. That way, even though we could only fit thirty quilters in the shop, anyone who wanted to could still make a quilt block. She suggested we put video monitors in the gym and station a remote camera crew there as well, just like we had on the Green, then sweetly asked if Dale would mind serving as the emcee there, reporting on the quilterss' progress and chatting with Mary Dell during the cutaway shots to the gym.

And what do you know? Turned out Dale didn't mind, either.

"And Dale, darlin', do you have any thoughts about how ya'll could get a little publicity from the local paper there? Just so they know you three are the lead dogs on this hunt and all working together? I understand you know the editor."

Dale was sitting next to me at the conference table in Porter's office. I looked at him out of the corner of my eye.

"Umm . . . well . . . yes. I think so. I'll call the editor and see what I can do."

"Wonderful! I knew you were the man for the job! I'm just so excited that you're part of this. Do you know I've seen every single one of your pictures twice?"

From there on out, Dale was putty in her hands. And when I scolded Mary Dell later for telling lies, she assured me that what she'd said was absolutely true. Her ex-husband, Donny, had been a huge fan of Barrow's films and dragged her to see every one of them at least two times. "That may help explain why Donny is my ex-husband, but no need to say that to Dale, is there?"

No indeed. It was all to the good. Another ego salved. Another problem solved. And best of all, I could see that by cooperating, each working to our strengths, we really would make the show and the whole Quilt Pink Day better, a real community event.

Just when I thought it was as good as it could get, Mary Dell plopped a big red cherry on the cake of my day. To make sure none of the quilters in the satellite studio felt left out, Mary Dell said she and Howard wanted to give copies of their most recent book, *The Quintessential Quilter,* a companion guide for the show, to everyone who stitched a Quilt Pink block that day. Furthermore, after the broadcast wrapped up, they would go to the gym to meet the quilters and sign their books.

I was sure even my most disgruntled customers, including Mavis Plimpton, would be satisfied by this solution. Too, we'd have more Quilt Pink blocks than ever before, which would let us make more quilts, and raise more money to find a cure for breast cancer. It was a great plan. My only concern was that my dear, generous friend might be biting off more than she could chew.

"Mary Dell, are you sure?" I asked. "Quilters are really excited about this. There could be three or four hundred of them at the gym.

That many books could run into some real money. Not to mention how much time it will take to sign them."

"Oh, don't worry about that. I bet the cable network will donate the books and if they won't? Well, it's all for a good cause. And Howard and I don't mind spending time with the folks. We love meetin' new people. You know that."

And that was that. In the course of a ninety-minute conference call, Mary Dell had used her charm and leadership to get everyone to work off the same page and find a solution to every problem and conflict that, up until then, had seemed unsolvable. Amazing. I couldn't help but wonder what would happen if we put her in a room with the leaders of the Middle East.

"Mary Dell, you're the best. Have I told you that lately?"

"I believe so but I don't mind hearing it again. I feel the same way about you, Baby Girl. Oh! I almost forgot! You know, we go on hiatus after we finish filming with you. Howard and I were thinking of taking a week's vacation, maybe see that fall foliage you keep going on about. Know of a good hotel we could stay in?"

"I do. Twenty-eight Marsh Lane—my guest room. Howard will have to sleep on the rollaway, but the price is right, free. And breakfast is included."

"I was hoping you'd say that. Sure you don't mind? You might get sick of us after a whole week."

"Not a chance."

"Good! I can't wait! I love doing the show, but I am *so* ready for a vacation. I just want to sit down with you and quilt and yak 'til we run out of things to say and just sit there staring at each other."

"That might take more than a week."

"Hope so. I can't wait. The way you talk about them, I feel like I know everybody in New Bern already, but it'll be nice to spend more time with your friends. And speaking of that, how is Franklin feeling? And Abigail? Has she calmed down about the wedding?"

"Oh, yes. Franklin is out of the hospital and Abigail has moved into his place, at least for now. Everything is on one floor, so that's a little easier for Franklin. I don't think they've figured out whose house they're going to live in yet."

"Very interesting," Mary Dell said slowly. "So tell me, have they done it yet?"

"Mary Dell!" I made a scolding noise with my tongue.

"Well," she said innocently, "inquiring minds want to know. Personally, I think a good roll in the hay would do Abigail a world of good. Help loosen her up some."

I laughed, thinking Mary Dell might be right about that, though I didn't say so. "I imagine that's a still a good way off. Franklin's only been out of the hospital for a couple of weeks. But, they really seem happy together."

"That's sweet. Good for them. And what about Ivy? How's it going with the divorce?"

I sighed, wishing the news were better. "They just got a court date, first of September. That's good because usually it takes a lot longer but, on the other hand, I'm worried about the outcome. Arnie and Margot have been burning the midnight oil trying to build a case, but I don't know . . . Arnie is sure Hodge is hiding something. He just can't believe the nursing home has made so little money, but so far Hodge's records back up his claims. According to the accountants, Hodge Edelman is flat broke. In a way, that helps. It helps even the financial playing field for Ivy. He'll have a harder time arguing that he'll be a better provider for the kids this way, though he does have a better earning history. But it's the doctor's accusation that Ivy was a drug abuser that's really damaging. Plus, he's going to swear that he saw no signs of physical abuse during the time Ivy was his patient. We know he's lying, but unless we can find better proof, it really comes down to Ivy's word against his."

"And you think that judge will find the doctor more convincing?"

"Well, can you blame him? I would, if I didn't know Ivy. So, in spite of everything we've tried, Ivy may lose her kids to that monster. And even if she doesn't, it's possible she won't get a dime's worth of support from Hodge to help raise them. And get this. He's claiming that she should pay alimony to him! He says he's just about bankrupt and wants to garnish part of her wages from the shop. Can you believe this guy? What gall!"

"As my old granny used to say, 'there's some men on God's good earth that was just born to be shot.' Sounds like old Hodge is one of them." Mary Dell clucked her tongue sympathetically. "Well, you tell Ivy I said hello. I sure feel bad about all this. None of this would have happened if we hadn't aired that video with her in it."

"Oh, Mary Dell, don't say that. This isn't your fault. It had to happen sooner or later. Ivy couldn't go on hiding forever; she knows that. Just the other day she told me what a relief it is to get up in the morning and know she's not going to have to lie about anything. One way or another, she'll get through this. She's tougher than she looks. Did I tell you? I gave her a promotion."

"Did you? That was sweet of you."

"Sweet, nothing. She deserved it. She keeps that order department running like clockwork. I don't know what I'd do without her and that's the truth."

"She sounds like a great little gal. I hope everything works out for her. Tell her I'm praying for her, will you?"

"I will."

❧ 29 ❧

Ivy Peterman

While I was in the kitchen getting her a glass of water, the social worker dragged her finger across the table looking for dust. She didn't find any; I've always been a good housekeeper, but it would take more than a tidy family room to win her over.

Because Hodge and I are both suing for custody of the kids, we each have to undergo a court ordered home study by a social worker. They look at each parent's living situation—housing, employment, schools—and make recommendations as to which home would be better for the children. I could tell she wasn't too impressed with our apartment, especially when she found out I'd have to find another place to live soon.

She smiled woodenly as I handed her the glass and sat down across from her. "Thank you. Now, tell me about your job. You work in retail?" The look on her face said that this was not a strike in my favor, that in her mind working in retail meant a dead end and minimum wage.

I didn't answer her directly, opting instead to hand her one of my brand new business cards, the ones Evelyn had surprised me with when she told me I'd been promoted.

IVY PETERMAN
COBBLED COURT QUILT SHOP
MANAGER
ORDER FULFILLMENT DEPARTMENT

For the first time since coming into my home, the social worker smiled—genuinely. "Cobbled Court Quilts? Really? I've heard of them. That's the shop they keep talking about on television, isn't it?"

"Yes," I said. "When I started there we only had four full-time employees for the whole shop. Now there's more than that just in my department."

I could feel heat rising to my cheeks. It felt uncomfortable blowing my own horn but I knew Hodge would have no similar qualms so I added, "And we're adding new employees all the time. By this time next year we could double in size."

It wasn't exactly a lie. That qualifying "could" made all the difference. By next year Cobbled Court Quilts could double in size. Or Hodge could suddenly decide he was wrong and had been for a long time, give up his custody fight, and write me a check for one hundred thousand dollars by way of apology. Or George Clooney could wander in the shop one day and propose marriage. Anything could happen.

"Really?" she said and scribbled down a note on her clipboard. "So would you say you have good opportunities for advancement?"

"Oh, yes. Absolutely." I said and nodded gravely, then threw in a phrase I'd heard Hodge use one day when he was talking to a potential investor. "This company has tremendous upside growth potential."

I felt like an idiot saying that, like a little girl walking around in her mother's high heels playing at being grown-up. But I guess she bought it because she smiled when I said it and wrote down a bunch more notes on her clipboard. No matter how foolish I felt, seeing the social worker's approving nod made it worth it. That nod could be the difference between keeping or losing my children.

Three weeks from today, whether I'm ready or not, I'll be in a courtroom, sitting at a table next to my attorney, trying to keep custody of my kids. Hodge will be sitting at another table with his attorney trying to take them from me. Three weeks from today. Ready or not. Right now, we're not.

Arnie keeps telling me not to worry, that he's still going to find that elusive loose thread, but it hasn't happened yet. As the court date gets closer, I can tell he's wondering if he ever will. Even Margot's optimism is beginning to flag. She doesn't say so, of course, but I can see it in her eyes.

I'm scared.

Some days it's everything I can do to keep myself from grabbing my kids and running, but it's too late for that. Before, I was able to melt into the background without anyone taking much notice. In fact, I've learned that Hodge never even reported my disappearance to the police. Isn't that something? There I was, shuffling my kids from one town to the next, sleeping in cars, always afraid that the law was after me, and Hodge never even so much as filed a missing persons report. Here he is, fighting me tooth and nail for custody, but he doesn't care about the kids. He never did. He's only doing this as a way to try to punish and control me. Even so, it's hard to understand why he didn't report me to the police. Did he just figure he had me so well-trained that I'd come crawling back to him eventually? That sounds like Hodge. Smug.

Once he did find me, he tried to have me charged with kidnapping but since he'd never filed a report, he couldn't make it stick. Lucky for me. But I wouldn't be that lucky if I disappeared a second time.

And then there's Bethany. After Margot talked me out of running, Bethany wouldn't get out of bed the next day. I mean, she absolutely refused to leave her room! I didn't know what to think. When I told her to get up and get ready to for school she screamed at me! She said she wasn't getting in that car no matter what I did. I was really mad, not to mention late for work, so I went in there and tried to make her get dressed but she fought like a tiger. Poor Bobby stood in the corner with his thumb in his mouth, clutching his blankie and watching me trying to wrestle his sister out of bed.

Finally, I gave up. I told Bobby that if Bethany wouldn't get out of bed, then I guessed none of us should. I said, "Shove over, peanut. Come on, Bobby, you, too." And we huddled under the covers together, crowded like sardines into Bethany's little bed.

Bethany thought it was funny that I was in bed with all my clothes on. We had a tickle fight under the quilts, all three of us. Once things calmed down we started talking. Bethany told me that she didn't want to get in the car because she was afraid if she did I'd take her away from New Bern and she'd never see her friends, or her school, or Abigail, Margot, or Evelyn again.

I promised her, then and there, that I wouldn't do that. I told her that New Bern was our home and she never had to leave. I promised.

Dear God, I hope I wasn't lying.

I won't run away. I can't because I promised Bethany, but that's just me. I don't have any control over Hodge and what he's going to do. And, as the days tick down to the divorce hearing, I feel less and less in control. I don't care about the money. Whatever there is or isn't, Hodge can have. The only thing that matters to me is my kids, which is why Hodge is so determined to keep me from getting them.

Evelyn, and Margot, and Abigail, and Arnie, and all these wonderful, good-hearted people in this picture perfect town have assured me that, in the end, good will triumph over evil, lies will be found out, and the truth will set me free. And maybe, if you grow up in a place like this, it does. But I was born a million miles from here. I'm from the places that Norman Rockwell never wanted to paint. And I know that sometimes the bad guys win.

I've started praying. I can't say that I have much faith that my prayers are being heard, let alone answered. But Margot is always talking about what can happen if you have faith the size of a mustard seed—in other words, little, puny, pinpoint tiny faith. Well, that's a pretty good description of mine, so I pray. Why not? It's all I've got left.

Work is a great distraction for me. When I'm at the shop I'm too busy to think about anything except cutting fabric, assembling orders, and getting them packaged and mailed. I like being busy.

And the closer we get to the big Quilt Pink broadcast, the busier we get. There are now five people working in order fulfillment: me, two of my friends from the Stanton Center, Karen and Jeni, plus two local teachers, Roseanne and Bryan. They were looking for work over the summer, so Evelyn hired them. She thinks that, after the broadcast, business might slow down, so hiring teachers makes sense. If it does, she won't have to lay anybody off after the show, because Roseanne and Bryan will go back to their old jobs. If we're still busy, she won't have any trouble finding replacements. Evelyn is a great boss.

When Evelyn told me that I was being promoted to department manager, I had to excuse myself to go to the bathroom. I didn't want her to see me cry. I know it's not that big a deal, but this is the first time in my life that I've ever really succeeded at anything. I felt the way I used to feel when I was in grade school and the teacher would put a gold star sticker on the top of my spelling test if I scored one hundred—like I wanted to take that star and pin it to my chest where everyone would see it and know that I was good at something.

Evelyn didn't give me a gold star, but I did get a four-hundred-dollar-a-month raise. I sure can use it. Arnie keeps saying that, after the divorce, I'll have plenty of money, maybe even enough to buy a little house, because the judge will order Hodge to pay child support, to sell our assets and give me half.

Yeah. Like that's going to happen. Arnie doesn't know Hodge like I do. There is no way I'm ever going to get a dime from Hodge. He'd die before he'd let that happen. Even when we were together, he made me account for every single penny I spent. I used to tell myself that was because he had such a good head for business and liked to keep control over his accounts, but now I see what he really wanted to control was me. I'm starting to see all the ways Hodge tried to control me. And all the ways I let him.

Anyway, like I said, over Hodge Edelman's dead body will I ever get one red cent of the money. Arnie keeps scratching his head over Hodge's financial disclosures. According to the records, Hodge doesn't have anything; the nursing home is losing money, the entire business is mortgaged up to the eyeballs, and it turns out our house is in foreclosure because Hodge has missed payments. Funny how the first missed payment came in the month he found me. That's Hodge. He's that vindictive. He'd rather lose the house than risk having to give me half the proceeds from it.

I'm not stupid. Neither is Arnie. We know Hodge is lying. He's figured some way to hide the money and cook the books so the losses look legitimate, but we can't prove anything. It's driving Arnie nuts. He told me yesterday that he's hired some kind of special investigator, Annie Fielding, a forensic accountant. That's someone who specializes in figuring out how and where dishonest businesses hide their ill-gotten gains. Arnie was really excited about her, but I don't think she'll find anything. Wherever that money is, I guarantee Hodge has made sure it can't be traced. He's thorough.

So, wherever we live after we leave the Stanton Center, it's going to have to be somewhere we can afford on my salary alone. I haven't actually gone looking for new apartments yet, but I have been reading the "for rent" section of the classifieds. Even with a raise, it's going to be tough to find a two-bedroom place within my budget. Of course, if Hodge gets his way I won't need two bedrooms. If Hodge gets his way, I'll be living alone.

∽ 30 ∽

Ivy Peterman

I keep having this dream.

I'm at home doing something—ironing, or cooking, or watching television; once I was quilting—and the doorbell rings.

The thing that's weird is, I know it's my house but I've never been there before, except in my dreams. There's a big stone fireplace in the living room, and built-in bookshelves under the windows, and a low-beamed ceiling that makes everything seem snug and safe, like a cottage in a Beatrix Potter book, a cozy den for a family of bunnies. The kitchen has blue and yellow tile, distressed white cabinets with glass fronts, and fresh, crisp curtains at the windows.

A pretty kitchen, but I've never seen it before. I guess that's the way things happen in dreams.

It's dark outside, late. I'm surprised to hear the bell because I'm not expecting anyone, but I'm not afraid to open the door, so I leave what I'm doing to answer it. And when I do, it's my dad! He's just standing there and he looks great. I'm so happy to see him. I say, "Dad, what are you doing here?" But he just smiles and doesn't say anything. So I wait.

After a while he gets this look on his face. He's sad. Disappointed. I can tell he wants something but I don't know what. He's looking at me and there are tears in his eyes and then I feel sad, too. Finally, he turns and walks away. It's so dark that he just disappears.

I wish I knew what he wanted.

Could my life be any stranger?

On one hand, things are better than they've ever been. I love my job. I love the people I work with and the feeling that, for the first time in my life, I'm actually good at something. I love my friends and this town. We're safe here.

The kids are happy. We live in a nice apartment with quilts on the bed and crayoned drawings hanging from magnets on the refrigerator door. Other people might think it's boring, but I love the routine and rhythm of our days.

After work, I pick the kids up from day care and they jabber the whole way home. They are allowed to watch one video while I cook dinner. We eat sitting together at the table. After the dishes are done we make popcorn and eat it at the kitchen table while we play Candy Land. Bethany and I let Bobby win. At bedtime I tuck them in with a story and a kiss. Then I go into the living room and pull up a chair next to the round wooden quilting frame Evelyn let me borrow.

The quilt top is finished. The quilt circle will sew on the binding together, but I wanted to do the quilting myself and by hand. The house block I made, the white clapboard cottage with its blue wide-eyed windows and garden of cheerful flowers, marks the center of the quilt. The other four blocks, made by Abigail, Margot, Evelyn, and Liza, stand at each corner like mismatched sentries on a guard, points on a compass, fixed and immovable. I sit in silence, rocking my sewing needle up and down, up and down, up and down in a smooth, even rhythm as steady and comforting as the sound of a beating heart, pausing only occasionally to check my stitches and see how I have progressed, or to rethread the needle and begin again. When it is time for bed, I turn out the lights and stop to linger by the door of my children's bedroom, opening it quietly and peering in at their peaceful, sleeping faces and thinking, "it doesn't get better than this."

And on the other hand, in three weeks all of that, everything I hold dear today, could be taken from me; this life I love could collapse like a column of ash.

Bobby does this thing that cracks me up. Whenever something is going to happen that he doesn't like, say I tell him that it's time to turn off the television and take his bath, he covers his eyes with his hands and yells, "You can't see me! You can't see me!"

He's so cute! He actually believes that if I'm invisible to him, then he's invisible to me. Of course, it doesn't work. No matter how tightly he shuts his eyes or how loudly he yells, "You can't see me!" the TV still gets turned off, the bathtub still gets filled, the clock still strikes eight, and the day ends.

Hiding from your fears doesn't make them disappear.

Bobby doesn't know that yet, but he will. You don't have to be a lot older than four to realize this. Still, sometimes we regress. Like Bethany did on that day she refused to get out of bed. Or like me, clinging to the topmost branches of the tree, hoping the shadow of leaves would conceal me from the world. Or my mother, losing herself in books, booze, and the arms of another man.

I've been thinking about my mother a lot lately—more than I ever did when she was alive. Dreams of my father permeate my nights, but the days belong to my mother. During the final, hushed hour of the day as I sit before the quilting frame, putting my needle steadily through its paces, physically engaged but mentally free to float on the wind of memory, I cannot help but think of her. I never wanted to be like her, swore I never would be, but it hasn't worked out that way.

My mother never volunteered much about her past, but in her own way, in fragments of sentences that trailed off into nothingness, italicized with sighs, and shrugs, and the set of her shoulders, she sketched a smudged outline of her early life for me, hints of her history, clues to a puzzle I didn't care enough to solve, not then. I feel bad about that. Now I wonder if, in her own way, she was trying to connect with me, or perhaps to warn me? I don't know. But I was too wrapped up in myself to notice. In my close little world there was room for me and for Daddy; no others need apply. Yes, I was a child and sometimes that is the way children are, but I wish . . . I wish I had heard her. I wish I had been better.

If I had things might have been different for all of us.

It's too late to change what has been. But is it too late to change what will be? To change myself? Maybe. Maybe not. I'm trying.

Using imagination, experience, and what maturity I have, I try to color in the lines of that smudged outline. I conjure my mother's face, her eyes hollow and longing, her long, thin body, curved in on itself, tucked tight into the sharp right angle of the sofa corner, protected on two sides and with her knees drawn in and up. Or sometimes I see her standing, arms hugging her shoulders, staring out the window with the stagnant, gray streetscape before her and all her dreams behind, wondering how she ended up there, trapped in a life that was, for her, worse than the one she'd thought she was escaping.

She didn't understand, but I do. I think I do.

My mother was born poor and bright. She once told me that she knew how to read by the time she was four and that no one taught her how. She said it plain, a fact with no pride attached, just laid it out like bait, waiting to see if I'd take it and ask the next question. I didn't.

If I had, I imagine she'd have told me the story of the house she grew up in, far and away up a hollow, off a dirt road, miles away from the small cluster of buildings they called "town" where her family carried on what little trade they did, miles more from a library. But she loved to read and when she exhausted the tiny collection of worn volumes at her school, she found a box of used paperback books for sale at the general store in town. She saved her nickels and dimes and quarters to buy them one by one until the woman behind the counter took pity and told her go ahead and take the whole box. She carried the heavy box up the road to a shortcut through the woods, over rocks and under brush, sweating and flushed because it was summer and hot and the best day of her life.

Maybe that's how it happened and maybe not. There is no one left to tell me, but this is how I've pieced it together in my mind.

Some things I know for sure. My mother was poor and brighter than those around her, bright enough to be dissatisfied, bright enough to know there was a world beyond the boundaries set by birth. She was certain that somewhere down the road there was a better life. There had to be. After all, she'd read about it in books, so it must be true.

And maybe, if she'd liked books about girls who have adventures and make their own way, maybe if she'd read about Jo March, or Scarlett O'Hara, or even Stephanie Plum, things might have worked out differently for her. You can find plucky, independent heroines in every genre. Why didn't she? Instead, she gravitated toward the heroine whose every dream and desire was fulfilled by attaching herself to a man who gave her life the storybook ending she didn't know to write for herself, and so that's what she set her mind on—finding the man who would give her the life she wanted.

She left school at fifteen, took a job in the general store, and saved enough money to buy a new dress and a bus ticket to White Sulphur Springs, where she'd heard there was a fancy resort that rich people went to on vacation. She got a job serving bread and rolls in the dining room and smiled sweetly at every eligible-looking man she served, and even some of the ineligible-looking ones, hoping they'd notice her but they never did, not unless they wanted another roll.

But one day, one of them did smile back, my father. If she'd have been there longer maybe she'd have realized that he didn't belong in that place, noticed that the suit he wore was secondhand and his best shoes were worn down at the heel, and realized he couldn't have been paying that bill on his own steam, but she was too inexperienced and too giddy with success to realize. So when he came again the next night, she smiled with her eyes open wide to let him know she was interested, available, and open to anything that was on his mind, anything at all.

That's enough. I have to stop here.

It's hard to think about my own parents like this. There was no love lost between my mother and me, but I wish there had been. It's hard to think of her as being so cheaply had, so conniving. It's even harder to think of the daddy I thought hung the moon for me alone taking advantage of a young woman, even one who was so willing to be taken advantage of. And it is hard to understand that what I considered the best years of my life, living with the daddy I adored in the house that was no better or worse than those of the other families with a man in the mill, was my mother's own private hell.

Why did it have to be like that? If she had only read different books. If she had only had other dreams. If he had only eaten his roll and listened to the voice in his head that told him the girl was too young. If he had only kept his room key in his pocket instead of slipping it into hers. If only she had learned to appreciate what he was instead of resenting what he wasn't. If only he had pulled me off that pedestal he'd placed me on as means of punishing her. If only they could have talked it out. If only he had made me stand on my own two feet. If she could only have loved me.

Then I might have seen where she made her wrong turn, instead of repeating her mistakes. Maybe I'd have learned to rely on myself and had a little faith in my own abilities. Maybe I'd have understood that I even had some abilities to put faith in, instead of waiting for twenty-six years and the gift of a woman named Evelyn to let me in on the secret. Maybe I'd have listened to my instincts, looked harder at Hodge, asked more questions, seen the evidence that was right in front of my face. Then maybe I'd have asked myself that most important question, "Do I love him?" Because I see now that the answer was no.

I didn't want to be like my mother, so cheaply had, so I made him wait a while for what he wanted, telling myself his patience proved his care of me. And when I ceded to him those things he most desired, the things he'd known would be his eventually—my body, my will, my utter dependence upon him—I told myself it was love. But it wasn't. It never was. I didn't love him; I *needed* him. I believed that then.

I don't anymore.

If only one of two hundred different lies had been rejected or recognized, I might have figured that out a long time ago. But there is no end to "if only," unless you decide to end it yourself. I have.

It's hard to think about my parents the way I have been, to delve deeper than the childish, stereotypical roles I'd cast them in—saint and sinner, hero and harlot, villain and victim—and try to look at them with the eyes of a woman instead of a child and to see them for what they were: two flawed, imperfect beings who could have done a million things differently and didn't. Yes, there were reasons and history and circumstances, but in the end they lived the lives they chose for themselves.

It is harder still to look at myself and see that I have done exactly the same stupid, stupid, stupid thing. Hardest of all is to forgive. I do. I have. I think I have.

But, some mornings I wake up and there it is again, like those mushrooms that grow in the damp, dark spots of your lawn. You pull on the stems and throw them away but when you go out the next day, there they are again, resentments like fungus, just as ugly and persistent as that word sounds. I guess this takes a while, but I'm not giving up.

I want to see things—my parents, my past, myself—for what they really are, the truth of it, not the almost version.

People act like little kids sometimes, hiding their eyes and refusing to see. Maybe, if you only do it once in a while, it's okay. But I've made a career of it. Not anymore. I'm ready to grow up. From here on out, whatever happens, good or bad, I'm facing it with my eyes open.

❧ 31 ❧

Evelyn Dixon

Labor Day has come and gone. The tourists have gone home. What a relief.

Don't get me wrong. I like tourists and I depend on them, like every other business owner in New Bern. When they return for the fall foliage season near the end of September I'll be happy to see them again, but it's been a long, crazy summer. I need some time to catch my breath.

This year the tourists will return a week earlier than usual, for Quilt Pink Day. When I went to the monthly meeting of the New Bern Business Association, I was greeted by a round of applause. The innkeepers report that they are one hundred percent booked for that weekend with extensive waiting lists. The restaurant owners, including Charlie, say that their reservation books are full for Friday, Saturday, and Sunday nights. But if anyone deserves to be applauded, it's Mary Dell. After all, if she weren't coming I know we wouldn't be anticipating crowds like this. Still, it's nice that people are so excited.

Now that I'm not trying to carry the load on my own, I'm starting to get excited myself. That is, until I start to think about actually having to get in front of a television camera; then I start to feel sick to my stomach. But I've decided to pull a Scarlett O'Hara on that subject; I'll think about that tomorrow.

The exciting part is that we are going to be able to raise a ton of money to find a cure for breast cancer and that thousands upon thousands of people are going to learn about prevention and early treatment of the disease. We've already filmed the segment with my breast surgeon, Dr. Finney. I only had to be on camera for a second to introduce her, so that wasn't too bad. The rest of the tape is the doctor using a model to show women how to perform a self-exam and encouraging them to try it on themselves, right at that moment, while watching the program.

Dale showed me the edited tape and it gave me goosebumps. With so many thousands of women watching, many of them are going to follow the doctor's advice and a small percentage of them are going to find a lump. That will be a terrifying moment for them, I know. I hate to think about that moment of shock when their tentative fingers find the lump. My eyes tear up as I imagine the mounting panic of a woman who has no connection to me except that she is about to embark on that journey called cancer that no one ever wants to make. I don't know these women nor do I know where their journeys will lead, but for some of them, that show, the sound of Dr. Finney's gentle voice guiding them through the steps of self-examination, may be the lifeline they didn't know they needed. Think about that. This show will save someone's life!

That's the exciting part.

If this helps the cause of commerce in New Bern—great. I'm happy to be of assistance. And I'm very grateful that all this publicity has turned my shop's accounting ink from red to black, and that I'm able to support myself and provide good jobs to more people in New Bern, especially Ivy and the other women from the Stanton Center. But that's not why I decided to risk humiliating myself on national television. I did it for the chance to help save a life.

Somewhere during this insane summer, between the never-ending stream of customers, Ivy's divorce, Charlie's insistence that we find more couple time, Franklin's heart attack, and getting smacked on the editorial page of the *Herald*, I lost sight of that.

Years ago, Charlie asked me what my vision was for Cobbled Court Quilts; why I tried to make my living as a quilt shop owner when there were about two hundred easier, more certain ways to make money? I didn't have to think long before finding my answer. When I took an accidental turn into the alley that led to Cobbled Court and spied the ruin of a building that would eventually house my shop, I envisioned something more than just a place to buy fabric or give sewing classes. I envisioned a community; a place where all kinds of quilters, novice to expert and everyone in between, could join for conversation, companionship, support, self-expression, growth, and healing in whatever measure they needed it.

That was my dream and it's all come true. And when the cameras roll on Saturday at noon, a little over two weeks from now, the Cobbled Court Quilts community will expand beyond even my wildest dreams, reaching out to thousands of people who never have never set foot through our doors and probably never will. Fantastic!

But tonight, Friday night, is about community with a small *c*. Our small circle is coming together to finish a quilt for the one who needs it most right now—Ivy. During this wild ride of a summer, we've missed a few meetings. Things haven't always worked out the way we planned and, as the days wind down to Ivy's court date, we're more and more aware that it could happen again. I keep praying for a miracle. I think we all are, but miracles don't always appear on demand. I suppose that's what makes them miraculous.

So, in the absence of miracles that appear on cue, we do what we can—we come around our friend, flanking her on every side, encouraging her and letting her know through our words, our laughter, our presence, and the gift of a quilt, that no matter what comes, she isn't alone.

We sat facing each other, Ivy and Liza on one long side of the quilt, Margot and Abigail on the two short ends, with me on the other long side, as we prepared to sew the binding on Ivy's quilt.

"It's like a little village!" Margot squealed, then pointed to the green medallion. "Look at that! Ivy's house even has a little appliquéd pail and shovel by the sandbox. Isn't that the cutest thing?

And the flowers! They're all made with buttons and ribbon. So sweet!"

She looked up at Ivy and her eyes sparkled. "Tell us about your house. Tell us how you imagine it."

"No," Ivy said curtly.

Margot's eyebrows arched in surprise at this rebuff, but then Ivy smiled. "You tell me first. I've been working on this every night after the kids are in bed quilting each of your blocks and it's made me curious. I'll tell you about mine, but the rest of you have to go first. That's the deal."

Everyone looked around to see who would start. After a moment, Liza took the plunge. "Mine's the weird-looking one, naturally." She pointed to a tall, thin column of a house that bore no resemblance to the others.

"That's what I like about it," Ivy said. "It has Liza written all over it."

Liza lowered her chin and raised her eyebrow in perfect imitation of her Aunt Abigail's 'what did you mean by that?' face.

Ivy rolled her eyes. "In a good way. It shows off your artistic sensibility. Stop looking at me like that." Ivy clucked her tongue and Liza laughed, teasing.

Sometimes, with the load of responsibility she carries, I forget how young Ivy is. She and Liza are closest in age of all of us, close enough that they might have been sisters. It's nice to see them joking together, nice to see Ivy acting her age.

Liza continued, "Yes, well. Here it is—my dream house. As you can see, it's very simple on the outside, very modern, concrete walls painted white and huge windows that let in a lot of light. And, as you can see from the bright blue that surrounds it, my house is on the water."

"The ocean?" Margot asked.

"Maybe. I'm not sure. It could be a big lake. There are three floors and each floor is just one big room. The ground floor has living/dining/dancing area with a very, very small kitchenette," she said with a grin. You couldn't tell by looking at her but Liza loves to eat though she is no more interested in cooking than her Aunt Abigail. If it weren't for Abigail's housekeeper, the notorious Hilda, whom

Abigail complains about continually but is truly devoted to, it's possible Abigail would starve to death. No, I take that back, she'd just eat every meal at the Grill.

"The second story is for sleeping and bathing, no walls, just a giant bed, a bathtub carved out of a single enormous rock, and a waterfall shower from the ceiling."

Ivy scratched her nose doubtfully. "No walls. Not even around the toilet? You've got a lot of windows there."

"Okay, good point. I don't really care about the neighbors because I'm not planning on having any, but I might have guests over sometimes. I don't want to gross them out. There are walls around the toilet, " Liza said with a nod to practicality. "And on the third floor you will find, drum roll, please . . ."

We chimed in one cue. "Your art studio!"

"Yes! A big, big space with the most amazing light ever—windows on every side that slide open to let in the breeze and the sound of the birds. And there's a balcony too, but you can't see it. It's on the back of the house."

"Sounds beautiful," Ivy said.

"It is. Oh, and one more thing. Needless to say, the fabulous huge, white walls of my beautiful house are filled with huge, gorgeous murals painted by me. Like living in my own gallery," she sighed contentedly, then turned to Abigail with an impish grin.

"Bet you're relieved to hear that, aren't you Abigail? Then you don't have to worry about me hanging them up at your place."

When Liza first moved in with Abigail, she'd wanted to hang a self-portrait made of old bottle caps in Abbie's foyer, next to the antiques and Abigail's collection of paintings from the Hudson River Valley school. Suffice it to say, Abigail and Liza have somewhat different taste in art.

"Don't be silly. I'd be proud to have one of your paintings hanging in my house," Abigail said so magnanimously that I thought she actually meant it. "You've become quite good."

"Thanks. I was wondering when you'd notice."

Abigail gave her a motherly slap on the wrist. "Always ready with a sassy comeback. Your mother was just the same."

Liza smiled, pleased with the comparison. "Okay, you're next, Abigail. Which one is yours? Everything that's left seems too small to be the abode of Mrs. Abigail Burgess Wynne Spaulding."

Abigail pointed to her block, a simple red saltbox with double chimneys, a gazebo, and an orderly line of flowering hedges flanking a white picket gate—modest but stately, classic New England architecture. It was the largest but, Liza was right, it was surprisingly small and simple by Burgess Wynne Spaulding standards.

"That? Really?" Margot sounded surprised. "Your house on Proctor Street is so beautiful. I know you'd hoped to donate it to the Stanton Center, but I just figured you were being generous, as usual."

"That was Woolley Wynne's dream house; it was never mine. I'm aware of how fortunate I've been to live there for the last few decades, but it was always too grand for my taste, now more than ever."

In a way, this made sense. The Abigail who was sitting next to me now, wearing a simple white blouse with her shining, platinum-gray hair drawn back into a smooth ponytail at the base of her neck, was a different person from the tight-laced, status conscious, island-unto-herself woman Liza had blackmailed into taking an unwilling part in our first Quilt Pink Day nearly three years ago. I don't know if I quite believed her assertion that she'd never cared for her enormous house on Proctor Street or craved the status that being the mistress of such a large estate conferred, but I could see that this new and improved Abigail didn't need such unwieldy accessories to confirm her place in the world.

"Don't misunderstand me, I don't have anything against grand houses or beautiful things, but I've had more than my fair share of them. When I die, I'd like to leave behind more than a big house filled with expensive things."

Liza, for once, was ready to give Abbie a little full-faced praise, no quips or double meanings attached. "What are you talking about, Abigail? You've got years and years of life left in you, make that decades and decades, but even if you died today you'd leave an amazing legacy." Liza ticked off a list on her fingers. "Wynne Memorial Library, the Burgess Wynne wing at the Art Museum, the Historical Society, your donations to the Women's Shelter, a floor at the hospital named after you—New Bern wouldn't be New Bern without your influence."

"And then, of course, there's me. Without you I'd probably be doing ten to fifteen in the big house as the county's most notorious sweater thief. Or maybe I'd be the headliner on one of those true crime shows." Liza's lifted hands met in front and swept to opposite sides, underlining her point as she feigned an overly dramatic voiceover. "Tonight on America's Most Wanted—Liza Burgess: The Cashmere Crook!"

Abigail smiled. "But you'll remember, I didn't exactly 'take you in.' Judge Gulden forced us on each other."

"That's doesn't matter. The end result is what counts. You helped me. You do help me."

"And me," Ivy chimed in. "You helped me get a job. And if it weren't for Franklin handling my divorce for free and you picking up the bills for the investigators and everything else, I wouldn't stand a chance up against Hodge and his legal team. The outcome isn't looking too favorable right now, but you've leveled the playing field, Abigail. I appreciate it so much."

"Well, you can't think I was going to stand by and let that monster take Bethany and Bobby, did you? And don't sound so negative about your divorce," she commanded. "You've got to think positively! You're going to keep your children and send that sorry excuse for a man limping out of this town with his tail tucked between his legs, do you hear me?"

"Yes, ma'am," Ivy said, but not with any real conviction.

"And what about me?" I asked. "If you hadn't rented the shop and warehouse space to me at such a ridiculously low price, Cobbled Court Quilts would have gone out of business a long time ago."

"And if that had happened," Margot added, "I'd be out of a job—again."

"By the way, now that we're actually making money, it's time we renegotiated the lease. I can afford to pay the market price for rent now and I intend to."

Abigail waved me off. "I don't like talking business at social events. It's rude. We'll discuss it another time."

Somehow I knew that it would be hard to pin her down as to what time would be more appropriate.

Liza turned to conversation back to her aunt. "But do you hear what everyone is saying? In one way or another, you've touched the lives of everyone in this room."

Abigail bent her head, looking, for the first time in my memory, sincerely humbled. "Thank you for saying so, Liza. Perhaps it's my age. I find myself increasingly anxious to make the rest of my life useful. Funding libraries and hospitals is important and I certainly have no intention of lessening those efforts; I've got plenty of money to continue that," she said honestly. "But more and more I believe it's our impact on individuals that matters most. I want to use my wealth and my life for that purpose, not to add to my personal comforts. I've got too much of everything as it is. Every single thing we own actually owns us in some way or another—they all have to be cleaned, or maintained, or fixed, or appraised, or insured, or some such thing. It all takes time and that, I've realized, is an absolutely finite commodity. Wasted time can't be redeemed. And a wasted life? Well, that's a tragedy."

I'd never heard Abigail talk like that before. I don't think any of us had. Like everyone else, I just sat looking at her. I couldn't help but think how lucky I am to count Abigail as my friend. She is truly one of a kind.

Abbie coughed. "Anyway . . . my point is . . . people are what matter. Family and friends most of all. That's why my dream home would be something smaller and simpler, something like this." She nodded toward her quilted saltbox. "A pretty house with nice gardens but nothing too complicated—just a nice long lawn in the back where we can have parties in the summer. The inside should have a big living room on one side, room to entertain, but it doesn't have to be bigger than is comfortable for forty or fifty guests."

I nodded. "I see. Just enough room for intimate gatherings." Across from me, Ivy pressed her lips together to hide her smile.

"Yes," Abigail said, not picking up on the joke. "Exactly. Bigger affairs can wait until summer or, if they can't, we can always rent a room at the club. I'd like a nice dining room, an adequate kitchen, and a library for Franklin. Upstairs there should be four or five bedrooms, ensuite, and an office for myself. Marriage, I've found, is a wonderful institution, but when you've lived alone as long as I have, it's important to have a room of one's own. The whole thing would probably be about a third the size of the Proctor Street house."

Margot squashed her eyebrows together. "But doesn't Franklin's house have most of that? Why not just stay there?"

"Yes, Franklin's house is comfortable and I've considered that but . . ." Abigail sighed. "I knew Franklin's late wife, Mary. She was a sweet woman and I liked her but I can't help but feel that house still belongs to her. I'd like to make a fresh start with Franklin. It's a new life, a new beginning, for both of us. I'd like a lifestyle and a home that reflects that.

"And," she said, giving Liza an arch look, "to those ends, I've made a decision. You're quite right, Liza. Mrs. Abigail Burgess Wynne Spaulding is too pretentious and too long. So I've decided to change it to Mrs. Abigail Spaulding." She sniffed. "Much more practical. Think of the hours I'll save answering my correspondence."

I think we were all stunned by this announcement. I certainly was. The name Burgess Wynne carried weight in New Bern and while I didn't doubt for a moment that Abigail was and always would be an influential figure among New Bern's elite, her willingness to abbreviate her surname said something about the depth of change she had undergone as well as the depth of the feelings she had for Franklin.

"I think that's wonderful, Abigail. Very sensible."

"Thank you, Evelyn. But enough about me; tell us about your block. It looks exactly like the house you're living in now."

"It is," I laughed. "At the moment, I love my life. I love my little yellow cottage and the little garden out back. I love that I can walk to work. It's perfect for me."

Margot tipped her head toward my block. "But, what about Charlie? Is there room for him in there?"

"We'd need a bigger kitchen, that's for sure. Someday—if he's not sick of me by then—yes, there is room for Charlie. But right this second I'm content with my life. I don't feel the need to change a thing."

"That must be nice," Margot said, in a slightly disbelieving tone. "I'm not sure I've ever felt that way."

"Until recently, neither have I, but yes, it feels pretty good."

"Well, I guess it's my turn," Margot said. "I've got the Dutch Colonial with the four dormers on the front."

"It's very pretty," Ivy said. "I love the way you quilted all those different shades of gray, so the chimney looks like it's made out of stone."

Margot tried to smile, but all she could manage was a sad little smirk. "Thanks. It's a big house, three bedrooms, two-and-a-half baths with a river rock fireplace in the living room, bookshelves on both sides, and a big country kitchen with a pantry and upstairs, in the bedrooms, there are window seats in front of all the dormers with cushions that match the curtains. It's a big house," she repeated softly. "A family house."

Her eyes moved around the circle, making contact with each of us in turn. "I know what you're thinking. You're wondering why I made it so big."

"We're not wondering at all. You want a family," I said. "Why shouldn't you?"

Margot's usually tranquil eyes sparked angry blue, like the sapphire flash that comes when live wires connect. "Because I'm never going to have one, that's why! I'm thirty-eight years old. I'm single and I'm always going to be single. I've wasted too much of my life dreaming about honeymoon cruises and nursery wallpaper, that's why!"

Our sweet, soft-spoken Margot was almost shouting. For a moment everyone fell into awkward silence, not knowing how to respond. Then Liza managed to say exactly the wrong thing at exactly the wrong time.

"So . . . how is Arnie?"

"Liza, shut up!" Margot snapped her head toward Liza and glared at her. Liza shifted backwards in her seat as if trying to move out of the line of fire. "I told you before, Arnie isn't interested in me like that! Men are never interested in me like that! I'm a spinster and it's time everybody got used to the idea! I've never been married and I'll never be married. I am sick and tired of getting my hopes up every time a man so much as says hello to me only to have them smashed against the rocks when I find out he is married, or gay, or 'just wants to be friends.'

"I'm up to here with all of you making it worse by pretending that love is just around the corner for me. It's not! It never was and it never will be! I know you think you're helping, but if you really want to help, help me learn to get used to the idea of being alone for the rest of my life because we all know that's what is going to happen. The sooner I give up all these silly, impossible dreams and face the facts, the better off I'll be. So shut up about Arnie, will you, Liza? Just shut up!"

As she spoke, Margot's grip on the edges of Ivy's new quilt tightened, crushing the pine tree border so it looked like a row of squat, misshapen bushes. When she finished, she flung the quilt away from her body as if it were on fire and covered her eyes and mouth with one hand.

"Okay," Liza said quietly. "I'm sorry."

Margot wasn't crying. She was too angry for tears. Her shoulders heaved as she took in big gulps of air, trying to compose herself. After a long minute, her hand lowered until only her mouth was covered. She took a final deep breath and released it in an even, controlled whoosh of air, dropped her hands, and took a fresh grip on her end of the quilt.

"I'm sorry," she said in a clipped voice. "I shouldn't have gone off like that. But I meant what I said. I don't want to talk about this anymore." She looked at each of us in turn, beginning with Liza and ending with me. "Understand?"

I nodded acknowledgment along with the others.

"Good. Anyway, tonight isn't about me. It's about binding Ivy's quilt. We've been sitting here for half an hour without sewing a stitch and I still haven't heard about Ivy's house." Margot's glance shifted from the quilted clapboard cottage with the bright red door to Ivy's face.

"Go on," she said. "Tell us about it."

32

Ivy Peterman

The evening had gotten off to a rocky start but by the time we finished stitching the binding on my quilt, things were more or less back to normal.

After Margot's outburst Abigail took charge and helped us shift gears, saying she didn't see why we couldn't sew and talk at the same time or, for that matter why we couldn't drink, sew, and talk at the same time. "We're all accomplished multi-taskers here. Thread your needles and get to work. Ivy, you tell everyone about your block while I pour the wine."

We finished binding the quilt just before nine, but before I left I pulled four packages wrapped in tissue paper and ribbon from my tote bag and handed one to each of my circle sisters. Each package contained four quilted placemats.

The pattern was the same, a big star block in the middle with two bands of fabric on either side to make a rectangle, but the fabrics varied according to the tastes and favorite colors of the recipient. For Abigail, I'd picked a blue toile with complementary pale yellows and blue; for Evelyn, jeweled-toned batiks in turquoise, green, and eggplant; for Margot an assortment of 1930s reproduction fabrics in pinks, greens, and creams; and for Liza, a jazzy novelty print of bright jelly beans on a black background with yellow, red, and purple fabrics that matched the candies. Included with each gift was a card with pictures drawn by Bethany and Bobby and a note from me.

The gifts I made them weren't expensive or exotic, but they were one-of-a-kind and from my heart.

When she read the note, Abigail lifted her hand, rested it lightly on her chest, and actually got a little teary-eyed. "Thank you, Ivy. This is just about the nicest gift I've ever received."

Liza loved the jelly bean theme. "These are so cute! They actually make me want to cook something just so I can use them."

"Pink and green are my favorite colors. How did you know?" Margot asked, adjusting the new pink and green knitted scarf she wore around her throat. I just laughed.

Ever the quilting teacher, Evelyn lifted her placemats close and studied the stitching. "Just look at the points on those stars. They meet perfectly!"

Like I said, they weren't fancy gifts but everyone seemed to like them and I was glad. After all they'd done for me, it was nice to be able to return the favor, if only in a small way.

When everybody was done opening the gifts, I looked at my watch. "Yikes! It's almost nine. I've got to scoot. I told Karen I'd be home by ten after. I'll take the dishes downstairs and wash them."

"Don't worry about it," Evelyn said. "You go pick up the kids. We can take care of this."

I hated leaving the mess for everyone else to clean up, but I really did have to go. "Are you sure?"

Margot started collecting the empty wineglasses and plates. "It's fine. Go on. We'll be right behind you."

I gave everyone a hurried hug and headed for the stairs. "Wait!" Abigail called. "You almost forgot something." She folded up the quilt and handed it to me.

"Thanks. I can't wait to get home and hang it up. Thank you all so much. Really. I wish there was some way I could . . ." My voice caught in my throat.

Abigail fluttered her hands like she was trying to shoo away a pesky fly. "Enough of that now. Go on! Go pick up your children."

"Okay." I smiled as I ran down the stairs and out the rear door into the back alley where I'd parked. I locked the door, double-checking to make sure it was secure. The others all lived close enough to walk home and on such a pleasant evening they would, going out the front door of the shop and locking it behind them.

It was a lovely night, warm for September. The moon was full and bright, streaming a beam of bluish light into the alley.

That's why I was able to see the man. His back was toward me and he was hunched over the side of my car. The strained play of muscles under his shirt told me he was trying mightily to jimmy open the car door.

For a split second my mind raced back to that night so long ago when I had been startled awake by the sound of a stranger trying to break into the backseat of the car where Bethany and Bobby were sleeping. Then, my heart had pounded in terror. Now, it pounded again, in anger. I recognized that head of hair, the set of those shoulders. This was no stranger.

"Hodge! Get away from my car!"

He flinched ever so slightly, startled by the sound of my voice, but then his shoulders dropped and he turned, smooth and slow, to face me. "Ivy. I've been waiting for you. Did you have to work late?" He smiled.

"What are you doing?" I asked and then answered my own question. "You were trying to break into my car."

His head hinged back on his neck and his brows drew together to signal his surprise at my accusation, but I knew what I'd seen. "No, I wasn't. I was just trying the door to see if you'd left it open. I've been waiting out here for a while and it's cold. I just thought I'd be warmer waiting in the car."

It was close to seventy-five degrees outside, but I didn't bother pointing that out. Something I'd learned about Hodge years ago—the less I let him talk the better. If you let him talk long enough, he could convince you that water ran uphill.

I pulled my car keys out of my pocket and readied them in my hand. "Get away from my car. I have to go home."

He grinned. "Well, actually it's my car. I paid for it. Remember?"

I didn't say anything.

Hodge leaned back against the driver's side door, casually crossed his right foot in front of his left and his arms across his chest, like a teenager hanging out on a street corner, and smiled broadly. "Ivy," he said, drawing out my name and then laughing. "Come on. Don't look at me like that. I was just kidding. Though, it actually is my car, but big deal. I don't care about the car."

He paused for a moment, gauging his timing, and let the smile fade slowly from his face and melt into a mask of concern tinged with regret. He was very, very good. Utterly convincing. Or would have been if I didn't know him so well. He sighed heavily, a sound that even a year ago would have made me sorry I'd doubted him.

A year is a long time.

He shifted his weight from the car door to his feet, stood again, uncrossed his arms and opened his hands expansively. "Listen, I know you're upset at finding me out here, but I'm not trying to scare you and I wasn't trying to break into your car. Honestly. We need to talk, don't you think? I tried to call you but couldn't find your number."

"It's unlisted. I don't want to talk to you. If you have something to say, you can call my lawyer. He's in the book."

"Yeah, I know. I know all about your lawyer. And mine. That's why I want to talk to you. Ivy . . . baby, we need to talk. This whole thing has gotten out of hand, you know? Lawyers. Social workers. I just . . ." He swallowed hard, as if trying to keep his emotions in check. "I just want you to come home. You and me and the kids— we're a family. We're not exactly Ozzie and Harriet, but we belong together. I don't want a divorce. And if you think about it, you don't really want one either, do you?"

"Yes, I do, Hodge. I want a divorce. Now get away from my car."

"You're mad at me." He lifted up open hands, an admission. "I know. I know. That night you left . . . I was wrong, one hundred percent. I'm sorry. But I was crazy, jealous. I thought you were fixing yourself up for somebody else, you know? Ivy, baby," he pleaded, "I love you so much it hurts. That's what made me act like that. But, it won't happen again, I swear it won't. You wanted to teach me a lesson and you did."

He tilted his head to one side and shrugged as if conceding the point. "When I came home that night and you weren't there, I was so mad. I punched a hole through the bathroom door. Had to get Kittenger to come over and stitch me up."

He rolled his eyes and chuckled, as if embarrassed by the image of his younger, more impulsive self now seen through older and wiser eyes. Out of everything he'd said so far, this was the one detail I found believable, that upon coming home and finding us fled, he'd put his fist through a door. I had no doubt he was capable of doing so again.

"Don't worry. I fixed it." He looked at me with smiling eyes, searching for signs of softening in mine, and then went on. "Anyway, after you left, I was really mad for a couple of days, but it was good, you know? It gave me some time to think about how I'd acted and then I felt really bad. I shouldn't have let myself fly off the handle like that, Ivy. I figured that's why you left; you wanted to let me stew in my own juice for a while. I kept thinking you'd be back any day. But when a week passed and then two, I thought maybe something had happened to you. I was so worried about you and the kids. You have no idea. I missed you so much."

It was a mistake to engage him, I knew that, but the enormity of this lie shook my resolve. I couldn't let him get away with it.

"Really? Is that why you never even bothered to report us missing? Or why you haven't shown up for any of your scheduled visits with the kids?"

Hodge wasn't used to me challenging him. He pressed his lips together, trying to keep his temper under control. "You mean my *supervised* visits with the kids? Yeah, Ivy, I was really anxious to abandon my business responsibilities and drive five hours so I could sit in some government office and visit my kids with some snotty social worker watching to make sure I don't smack them or look at them sideways! Yeah, I was real excited about doing that, Ivy. What father wouldn't be?"

His voice was raised. I knew I should tread more lightly, but part of me was happy to see him angry, happy to know that, for once, I was the one holding the strings and making him dance to my tune, piercing holes in the mask of composure he was working so hard to maintain. He took a deep breath and let it out slowly. I could almost hear him mentally counting to ten as he told himself to calm down.

"And I did report you missing," he insisted. A lie. "The police must have lost the paperwork or something, but I did file a report. Not at first, I didn't want cops chasing after you like you were some kind of criminal or something. After all, it was just a little marital squabble."

I remembered hurrying between the chest of drawers and the bed as I'd filled a suitcase with clothes, rushing to make sure we were gone before he returned, blood dripping from my lacerated hand onto the carpet, the pain, catching a glimpse of my left eye in the mirror above the dresser, swollen purple turning to black. A marital squabble.

"And anyway, I really thought you'd come back. I didn't think you could make it without me, but I was wrong. Okay? I admit it, I was wrong. You found a job, a place to live. You proved your point. Now it's time to come home."

"I am home."

"Yeah," he said. "Sure you are. Come off it, Ivy! You can't seriously mean you'd rather live here, in this crappy little town, in your dingy little apartment, working at your dead-end job, than go back to your beautiful house right on the golf course with the Jacuzzi and three-car garage?"

"Yes, I can. I do."

He shoved his hands in his pockets and decided to try one more time. "Ivy, I know you're mad. I know you're trying to punish me. I get it. I really do. But, you have to believe me. I love you and you have to come home now." I shook my head but he ignored me. "It's all going to be different, I promise. A whole new start. We're going to go on a second honeymoon, back to the Caribbean. I already bought the tickets. I called the hotel and reserved the same bungalow we had on our honeymoon. It'll be a fresh start for us. And when we get back, I'm going to buy you a new car. Any model you want. And I'm going to hire a housekeeper, so you have more time for yourself. And, if you want, we can even go to one of those marriage counselors. You'll see. I'm a changed man. From here on out, it's going to be a whole new ballgame, but I don't want to hear one more word about divorce, ever again. Do you hear me?" His nostrils flared, white with frustration in the face of my silent refusal.

"Do you hear me? You're coming home," he declared. "And you're doing it now! You belong at home."

"I belong where *I* say I belong. I belong to myself. I'm nobody's property. Not anymore. Now get out of my way."

With my keys still in my hand, I took three long steps toward the car and turned my shoulder slightly, trying to shove Hodge away from the car door. The heat of my anger made me feel powerful and strong, deceptively so. He never supposed I'd have the nerve to challenge him physically. The surprising force of my body against his muscled torso caught him off-guard and he lost his balance, tottering a good four feet from the door he'd been blocking. Seeing my chance, I clicked the keychain to unlock the car door, accidentally dropping my quilt in the dirt as I sprang for the door and wrenched it open. I tried to get behind the wheel and slam the door, but I wasn't fast enough.

I felt a searing pain in my scalp as Hodge grabbed hold of my hair and dragged me from the car. I tried to grab on to the interior frame of the car, but it was no good. He hauled me out of the car. My flat-soled tennis shoes scuffled on the loose gravel as I scrambled to keep my feet under me; if he got me on the ground I'd have no chance of escape and escape was the only thing on my mind.

The sense of power I'd known a bare moment before fled; terror rushed in to fill the void. I fought back my fear, tried to get a grip on myself, watching for an opening. I knew there would only be one.

Still holding my hair with one hand, he dragged me away from the open car door toward the hood. He twisted his left hand backwards, slapping me as hard as he could with his knuckles and wedding band leading the blow, knocking my head sideways so the pain ripped through my cheeks and my scalp simultaneously.

He shoved me back against the hood of the car, grabbed the

waist of my jeans, unsnapping the closure and opening the zipper in one movement. "You don't belong to anybody? Is that what you said? Is that what you said to me?" he bellowed.

Jerking my hair, he pulled me off of the car and then twisted me around to face the hood, tugging the fabric of my jeans and underwear down around my hips with his free hand, while simultaneously pushing down on my head, forcing me to bend over the car.

My mind screamed out, No! I wasn't going to let him do this to me. Not ever again. I wanted to shout with rage but instead I made my voice soft and pleading. "Hodge, don't. Please, Hodge, don't."

"Oh, now it's please, Hodge? Please? You should have thought of that before you made your little declaration of independence, baby. I'm going to remind you who you do belong to. By the time I'm through with you, you're going to say please like you mean it."

There was nothing Hodge enjoyed quite as much as my fear. It gave him a sense of power that went to his head, made him a little drunk and, if I was lucky, distracted.

I let a sob escape from my throat, which didn't require much acting on my part, and though it sent a fresh shock of pain to my scalp, as he pushed me closer to the hood of the car, I pretended to stumble. That gave me a chance to flex my knees, center my weight and blast upward like a submarine performing an emergency blow, exploding to the surface without warning. With the silvery tip of the car key wedged tight between the middle and forefingers of my left hand, I concentrated every ounce of primal energy I could into my arm and gouged the pointed key into the orbit of his eye.

He screamed, let go of my hair, and clutched at his eye. I howled, "No!" and spun my body to the left and pumped my arm like a piston, driving my elbow into his stomach as hard as I could. He doubled over. I ran toward the open car door, hitching my jeans up as I did.

I almost made it. I was behind the wheel with my fingers wrapped around the door handle, ready to slam it shut, when Hodge wrenched it open with such power that my arm jerked and I could feel a burning sensation in my shoulder socket. He grabbed me again, by the arm this time, and pulled me from the car. I could feel the firestorm of rage in Hodge's powerful right arm, more violent and uncontrollable than before, and instinctively knew that, at that moment, he was absolutely capable of killing me.

He was a monster, furious and snarling. Once he had me out of the car, he grabbed the keys from my hand, and flung them across the top of the car. I heard a dull clink as they fell onto the gravel far out of reach.

Hodge pushed me against the side of the car, pinning me against the metal frame, and shoving the hard edge of his hip into my stomach. He gripped my left arm and stretched it out so my fingers hung over the edge of the doorframe.

"You want to play with the car door? Is that right? You want to shut the door on me?"

He clutched the door handle with his right hand and, as hard as he could, slammed it shut on my hand.

There was a sickening crack of breaking bone. I screamed in agony.

Hodge screamed, too.

My eyes were screwed shut in pain, so I didn't see what happened, all I knew was that Hodge let me go. The car door opened, releasing my broken, bleeding hand. I crumpled to the ground, overcome by pain.

And suddenly Margot was on the ground next to me, shaking, crying, and wrapping my hand in her pink and green scarf.

I opened my eyes and saw Hodge doubled over, howling with his hands covering his face and Liza standing in front of him, eyes blazing, her feet planted wide apart, both hands fully extended, gripping a tiny metal canister, and pointing it straight at Hodge.

Just behind Liza stood Evelyn and Abigail, armed and dangerous, each holding a big sixty millimeter rotary cutter with new, sharp blades that glinted in the moonlight, and expressions that made it clear that if Hodge made one wrong move, they'd give no more thought to using those blades on him than they would to slicing through a bolt of fabric.

Groaning, Hodge rubbed his eyes and raised himself upright,

blinking as he looked from one female face to the next as if his eyes might be playing tricks on him.

Keeping her eyes trained on Hodge, Abigail called out. "Ivy, are you all right?"

"Yes," I said, swallowing back the pain. "I'm okay."

"Good. Mr. Edelman, move slowly back to the wall. Spread your feet apart, lift your hands over your head and keep them there."

Hodge stopped for a moment, assessing the situation. His eyes shifted from Abigail to Evelyn and back. His mouth twisted into a sneer and he laughed. He thought they were bluffing. Reaching out both arms, he took one quick, large, lunging step toward me, daring anyone to stop him, certain that neither woman had the guts to do so.

He doesn't know them the way I do.

Striking like a cobra disturbed in its lair, uncoiling in one fluid motion, Evelyn took her right hand off the cutter, sprung toward Hodge, swung her arm behind her head and brought it back down again as hard as she could, slapping him for all she was worth! The crack of her palm against Hodge's shocked face echoed off the alley's brick walls, a sharp, stinging sound, decisive and startling as a gunshot.

"Ahh!" Hodge's eyes widened with surprise. His hand instinctively flew to his cheek to absorb the shock of the slap. He retreated a step as Evelyn, all flashing eyes and fury, crouched down into a stance like a sumo wrestler, menacing him with the glinting, circular blade of the cutter, thrusting it forward like a gangster brandishing a switchblade and forcing him backward, step by step, until his back was against the wall.

"Hands up!" Evelyn commanded. Her chest was heaving and her breath was ragged. Hodge hesitated just a moment, trying to decide if this delicate-boned, fifty-year-old quilter was as dangerous as she looked.

As if reading his mind, Evelyn hissed, "Go ahead. Just try it. Right this second, there is nothing that could make me happier than having an excuse to slice you up like a leftover pizza pie. But remember—there's one of you and five of us. Think about that, you cowardly, pathetic louse, before you try to take one more step toward Ivy." Her voice dripped with disgust and anger. She looked at him as if he were vermin, a bug to be squashed.

For once in his life, Hodge did the smart thing. Slowly, he raised his hands over his head, keeping both eyes on the blade Evelyn held clutched in her hands but refusing to look her in the eye, as if afraid doing so might provoke her.

He was afraid! Hodge Edelman was cowering with his back against a wall and his hands raised helplessly over his head, too frightened to move a muscle, and Evelyn Dixon, a woman, was the one who'd put him in his place! I could hardly believe it. If not for my mangled hand, I'd have jumped up and given her a high five.

Abigail stepped forward. "Very good, Mr. Edelman. Wise move. Margot," Abigail said in a deliberately steady voice. "Come over here and hold this cutter. I need to you keep an eye on Mr. Edelman while I make a phone call."

Sniffing, Margot got to her feet and took over for Abbie.

"Thank you. If he moves, just lunge for him. You don't need to be particular about your aim. That blade is brand new and sharp enough to cut to the bone. If you have to use it, anything you hit will cause serious damage. But do try to stay away from the major arteries, dear. If you hit one, he'll probably bleed to death before our eyes."

Hodge's eyes shifted from Evelyn to Margot and he swallowed hard. And somehow, in that hedging, frightened glace, I finally saw him for what he was—all the names that Evelyn had called him. A louse. Pathetic. A coward.

Abigail took her cell phone out of the pocket of her slacks and held it to her ear. "Franklin? What? Yes, I know I'm late, darling, but I've been delayed. We had a little problem over at the quilt shop. Could you come over here right away? We're in the back alley behind the shop."

She glanced at Ivy and then at Hodge. "And while you're at it, could you please call the police? We're going to need an ambulance and a squad car. Thank you, darling."

❧ 33 ❧

Evelyn Dixon

When you're standing in a dark alley with nothing except a canister of pepper spray and two rotary fabric cutters between you and a violent monster, five minutes feels like five years.

After the initial surge of adrenaline that had coursed through my veins when we burst through the back door of the shop into the alley, spotted Hodge and Ivy a split second too late to prevent him from crushing her hand in the car door, and "taken him down" as Liza would forever after refer to it, I felt drained. My hands, clutched so tightly around the handle of the cutter that it would have taken surgery to remove it from my grasp, began to tremble slightly, but I held my ground, praying that Abigail's sternly delivered warning had convinced Hodge Edelman not to move until the police arrived.

She wasn't kidding; those rotary cutters were sharp enough to slice through human flesh and if Hodge tried to get away or, worse, to harm Ivy or any one of us, I was absolutely prepared to do what I had to do. But that didn't mean I was anxious to prove it. I'm a quilt shop owner, not Rambo. I'd never before felt such anger, such rage as I did when I slapped Hodge Edelman. I hope I never do again.

Except for the whine of the town whistle that pulsed through the streets of New Bern whenever the fire department received an emergency call, the next five minutes passed in tense and uncomfortable silence. And then New Bern's finest arrived, all flashing lights and sharply issued instructions, telling all of us to drop our "weapons" and put up our hands until they figured out who was who. Such a relief.

Franklin arrived a minute later. The Fire Department EMT's were on his heels. That's another advantage of living in a small town; news travels fast and help arrives even faster.

Having sorted the good guys from the bad, the police officers handcuffed Hodge, read him his rights, and loaded him into the backseat of the cruiser. As soon as the police said we could put down our hands, Abigail, Liza, Margot, and I kneeled down on the ground next to Ivy.

Blood was seeping through Margot's hastily improvised bandage, turning the yarn of her scarf a dark red. "Sorry about that," she said to Margot. She looked a little pale and was breathing heavily but otherwise seemed all right.

The EMT, Denise Fraser, who had taken a table runner class at Cobbled Court, a beginner's project, after we first opened and had gone on to become a good customer and a good quilter, came up carrying a box with first aid supplies and knelt down on the ground next to Ivy. She gave Ivy a quick once over, making sure she wasn't suffering from shock or any hidden, more serious injuries.

The Denise I knew from the shop was always quiet, even a little on the shy side, but now she was professional, efficient, in command, and observant. "Ivy, your jeans are undone. Were you raped?"

My heart skipped a beat.

"No. He tried, but I fought him off."

Denise bent down to begin unwrapping the blood-sodden scarf from Ivy's hand. A trace of a smile tugged at one corner of her mouth. "Yeah, I saw that. My partner is over at the squad car bandaging up an eye. Seems somebody tried to pop it out the socket with a car key." She winked. "Good girl."

Ivy winced as Denise continued unwrapping her hand. She looked at the ring of solemn faces surrounding her. "Well, I just finished thanking you for one thing, make that months of things, and now you all come riding in like the cavalry to save me again. As soon as this hand heals, I guess I'll have to start working on some more placemats. Really, we've got to quit meeting like this."

Ivy laughed weakly, but no one joined in. Abbie looked like she wished Hodge had bolted so she'd have had an excuse to slice him into quarter-square triangles and Margot was on the verge of bursting into tears.

Ivy tried to reassure everybody. "Don't look so worried. It's just a hand. It'll be all right. Look!" She held up her fingers of her good hand and wiggled them. "I've got another one just like it. But thanks for showing up when you did. Your timing was perfect." ·

Liza frowned at Ivy's mangled left hand. "Not quite."

"It's nothing. Trust me, I know what I'm talking about. It's the same hand he smashed before. My sewing hand is still good, see?" She pinched an imaginary needle between the thumb and forefinger of her right hand and mimed a quilting stitch.

"Well, thank heaven for that," I said with a smile and reached out to brush a lock of hair from her forehead.

"Speaking of perfect timing," Ivy continued, "how did you find me? I figured you'd all leave through the front."

"We were about to," Margot said, "but then the phone rang in the shop. Even though it was after hours something told me I should pick up. It was Karen; she was wondering when you were going to pick up the kids . . ."

Ivy's already colorless face turned a whiter shade of pale. "Oh my gosh! The kids!"

Abigail patted her arm reassuringly. "Don't worry. I called her as soon as the police arrived. The children are fine with her for the moment. Franklin and I will go over and collect them later. They can stay with us tonight.

"Anyway," she continued, picking up the story where Margot had left it, "once Karen called, we started to worry. You'd had enough time to get home by then. Then we heard the sound of yelling in the alley, so we all started running for the back door. Liza had the presence of mind to dig her pepper spray canister out of her bag."

"A girl living alone in the big city has to be prepared," Liza said proudly.

"And as we were headed out the door, Evelyn grabbed two rotary cutters off the notions rack and handed one to me," Abigail finished. "Very quick thinking."

"Very quick. Thanks, Evelyn."

I nodded. "I don't think I'll ever look at a rotary cutter quite the same way ever again."

Franklin called Arnie and then Garrett, who was having dinner at the Grill. He and Charlie got there right after the police. Arnie arrived just as Denise finished cleaning Ivy's broken hand and rewrapping it in a less-improvised bandage. Ivy thanked her.

"My pleasure," Denise said. "And as an added service, we'll give you a ride to the hospital. I'll even turn on the lights if you want. No sirens, though. You're going to need an orthopedist, but it's not life-threatening."

"I'm her lawyer," Arnie said. "I'd like to come along in the ambulance."

"It's already pretty crowded with all the equipment. How about if you follow us instead?"

Arnie nodded. "That's fine. Margot, can you come, too? It'd be a big help if you could take notes while I interview Ivy."

"Okay."

Denise and her partner brought a gurney and strapped Ivy onto it for the ride to the hospital. As they prepared to load her into the ambulance, Arnie patted the white sheet covering Ivy's legs and said, "This isn't exactly how I'd have planned it, but you know something? This might be the break we've been looking for." Arnie glanced at the fat bandage around Ivy's hand and winced. "Sorry. No pun intended."

Ivy brightened. "Really? You think so?"

Arnie nodded. "It's going to pretty hard for him to claim he isn't an abuser when he intentionally slammed your hand in a car door in front of four reliable witnesses. And, in my experience, exposing one lie has a way of unearthing all the others. This might be your loose thread, Ivy. We've still got some work to do and this whole turn of events is bound to delay our court date—for one thing, the judge is going to have to decide what to do first, give Hodge a divorce or three-to-five for assault." Arnie grinned. "But I've got a feeling that after this, Hodge's whole story is going to come apart at the seams."

"I hope you're right."

The squad car left with Hodge in the back. Arnie and Margot followed the ambulance to the hospital. Abigail and Franklin went to pick up Bethany and Bobby. That left just Liza, Garrett, Charlie, and me.

"Gosh, Mom, I never realized that underneath that mild-mannered exterior, you were quite such a commando. I can't believe you actually hit him! Way to go, Mom! You could give Lara Croft a run for her money. Or James Bond. I mean, a rotary cutter that doubles as a dangerous weapon? Who knew? What else do you have up in the workroom? Quilt hoops that double as satellite tracking devices? Bolts of fabric that are actually invisibility cloaks?"

Liza approached, carrying Ivy's quilt. "That's Harry Potter, not James Bond. Keep your characters straight."

Garrett kissed her on the top of the head. "You did good tonight."

"Thanks." Liza grinned and held up Ivy's abandoned quilt. "I found this over by the side of the car. It's okay, just a little dirty, but it ripped in one spot. Mind if I go back inside the shop and get some thread to fix it?"

"Would you? That would be great. I just want to go home, climb into bed, and go to sleep. I'm exhausted. Oh, wait a minute! I just remembered. I never locked the doors."

"Don't worry about it, Mom. I can lock up." Garrett squeezed Liza's shoulders. "How about you? Are you exhausted or do you want to come up to my place and watch a movie?"

"Sounds good. I'm too jazzed to sleep, anyway." Liza grinned at me. "You know what? I'm kind of proud of us. I wish we'd gotten there before he broke Ivy's hand, but imagine what could have happened if we'd never shown up at all? It just goes to show you, you do *not* want to mess with the Cobbled Court Quilt Circle. Cross one of us, and you're going to have to face all of us."

"Good night, Liza." I gave her a hug and Garrett a kiss. "Good night, sweetie. See you at work tomorrow. Thanks for locking up."

They left, disappearing through the back door of the shop. A minute later, a light turned on in the window of Garrett's upstairs apartment.

"Watching a movie and eating popcorn. Think that's all they'll be doing up there?" Charlie asked.

I shot him an irritated glance. "I don't know and I don't want to know. None of my business. They're of age and I'm too aged to want to think about it."

Charlie smiled. "Sorry. Probably not the sort of question I should ask a woman who's worn out after a long day of crime fighting and all."

"Probably not the sort of question you should ask a mother— ever."

"I stand corrected. Now, can I take you to the Grill and buy you a drink, or are you really too tired?"

"I'm really too tired. But thanks for the offer."

"In that case, I'll walk you home. You shouldn't be out on the street alone at night. Not that I'm worried about you, mind you; it's everybody else I'm concerned about. Nobody should have to meet up with you in a dark alley."

"You're hilarious."

"I know. A comic genius."

"Yes, but only in France."

I picked up the abandoned rotary cutters up off the ground, making sure the blades were on safety before shoving them in my back pocket.

"Wait a minute. Let me see that." Charlie whistled low. "Whoa. These are lethal. You could've cut him to ribbons with one of these things, you know that?"

I felt a lump in my throat and hot tears in the corners of my eyes. "And if he'd so much as blinked . . . if he'd taken one more step toward, Ivy, I would have. Happily." Fear and anger and exhaustion pooled in my heart and spilled out my eyes.

"Why did he do that to her, Charlie? He hit her. He tried to rape her. And then he purposely slammed the car door on her hand. Why? What's wrong with some men? Why are they so cruel?"

Every trace of humor faded from Charlie's face. "Oh, Evelyn. Sweetheart. Come here, my brave one. I'm so proud of you. It's all right. Everything will be all right now." He folded me into his arms and I cried until I couldn't cry anymore, until his shirtfront was soaked through with my pity and my tears.

∞ 34 ∞

Ivy Peterman

Luck is a relative term.

X-rays showed that my thumb and two of the other fingers in my left hand were broken, but the orthopedist was able to set the bones without surgery, so that was lucky. He did have to use external pins to make sure the set bones stayed in place, but that's where painkillers come in. After that, I was given a cast, a little brown bottle with more painkillers, and instructions to come back in two weeks for another x-ray.

Hospitals are boring and lonely. Sitting in white rooms with white lights under white sheets for incredibly long stretches of time gives you plenty of opportunity to stare at the walls and worry while waiting for someone to show up and perform potentially painful procedures on you. I was very glad Margot and Arnie came with me; they were a good distraction. After the initial x-ray and once-over by the emergency room doctor, we had to cool our heels until a hand specialist was located and arrived. Arnie used that time to quiz me about the confrontation with Hodge while Margot scribbled notes, but that didn't take too long. In an effort to keep me entertained, Arnie inflated two examining gloves, drew feathers and beaks on them with a Magic Marker, and staged a latex chicken puppet show/cockfight. Margot supplied appropriate and frantic clucked barnyard sound effects while Arnie hid behind a screen to handle the puppets and narrated play-by-play for the entire battle in a convincing impression of an ESPN announcer. Arnie was hilarious. Who knew?

When the orthopedist finally arrived, I was laughing so hard tears were running down my face. Concerned, he called for a nurse to get me more pain medication. I assured him I didn't need any and tried to explain what made me so giddy, but he just looked at me blankly.

"Never mind, Doc," I said, wiping my eyes. "I guess you had to be there."

After the doctor patched me up, Arnie and Margot drove me home. It was after two. I'm sure they were exhausted, but they insisted on coming inside and getting me settled. That turned out to be a good thing.

The apartment had been ransacked.

Every drawer and cupboard was open, the cushions were off the sofa, and the mattresses had been overturned as well. There were a couple of things missing—the television, my jewelry box, as well as several bottles of nonprescription medications from the bathroom—nothing of real value because, frankly, I don't own anything of real value. Though it was obvious that it was intended to look like a robbery, I knew Hodge was the intruder.

"I don't get it," I said as I picked up a sofa cushion. "Hodge has a number of bad traits, but I never thought stupidity was one of them. He's got to realize that he'd be the first person I'd suspect. What's he thinking? Is he trying to scare me? Or was he actually trying to find something? This is crazy. Even for Hodge."

Arnie pulled his cell phone out of his pocket. "Ivy, put down that pillow and don't touch anything else until the police get here."

I was so tired and the pain pills were starting to wear off. "Oh, Arnie. Can't we wait until morning?"

"Sorry, kiddo." Arnie didn't look up as he dialed the police. I pulled out kitchen chairs for Margot and I to sit on.

"They'll be here in a few minutes," Arnie said after ending the call. "Now, to answer your previous questions. Was he trying to scare you? Definitely. Look at this mess. He wanted you to know he'd been here."

"But that's crazy. He had to know I'd call the police and put the finger on him."

"Maybe," Margot said, "but think about it for a minute. Today, you'd call the police, but would a few months ago, would you? I don't think so. Hodge hasn't seen the newer, stronger, braver, Ivy. Maybe he thought you'd be too frightened to report the break-in. But I'm wondering how he got in. There's a security system, right?"

"Yes," I answered, "you need a special card to open the main door, but if he timed it right, he could probably have snuck in behind someone else. It's dark. Maybe he hid in the bushes and waited until someone opened the door. If that someone was a mother with two or three chattering kids, she might have been too distracted to notice. It's possible."

Arnie leaned back against the kitchen counter and crossed his arms over his chest. I'd spent enough time with him over the last few months to recognize this stance. It was his thinking pose.

"Okay, so let's assume that's what happened. Tomorrow, I'm going to call around to the local inns to find out where Hodge is staying and when he checked in. I'll bet you ten dollars he's been here for several days, watching you, figuring out your schedule and work hours so he'd know when you'd be out of the house.

"Ivy, when you saw him in the alley, you said he was hunched over the door of your car, like he was trying to break in. I think you were right. He was trying to scare you, but he's also looking for something. He came here first and, when he couldn't find it, he tried to break into the car, thinking it might be there."

Arnie narrowed his eyes, considering the evidence. A smile spread slowly across his face and widened into a broad grin. He uncrossed his arms, rocked forward to shift his weight to his feet and laughed. "That's it," he said to himself and then looked at us. "That's it! He was looking for something. First in the apartment, then in your car but he didn't find it and do you know why?"

"No," I said. "Why?"

"Because what he was looking for wasn't here or in your car, that's why. What he's looking for is in my office. Now aren't you glad I insisted you store them with me?"

"The files!" Margot cried. "He was looking for Ivy's files!"

"Bingo! Margot, this is why I have pledged my eternal devotion to you. You're as brilliant as you are beautiful!" Arnie made his hands into fists and pounded a drumbeat on his thighs, thrilled by the genius of his discovery. I was less convinced.

"But you've looked through those papers fifty times and haven't found anything."

"I know." Arnie pulled up his shirtsleeve and checked his wristwatch. "After we file this report, we're all over going to the office and look through them again."

"Arnie, are you kidding?" I protested. "It's almost three in the morning. I've got to get some sleep before I have to pick up the kids tomorrow. Aren't you tired?"

Arnie's face lit up. He was the epitome of bright-eyed and bushy-tailed enthusiasm. "Nope."

He clapped his hands together and rubbed them eagerly. "But, you're right. You've got to get some sleep. Margot too. But, Margot, as soon as you're up to it, could you come into the office? We're going to go over those files with a magnifying glass until we find whatever it is Hodge Edelman was so very anxious to get his hands on. I don't know what it is but it's in there somewhere. Mark my words, Ivy! Somewhere in those papers is what we've been looking for. The loose thread."

"Seriously?" I asked. "You really think there's something there that will help us?"

"There has to be. Otherwise, why would he risk so much trying to find it?" He laughed. "Thank God, Hodge Edelman is such an arrogant, ham-handed burglar. It's been right under our noses all this time, but if he hadn't made such a show of searching for it, we might never have known it."

Arnie looked at his watch again and sputtered, impatient as a horse in the starting gate. "Where are these guys?"

∽ 35 ∽

Ivy Peterman

Bobby is too little to understand but, Bethany is old enough to know what the word divorce means. And if there was any chance she'd forgotten why we'd left Hodge and come to New Bern, when I arrived at Frankin's and Abigail's to pick her up the next morning, the sight of my left hand in a cast brought everything back.

As soon as she saw me, her eyes filled with tears. I knew what she was thinking. I got on my knees, wrapped her in my arms, and said, "It's okay, peanut. I'm fine."

Trying to blink back the tears, she searched my face with her eyes. "I didn't say anything, Mommy. Not this time. I promise, I didn't."

"I know."

"Was it Daddy?" she whispered.

I wiped the wet from her cheek. "Yes. But everything is going to be all right this time. Mr. Kinsella is going to go with me to see the judge and tell him what happened and make sure that Daddy can't hurt us anymore." I hoped I wasn't lying. Arnie seemed so sure.

"We're getting a divorce?"

"We are."

"Good." Bethany looked down at my hand. Her lip quivered. "I didn't say anything to him, Mommy. I didn't."

"I know. It wasn't your fault, sweetheart. It was never your fault. Never."

After the break-in, Franklin and Abigail insisted that the children and I move in with them until the divorce was final. I didn't like the idea of imposing on them, but in the end, I agreed and it was something of a relief. Margot might think of me as the newer, stronger, braver Ivy, and in many ways I was, but the attack in the alley and coming home to find my apartment broken into and ransacked had scared me, just like Hodge hoped it would. He was in jail for the moment, but there's a little thing called bail. Bottom line was, I didn't want to be in the house alone.

Franklin said he'd go over to the apartment and help me pack some things but Abigail insisted she go in his place. "You're not supposed to be lifting anything heavy, Franklin, not until the doctor gives you the all clear. And if I know you, you'll be hefting boxes and suitcases and I don't know what all. You stay here and watch the children. I'll go to the apartment and help Ivy pack."

"You see what it's come to, Ivy? Married less than a month and I'm already a hen-pecked husband," he said, but he didn't look too upset about the arrangement. He kissed Abigail on the cheek and went into the living room with Bethany, who wanted to know which Barbie he liked best, Mariposa or Island Princess.

Staying with Abigail and Franklin turned out to be a nice break. Abigail treated me like a guest and, I have to admit, I enjoyed it. It was nice to be fussed over, especially with my left hand out of commission. As I'd feared, Hodge made bail. Arnie got a protective order issued against him, which was supposed to ensure that he steer clear of me, but Franklin insisted on accompanying me to and from work every day just the same and I let him. I wasn't convinced that a piece of paper would protect me from Hodge. Franklin's presence seemed much more substantial.

Another advantage to staying with the Spauldings was that Franklin and Abbie adored the kids and were happy, even eager, to babysit. That made it easier for me to spend my non-working hours at the law office helping Arnie and Margot go over those files with a fine-toothed comb. We did so again and again and again, but I didn't see anything new and neither did anyone else. After a week of it, even Arnie's enthusiasm was beginning to flag.

One night, just two days before we were due in court, when the clock was getting ready to strike eleven, Margot pulled a piece of paper out of a pile and said, "Ivy? What's this?"

Yawning, I walked over to the desk where she was working and peered over her shoulder. "This notation on the back of this piece of paper, this series of numbers and letters, what is it?"

"I don't know. That Hodge's handwriting, not mine."

"No clue?"

"None."

Margot stared at the wall and drummed her fingers on the desk, thinking, and then copied the numbers and letters onto a legal pad.

"You think it means something?"

"Everything means something, the question is whether or not this means something important. At the moment, nothing comes to mind but . . ." she shrugged, "You never know. I'm going to make a couple of calls."

On the day of the divorce hearing, I wore a nice dress with a jacket Evelyn lent me. I sat at the table, flanked on either side by Arnie and Franklin. Arnie was in charge of the case, but Franklin was sitting in the second chair just in case Arnie needed him and also as a show of strength to the other side. Apparently two lawyers are more intimidating than one. Franklin conferred with Arnie before the judge came in, giving him some last-minute advice and warnings, but told him he had every confidence in him.

Margot sat behind us on the first bench of the gallery, so she would be close if Arnie needed anything. Abigail was there with Evelyn and Charlie. They'd had gotten Garrett and Gina to cover for them at work.

As Arnie had advised, I sat without looking at Hodge, keeping my gaze focused ahead. But Hodge had either received no such advice from his attorney or discarded it. I could feel his eyes on me and it made the hair stand up on the back of my neck but I stuffed back my fears. I refused to be afraid of Hodge. I wouldn't give him the satisfaction.

As Arnie predicted, our court date had been pushed back but only by a couple of weeks.

I had filed charges against Hodge for the attack in the alley, but that would be dealt with in a criminal trial later. Arnie explained that we could and would talk about what happened in the alley, but because Hodge hadn't yet been convicted, there were certain legal technicalities he had to observe.

"For instance, I can't try to force him to admit to attacking you, though I can push him to take the Fifth, refusing to speak on the grounds that he might incriminate himself. That won't look good for him, but doesn't help us as much as an outright conviction would. At this point, Hodge is only an 'alleged' attacker."

"Even though I'm wearing this thing?" I lifted my hand, heavy in its white cast.

Arnie nodded. "Afraid so. Hodge's side is going to try to argue that your injury was self-inflicted, a desperate attempt by a drugged-out mom who would do anything to keep her kids."

"But how can he say that?! We have witnesses! Abigail and Evelyn and—"

Arnie held up both his hands to stop my stream of protest. "I know. I know. It seems crazy, but that's just the way things are. I'm just telling you so you'll understand that I have to be careful about using the attack as evidence against him. We don't want it to blow up in our faces, okay?"

"Okay," I said, but I wasn't happy.

"Even so," Arnie said as he adjusted the knot in his tie, "try to keep your cast on the table as much as possible when we are in the courtroom—out where the judge can see it. Nothing wrong with sending a few subliminal messages—every little bit helps."

Standing in my ransacked apartment, Arnie had been so sure that everything was about to go our way, but now that our day in court had finally arrived and we still hadn't found a smoking gun among my files, he was less euphoric. Still, he was pretty sure it would be impossible for Hodge to get complete custody of the children now. And while that was an enormous step in the right direction, this most recent reminder of what Hodge was truly capable of had me in a panic. The kids wouldn't be safe in his care, I knew that. Hodge was a violent man and shouldn't be allowed to spend even one unsupervised hour with Bethany and Bobby.

But there was no guarantee the judge would agree and, if he believed the testimony of the first witness, chances were the court would have as many misgivings about placing the children in my custody as in their father's.

Dr. Kittenger was just as smug and self-satisfied as I remembered. Hard to understand given that he also was just as unattractive as I remembered. He sat in the witness chair, smoothing one hand over his nearly balding head to make sure his comb-over was still in place and sniffing loudly after he repeated the words "So help me God," then proceeded to tell as big a bunch of lies as has ever been uttered under oath.

At least that's what I thought. Later, Arnie said he thought it seemed like a pretty average day in divorce court. I'm glad I'm not a lawyer.

According to Dr. Kittenger, I am a drug addict. Or at least I was in Pennsylvania. When Arnie confronted him with the negative drug test results, he asserted that perhaps I had since given up the habit (yeah, because if you've got a drug addiction, running away and living in a car with two small children is the thing that will make it easy for you to quit) but that when I was under his care, I was definitely an addict.

"I had suspected as much for some time," he said, "but I didn't realize how big an issue it was until the day she kidnapped the children . . ."

"Objection!" Arnie leapt to his feet and looked at the judge. "My client has not been charged with kidnapping."

"Sustained. Dr. Kittenger, please refrain from accusing Ms. Peterman of kidnapping."

"I'm sorry, Your Honor," he said, but he didn't look as if he meant it. "On the day she . . . left town . . . Ms. Peterman came to see me at the nursing home. Of course, my primary job is to oversee the medical care of the residents of the Shady Brook Care Center, which I own with Mr. Edelman. However, as a courtesy to Mr. Edelman, I have served as the Edelman family physician for some time.

"On the day she left, Ms. Peterman came to see me with what she said was a respiratory complaint, but I couldn't find anything wrong with her. During the examination, my pager went off and I had to tend to one of our patients. I left Ivy in my office briefly. When I returned, she wasn't there. My desk drawer was open, the one where I keep the key to the cabinet that contains the schedule C drugs."

"Schedule C?" The attorney asked innocently, though he already knew the answer.

"Those are drugs whose use is restricted and controlled by the government, narcotics and such, drugs with the greatest potential abuse risk. That's why we keep them under lock and key; they're prime targets for addicts."

Kittenger paused, letting the word addicts hang in the air, then took a handkerchief out of his pocket and trumpeted into it loudly, apologizing for the effect autumn pollens had on his system. "Anyway, when I got back to my office the key was missing and so was Ivy, but it didn't take me long to locate both of them. I found her in the storage room. She'd opened the drug cabinet and was stuffing bottles of pills into her purse."

George Caldwell shook his head as if he genuinely regretted hearing this news. "And then what happened?"

"Well, I confronted her, naturally," Kittenger said. "At first she admitted she had a problem, but when I said she needed to go in for treatment, she started backpedaling, denying everything she'd said before. She called me some terrible names and then walked out. Of course, I had to call Hodge and let him know about the situation. I didn't want to, but there were the children to be considered. It simply wasn't safe to leave them in the care of an admitted drug addict."

He blew his nose again; it was a strange coincidence that he did so every time he uttered a particularly loaded phrase.

"When I told Mr. Edelman what happened, he was terribly upset, naturally, and very concerned for his wife. I advised him to check her into a rehabilitation program as soon as possible and he agreed, but he never had the chance. By the next day, she was gone and so were the children."

Dr. Kittenger started to tell about what had happened when Hodge confronted me about my "addiction" and, of course, Arnie objected. But, it didn't matter. The judge didn't need Kittenger to fill him in on the details. Hodge was in the warm-up pen, waiting for his chance.

Before he did, Arnie cross-examined Kittenger, quizzing him about the incomplete nature of my medical records, asking him how it was possible that he hadn't noticed or noted my previously broken arm, or collarbone, old injuries that my physician's deposition stated must have occurred while I was under Dr. Kittenger's care. He mumbled something about it being hard to accurately date such things and suggested those breaks were from childhood injuries.

Arnie went on to question him about a few other oddities in my medical records. In the original records, there were many places where the doctor had added extra notes in the margins, squeezing in comments that supported his version of the story. Interesting, Arnie noted, that all these observations were written in different ink than the rest of the record, just the sort of thing you'd expect to see if someone were adding things to the records after the fact. This seemed to catch Kittenger off-guard for a moment, but then he countered that he was a busy man with many patients to tend to. Sometimes he got called away for emergencies and had to finish his record keeping in the evenings. "I take quite a lot of work home at night. I suppose that's what happened. Possibly I added some extra notes later at home, using a different pen."

Then Arnie pulled out a pile of papers, billing records from Shady Brook, noting scores of dates when the good doctor had billed our insurance for office visits with me and then wondered aloud why there weren't any accompanying notes of those visits in my medical file.

I had to press my lips together to keep from smiling. The forensic accountant Arnie had hired had uncovered this during her investigation. I remembered most of those appointments, all times when I went in to have Kittenger patch me up after Hodge had given me another pounding, but he'd never kept any records about that. Kittenger knew what side his bread was buttered on, Hodge's, and he wasn't going to keep records on anything that might make his partner look bad.

Kittenger was really flustered by this. The best explanation he could muster was that there must have been some kind of error in the accounting department or that perhaps there had been a mistake and those bills were for visits by Bobby or Bethany instead. Arnie quickly produced the children's records, noting that there were no indications that Kittenger had seen them on those dates, either. In the end, the best Kittenger was able to do was assert that it was indeed highly irregular.

Arnie had done a good job. When he got back to the table, Franklin leaned over and told him so, but I was concerned. Arnie had punched some major holes in Kittenger's credibility, but something about the look on the judge's face made me wonder if he'd noticed.

✦ 36 ✦

Evelyn Dixon

After Hodge got off the stand, a late summer thunderstorm blew into town and knocked out the lights in the courthouse, so the judge adjourned court early for the day, telling everyone to be back at ten the next morning.

Charlie invited everyone to the Grill. It was just after three and the kitchen staff was on break between lunch and dinner, but Charlie assured us he could come up with something in the way of sustenance. Ivy begged off, saying she wanted to go and pick up the children from day care. Arnie went back to the office to prepare for the next day and Margot went with him, so, in the end, only the Spauldings and I took Charlie up on his offer, running between the raindrops to get to the Grill.

The lights were off and there was no one inside the darkened restaurant. We went into the kitchen and pulled up stools by the counter, sipping iced tea as we watched Charlie pull lettuce, tomatoes, basil, a block of feta cheese, and various other ingredients out of the big commercial refrigerator. He'd decided that a big salad with a loaf of fresh bread would be just the thing for an early supper.

It had been hard sitting in the courtroom all day, being forced to listen to the mythology woven by Hodge Edelman and that toadying doctor friend of his without leaping to my feet and shouting, "Objection!" I object to liars on all possible grounds. I'm sure Abigail felt the same but we'd had strict instructions from Franklin and Arnie that, no matter what happened, we were not to say a word, not even to each other.

Now, released from our gag order, we were anxious to discuss the day's events, but first, apparently, I had to slice cherry tomatoes into halves.

Charlie set a big bowl of perfectly round little globes down next to my place at the counter and tilted his head toward the knife block. "I need a sous chef."

"It's a salad," I balked. "Why do you need a sous chef to make a salad?"

"Because it's not just any salad—it's *my* salad. A very special recipe that my . . ."

I rolled my eyes and finished the sentence for him, one I'd heard on many occasions. ". . . my mother made back in the old country. I know."

"And so it is." He grinned and began whisking a stream of balsamic vinegar into a bowl of olive oil. "Now, slice."

"Here," Abigail said as she reached for a second knife. "I'll help you. That doctor was such a odious little man, wasn't he?" She shuddered. "I'd hate to think of him examining me. Poor Ivy. At least she's in with Dr. Carmen now. He wasn't taking new patients but after I called and told him about Ivy, he made an exception."

I smiled to myself, thinking about how long the list of people who were willing to make exceptions for Abigail must be. "Well, his deposition was certainly helpful. And the way Arnie took apart Kittenger's testimony, piece by piece, was great. It was all I could do to keep from standing up and cheering. That scored a few points for our side. I mean, the judge has to think twice about Kittenger's testimony now that Arnie finished with him, don't you think? "

"Oh yes," Abbie concurred. "Certainly. Though it bothered me that the day ended with Hodge's story. Very interesting to see how he operates. He kept enough of the details of how he met Ivy so it sounded convincing, but he twisted the tale so he came off looking noble, if a bit naïve, while making sweet, underage Ivy appear . . . well . . . unsavory. I don't like the idea of the judge going home with that impression in his mind. But, perhaps that's better. Arnie will shred that story once he gets the floor. I thought he did a brilliant job today, didn't you, Franklin?"

Franklin nodded. "He did. Arnie is a very good lawyer. I couldn't have handled things better myself and that's the truth."

The expression on Franklin's face had me worried. All you had to do was look at him to know he was worried himself. "And? What aren't you telling us?"

Everyone was quiet. I put down my knife and Charlie stopped whisking his vinaigrette. Franklin took in a breath and let it out slowly.

"I didn't want to say anything to Arnie because I didn't want to undermine his confidence. I hoped that it wouldn't be an issue but, after sitting in that courtroom today, I'm afraid it may be."

Abigail let her fingers rest on her husband's arm. "What is it? Franklin?"

"When Hodge attacked Ivy and we got a new court date, we got a new judge as well. We lost Harry Gulden and got Joseph Maynard instead."

"So?" Charlie commented. "I know Judge Maynard. He's a nice enough man. Comes in for dinner with his wife every month or so. Likes an appetizer for himself and Mrs. Maynard, a strip steak, medium rare, and leaves good tips. Twenty percent. More, sometimes."

In Charlie's world, this was the measure of a man. Was he skimpy about ordering? Did he skip courses or split entrees with dinner partners? And was he a good tipper? These were the traits that displayed a man's character.

"Are you saying Maynard is a bad judge?" I asked

Franklin lifted up one hand. "Oh, no. The furthest thing from it. I've known Joseph for years and appeared in his courtroom on numerous occasions. He's an excellent jurist and a good man. In any other case, I'd be thrilled to have Joseph Maynard on the bench."

"So why not this time?"

Franklin's eyes flickered. He weighed his words before speaking.

"Joseph is a good judge and a fair one. But," he said slowly, "when he hears drug cases, it seems to me that his sympathies are set against the accused and he tends to give their testimony less weight. Drug addicts are notorious liars. Any judge knows that and takes it into account when hearing a case. Joseph knows this from personal experience. I'm concerned it might color his judgment. His daughter, Laurel, is an addict."

❧ 37 ❧

Ivy Peterman

It was pouring rain, but after picking Bobby and Bethany up from day care, I took them to Maxine's, our local ice cream shop. Maxine has twenty-two kinds of ice cream, all made on the premises. The flavors change depending on Maxine's mood but, no matter what's on the menu, Bethany orders vanilla. I got two scoops of fresh peach and Bobby wanted a scoop of "Dirt" which is dark, dark chocolate laced with gummy worms—the flavor of choice for three-to-five-year-old boys.

I knew the ice cream would spoil the kids' appetite for dinner and I was right, but I don't do it very often and I had an urge to spoil them a little. Supper was spaghetti and meatballs. After eating the prescribed five bites that is the rule at our table, they mostly pushed the noodles around the plate until I said they could be excused.

Abigail, reveling in the role of indulgent grandmother, had gone to the toy store and bought the kids a stack of new board games, so after dinner we played Chutes and Ladders, Memory, Hi-Ho Cherry-O, and Zingo, one after the other. The kids loved them all, but at the end of the night they still wanted to play the old standby we'd brought from home, Candy Land. We did and, of course, I got stuck in the Chocolate Swamp forever. This always happens to me and the kids think it's hilarious.

I let them stay up an hour past their bedtime. Bobby wanted me to read *Goodnight Moon* for the ten thousandth time. Bethany groaned about that, but sighed and snuggled in close when I began reading, comforted by the familiar bedtime ritual.

Bobby was already asleep when I tucked in their quilts and went to the door, but Bethany yawned and said, "I love you, Mommy."

I turned out the light and said, "I love you, too, Bethy." And I do. So much it makes my heart hurt.

My kids are my world. I would walk over hot coals for them. In some ways maybe I have, though I should have done it a lot sooner. But, the bottom line is, I'd do anything for them. My whole reason and purpose in life is to raise them in a safe, secure, loving home. But that judge doesn't believe that, I can tell. His eyes give him away.

Franklin and Abbie came home right after I put the kids to bed. They had picked up a video at the store, *Annie Hall*, and asked if I wanted to watch it with them. It's a great old Woody Allen comedy, about a woman, Annie, who starts out insecure, needing the approval of her boyfriend to define herself, but appears to comes into her own by the end of the film, rejecting the boyfriend, who has ended up needing her more than she ever needed him. It's a good movie and probably Abigail and Franklin thought it was an appropriate one. I find the ending a little frustrating because, to my way of thinking, Annie just leaves one dependent relationship to enter into another one, albeit with a more enlightened man at her side. I begged off.

I was tired, but couldn't sleep. I kept thinking about everything that had happened in court that day—the testimony of lies that Hodge had delivered with a completely straight face. How could he have said those things about me?

The story he told about how he'd met me left out the part about how I'd frozen on the stage and not been able to go through with the strip. In Hodge's version of events, I was an experienced stripper and he, misguided by love and a foolish desire to reform me, had rescued me, paid off my debt to Jerry (which he implied was money I owed for drugs), and taken me home. According to Hodge, once I was installed in his home I recognized a good thing when I saw it, had practically dragged him to bed, and then purposely gotten pregnant so I could keep my hooks into him. By that time, Hodge had realized what a calculating, drugged-out little tramp I was but had manfully struggled to hold our marriage together "for the sake of the children." In all this, Hodge's only sin was apparently an erroneous belief in the redemptive powers of love.

And, according to Hodge, the only reason I had left him was because, after his talk with Dr. Kittenger, he'd confronted me about my supposed drug addiction. It was an angry scene with me denying everything, the way addicts do, and Hodge telling me that in the morning he was checking me into a residential drug treatment program. He said I was so angry that I'd attacked him with a broken vase. He pointed to a thin white scar on his cheek as proof. Finally, he said, things calmed down and I agreed to enter treatment. Then, hard-working breadwinner that he is, he'd gone back to the office to clear up his desk so he could take me into rehab the next day, but when he'd returned to the house, I was gone and the children with me.

The last line was delivered in a raspy, supposedly emotion-choked voice. When he "pulled himself together," he claimed that he'd never abused me, that I'd pretended to be a victim of domestic violence so the Stanton Center would take me in. I was crazy, he said. Drugs had fried my brain. And, according to him, my broken hand was a self-inflicted wound, a sick attempt to gain attention and support my erroneous claims of abuse.

Fascinating fiction.

How he was able to sleep at night? But, knowing Hodge like I did, I had no doubt that at this moment he was in his hotel room, snoring like a band saw.

On the cross-examination, Arnie had confronted Hodge about the abuse in our home, which he vehemently denied, jumping to his feet, pointing to me and saying it was all a lie I'd concocted, that he'd never laid a hand on me and I was falsely accusing him to give myself leverage in the divorce.

The judge told him to sit back down, that he would not tolerate histrionics in his courtroom. Hodge obeyed, but I couldn't help but wonder how effective that little performance would be. Later, when questioning him about the attack in the alley, Arnie backed Hodge into a corner just as he'd planned, until Hodge had to plead the Fifth Amendment. That certainly couldn't help Hodge's side, but I was still worried.

Standing at the table after court had adjourned for the day, I questioned Arnie about it. "Aren't you worried that that's what will stick in the judge's mind? After Hodge's outburst, doesn't his mumbling that he pleads the Fifth seem a little anticlimactic?"

"Not at all," Arnie said as he stacked up his files and stuffed them into his briefcase. "Judges see this kind of thing all the time. Judge Maynard is a good judge. He's not going to be swayed by amateur theatrics."

"You don't think so? I don't know, Arnie. I don't think Judge Maynard likes me. Every time he looks at me the hair stands up on the back of my neck."

Arnie rolled his eyes. "Now who's being dramatic? Today went well and tomorrow will be even better. You'll get to tell your side. And, later, Donna Walsh will take the stand to corroborate your story, just like we planned. All we have to do is stick to our game plan."

He snapped his briefcase closed. "Oh, that reminds me. Meet me at the office at nine tomorrow. I want to go over your testimony one more time."

"Nine o'clock. I'll be there. But, Arnie . . . the judge . . . don't you think that . . ."

Arnie laid his hand on my shoulder. "Everything is fine. Really. I told you before: Judge Maynard is a good judge. No matter what the hairs on the back of your neck are telling you, I assure you that he is approaching this case the same way he would any other, with complete impartiality."

"But, Arnie, if the judge believes Hodge . . . I've got to have full custody of the kids, Arnie. I've just got to! They wouldn't be safe with him. Especially Bethany . . ."

"Ivy," he said wearily, "we've been over this a million times. We're going for full custody. You know that. I'm doing everything possible. Later, we're going to bring in Donna Walsh, your counselor from the Stanton Center, the whole slate of people who can corroborate your story. And I still haven't given up that we'll find that loose thread. Margot is at the office right now, going over the files again. Believe me, I am doing absolutely everything I can to get you full custody of the kids, but it just isn't something I can guarantee."

"I know, Arnie. I'm sorry. I wasn't saying that you weren't doing a good job. I know you are. You've been incredible. I'm just so nervous. The idea that Hodge could get even partial custody has me so . . ."

I stopped myself. There was nothing to say that I hadn't said before. I had the best lawyers in town and truth on my side, but as Arnie said, there were no guarantees. Everything that could be done was being done. Now, my fate and my children's fate lay in the hands of Providence and the judge whose every glance made the hairs stand up on the back of my neck.

"I'm sorry, Arnie. Don't mind me. I'm just a little crazy right now."

"It's all right. I understand." He looked at his watch. "Listen, I've got to run. I need to go to the office and revise my notes for tomorrow, but I'll see you in the morning. Until then, just go home, play with the kids, and quit worrying. That's my job. Okay?" He smiled reassuringly.

"Okay."

After I put the kids to bed, I tried to heed Arnie's advice and quit worrying, but Judge Maynard was still on my mind. I couldn't shake the feeling that, for some reason, the man just didn't like me.

Still, he didn't seem to be particularly taken with Hodge, either. When Hodge had been on the stand, Judge Maynard's eyebrows had taken on a particularly skeptical slant, but I didn't believe that necessarily boded well for *me*. Probably all it meant was that he thought we were *both* lower than slug slime on the forest floor. I guessed that if he'd had the option, the judge would have preferred to put Bethany and Bobby into the custody of almost anyone in that courtroom rather than Hodge or myself, but that didn't do me any good. One way or another, he was going to have to award the children's custody either to me, or to Hodge, or split it up between the two of us.

No! I had to get custody of my children. Full custody. I just had to!

Somehow I had to make the judge believe me. Tomorrow would be my turn on the stand, but the courtroom, I had seen, is all about questions that can be answered yes or no and the road that had brought me to New Bern was long and winding.

It didn't just start with me and Hodge; it began long before. My life, my parents' lives, my kids' lives were all connected. Lying in Franklin's guest room, listening to the thunderstorm that cracked the night sky and sent strobe-like flashes through the slits in the window blinds, I thought about the moment the lights turned on for me.

I'd gone to the mall, with Bethany and Bobby in tow, to buy new shoes for them and some face cream for myself.

After we got the shoes, I stopped by the cosmetics counter to buy moisturizer. They were giving free makeovers for a new cosmetic line that day.

I've never worn much makeup but when the porcelain-skinned saleslady in the black smock said, "What do you think, princess? Shouldn't your beautiful mommy sit down here so I can make her even more beautiful?" Bethany was sold.

"Come on, Mommy. Do it. Daddy will be so surprised!"

There were plenty of reasons for me to pass. Bobby was already yawning, ready for his nap, but Bethany was so excited about the idea of a makeover that I hesitated.

Seeing her opening, the pretty saleswoman laughed. "Come on, Mommy. You owe it to yourself and you're going to love the products. I've got a lipstick that'll change your life."

I knew better. No matter what the magazines say, there is no such thing as the lipstick that will change your life, but I wanted to believe there was. We all want that, don't we?

Hodge was always complaining about my appearance. According to him my butt was too big, my hair was too frizzy, and my clothes made me look too dowdy. Silly to think that a new shade of lipstick and a mascara that would make my lashes appear one zillionth of an inch longer than nature had made them would melt my husband's heart, but I wanted it to be true, so I sat at the makeup counter and told the lady to have at it.

Fifteen minutes later, she spun the chair around so I could see the mirror and said, "Voilà! What do you think?"

I gasped and Bethany jumped up and down. "Mommy, you look bee-ooo-tee-ful!" she exclaimed, drawing out the adjective the way I always did when she modeled an outfit from her dress-up trunk.

And it was true. I did look beautiful. Like me, but better. Sitting in the chair, I'd been a little nervous, afraid that the woman would overdo it with the makeup and I'd end up looking like a clown, but she'd used a light hand, applying just a little blusher to accent my cheekbones and jaw, a soft black/brown mascara on my lashes, and a peachy colored shadow that magically made my eyes appear larger and deeper in color, and, of course, the golden peach lipstick that was supposed to change my life.

And now that I think about it, in a way, it did. Just not in the way I'd planned.

Pleased with the results, I ended up buying the lipstick, mascara, and blush. The eye shadow was pretty and fun for a special occasion, but I knew I'd never really use it. With two children under the age of six, any makeup that couldn't be applied in two minutes while holding a toddler on my hip was destined to gather dust in a drawer.

I paid for everything and looped the bag on the handle of the stroller where Bobby sat half-asleep with his head lolling to one side. Bethany skipped as we headed for the car. Maybe it's silly to get excited over a little makeup, but I was. I felt really pretty and was anxious to get home and show off my new look for Hodge.

Walking down the center of the mall, one of those great-looking men who are always trying to sell hand cream approached. He whistled low and said, "Lady, I'd try to sell you some of this but, honestly, I don't think anything could make you look any better than you do right now. You are beautiful."

With two kids hanging on me, I knew he was just engaging in a little harmless flirtation, but couldn't help blushing a little at the compliment. It was nice to be noticed by an attractive man, even if he really was going to try to sell me something.

Bobby woke up for a moment and looked at the man, a little dazed. "Daddy?" he questioned.

The man grinned and winked. "No, kid. But I sure wouldn't mind."

I rolled my eyes, grabbed Bethany by the hand, and continued on my way.

At home, I put Bobby down for his nap. Bethany sat down to watch an episode of *SpongeBob SquarePants* while I started making dinner, a southwestern-style chicken dish I knew Hodge liked.

When he left that morning he said he'd be late, but I heard the mechanical groan of the automatic garage door a little before four. The sound caused me a pang of anxiety. Him coming home early meant he wanted to check up on me and perform one of his surprise inspections, the kind I never managed to pass. If I'd been thinking clearly, I'd have rubbed off the makeup, knowing he wouldn't be in the mood for me to surprise him with a new look.

Instead I ran into the bathroom, straightening up the towels that were hanging askew on the rack and rinsing the slimy soap off the dish, things that drove Hodge crazy, and yelled out to Bethany, "Pick up your toys! Quick! Daddy's home!"

I heard the car door slam and sped into the kitchen to scoop up discarded bits of onion and peppers from the cutting board.

Hodge came in through the garage, scowling. "It smells like garlic in here. How many times do I have to tell you to turn on the fans when you cook? What the hell is that on your face?"

I lifted a hand to my lips, remembering the lipstick, and swallowed hard. "Oh. I got some new makeup at the mall today. Do you like it?" I tried to sound casual, knowing from experience that signs of fear only fanned the flames of his anger.

He let his briefcase drop to the floor with a thud and loosened his tie with one hand. "No. I don't like it. Why would you think I'd like it?"

He slapped me hard across the face. I told him I was sorry, that I'd take it off, but it didn't do any good. He slapped me over and over, calling me names that I don't say and won't write; names that no one should ever be called.

Bethany heard the noise and ran into the kitchen with her eyes blazing. Usually when Hodge started beating me, the kids ran for cover. That's what I'd told them to do when daddy "lost his temper." Hard to believe now that's what I used to call it. What kind of confused message was I sending to them, giving them the idea that a man who hits a woman has just lost his temper? I'd never tell them that now. I'll never tell them that again.

Seeing what was going on, Bethany ran to Hodge and pounded on his leg with her little fists. "Don't you say that to Mommy! Don't you call her names! She looks beautiful!"

Hodge looked down and bellowed, "Bethany, get out of here! Ivy, tell her to get out of here right now!"

I did as I was told, but Bethany wouldn't budge.

"No! You stop hurting her! She's beautiful! We don't need you. The man at the mall said she was beautiful. He wants to be our daddy, so we don't need you anymore!"

Hodge spun around and started slapping Bethany, screaming at the top of his lungs and demanding to know who the man was, what was his name, and calling her the same horrible names he'd called me, saying she was growing up to be a little tramp just like her mother.

I was screaming, too, begging Hodge to stop, then demanding. When that didn't work I grabbed a heavy crystal flower vase from off the kitchen counter, dumped the carnations on the floor, and held it up high over my head. "Stop it, Hodge! Leave her alone! Stop it or I swear to God, I'll kill you. I'll kill you if you touch her again!"

Hodge spun around to face me. When he did, I screamed for

Bethany to run, run into the bathroom and to take Bobby with her. She hesitated for a moment but when I yelled, "Do it!" she obeyed. I heard Bobby cry, mad at being woken from his nap so abruptly, followed by the slam of a door.

Hodge sneered and walked slowly toward me, forcing me to back around the kitchen island, circling me like a panther. Tears streaming down my face, I told him to back off, but he lunged for me. We struggled for the vase but he was stronger.

He ripped it from my hands, then grabbed my left wrist, pinned my hand down on the granite countertop and smashed the vase down on it as hard as he could, breaking my little finger and shattering the top of the vase. Shards of glass cut my hand.

I was bleeding, in pain, furious. It was one thing for him to beat me, but when he hit Bethany, something inside me snapped.

Reaching my right hand across the countertop, I grabbed the jagged base of the broken vase and sprung at Hodge, cutting his face with the broken glass. That part of his story was true; the thin, white scar on Hodge's face was my doing.

He wasn't expecting me to come at him like that. He cursed, let go of my wrist, and grabbed his bleeding cheek. I saw my opening and ran toward the bathroom, screaming for Bethany to open the door. She did. I had just enough time to run inside and lock the door before Hodge reached it, pounding and bellowing at me to open the door.

You know the rest of the story—most of it—all except the part when, sitting on my lap on the bathroom floor with the angry red outline of her father's fingers still visible on her cheek, my little girl put her arms around my neck and sobbed, not from the pain of the slap but from a childish, undeserved guilt she felt at having given me away, innocently sharing the image of another man's interest in me, not understanding the consequences that her actions might bring.

And with Hodge raging on the opposite side of the locked door, and my baby sobbing in my arms, I remembered another little girl, sobbing her guilt into the branches of an old oak tree, and realized how easily history can repeat itself.

❦ 38 ❧

Ivy Peterman

During the night the thunderstorm knocked out the power. Abigail's urgent knock woke me. "Aren't you up yet? Arnie just called wanting to know where you are."

I rolled over and saw the radio alarm clock blinking twelve. The last time I'd looked at it the clock said three-forty. I felt rummy, almost drugged. "What time is it?"

"Nine twenty-six. Doesn't the court reconvene at ten?"

It did.

I jumped out of bed and asked Abbie to call Arnie, explain what happened, and told her to go ahead, saying I'd meet everybody at the courthouse as soon as I could.

I showered, dressed, put on my makeup, grabbed my car keys, and ran out the door at nine minutes before ten. Naturally, the car decided not to start. I ran the four blocks to the courthouse and arrived just as the clock was striking ten. My blue pumps will never be the same.

In the courtroom, Arnie was standing lookout. He closed his eyes and sighed with relief when I came in. "Thank God! The judge will be here any second."

"Sorry." Abigail and Evelyn gave me an encouraging wave from the gallery and I waved back. "Hey, where's Franklin? And Margot and Charlie?"

"They'll be here soon. There've been some new developments. Good ones. When we got to the office last night there was a . . ."

The bailiff announced the arrival of the Honorable Joseph Maynard. Arnie leaned toward me and whispered, "I don't have time to explain now, but whatever I say to you, just go with it. Okay?"

I was the first witness. I told my story just the way Arnie and I had discussed, beginning with how I'd come to the Atlantis Club looking for a job and ending with story about the lipstick that changed my life and brought me to New Bern.

Arnie asked a lot of questions, more than he had when we rehearsed my testimony. I had the feeling he was stalling for time and remembering what he'd said about following his lead, I dragged out my answers until it was time to break for lunch.

As soon as the judge left, Arnie turned on his cell phone, waving off my questions until he could listen to his messages. With the phone at his ear, Arnie's face broke into a broad smile. He clutched his hand into a triumphant fist over his head, pulled it down sharply like a trucker tugging on his horn, and hissed. "Yesssss!"

"What?"

Arnie grabbed my arm. "Come with me."

Leaving Abigail and Evelyn to follow, Arnie hurried me to the Grill on the Green. Charlie was standing at the front door. "In the back room," he said. "I didn't think you'd want anyone from the other side to know she's here."

"You thought right."

Still tugging my arm, Arnie led the way through the restaurant to the back room that was usually reserved for private parties. I came through the door and heard a voice from the past.

"Well, bless my bloomers! There she is, in person. Miss Cracklin' Ivy Rose."

I covered my mouth with my hand and laughed. "And there *you* are, in person," I echoed. "Miss Carmel Sunday!"

* * *

Everybody—Charlie, Evelyn, Franklin, Abigail, Arnie, and I—
sat at the big round table watching Carmel Sunday enjoy the lunch
Charlie had prepared just for her.

Carmel clutched a hand to her ample bosom and groaned with
pleasure. "Oh!" she exclaimed through a mouth full of food. "This
is the most unbelievable thing I have ever eaten in my life! What is
it?"

Evelyn gave Charlie a coquettish glance and answered for him.
"That would be the duck that makes food critics cry. For joy."

"Amazing," she murmured, closing her eyes as she swallowed.

"Isn't it?" Evelyn agreed. "That's the recipe Charlie pulls out of
his back pocket when he's trying to impress the ladies."

Carmel opened her eyes wide and turned to Charlie. "It works! I
am duly impressed." Charlie blushed.

Arnie cleared his throat. "Can we continue this meeting of the
gourmet society later? We've got to be back at court in fifteen minutes. Carmel, remember what we talked about. Just answer my
questions and then tell exactly what you saw that day at the club.
No embellishments. Stick to that and you'll make a very believable
witness."

Carmel put down her fork and sat up straight in her chair, a hen
with ruffled feathers. "Well, I should hope so. Hey! I may take my
clothes off for a living, but I'm as honest as they come. Check my
record; the only thing you'll find there is a traffic ticket from 1988."

She turned to Evelyn to explain. "The cop said I was going forty
in a twenty-five, but I swear I wasn't. You tell that to the judge,
Arnie! I'm an honest person. Nobody can say I'm not."

Arnie nodded and tugged at his shirt collar. "I'm sure he'll realize that, Carmel."

"Carmel, thank you so much for doing this," I said. "Really, this
is going to be a huge help."

"Don't mention it," she replied with a wave of her fork. "You
were such a sweet kid. The minute I saw you I knew you were in the
wrong place, but what could I do about it? After you left with
Hodge that day, I wondered if you wasn't jumping out of the frying
pan and into the fire."

She took a last bite of duck and dabbed her mouth with her napkin. "When my friend Sheila told me some people had come to the old neighborhood wanting to talk to anybody who remembered you, I called as soon as I could. Sorry I didn't hear about it sooner, but I just got back from visiting my sister in Idaho. Sure am glad to be back. Don't know what Vesta sees in that place. There's not a shopping mall within fifty miles. Just scenery. Gave me the creeps." She shuddered.

There was a knock on the door. Margot came in grinning from ear to ear. "I was right! It all checked out! Annie just called from her car. She's on her way. She'll be here a little after one and she's bringing company with her."

Arnie jumped up so quickly the chair he was sitting in fell over. He grabbed Margot around the waist and spun her in a circle. "You're a genius!"

"What's going on?" I asked. "Who's on the way?"

"Annie Fielding, the forensic accountant we've been working with. I'm going to put her on the stand right after Carmel."

"Wait a minute," I said. "I'm confused. I thought Donna Walsh was going to testify after Carmel."

Arnie put Margot down and picked up his briefcase. "Change of plans. Carmel? Ivy? Let's go. Franklin, I haven't had time to prep Annie; can you do the cross? Margot will fill you in on the details. Can you be ready to go by two-fifteen?"

Franklin ran a hand over his shirtfront, making certain his necktie was smooth. "Absolutely."

"Franklin, are you sure this is a good idea?" Abigail said. "It's another week until your doctor appointment. You know what the doctor said about avoiding stress."

"Abbie, the only thing that's been causing me stress lately is having to sit on my hands while Arnie gets to have all the fun. I like being a lawyer! I'm good at it. I know I was overdoing it before, but prepping and cross-examining one witness is not going to propel me to cardiac arrest. Besides, I have to do it. This is for Ivy. And the children."

"All right," Abigail assented. "Just don't get too worked up."

"I won't." Franklin picked up his wife's hand and held it to his lips. "I promise. Getting worked up is something I save for you, my love."

Margot's eyebrows shot up as she tried, unsuccessfully, to stifle one of her signature giggles. I didn't blame her. Apparently returning to work wasn't the only activity Franklin hadn't waited to clear with the doctor. No wonder Abigail seemed so cheery recently. I gave Evelyn a knowing look across the table. She raised her hand to her mouth, trying to cover a smile.

Abigail glared at the three of us, making Margot giggle again.

"Margot," she said, carefully enunciating her words, "shut up."

Carmel was an excellent witness, clear in memory and quick with her answers.

Hodge's lawyer tried to get her to backpedal, suggesting that it would be impossible for her to remember all the details of something that happened so many years ago, but Carmel countered back, "Not for me. I've got a mind like a steel trap. I can still remember everything I learned in school: state capitals, algebra formulas, you name it."

"Is that right?" George Caldwell asked with a smirk. "Well, how about this. Who was the thirteenth vice-president of the United States?"

"Millard Filmore," Carmel answered proudly. "From 1850 to 1853. Then the president, Zachary Taylor, died and Filmore took over as president, but that was it for him. He never got elected president on his own." George frowned, realizing he'd gambled and lost.

Carmel continued, "That's what I'm saying. I'm like an elephant. Never forget. And I remember everything that happened when Ivy showed up at the club. I knew Hodge already. He was one of the regulars. Always buying drinks and girls for those doctors, but plenty of times he came in on his own. Even after he took Ivy home with him he used to show up at least a couple of times . . ."

"Thank you, Miss Sunday," Caldwell said grimly. "You're excused."

Carmel winked at me as she left the witness box and I smiled.

She'd done well. As she'd been speaking I'd seen the judge glance at me a couple of times with an expression that seemed to be wondering if maybe, just maybe, I might be telling the truth.

Hodge and his lawyers were starting to look grim. Carmel's testimony hurt them, but it was Annie Fielding who would deliver the knockout punch. And she did it without ever taking the stand.

At two-fifteen on the nose, Franklin entered the courtroom followed by Margot and a petite brunette in a navy blue shirtdress, Annie Fielding, and two men I didn't recognize, who wore dark suits and even darker expressions.

Arnie requested and was granted a moment to talk with his colleague.

"Change of plan. I'm going to put Ivy back on the stand," Franklin said.

Arnie looked puzzled. "Yeah? You don't think it would be better to go straight to Annie?"

Franklin shook his head. "No. If things work out the way I hope they will, we may not even need to call Annie. We've got to do this in such a way that there can be no question of Ivy's involvement. We have to show she had no idea what was going on."

"That should be easy. I don't have any idea what's going on. What *is* going on?"

"You'll know in a minute. You've just got to answer a couple of questions. Just get up there and tell the truth. Trust me, Ivy. I know what I'm doing."

After the judge reminded me that I was still under oath, Franklin began.

"Ms. Peterman, we haven't discussed the testimony you are about to give, have we?"

"No," I shrugged. "As far as I knew I was done when we broke for lunch."

"Well, this will just take a few more minutes. Ivy, about two weeks ago just before nine PM, you left Cobbled Court Quilts and went to your car to find Hodge Edelman waiting for you, is that right?"

"Yes. He said he wanted to talk to me."

"What about?"

"He was trying to talk me out of getting a divorce. He told me he wanted us to get back together and for the kids and I to move back home to Pennsylvania."

"Did he offer to give you anything special if you complied with his request?"

I had to stop and think for a minute. The searing pain that coursed through my hand as he'd slammed the car door on it loomed large in my recollections of that night. I'd told Arnie and the police about it at the time, but now it was harder to remember much about the conversation that had taken place before Hodge attacked me.

"Ummm . . . he said that if I came home he'd buy me a new car, and get me a cleaning lady."

"Anything else?"

"Oh yeah. He said we'd go on a trip. Back to the Caribbean. He said he'd already bought tickets and made a reservation at the same hotel we'd gone to on our honeymoon."

Franklin pulled on his nose and nodded. "All right. Let me ask you something else. Do you have any bank accounts?"

"Yes. I've got a saving account at New Bern Mutual."

"How much money is there in that account?"

"About twenty-five hundred. I'm saving for the deposit on a new apartment."

"Is that all? You have no other bank accounts in your name?"

"No," I said.

"Are you sure? Isn't there an account registered in your name in the Cayman Islands?"

I thought for a moment. "Oh! Wait a minute! I do have an account there! A savings account. I forgot all about it. I was already pregnant on our honeymoon and Hodge helped me open a bank account in my name, a college account for the baby. He said the interest rate was better than in the States."

"How much would you say is in that account today?"

"I don't know. Hodge handled all the financial stuff. We opened it with three thousand dollars ten years ago, so I'd guess now it's worth . . . maybe four thousand?"

The shadow of a smile that played at Franklin's lips told me I'd said the right thing. "So, Ms. Peterman, you didn't know that the offshore account your husband had you open in your name contains, at the opening of business today, three million two hundred and thirty-eight thousand dollars and sixty-four cents?"

For a moment I didn't breathe. My jaw actually dropped open. Sandwiched between his lawyers, I saw the veins pulse in Hodge's neck and his jaw tighten. Kittenger was sitting in the gallery behind Hodge. His face went suddenly white.

"Three million dollars! Are you kidding me?"

Franklin was done playing straight man. He smiled openly and said, "I take it this information comes as a surprise to you?"

I let out an incredulous laugh. "Yeah, I'll say it does! Three million dollars? If I knew I had three million dollars, do you think I'd be living at the Stanton Center and worrying about how I'm going to scrape together enough money for the deposit on a new place?" I laughed again. "Really? Three million. Are you sure?"

"Thank you. You may step down."

Next, Franklin surprised everyone by calling Dr. Kittenger back to the stand.

The good doctor looked nervous when the judge reminded him that he was still under oath. Beads of sweat pearled on his brow.

"Dr. Kittenger, you stated before that you and Hodge Edelman are joint owners of the Shady Brook Care Center?"

"Yes."

"How much money did you have to put up for your half of the partnership?"

Kittenger swallowed. "Nothing. My expertise in medicine was what I brought to the partnership."

"Ah," Franklin nodded understandingly. "I see. I did some checking and found that you undertook your medical studies in South America and that you graduated eighty-fifth in your class. Is that right?"

Kittenger looked at Franklin with loathing. "Yes."

"Eighty-fifth. Out of a class of eighty-nine. I guess Mr. Edelman saw some medical expertise in you that had gone undiscovered by your professors."

Caldwell objected to that, naturally. Franklin apologized and asked that his comment be stricken from the record before he continued.

"So you oversee the medical aspect of the business and Mr. Edelman is in charge of finances, is that right?"

"Yes, that's right." Kittenger squirmed nervously in the witness chair. His eyes darted from Franklin to Hodge and back again. "I have nothing to do with the business side of things. Billing, record-keeping, and such, that's all Hodge's domain. I just take care of the patients."

"So, that would explain why you didn't know anything about the billing errors for Ms. Peterman? All those bills for appointments you kept no records of?"

"Like I told Mr. Kinsella, I have nothing to do with that," the doctor snapped. "There must have been some sort of accounting error."

"Well, that's certainly possible. Over the past several years, there've been all kinds of accounting errors at Shady Brook. My next witness, Annie Fielding, is a forensic accountant. She's found over three million dollars in billing errors at Shady Brook, most of them for Medicare patients—patients whose bills are paid by the government. In fact, it's almost exactly the same amount as is contained in the offshore account that Mr. Edelman had his wife open in her name."

Franklin stopped for a moment, smiled and scratched his cheek with his index finger. "You know, it's amazing what these forensic accountants can find out once they start digging around. Miss Fielding is very skilled at her job. Tell me, Dr. Kittenger, you like to travel, don't you? Aren't the Cayman Islands one of your favorite destinations?"

And that was it. The loose thread. Franklin gave it a good tug and, right in front of everyone, Kittenger unraveled. The doctor's eyes bulged out of their sockets. He jumped to his feet and pointed at Hodge. "It was Hodge! It was all his idea! I just made the deposits! He talked me into it, all of it! It was never supposed to go this far. He promised me that all I had to do was make the deposits. That's was all! I never agreed to the rest of it. The stuff with his wife. Altering the records and saying she'd taken drugs. That was all Hodge's idea! He made me do it!"

Hodge leapt from his chair and screamed. "Sit down, Kittenger! Just shut up and sit down!"

Kittenger took his partner's advice, but it was too late. Wild-eyed and weak, he dropped into his chair and said. "I want a lawyer." He pointed at Franklin and said, "You! I want you. I plead the Fifth!"

Franklin smoothed his necktie. "We'll discuss that in a moment. In the meantime," he said turning around to face the gallery. "There are some gentlemen here who would like to talk with you and Mr. Edelman."

The two dark-suited men who had been sitting with Annie Fieldman got to their feet. Franklin turned his attention toward Judge Maynard. "Your Honor, allow me to introduce Mr. Dowling and Mr. Kirkpatrick. They work for the government, investigating Medicare fraud."

ꙮ 39 ꙮ

Evelyn Dixon

"Back to you, Mary Dell!"

"Thank you, Dale. And be sure and tell all those quilters over at the high school that I'll be heading over to see them in just a few minutes because you know what? It's already time for us to say good-bye!" Mary Dell looked at me, seemingly shocked.

"Evelyn, I don't know how that hour flew by so fast. Do you?"

I shook my head, hoping this was a rhetorical question. As far as I was concerned, this had been the longest hour of my life.

"This has been such a special show. On behalf of Howard, myself, Evelyn, and everybody here at Cobbled Court Quilts, thank you for tuning in. With your help and the help of thousands of Quilt Pink quilters across the country, we can play an important role in detection, treatment, and finding a cure for breast cancer. So spread the word!"

Mary Dell turned in her chair to face camera two so smoothly that you'd never have known the floor director had given her the cue to do so. It was as if her brain had taken a notion to twist to the left and her body followed quite naturally. "But, as always, before we sign off I want to leave you with a little bit of quilting wisdom from one of our viewers. Today's quilter's quote was sent in by Betty Jura of Fullerton, California. Evelyn, would you share Betty's thought with everybody?"

I hesitated for a second and Mary Dell said, "It's right there on that card, Baby Girl. Just go ahead and read it."

I cleared my throat. "When life gives you scraps, make a quilt."

Mary Dell threw back her head and laughed. "Oh, I love that one! Good advice from one who knows! Thank you for sharing that, Betty."

The *Quintessential Quilting* theme music began playing softly in the background. "Thanks again for watching. And remember . . ." Mary Dell's expression became serious as she held up an admonishing finger, ". . . behind every great quilter is a great big pile of fabric. So get back to work! Bye ya'll!"

She laughed and waved. Everyone in the shop, quilters and observers, broke into applause as the theme music increased in volume. I clapped and grinned idiotically at the camera I hoped was the right one.

The floor director held up three fingers, then two, then one. "And we're off the air. Good show, everybody!"

Excited chatter and a few cheers mixed in with the sound of applause. I slumped into my chair, utterly exhausted.

"Baby Girl! You did it!" Mary Dell beamed as she reached over to clasp my sweaty hand. "Now that wasn't so bad, was it? Admit it; you had fun."

I tilted my head and looked at my friend sideways. "That was, without question, the most miserable sixty minutes of my life. Don't ever ask me to do that again."

Mary Dell clucked her tongue and blew out a long, disbelieving breath. "Come on now. You did just fine. I was proud of you. You didn't puke once!"

"No," I chuckled and hoisted myself upright in the chair. "I managed to take care of all that before they turned on the cameras."

Mary Dell slapped her thigh. "Well, see? There you go! And it'll be even easier next time."

I gave her an evil glare. There she was, practically a force of nature, feeding off the energy of the cameras, cues, and crowd like a dead battery sucking up volts from a charger and me? All I wanted to do was lie down and take a nap.

Still wearing her headset, Sandy wended her way through the web of camera cables. "Good show, Evelyn. Everything looked great on the monitor, really. I'll play back the tape for you."

"Must you?"

Sandy grinned. "Mary Dell, the car is waiting. Howard's already inside. You two had better get over to the gym and start signing those books. We handed out five hundred copies, so it'll take a while. Then you've got to do your thing over at the Green. The barbeque is supposed to start at five but if the signing is taking too long, you can show up late. Porter says they've got it all worked out." She grabbed a coiled extension cord from one of the camera people and headed toward the back door to load it into one of the trucks parked in the alley.

"Thanks, honey. Hey! Is there anything to eat around here?"

"There's a six-pack of Dr Pepper and a box of Moon Pies in the car," she called without turning around. "I already gave them to the driver."

"Sandy thinks of everything." Mary Dell said admiringly. "I'm starving! Nothing personal, Baby Girl, and I appreciate the thought but no matter what Porter says, I just don't have a lot of faith folks around here know how to make decent barbeque."

"They don't," I said with a yawn. "Mary Dell, you'd better get over to the gym like Sandy said. I'll see you later. Are you sure you still want to come tonight? Won't you be too tired?"

"Too tired!" she scoffed. "Are you kidding? Skip out on a special meeting of the Cobbled Court Quilt Circle held in my honor? Are you loco? Wild hogs couldn't keep me away."

Mary Dell and Howard went off the gym to meet the other quilters. I trudged up the stairs to Garrett's apartment, intending to pass out on the sofa until it was time for the barbeque on the Green, but made a visit to the bathroom first. After washing my hands, I peered into the mirror. The face that peered back at me was completely exhausted, but that was all right. I didn't mind.

When I was a little girl, my father liked to begin every family dinner with the same question, "What did you do today?"

My brothers and I would go around the table, in turn from oldest to youngest, and report on our activities. Some days the news was all good, other days it was punctuated by frustrations with friends, injustices by teachers, or complaints of overwork.

But no matter how good or bad our day, my father's closing question never varied. "And did you do any good for someone else today?"

Sometimes, we hadn't and that always got us thinking. Other times we had, and that always brought a smile to Dad's face. "Well, then," he'd say. "I guess it was a good day after all."

The road to Quilt Pink Day had been a weary one, potholed with long hours, hard work, stage fright, misunderstandings, and more than a few petty jealousies. But as I splashed cold water on my face, I didn't remember any of that. Instead I thought about the quilts we'd made, the money we'd raise, the women we'd encouraged, and the lives that might be saved.

Toweling the water from my tired face, I looked into the mirror and smiled. "I guess it was a good day after all."

40

Evelyn Dixon

Pulling a naked pork rib from her mouth, Mary Dell leaned over and whispered into my ear, careful to make sure that no one overheard her, "You're right. These Yankees don't know the first thing about barbequing a pig."

"Told you. Here. Give me your plate and I'll get rid of it for you."

Mary Dell surreptitiously pushed her plate toward me. "Don't let anyone see you. I wouldn't want to hurt anybody's feelings."

"Don't worry. I'll give it to Garrett. He'll eat anything." Holding Mary Dell's plate in my hands, I got up from the picnic table and started looking for Garrett just as Lydia Moss pushed through the crowd, waggling her fingers over her head to flag us down.

"Yoo-hoo! Evelyn! Mary Dell! There you are! I've been looking for you everywhere. I know you've barely had a chance to catch your breath today, Mary Dell, but Porter asked me to find you. He's just about ready to call you up on stage. Are you ready? Did you get enough to eat?"

"More than enough," Mary Dell answered.

"Wonderful! How did you like the barbeque sauce? That's my grandmother Lydia Lystrom Post's secret recipe. Normally I only make it for family, but the hospitality committee asked if I wouldn't mind parting with the recipe just this once and since it was for you, of course, I said yes."

"Really? Well, Lydia, you didn't have to do that. Bless your heart. I've never tasted anything like it."

Lydia beamed. "Oh, good! Really, it couldn't be easier. You just take a bottle of ketchup, a jar of grape jelly, a teaspoon of chili powder, and . . . oh, darn it. There's Porter coming up to the microphone. I'll write the recipe down and give it to you later."

"Thank you, Lydia. That'd be real sweet of you. But right now, I'd better scoot."

Just before wending her way through the crowd, Mary Dell turned to me with a grin and said, "Baby Girl, aren't you going to finish your barbeque? You've just got to, honey. It's like I told Lydia. You've just never tasted anything like it." She winked and started making her way to the stage, shaking hands as she did.

"Thanks, Mary Dell. Thanks a lot."

Lydia turned to me with an expectant look on her face. I picked up a pork rib and started gnawing on it.

After the signing at the gym, a few of the kids from the church youth group had drafted Howard onto their team for a softball game. Porter must have pulled him away from his fans because I could see him mounting the stairs to the stage, following right behind the First Selectman, smiling and shaking the hands of people who were standing nearby and clearly having the time of his life. Porter had to keep a hold on Howard's arm just to make sure he wasn't completely waylaid by admirers.

When they reached the microphone, Porter tapped it a couple of times to make sure it was on, then said, "Ladies and gentlemen, as First Selectman of the village of New Bern and on behalf of the citizens of New Bern, let me thank you all for coming out today in support of such a . . ."

The microphone squealed, making a sound like nails on a chalkboard. The crowd collectively covered its ears until the squealing stopped. Then someone shouted, "Come on, Porter! You've made enough speeches today! Let Mary Dell and Howard talk already!"

Lydia clucked her tongue with annoyance. "Really. People can be so rude!" she exclaimed, her attention fixed on the stage and her husband's face.

I murmured something agreeable and, taking advantage of the diversion, quietly slipped a piece of pork to a Labrador that was ambling through the crowd, sniffing the ground for scraps.

"All right, all right!" Porter said, lifting his hands and grinning with good humor. "I can take a hint, Steve. Ladies and gentlemen, without further ado, allow me to introduce the people you've all been waiting to see! The hosts of the cable television's most successful craft show, *Quintessential Quilting*, Mary Dell and Howard Templeton!"

The crowd broke into thunderous applause as Mary Dell, who reached the top of the stairs on the opposite side of the stage just as Porter finished the introductions, waved, stepped up to the microphone, and said. "Well, thank you, Porter! It's so wonderful to be here! Hello, New Bern!"

A fresh wave of applause swelled the air as the citizens of New Bern acknowledged her greeting.

Howard took the microphone from his mother, jumping into the little act they'd worked out between them without missing a beat. "Excuse me, Mama, but that doesn't sound right. What do you say we teach the folks how to say hello Texas style?"

"Howard, that's a wonderful idea. Why don't you do the honors?"

Howard's face broke into a wide grin. He waved his arm over his head like he was signaling a ship and shouted, "Howdy, ya'll!" Then he cupped his hand to his ear and leaned toward the audience, mutely inviting them to follow his lead.

They did, enthusiastically mimicking Howard's greeting, complete with waving arms.

Mary Dell took the microphone next, smiling. "Well! That was just wonderful! I tell you, you've made me feel right at home. And I do want to thank ya'll for inviting us here today and for everyone who has gone to so much trouble to make New Bern's Quilt Pink Day such a big success. Porter Moss, Dale Barrows, and everyone on the planning committees, thank you so much. And I want to give an especially warm and heartfelt hug of a thank-you to my dear friend Evelyn Dixon, owner of Cobbled Court Quilts and the one responsible for bringing Quilt Pink Day to New Bern in the first place. Let's give her a big round of applause!"

I'm not a shy person, but after the broadcast, I'd had enough notoriety to last me a lifetime. Still, Mary Dell meant well, so I got up from my seat on the picnic bench, waved, and quickly sat down.

After the applause died down, Mary Dell continued. "I'm going to let ya'll get back to eating your barbeque in just a minute, but first, Howard and I want to thank you again for treating us right and making us feel so at home. And, to show our appreciation, we want to teach you a little song we like to sing back home called 'Deep in the Heart of Texas.' Ready, ya'll?"

Nobody else could have pulled it off, not with a crowd of buttoned-up, no-nonsense, dyed-in-the-wool New Englanders, most of them directly descended from the purest of Puritan stock, but Mary Dell Templeton was the woman who put the celebration in the word "celebrity." After a little coaching, she had that audience eating out of the palm of her hand, singing at the top of their lungs and, between choruses, clapping out the song's familiar four-beat rhythm with the gusto of cowhands on rodeo day.

Sitting on my bench, clapping along with everyone else while a fat yellow Labrador stood nearby and wolfed down the leavings of my lunch, I smiled with my whole heart, the kind of smile that brings tears to your eyes, as I watched my dear friend Mary Dell.

Let me tell you: She was a sight to see.

After the public revelries wound down, Franklin, Garrett, Bethany, Bobby, and Howard drove to Waterbury for a movie while Mary Dell came back to the shop with me and the rest of the quilt circle for our own private party.

Though he had a strict rule against serving bar food at The Grill on the Green, Charlie put aside principle and made a special batch of buffalo chicken wings for me to serve at the circle meeting. He'd also arranged for his beverage supplier to bring in two cases of

Dr Pepper, enough to get Mary Dell and Howard through their week-long vacation in New Bern.

When I came out up the stairs carrying a platter of wings, Mary Dell dropped the scissors she was holding and practically hooted for joy. "Are those what I think they are?"

She grabbed a chicken wing, dipped it in the accompanying bowl of blue cheese dressing, and took a bite. "Oh my gracious me! I tell you what, I have died and gone to heaven. Girls! Get over here and try some of these. You too, Abigail. You're going to love this."

Five minutes later, our individual quilting projects abandoned, all of us were sitting at the worktable sucking the meat off chicken wings, our fingers stained red with the hottest of hot sauce—all except Abigail, that is, who insisted on eating hers with a knife and fork.

Between the broadcast and the barbeque, I had managed to sneak upstairs to Garrett's apartment for a refreshing twenty-minute catnap, otherwise I'd have been dead on my feet. Mary Dell had had no such opportunity, but it didn't seem to matter. She was still bright-eyed, bushy-tailed, and anxious to catch up on all the second-hand news she'd heard from me. She wanted to hear the real scoop, straight from the horses' mouths.

"You are kidding me! So they'd been bilking the government all those years, charging for charging for procedures they'd never performed . . ."

Ivy nodded confirmation. "Sometimes on patients who had died months before."

". . . and then that little toad of a doctor would fly to the Caymans every month and put the money in your account?" Mary Dell narrowed her eyes and made a hissing noise. "That man is lower than flea skis."

"That sounds about right," said Ivy with a grin. "The plan was to keep working until they had six million in the bank, three for each crook, then Hodge was going to pretend to take me on a second honeymoon, and trick me into withdrawing the money for them. And if anything went wrong, they figured they could pin the whole thing on me since the account had my name on it. Kittenger told the Feds everything.

"Hodge had it all worked out. The one thing he didn't plan on was me growing enough of a spine to actually leave him. Kittenger said Hodge didn't report us missing because he didn't want to attract the attention of the police. He figured I'd come crawling back on my own, but when months passed and I still hadn't turned up, they got nervous. Then one of our neighbors, who knew I'd disappeared with the kids but didn't know why, saw the promotional video and told Hodge where I was . . ."

Mary Dell's face fell. "Honey, I'm real sorry about that. I never meant to cause you all that trouble."

"Are you kidding?" Ivy took a sip of her Dr Pepper and paused a moment, waiting to see if she liked it before taking another. "I didn't know it at the time, but that was the best thing that could have happened. If not for that, I'd still be on the lam, dragging my kids from pillar to post, and living a life of lies."

"Now, I've got a career, good friends," she said, smiling as her eyes scanned the ring of faces, "and a home."

"And a bank account worth three million dollars!" Mary Dell exclaimed.

Ivy tipped her head to one side. "Not quite. That money was stolen. The government has frozen the account. In fact, they've frozen all Hodge's accounts, everything. It turns out that there's one thing he wasn't lying about. Other than that money in the Caymans, Hodge was dead broke. He borrowed money like there was no tomorrow, which I guess makes sense if you're planning on skipping the country and you're a thief. But, that means I'll get nothing from the divorce. No settlement. No alimony. Zero."

Mary Dell made a tsk-tsk sound with her tongue. "Ivy, that's terrible."

"Oh, I don't know." Ivy said. "I don't have any money, but I didn't have any before, either. Nothing has changed. We'll manage. Evelyn has taught me that I'm perfectly capable of supporting my family."

"You certainly are," I agreed.

"It's all good," she said. "The Petermans are home, in New Bern to stay. And no one can take my kids away from me, especially Hodge Edelman, because from what I understand, he's going to be in prison for quite some time—years and years. Maybe everything didn't work out the way I planned it, but in the end, it worked out better than I ever could have planned. It's like Margot says, 'all things work together for good . . .' "

"To them that love God, to them who are called according to his purpose," Mary Dell finished phrase and her eyes misted. "Romans 8:28. That was my old granny's favorite verse."

"Mine, too," Margot said with a smile.

"So, Margot, honey, how'd you crack this thing open?"

"Well," Margot said modestly, "it really was a team effort. When Hodge broke into Ivy's apartment and then her car, it was Arnie who figured out there must be something in Ivy's personal papers that Hodge didn't want anyone else to have. I was just lucky enough to turn over a sheet of paper and see a string of numbers and letters that Hodge had written."

Liza pulled a chicken bone out from between her lips and made a "get real" face. "Come on, Margot. There was more to it than that. You're the one who finally put two and two together."

Liza's eyes brightened as she leaned in to fill Mary Dell in on the details. "For the next couple of nights, Margot couldn't sleep. She kept thinking about those numbers, thinking they had to mean something, so she got up in the middle of the night and started reviewing the notes she'd taken when she and Arnie were at the hospital with Ivy. And then, all of a sudden—Bam! It hit her! The part about Hodge wanting to take Ivy to the Caribbean, and wanting to do it so bad he'd already bought the tickets!"

"Well, it wasn't quite—Bam!" Margot said. "But it got me to wondering. First thing the next morning, I called Annie Fielding and asked her if those scribbles from Hodge couldn't be some kind of account or password. Annie had already noticed some enormous problems with the books at Shady Brook. She thought Hodge was hiding money somewhere, but couldn't trace it. So she started pulling up online banking sites for every bank in the Caribbean, plugging

the numbers into every password prompt she could find until, finally, she found the right one. There it all was! Every deposit, every
transaction for the previous eight years! And Franklin took it from
there. Arnie had to get back to court, so Franklin only had one hour
to talk to Annie, look over the financial evidence, and figure out a
strategy. Abigail, your husband is some lawyer!"

"I've always known that," Abigail said with a proud little smile.
"He's handled my business affairs for thirty years. Of course, now
that we're family I get a reduced rate on billable hours."

Abigail, who had poured her Dr Pepper into a glass, took a tentative sip and pinched up her face in disgust. "Something must be
wrong with mine; it's like drinking cherry perfume."

"No, that sounds about right," Mary Dell said and took another
swig from her soda can. "It's an acquired taste."

Abigail pushed her glass away and got up to pour herself a glass
of water from the pitcher that was sitting on the end of the table.
Margot picked up where she'd left off.

"The really amazing part was how Franklin tricked Dr. Kittenger
into spilling the beans. We didn't have access to Kittenger's travel
records at all, but Franklin had been watching him in the courtroom and noticed how nervous he was. He figured that, some way
or other, Kittenger had to be directly involved. Somebody had to
make those deposits and, from what Ivy told us, we knew that
Hodge never traveled out of town overnight. Franklin guessed Kittenger was the mule, but he didn't know for sure. All he did was ask
Kittenger if he liked traveling to the Caymans and that was it! He
cracked like an egg."

Mary Dell whistled her admiration. "That is some story, Margot.
And I particularly like the part where you and that cute little Arnie
got to work side by side the whole time, smokin' the midnight hour
just like Perry Mason and Della Street." Mary Dell rested her chin
on her elbow and raised her eyebrows suggestively. "So tell me,
Della. Did any sparks fly between you and Mr. Mason? Any foolin'
around with the legal briefs?"

Margot turned bright red and the smile faded from her face.

Oh no, I thought. *Here we go again.* The last time anybody hinted at any possibility of romance between Arnie and her, Margot had burst into tears. Ivy and I both started to say something, anything to deflect Mary Dell's imprudent inquiry, but Margot beat us to it.

"Actually," she said softly. "He's asked me to go with a picnic with him tomorrow afternoon. A date. A real date."

"He asked you out?"

"Margot, that's wonderful!"

"Arnie is such a great guy!"

The smile slowly returned to Margot's lips. "I know. But I told him I couldn't go."

I stared at Margot, completely confused. "Why not?"

"I'm on the schedule tomorrow. You and Mary Dell and Howard are going up to the lake to see the leaves and I said I'd cover for you, remember?"

"Margot! Are you kidding? Don't worry about that. We've got all week to see the leaves. You go on your date with Arnie."

Margot's face lit up. "Really? Are you sure?"

"Heck, yes!" Mary Dell affirmed. "We can watch the store. Evelyn can run the register, I'll cut yardage, and Howard can help people figure out what color fabrics go together best. We've got you covered, honey. So you get on the horn and tell Arnie you're going on that picnic. Scoot! Young love can't wait."

"Well, I wouldn't know about *young* love, but thanks, Mary Dell. Thanks, Evelyn." Margot let out a little squeal of excitement and ran out the door and down the stairs where she could talk to Arnie in private.

Mary Dell smiled as she reached toward the serving platter and piled her plate high with dripping, spicy chicken wings. "Well, that worked out, didn't it? I'm glad. She seems about as sweet as tea."

"She is," Liza confirmed.

"And speaking of young love, Liza, how are things going with you and that good-looking Garrett?"

"Mary Dell!" I gasped. "You can't ask her about that! Not when I'm sitting right here!"

Mary Dell hinged back, offended. "Well, why not? Heaven knows you're never going to ask, you're much too polite for that, and in-quiring minds want to know. So come on, Liza, what's the scoop?"

I started to protest—she shouldn't have to answer personal questions about her boyfriend in the presence of his mother—but Liza waved me off.

"It's okay, Evelyn. I don't mind. The scoop is that we're in an ex-clusive relationship, but"—she shrugged noncommittally—"that's it for now. I've got a year to go before graduation, then I've got to figure out how to make some kind of living with a degree in studio art. So for right now that's about as far into my future as I can see."

"Well, you've sure got an eye for color," Mary Dell said. "Not that I'd know personally, of course. Everybody knows I got no more taste than a hothouse tomato, but Howard was bragging on you. He just loves all the displays you did for the shop and the way you arranged all the stock into seasons. Said it helps people imagine way more possible color combinations than they would if the fabric was just sorted like a color wheel. You've got a real special talent."

"Thanks. It's not a big deal, really, but I do like working with fabric."

"Well, darling," Abigail interjected, "maybe that's how you can make a living with a degree in studio art. All these fabrics must be designed by someone. Perhaps you could do that after you gradu-ate. If you'd like, I could make a few calls . . ."

Liza held up a hand to stop her aunt. "Thanks, Abbie, but let's not go calling in any favors yet. Besides, whatever it is I end up doing, I want to do get there on my own, because of my own talents and hard work, not because I'm your niece. Okay?"

Abigail's mouth flattened into a line. "Fine. Have it your way. I just don't see what so wrong about using connections if you've got them. A million girls would . . ."

"Abbie," Liza warned.

"Fine."

Mary Dell wisely changed the subject. "Ivy, what are your plans now?"

"Things have been so crazy the last few months I haven't had much chance to think about the future. I'll stay on at Cobbled Court—at least, I will if Evelyn still wants me."

"I do," I assured her. "You're not going anywhere. Don't even think about it."

Ivy smiled. "Other than that, my biggest concern is finding a new place to live. But you know, I'm not really that worried about it," she said in a voice that sounded almost surprised. "One thing I've learned recently is that, one way or another, things have a way of working out. It's good to know what direction you're heading in, but it's better to be flexible about your route. Sometimes the back roads turn out to be the fastest way home."

"In other words," Mary Dell said sagely, "when life hands you scraps, make a quilt."

"Right," Ivy said.

Abigail narrowed her eyes and tapped her fingernail on the table thoughtfully. "Speaking of homes. I heard some very interesting news today. Homes," she mused. "You know something Ivy, I just might have an idea about that . . ."

∽∾ 41 ∽∾

Ivy Peterman

It's a good thing there aren't many cops in New Bern. If there were, Franklin Spaulding would have to give up his regular practice in favor of spending his days clearing up his wife's tickets.

"Ivy! Quit being such a Nervous Nelly. Open your eyes. I wasn't within a mile of hitting that man."

I followed orders. She was right. We'd missed the pedestrian but only because he had quick reflexes. I looked in the rearview mirror and saw him standing on the side of the road, shaking his fist at Abigail's car.

The tires squealed as she made a hard left onto Proctor. "There it is. On the right." Abigail pointed to the right and swerved the car in the same direction, finally coming to a jerky stop in front of her enormous white mansion.

"But . . . this is your house. I can't afford to rent your house. I can't even afford to heat it."

Abigail sighed, impatient that I was so slow to catch on. "No, not the main house, Ivy. I told you, I sold the main house. The Wyatts have wanted a house on Proctor for years, but they almost never come on the market. When I called and offered to sell them mine, they jumped at the chance. Everything worked out beautifully. I called Donna Walsh and told her to make an offer on the old elementary school before some wily contractor beat us to it. The proceeds from my house enabled her to make a fifty percent down payment on the school. So everybody's happy—me, Donna, the Wyatts, the school district, not to mention the families who will live in the newer, bigger, better Stanton Center!" Abigail beamed, entirely pleased with herself.

"Even those unimaginative drones in zoning have agreed it's a perfect solution! I'm still irritated that they blocked my original plan, but when I heard that the school district was building a new elementary school and wanted to sell the old one, I realized it was perfect for our purposes—even larger than my house and in a more convenient location. Isn't it lovely how everything worked out? Of course, we still have a good bit of money to raise, but I've already made a few calls. People have been very generous with their pledges. When the bell rings to dismiss the students in June, we'll have a construction team standing by ready to tear out old walls, electrical, and plumbing and rebuild the top two floors of the school into fourteen new apartments! Isn't it exciting?"

"It is," I agreed sincerely. "I'm just having a hard time understanding where I fit in to all this. You said you found a perfect, affordable rental for me and now we're sitting here on Proctor. Abigail, there is nothing on this street that I can afford to rent."

"Oh yes, there is." She pointed to a spot slightly behind us. "There. The carriage house. I still own it. I had it subdivided from the rest of the property. Remember?"

I twisted to my right to see where she was pointing. And there it was; the red door like a laughing mouth, two winking windows for eyes. "Oh my gosh," I whispered. "The house that smiles . . ."

"What?"

I turned. Abigail was staring at me. "Never mind. It's just . . . it's just something that Bethany said one day. It doesn't matter. Abbie, *this* is the house you wanted to show me?"

"Yes. Of course. Why else would I have brought you here? Really, Ivy. Do try to keep up. Focus. You're beginning to make me wonder about you."

"Sorry. I knew the big house was yours, I just never made the connection that the little house went with it."

"Well, it does," she said, absentmindedly picking up the reading glasses she wore on a chain around her neck and examining the lenses. "Originally, I'd planned on moving here myself, but that was before the wedding and, really, it's too small for both Franklin and me; besides, I've found a piece of property that will be just right for the house I'd like to build. Very similar to the one I designed for your quilt. I've already got an architect working on plans."

She found a spot on her glasses, breathed on the lens, and rubbed at the smudge with the sleeve of the sweater that hung carelessly over her shoulders. "I thought about Liza, but she's not interested. You saw her quilted house, all soaring expanses and walls of glass. She doesn't want to live in an antique with squat ceilings and six over six windows."

"Well . . . couldn't you just sell it?" I spoke hesitantly, not wanting her to agree with the idea but knowing that, in all fairness, I had to put it out there. Selling would certainly be the most logical solution.

"I could, but honestly, I don't want to. Call me sentimental, but I've lived here a long time. Woolley and I may not have been madly in love, but we did have some good times together. I guess this is my way of honoring those memories." She shrugged, unable to put her feelings into precise language, but I understood what she meant.

"Then, when we were at the quilt circle meeting last week, I realized it would be perfect for you and the children. At least," she smiled, "that's my opinion, but you'll have to judge for yourself. Shall we go inside?"

Abigail turned the key in the lock and opened a door that led into a living room with a beamed ceiling, built-in bookshelves under the windows, and a deep stone fireplace. I couldn't breathe.

"Well," Abigail said brightly. "What do you think? It needs painting, but it's solid and the roof is practically new. There are three bedrooms upstairs and two baths. There's a half-bath off the kitchen and . . ."

I swallowed hard. "Abigail. The kitchen. Does it have blue and yellow tile?"

She nodded slowly. "Why yes. Yes, it does."

"And distressed white cabinets with glass fronts?"

"That's right. How did you know? Have you been here before?"

I turned in a slow circle, taking in every inch of this oh-so-familiar room until I faced the open door. For a moment, I could have sworn I saw my father standing on the stoop, smiling, and waiting . . .

Epilogue

Ivy Peterman

If you wait until Christmas Eve morning to buy your tree and ornaments, you can get both very cheap. So we did.

Of course, by that time the selection was pretty limited, but the trunk of the tree is mostly straight and when I turned it to face the corner, you can barely see the bald spot in back. There were plenty of strings of lights left at the discount store but only odd boxes of ornaments. We dug through the pile and found one burgundy, one pearl, and one copper box of glass balls and decided that together with the white paper and silver glittered snowflakes we'd made, they would look beautiful. And they do, especially in the glow of the firelight.

Bethany took two of the smallest burgundy balls from the box of ornaments and looped them over the tops of her ears for earrings.

"Mommy, how do I look?"

"Oooh, very glamorous. There's just one thing missing." I took a pinch of silver tinsel from the box and sprinkled a few strands in her hair. "Perfect!"

Bethany giggled. "Mommy, you're weird."

"Yeah, I know. I get that a lot."

Bethany glanced at the clock that stood on the mantel and

creased her tiny brow. "Only an hour until they get here," she said. "I'll help you clean up this mess."

"No, peanut. That's all right." Bethany is always so good, so eager to please. More like an adult than a little girl and it worries me. I know that kids who've gone through the kinds of experiences Bethany has tend to be either too good or completely the opposite, angry and lashing out at everyone. Given the options, I suppose the former is better than the latter, but it's still a concern, one we're working on. These things take time.

"I can clean up. Why don't you go in the kitchen with Bobby and finish the oranges?" The kids made presents for everyone who was coming to the party—pomanders, oranges studded with spicy sweet-smelling cloves to hang in closets.

"Okay," she agreed, grudgingly. "Call me if you need help."

"I will."

"Should I check on the lasagnas?"

"I already set the timer. You don't need to worry about a thing. Go on and enjoy yourself. Be creative!"

"All right," she said slowly. "But are you sure you don't . . ."

"Bethany," I laughed. "Scoot! I've got everything under control. Trust me."

These things take time.

I still have the dream, but it's different now.

The bell rings. I open the door and there is my father, smiling, waiting. I invite him to come in. That's what he was waiting for all along. Behind him comes my mother, then Abigail, then Evelyn, then Margot and a long line of other people, Franklin, Charlie, Liza, Garrett, Mary Dell, and Carmel Sunday and, believe it or not, even Hodge. I have to tell you, that last one threw me at first but, in a way, it makes sense.

I spent so much time living a life that was almost true. I don't do that anymore. Now everything that's happened to me—the good, the bad, the mistakes of the past and my hopes for the future—is part of the life I'm living today. Nothing gets ignored, or denied, or left to lurk on the doorstep. I've invited it all in. I've embraced the truth and it truly has set me free. Maybe that's why we had to live in the Stanton Center for all that time. It's a place of transition, a way station for women on the road to learning who they are and what they can become. Until I faced my past, I wasn't ready to come home. Now I am.

Abigail refused to accept a deposit for first and last month's rent, tearing up the check I handed her. I want to stand on my own two feet and I am, but that shredded check really did make things easier. My savings bought three new mattresses. That was the biggest expense. The rest—dressers, sofa, coffee table, and a wonderful antique oak dining table with six chairs—we bought very cheap at tag sales. I could still use some more lamps and it would be nice to find a side chair, but that can wait.

I've been painting the house, room by room, giving Bobby's room a coat of sapphire blue, Bethany's a sweet princess pink. The other walls are now a sunny yellow that look cheery even on the snowiest winter days. For now, I've given up quilting in favor of drapery sewing. Soon there will be fresh, crisp curtains at every window.

It's all worked out pretty well for everybody—for me, for my children, and for Abigail, who, these days, is all about architects and blueprints. And not just for the house she is designing for herself and Franklin to live in, the house with the square footage that seems to get just a teeny bit larger with every updated set of plans, but also the blueprints for the new Stanton Center—make that the Stanton Center *and* the Spaulding Woman's Center for New Beginnings.

The bottom floor of the old school will house New Beginnings, a place where victims of domestic violence can get the education, training, encouragement, and support they need to begin life anew. There will be classes for women who want to earn their high school equivalency diplomas, or study for college entrance exams, or learn interview skills, plus counseling and recovery groups, parenting classes, and vocational training.

Eventually, they hope to have a wide range of vocational classes, each sponsored by a local business owner who has agreed to offer hands-on internships for interested participants, but to begin we'll just have three: an administrative assistant program sponsored by the law firm of Spaulding, Ketchum, and Ryan; a culinary arts program sponsored by The Grill on the Green; and a retail and quilting program offered by Cobbled Court Quilts. Everything should be up and running by this time next year.

Evelyn is very excited about the program and so am I. This is going to be a chance for women just like me to pick up the tattered scraps of their lives and stitch together a new vision of themselves and their future. Some will only pass through, learn to run a cash register or to make a quilt or two, and then move on, taking what they've learned with them, but others will stay on at Cobbled Court Quilts, taking jobs and staying here for a season, or a year, or forever. The way the business has continued to grow at the shop, we'll be able to offer jobs to many of our interns.

And the best part? Evelyn and Donna Walsh took me to lunch last week and asked if I would be willing to head up the Cobbled Court internship program. We're going to promote Karen to Assistant Manager for the department so she can fill in for the ten hours a week I'll spend at New Beginnings, but I'm going to be in charge of the whole thing! Isn't that something? I could never have imagined that the pain and trouble in my life could be turned around and used for good, but it will be.

It's just like that verse Margot taught me, the one that was her grandmother's favorite and now is mine, "all things work to good for those who love God and are called to his purpose." I believe that now. I believe that God can and is taking all the stuff in my life—my pain and past, my shame and sorrows, the lies and losses, all of it—and using it for a good purpose. And I believe it all started on that dark night, when I was lost and frightened and didn't know how to find the road. That was the night I tossed up a puny, mustard seed prayer, asking for guidance from someone who, at the time, I wasn't even sure existed. I don't feel that way anymore.

Soon, my doorbell will ring and the people I've come to think of as my family—Abigail, Franklin, Liza, Evelyn, Garrett, Charlie, Margot, and Arnie—will come through the door carrying armloads of presents to go under the tree and platters filled with food to lay on the table next to the lasagnas I've got baking in the oven. We'll share a meal, exchange gifts and love and laughter and, when it gets dark, we'll tromp through the drifted snow, up the street, across the Green, and into the church for the candlelight Christmas Eve service, packing into the pews cheek by jowl, kneeling next to the others who want to come this night and say a prayer of thanks for unexpected gifts.

I already know what my prayer will be. With Bethany on one side of me and Bobby on the other, I will kneel down, close my eyes and say:

Thank you. For everything. For my children, our family, my friends. For this beautiful little town, this city of refuge, and all the people in it. Thank you for helping me stitch a new quilt from the scraps of my old life.

Thank you for believing in me, even before I believed in you. And for the bend in the road that sent me one hundred and eighty degrees from my intended destination. Yes. Especially for that. Thank you for the wrong turn that led me home.

Author's Note

Dear Reading Friend,

Thank you for joining me on this armchair journey to New Bern. If this is your first visit, I hope you enjoyed getting to know Evelyn, Ivy, Abigail, Margot, Liza, and the rest of the Cobbled Court characters and will search out the first book in the series, *A Single Thread*. If you've read both books and are anxious for more, you won't have long to wait. The third Cobbled Court novel is set for release in the summer of 2010.

In the meantime, I hope you'll drop by my website, www.mariebostwick.com. You can check out my blog, send me a note (I always love hearing from readers), read excerpts from all five of my novels, or check out my calendar to see if I might be coming to visit your area. If you register as a "Reading Friend," you'll also be entered in my monthly Readers' Contest, be able to post in the forum, receive my seasonal newsletter and personal invitations for appearances in your area, and have access to special content available only to registered Reading Friends, including the free downloadable pattern for the "Broken Hearts Mending" quilt that was featured in *A Single Thread*.

If you don't have access to a computer or, like me, you still enjoy the pleasure of letter writing, you can write to me at the following address. . . .

Marie Bostwick
PO Box 488
Thomaston, CT 06787

Again, thank you for visiting New Bern. I hope you had as much fun reading this book as I had writing it and that you'll be back soon.

Blessings,
Marie Bostwick

A THREAD OF TRUTH

Marie Bostwick

ABOUT THIS GUIDE

The following questions are intended to
enhance your group's reading of
A THREAD OF TRUTH.

DISCUSSION QUESTIONS

1. An avid quilter, Marie Bostwick has been known to turn to quilting when working through tough life issues—not unlike the women in *A Thread of Truth*. What is it about working with one's hands that cultivates a sense of serenity? Can you recall a time when quilting, knitting, or some other handiwork helped you through a tough time?

2. Evelyn Dixon has built more than a successful small business in Cobbled Court Quilts—she's created a community of quilters. How did she accomplish this? What are the pluses and minuses of approaching staff and employees like an extended family? Does it work for Evelyn? What does she gain? What price does she pay?

3. One of the first people Ivy Peterman meets in New Bern is Abigail Burgess Wynne, and Ivy immediately is both dismayed by Abigail's refined intimidation skills and touched by Abigail's insistence that a place be found for Ivy and her two children at the women's shelter. Does Abigail's power come solely from being the richest woman in New Bern? If not, to what can one attribute her confidence? Would you welcome a friend like Abigail? What would it take to incorporate such a personality into your circle of friends? Is it fair that Abigail's wealth and power make it possible for her to get her way, even in the name of a good cause?

4. The specter of domestic violence forms the underpinning of Marie Bostwick's plot in *A Thread of Truth*. What moment in the story best captures the fear and helplessness Ivy feels about her situation? How else does Bostwick convey the reality of being a mother on the run from an abusive husband?

5. According to a 2005 CDC survey, one in four American women have been abused by a husband or boyfriend—and on average more than three women are murdered by their husband or boyfriend every day. What would you do if you thought someone you knew was being abused by a significant other? To whom would you turn if it happened to you?

6. The most dangerous time for a woman being abused is when she tries to leave someone. Does that explain why Ivy is less than forthcoming with the details of her life? Does that justify lying to her boss? To her caseworker at the shelter? Where would someone in your community go if she was trying to escape from an abusive spouse?

7. In *A Thread of Truth*, Ivy presents herself to the shelter intake worker as "poor, powerless, and poorly educated," counting on the stereotype of victims of domestic violence to quell any doubts the woman might have about her. Yet studies show abuse happens in all kinds of families and relationships, and persons of any class, culture, religion, sexual orientation, age, and sex can be victims—or perpetrators—of domestic violence. Why do such stereotypes endure? What would it take to change them?

8. What do you think about Ivy's reluctance to come clean with her new friends about her past? Is her reluctance reasonable? Or does it contribute to her problems? Why are people so reluctant to share the less-than-perfect aspects of their lives with others? With whom do you share your unvarnished truth?

9. Many people hesitate to delve too deeply into the lives of those around them, yet the 2004 Allstate Foundation National Poll on Domestic Violence found three out of four respondents personally knew a victim of domestic violence. And the American Psychological Association estimates 40

percent to 60 percent of men who abuse women also abuse children. Do those statistics make you more inclined to report suspected abuse? Do they make you more inclined to reach out to someone you suspect might be in an abusive relationship? Do you know the signs of abuse?

10. Evelyn set out to New Bern, Connecticut, all on her own from Texas, but when it came to opening Cobbled Court Quilts—and keeping it open—she had the support of a wonderful circle of women. Some of these women work for her; some are simply fellow quilters. Yet all pitched in to help in a way once seen only in families. What one thing had to happen before these women could come together? How would you go about building such a foundation of friendship in your own life? Or have you already done so? Given the mobility of Americans today, are those we work with and those we choose to let in our lives our new family?

Dear Reading Friend,

I hope you enjoyed *A Thread of Truth* and will want to read more of my stories. For a change of pace, you might want to pick up a copy of *Snow Angels*, a Christmas collection of four heart-warming Christmas novellas from four different authors, including my novella, *The Presents of Angels*, on sale from Zebra in November 2009.

The Presents of Angels tells the story of Kendra Erickson-Loomis, a retired Radio City Music Hall Rockette who has found love and a new life in the charming village of Maple Grove, Vermont. After falling in love with and marrying Andy Loomis, the handsome local minister, and becoming stepmother to Andy's adorable daughter, Thea, Kendra finally has the family she'd always longed for. Learning that she'll be welcoming a new baby in the New Year is just icing on the cake.

But when Andy's ex-wife makes an unexpected appearance in Maple Grove, Kendra fears that her dream of living happily might turn out to be just that, a dream. As the holidays approach, it seems that only a miracle will keep her dream from shattering, but fortunately for Kendra, Christmas is the season when miracles abound.

This Christmas, if you're looking for stories to warm your heart and put you in the spirit of the season, look no further than *Snow Angels*, on sale in November.

I so appreciate your support and wish you all the best at Christmas and in every season of the year.

Blessings,
Marie Bostwick